F
CLEEVE

Judith

D1292056

JUDITH

By Brian Cleeve

SARA
KATE
JUDITH

Judith

BRIAN CLEEVE

Coward, McCann & Geoghegan, Inc.
New York

First American Edition 1978

Library of Congress Cataloging in Publication Data

Cleeve, Brian Talbot, 1921-
  Judith.

  I. Title.
PZ3.C583Ju   1978   [PR6053.L43]   823'.9'14   78-5781
ISBN 0-698-10910-4

Printed in the United States of America

To Eleanor Corey
for all her help

JUDITH

Chapter 1

She stood listening. The wind battering at the house, the timbers creaking, cold whispers of air like the wind's spies, in the corridors, down chimneys, making the flame of her candle bend and darken, running the shadows on the kitchen floor, and cupboards. Her heart beating as she tried to listen, not to the huge buffets of the wind, the howling of it against roof and walls, the banging of loose shutters, the groaning of one of the great doors in the stable yard; not listening to any of those sounds, but trying to hear beyond them, under them, as if in such a gale she could hear their hoofbeats, men's footsteps, whispering.

But all she could hear was her own heart-beat, like a fist knocking to escape.

She went into the passage, the candle guttering, the cold whip of air from under the back door against her ankles, finding its way under her cloak. What time was it? One? Two o'clock? They would not come now. She put her hand on the bolt and thought that she could hear them outside, in the yard, and stood not moving, scarcely breathing. What have I done? Was afraid to draw the bolt, afraid to stay there.

I am a coward! she thought furiously. A miserable, wretched coward!

The door almost tore itself out of her hands, slamming inwards, forcing her back. Somewhere in the house a door swung open, banged. Martha would wake. Solomon. Her father.

She fought to close the door behind her and the wind dragged at it, fastened her skirts against her, filled the hood of her cloak, trying to tear it away. The knot of her hair loosened and her hair fell into the hood like a sheared fleece. Even here in the yard the wind was like a living thing, a great animal tearing about its cage.

She could not breathe for a moment and stood half sheltered in the doorway, the closed door behind her, the bulk of the rain butt protecting her. Across the yard, the massive shadow of the stables, and to her left, the barn.

She tried to imagine what they meant to do.

'Dunna be afraid, ma'am. Ye'll not know we're come nor gone. Stay asleep, an' dunna listen for us.'

Not to listen for them! To sleep!

She listened again, and there was nothing but the wind; now holding her against the door, now lulling for a second, then that sense of a living thing, clawing and snarling at the walls.

'We likes bad weather, ma'am. A wild night an' no moon, that's what we looks for. Old Gaultrip an' all the Customs lads lying up snug.'

He had a wry-neck, twisted to one side, and he had drunk the last of her gin as if it was water.

'We'll bring ye more o' this ma'am. A half-anker as hansel. The Master ann't mean wi' stuff. An' a drop o' good French wine for the poor gentleman, as 'ull put the strength back into 'em.'

Bad weather and no moon. But not so bad as this?

Another lull. She went to the gates, that she had wedged open with stones that afternoon, telling Solomon to leave them alone. Had he guessed what she was doing? But he would be too afraid to talk.

Across the causeway that filled the moat outside the gates the wind came at her again, sent her staggering. It seemed to be lifting her from her feet, wanting to throw her down. The avenue lay ahead of her, black shapes of trees against black sky, branches thrashing, the last autumn leaves torn free, thin black lace of the highest branches against starlight; rags of black cloud driven across the stars.

I will walk down the avenue, she thought. If they have not come by the time I reach the cart road—— And imagined meeting them and stood still. There was a sharp crack like a gunshot, and an elm branch fell, tearing its way through lesser branches. She went back across the causeway and into the yard, into the passage, forcing the door shut again. Stood in the sudden quiet.

The sounds of the house reshaping themselves, the creaking, the banging of a shutter, its latch too loose. She took the candle-stick from the wall-niche beside the door, and felt her way to the kitchen. The fire had died to a redness, a dull slumbering, and she pushed the tip of a paper spill deep into it. There was a sudden dance of flame, of light, and the kitchen woke; table and shelves, dark sheen of copper, pewter, white glisten of china; yet everything strange, alone, secret. She felt a sudden fear of it, of being alone, Martha not there, the house asleep, as if by what she had done, what she had entered on, she had destroyed a barrier of safety and nothing was as it had been.

She went out quickly, sheltering the candle, along the passage to the front of the house, up the stairs. They would not come, they would not come, and tomorrow she would send to them that she had changed her mind, that she could not, it was not possible, not—— She opened the door of her father's room, softly, shielded the flame again. Heard the stirring of his hand on the covers.

'Are you awake Father?'

She came and knelt on the cushion that was always there beside the great bed and drew back the curtain a little. He lay propped on his pillows as she had left him, his eyes open, reflecting the candlelight. His mouth drawn down to the left, the side that was paralysed, the covers over him so flat that there seemed to be no body under them. His eyes turned towards her, his mouth tried to smile. His hand moved, fingers shaping themselves to be held. She set down the candlestick and took his hand between hers to warm it.

'You are cold.'

He whispered something. She put her head closer, to hear him. 'Not now' he was whispering. 'I am not cold now.' She put his hand against her heart.

He shut his eyes. The shadows, of the curtains, of her head and shoulders against the wall, bowed and moved as the draught caught the candlelight. Moved on the rows and piles of books. On his desk, that was now hers. On the fire-place where the fire had died. On his arm chair. She let go of his hand, very slowly and carefully, and closed the curtain. What time was it? But she could not imagine sleeping. She went to the desk to find his watch. Ten minutes before three. She pressed the spring and the chimes sounded. Two. Then the three brief quarters. Then five more, swift and tinkling. It was as though she was listening to her childhood. The silver watch against her ear, chiming and magical. Stories. Supper. Bedtime. Her father writing, the

[3]

scratching of his quill, like a mouse, the sudden dash of words, then stillness, then the scurrying again. While she sat on the floor, sharpening his pens, or folding paper scraps into boxes, into boats and cocked hats.

She put down the watch and touched the letter she had been writing that afternoon. To Mr. Terry, the attorney in Urnford, about the Earl's claim against her father. 'My dear sir, I must beg of you most earnestly the favour of an early——' She had scratched out 'early' from the rough draft and written 'immediate' instead. As though Mr. Terry would do anything immediately. His little wax-coloured face like a bleached raisin, shrivelled up with apologies and helplessness.

She touched the ledger of accounts. She had been so proud of keeping it when she began it almost three years ago. Had thought, I am really helping. Really and truly helping him. Because he could write great books, but he could not keep accounts, and she had taught herself to keep them. Except that all the entries were on one side. Nothing to Credit. Nothing to Income.

She opened the cover and looked at the first page again. 'January 1st, 1796, Anno Domini, the 36th of His Majesty King George III, being the Accounts of Income and Expenditure of Guthrum's Farm in the County of Essex, the Kingdom of England, the Property of Jonathan Mortimer Esq., Gentleman, to be kept by his Daughter Judith, aetat 16. May God preserve us from all harm in this coming year.'

The first entry, in the same careful copybook writing, fine, thin upward strokes, thick downwards; 'To Martha Jacks, House-keeper, her year's wages, £6'.

There had been four servants then, and two years before that, when her mother had been still alive there had been nine, and it had not seemed many. Now there were two. Martha and Solomon. And next year?

She had sat down as she read. My desk, she thought. To sit here and write, to know that he lay quietly there behind her, to turn round to him when she had finished a letter, done the week's accounts, written new receipts into her Wise Housewife's Book, and see his eyes open, watching her. She spread her hands out across the wood. Inkwell, sand box, wafers, sealing wax and taper stick and box of tapers, tray of pens, pen knife. Like a friend. And above the desk the shelf of her father's books, all his life there on one shelf. 'On the Rights of Colonies to Throw off an Unjust Yoke.' 'On a True Education of Women.' She took the first volume of that book and lifted the cover with a half reluctance. The lock of her mother's hair fastened there on the flyleaf, under a transparency, that also covered the handwritten dedication. 'To my beloved wife and companion and true friend, who has been educated by Nature and needs nothing of what is contained in this small book, I offer this copy of it nonetheless, as a gift of my heart; August 15, 1787.' And written below the transparency, below the curl of pale, pale golden hair, like ripe wheat, or flax, the date of her mother's death. 'February 17, 1794.' And in an uncertain, sick man's hand, 'Half my light is gone out.' Two days later he suffered the first stroke of his illness.

She closed the cover, took down another volume. 'A Deist's Answer to the Church of England.' He had had such hopes for its success, not worldly, but moral. He had been so sure that it must persuade every rational being to turn away from superstition. That had been the beginning of their ruin, since her father had guaranteed the costs of printing, and insisted that five thousand copies should be prepared. Mr. Richardson had sold less than a hundred of them, and all the remainder had had to be sold for waste paper, or were on the shelves of what had used to be his study, along the corridor.

Oh my dear, she thought, my dear, holding the thick, squat volume in its calf and gilt, that even in appearance had a forbidding look, as if determined not to be popular, nor to court material success of any kind.

And his last book would be the same if it should ever come to print. Already close to a thousand pages of the manuscript lay in a drawer of the desk under her hands. 'A Treatise on Just Government'. He was still writing it. Every day she put the writing board, and fresh pages, beside him, carefully arranged; fastened the pencil between his fingers. And his hand would move. Hour after hour. Until there was a drift of pages on the coverlid. Pages fallen to the floor, scattered. And she would gather them together, let him see the care she took in ordering them, reading what he had written. Nodding. Smiling. While her heart seemed to tighten inside her until it was hard to breathe, let alone to smile.

[5]

'Mr. Richardson is impatient for you to finish, he cannot wait till all is complete. But at the same time he begs you not to spoil anything by haste.' Pretending to read Mr. Richardson's letter. Who had really written 'What you descibe to me of your father's unfinished work is very interesting indeed, if somewhat on the too scholarly side for the modern taste, but as your father's friend and yours, I cannot offer you the least hope that even should it ever be finished there would be any rational prospect of publishing it. The times have changed, my dear Miss Mortimer. If they were ever favourable to the Radical Cause they are the very opposite now, and grown more ferocious against all talk of reform. Your own projected book, that you mention to me, of receipts useful to poor households, does hold some prospect of reward, although, I hasten to warn you, not a great one. But I think you may count upon say ten guineas if it lives up to my expectations as I feel sure it will.'

Ten guineas! For what had already taken her the best part of a year, and must take as much again! Ten guineas! The owlers would give her that for a single use of the barn, and the stables to hide their goods.

And as she thought of them, the wind dropped, there was a stillness. They are coming! And she sat rigidly, the letter trembling in her two hands. Could see them, that dark flood of men and animals.

I cannot go out to them! And then the idea of staying in this room, knowing, thinking that they were outside, was even worse. The wind came again, drove against the shutters, rattled the window, stirred the ashes of the fire.

She listened by the curtains of the bed, heard his breathing quiet, asleep. Let them be there now! She went down the stairs, to the back door again. Nothing but the gusts and lulling of the wind. And then between one gust and another the heavy tread of horses. She had to support herself for a second against the door. And as she stood holding bolt and candlestick, the flame bending, smoking, guttering in the draught, there was a sharp knock, a whisper.

'Who's there wi' a light? Is that you, ma'am?'

She dragged the bolt open, stood back. The door slamming inwards. A man's shape. Dark and bent. Beyond him the yard was full of shadows; men, horses, donkeys, pouring into the yard

[6]

through the wide gates like a thick, urgent river; the shapes grotesquely swollen, hump-backed with their loads of casks and bales and oilskin rolls; a thick smell of horse-sweat, smell of men; of tarred canvas, of wet fustian sweat-steaming in the cold. A rush of shadows, loads falling, thudding, horses stamping, men's whispered curses, the sudden, terrifying trumpet bray as a donkey lifted his muzzle in relief at being freed from his burden. All this in a second as her candle flame went out, and the bent shape of the wry-necked man they called Slipgibbet dragged off his woollen cap, made a lame-legged bob to her.

'I told you not to wait up on us, ma'am. But the Master's here, an' 'ud like to speak wi' you, since ye're waking an' about. If you'll speak wi' him.'

Behind him a greater shape; two; two men, one with a darkened lantern, its yellow eye deep buried in a metal hood, that turned this way and that, staring at her, beyond her into the passage, into her face again, the man's face hidden, a dark outline in the dark.

'Mistress Mortimer, aye?'

She could not control her voice to answer him, could only nod.

'I'm Walt Barnabas, of Shotton, an' this is my son Robert.'

She whispered a greeting, hardly knew what she said.

'Can we step in a minute? we ha' money to give you an' we can settle all now, 'stead o' sending messengers. Ten guineas he arranged wi' you, eh? An' another five if we do leave things here more 'n two nights.'

She backed from them to the kitchen door, the wind seeming to drive her along the passage, and then the sharp stillness as the men closed the door against the yard and its monstrous rush and hurrying of shadows, of whispering, of stamping hooves. She lit her candle at the fire again and set it on the kitchen table.

'You take the lamp, Slip, and see all's stowed quick an' Bristol. I'll be out to 'um inside five minutes to pay off the tub-lads an' I want all done when I come.'

He sat heavily on the bench by the table, his son still standing. 'Sit, Mistress, sit ye, and you Robert. Get out the bag. Pay on the nail, I say. Where there's no debts there's no quarrels.'

He pushed back his tricorn hat that had left a thick red dividing trench across his forehead. Wind-burned brown below. Old man's white above. The edge of a grey wig showing, the thick, tight curls of it against the great blue collar of his heavy riding coat. An old man with deep-set eyes and a thick, powerful nose, his cheeks fallen a little, but his mouth set like iron. Grey twists of eyebrows. The eyes at once hard winter grey, and humorous, judging her fear of him, and amused by it, and not displeased.

She looked quickly towards his son, who was unfastening the neck of a leather bag. Brown hair, his own, drawn back and clubbed and tied behind his neck, long eyelashes lowered as he looked down at the knot he was untying; his hands square and powerful; a sailor's hands. Yet something neat about them, as if they were used to handling small objects and manipulating them with care. Despite his breadth and height he seemed as unlike his father as could be possible, his mouth sullen rather than hard.

'Push back your hood, mistress, let's see one another clear. Aye, a bonker, swacken lass, Slipgibbet said ye were an' he was right. Ten guineas, can ye nivva untie that bag, Rob? And a half anker o' gin, weren't that our bargain? Slip 'ull bring in the gin to ye.'

The knot gave, the heavy bag spilled open, gold ran. A hundred, two hundred guineas and half guineas there, a dark mouth of gold. Old Mister Barnabas reached out and scooped as if they were grains of corn. 'Ten.' He counted them, made a pile, pushed it towards Judith's hand. They both looked at her, the father still amused, the son impatient, already tightening the leather string of the money-bag, twisting the knot. His eyes suddenly full on hers. Dark. Unsmiling. Eyebrows like his father's, drawn down, knotted. A tenseness about his face, his expression, as if he was holding himself back from showing his thoughts, and his thoughts were fighting to show themselves. His face was tanned and wind-burned like his father's, but the skin so fine it showed the blood underneath. She had heard that his mother was French and there was what she imagined was a Frenchness in his face, the dark hair and eyes, the set of his mouth, the fineness of his skin.

'We'll be back tomorrow night, or t'latest the night after. An' they'll be some'un about watching to see as no 'un troubles you. Dunna fret, you'll be as safe as ye ever were, an' ten guineas the richer.' He heaved himself up. pulled down the point of his hat until it sat on his head like part of him, solid. A great dark blue mass of coat and wig and hat, like a thundercloud building, eyes glittering from under the grey fells of eyebrows.

'Will you—be coming again?'

'Aye! Dunna fear! A sound place like this, we'll use ye. An' if we dunna meet face to face for payment I'll have a lad as 'ull bring ye your money.'

'Mr.—Mr. Slipgibbet——'

'Mister Slipgibbet! There's a rich 'un! Cobb, his right name is, Benjamin Cobb, but Slip 'ull do. What about 'em?'

'He said I—I should have some wine for my father. He is ill and it would do him good.'

'Then ye shall have that an' all. Rob, mind me of it an' next time we'll bring a half cask o' Burgundy. Now, good night, ma'am. Dunna fear nor worry. I ann't lost a run o' goods in many a year, an' dunna mean to, eh, Rob? 't 'ull be an income for ye atween now an' Christmas an' mebbe ye shall ha' a bit o' silk then to go wi' your pretty hair.'

He leaned forward and touched it with a kindly hand, as if she was still a child.

'Put up your guineas safe. An' Rob, tell Slip to bring in the gin for her. Five gallons o' best Hollands, ma'am, none of your Roscoff stuff.'

They went out and after a moment or two the man Slipgibbet came in with the half anker of gin and set it where she showed him, on a low shelf by the dresser. Made his lame, ducking bob of the head, and was gone again. And she still sat, the small pile of gold coins in front of her, hearing the sounds outside. Lessening. Until she could hear nothing. Nothing but the gusts and crying of the wind. Were they gone? She wanted to get up and look out of the window and could not bring herself to move, to break the stillness of sitting there.

Even the wind had grown quieter, now dying away, reviving, dying. And then an utter stillness. She had grown cold with sitting. Shivered. Thinking of nothing, half asleep, as if in the past night she had made an enormous effort, and was now too tired to move, to go to bed, to sleep properly. Even the question, what have I truly done? seeming to take an immense time to form itself, and to be beyond her power to answer.

The mouse who lived in the hole beside the hearth came out to look for crumbs. Judith watched him, watched the tiny shadow move, stay still, scurry, dart with bravery and terror.

'Little mouse' she whispered, 'do not be afraid.'

But he was afraid, and ran pattering, and was gone.

Chapter 2

They went through the Great Gallery, the Summer Drawing
Room, the State Drawing Room, two ante-rooms, with footmen at
the doors of every one, each room desolate with emptiness, with
furniture standing like islands in a Dead Sea of polished floors,
the air still and chill and motionless; a dull glittering from
mirrors, chandeliers, silver; from gilt mouldings, ormolu; the vast
window curtains hanging in thick, stifling folds of velvet, brocade,
silk. Mr. McKennzie the Groom of the Chambers leading the
way, their footsteps echoing, the doors seeming to rumble like
distant thunder as they opened and closed in the silence. The
footmen like automata, a miserable little negro page half asleep
on a stool with his eyes open, starting to frightened wakefulness
and jumping up as they came by. She would have liked to pat him
and ask his name, she had never seen him before, but she could
only smile at him, her own lips already stiffening with terrors as
they came nearer and nearer the Earl's apartments. The Earl's
reception room, more footmen, a small ante-room with a stairs
leading down from it to gun rooms and the Orangery and the
Estate business room. And a door into the Earl's library.

Now God for Harry and for England Judith thought, they
cannot eat me.

'Miss Mortimer, your Lordship. Your Ladyship.'

Her Ladyship? The Countess here? Merciful God, they were
all—the whole family, every one—— And she felt herself hesitate,
and plunge, and hesitate again, not able to see quite clearly who
was where. The Earl, the Countess, Lord Claydon, Miss
Whittaker, Mr. Halliday, Mr. Massingham—— And Francis?
Was he not here of all of them, cousin Francis? And saw him by
the window, magnificent in his new uniform, Yeomanry scarlet
and buff and silver; gold lacing; glistening Hessians and tassels.
Sword belt. Oh Francis, help me, please.

And he did help, coming forward, eyes smiling, eyes bluer than her own, hair almost as fair, bowing as she curtsyed, not so much to him as to the room, the whole frightening phalanx of authority, of Matcham grandeur. Curtsying to the Countess, lying on a chaise longue with Mr. Massingham her secretary and factotum behind her, holding her prayer book and reticule and fan and lorgnette, ready for every service of piety or enquiry or comfort as it might be required, and baring his gapped, ugly, jutting teeth in a smile of condescending welcome; Miss Whittaker busy at her embroidery frame, peering up at Judith as if hoping for relief from wretchedness but already resigned to not receiving it; Mr. Halliday the Earl's man of business as well as Steward gaunt and dour in black behind the Earl's chair; Lord Claydon facing his father across the wide, marble expanse of the hearth; the fireplace so vast, and so deep, that the logs seemed lost in it, and to be burning far inside the depths of a cave, giving scarcely a glimmer of heat to the room; and the Earl himself, small and thickmade and fidgeting in his winged chair, his fingers drumming on the arms of it as he creaked to his feet for Judith, bowed, his face already showing anxieties, disapproval of the way she had come in, an old man's nervousness that she was going to do something sudden, or noisy, or knock something down. It was more than five years since she had done anything of the kind, but the Earl never saw her without seeming to imagine that she would overset a table or trip over the edge of a carpet.

'You are still growing! he said accusingly, looking up at her as she straightened from her special curtsy for him. 'You will be six feet tall if you are not careful. Your mother was too tall as well.'

Claydon giving her his hand, limp as fish. Mr. Halliday bowing. Mr. Massingham bowing and smiling, holding the Countess's prayer book against his heart as if to sanctify it, his tongue slowly touching a red mark on his lower lip; one of his eternal cold sores that she could never look at without wanting to shudder. Once, in a Christmas game of Forfeits he had kissed her, and afterwards she had scrubbed and scubbed at her mouth until it bled, in terror that the sore would come on her own lip. She looked quickly away from him towards Miss Whittaker, the Countess's dame de compagnie, who had upset her silks and was now bent over them in flushed anxiety, unsure whether to stand or sit.

The Countess extended her hand in its black silk mitten, her fingers white as ivory. Raising almost invisible eyebrows above the deep hollows of her eyes, their expression saying 'Look what you have done now, you have only to enter a room and it is in turmoil.'

'And how is your father to-day, child?'

'There is no real change, ma'am, one cannot hope for there to be a change for the better, I am afraid.'

'No change, eh?' the Earl said. 'Hah. Sit down, girl, sit down.'

The silence grew deeper, the Earl thinking of something to say next, or of how to say it. He cleared his throat at last, and leaned forward. 'But you are changing!' he said sharply. 'You are eighteen! Almost nineteen! That is an age when a young woman must begin to think—must begin to think of the future? Eh? Eh?' He drummed his fingers on the arms of his chair, stared at his elder son as if he disliked him, stared again at Judith, who could only stare at him in return, before lowering her eyes and flushing in embarrassment.

'Well, have you thought? Of the future?'

She sat afraid to breathe, she did not know why. She had expected a dozen unpleasant things from the Earl's summons to this visit; from his mention of 'family matters to be discussed.' But not that she should be challenged about her future, short and sharp like that.

'Why—I suppose sir—that my future is—to look after my father. I—have not thought beyond that except——'

'Except what? Except what, eh? Eh?' Seeming to creak as he leaned forward in his tight blue coat with its brass buttons, his old-fashioned nankeen breeches and his black silk stockings.

"Except that I—I should like to——' She wished that she had not begun. Everyone waited. Mr. Massingham leaned forward, one hand at his lips, his treasury of the Countess's belongings gathered against his breast by the other. '—to—to make myself useful in some—some way in the parish.'

'And what way might that be?' the Countess said, the slightest tones of suspicion in her voice that Judith might be imagining some charitable undertakings independent of her authority and protection.

'It—it is scarcely a thought as yet. Only—to teach a little——'

'To teach?' the Earl said. 'And who have you in mind to teach?'

Not suspicion in his voice but almost anger, outright indignation as if already he saw her continuing her father's crimes by teaching the infants of the parish to read and write, his mind leaping from there straight to Revolution and the guillotine.

'Oh—not children, sir, I—I should not be qualified, I am aware of that. But the women—the labourer's wives——'

'The labourers' *wives*?' Such wonder, such incredulity and horror in his voice that she felt herself blushing again, as though unawares she had made an improper remark.

'And—and their daughters of course. The young women. There is so much they do not know.'

Claydon staring at her. Mr. Halliday's long thin mouth slightly pursed as if to say I have heard many things. And now I have heard this. But I did not expect it, no, I did not.

Miss Whittaker holding up her skein of red silk like a mouse with a crumb, her mouth open.

'And what do not they know? If one may ask such a question? That they need to know?' The Earl's words dropping like stones into a well.

'Why! Almost everything! They know absolutely nothing. Not how to bake, nor to sew, scarcely how to wash clothes many of them. They do not know anything of diet, of—of hygiene for themselves, or—— You cannot imagine sir——'

'I do not wish to imagine it, Judith. Nor does her Ladyship. Nor Miss Whittaker.'

'Oh no!' Miss Whittaker breathed, 'oh no, indeed sir, I do not.' She held up trembling hands, ready to place them over her ears in protection against such dreadful knowledge.

'I never heard of such desperate folly!' the Earl said. 'A dame school for labourers' wives!'

'Oh no sir! It is—it is a book' she said quickly. 'Mr. Richardson the bookseller had promised already to consider it—if—if it fulfils his expectations——'

'A book? A *book*? Who is this—Richardson?' The Earl repeating the words 'book' and 'Richardson' as if she or he must be gone mad.

'She will mean the printer Richardson' Lord Claydon said, looking at Judith with a despairing wonder. 'The radical man that was tried with the Corresponding Society fellows.'

'I knew it!' the Earl cried. 'A radical! A printer! This is your

[14]

father's doing! He means to disgrace me to the last. I will not have it, Judith! A book! A radical book! You shall burn it with your own hands, you shall not leave this room until I have your solemn promise of it.'

'But sir! It is a book of receipts, not of politics! And of—of how to grow cabbage in their gardens—and—and how to keep their babies from the green diarrhoea—and——'

'JUDITH!'

'Oh mercy upon us!' Miss Whittaker shrieked, and did this time clap her hands to her ears.

'My dear dear Miss Judith' Mr. Massingham breathed.

'I have heard enough' the Countess said. 'A woman, a lady, cannot write a book, Judith. Nor can she concern herself with such matters as you have just described. It is very fortunate that his Lordship has already taken steps to put such things out of your reach.'

'But ma'am, indeed women can write books. Miss Wollstone-craft, Miss Burney——'

'Judith! Be silent!' The Earl held up his hand in warning, 'you are too quick to answer, I have told you of it before. You argue. You contradict. It is a most dreadfully wrong thing in a woman, above all in a young woman. Your father has many things to answer for, and not the least of them is your upbringing. To teach you Latin! To turn you into—into a—a——'

'A bluestocking, my Lord?' Mr. Massingham ventured.

'A bluestocking! A—a—a learned woman is a monstrosity, Judith. No man could feel affection for her, respect for her. She could not be a true mother to her children, a true wife to her husband, a—— But I have not summoned you here to scold you' the Earl said, with one of his swift alternations into kindness, or what he meant to be kindness. 'Far from it. Quite the opposite indeed. I have summoned you to talk about a much happier thing. Your future, my dear. Not books and such follies.' He paused for the greater effect, looking at the Countess, at Lord Claydon, at Mr. Massingham, at Miss Whittaker still stooped and flushed and breathless over her skeins of colour, as if he was sharing with them some ripe pleasure that he was now to reveal. 'Can you not guess to what I refer, Judith?'

'Why—why no, sir, I cannot, I confess, I—I did not presume to think that my future concerned you.'

His look sharpened for a second, and smoothed again, determined not to be provoked further.

'Of course it does, my dear. Is your father not my cousin? Who else should be concerned with your future if not I? And her Ladyship? Eh? Now, guess. Guess what I am about to broach to you!'

He was fastening her with that look of determined, ferocious jollity he had used to wear in his kindlier moments during her childhood visits, which in fact had been more terrifying to her than his usual remote, impatient irritability, since it must be answered, and played up to, and she had not known how to play up to it, what he might expect of her.

'I cannot, sir. How should I guess?'

'Why, your marriage, child. Your marriage! What other future does a young woman have? Your marriage.'

'My—marriage?' she whispered. She wanted to steal a look towards Francis, and dared not. Was this why everyone was here?

'Yes, yes child! You have not took against marriage, I hope, with all your other addled notions?'

Mr. Massingham widened his mouth in a silent echo of the Earl's jollity, and picked at his lower lip, his eyes grown very attentive on Judith's face. Even Mr. Halliday allowed his expression to soften slightly.

'Why—why no, sir, but—but I have not so much as thought of marriage.' Afraid to look at any of them, feeling herself begin to blush, knowing that they would misunderstand the reason, and furious for it, and blushing deeper.

'Heh heh heh!' cried the Earl. 'Such a crimson cheek! Eh Halliday, d'ye mark her blushing? D'ye mark her milady? Eh, Miss Whittaker, there's a rosy cheek for a maid, eh? Who has never thought of marriage! Heh heh heh!'

'I do promise you, sir, I have not.'

'And very proper. It is good to hear of it. Eh, my lady? An't it a good thing in her?'

'If it is sincere, yes' the Countess said. She had taken her fan from Mr. Massingham and spread it between her cheek and the fire. 'In my experience most young women of eighteen think of nothing else.'

The Earl leaned forward. 'Now, what is needful for a marriage, eh? Eh, Judith?'

'Needful, sir? I—I suppose a husband?'

'A husband she says!' the Earl cried, mercifully not in a mood to be angered by stupidity, but instead to be delighted with it, as something helpless and childish and feminine that he might set right. 'No girl, a dowry. A dowry! That is what is necessary. Eh, Halliday? Eh, Massingham? Ain't that what a young lady needs for a marriage?'

'It is indeed a most helpful attribute' Mr. Halliday allowed.

Mr. Massingham smiled, showed his teeth. 'Your Lordship has hit upon it exactly' he said. 'As always.'

'There, you see, Judith? But——' He changed his mauve jollity by some inner alchemy to a darker shade of seriousness—— 'But, Miss. How does a young woman of no fortune obtain one? Answer me that now.'

He means to give me a settlement, Judith thought, torn between humiliation at this public discussion of her affairs and poverty, and unwilling gratitude at his kindness. And behind both those feelings the nervousness, the irrational but growing fear that the Earl had in his mind chosen a husband for her already, and that his pleasure now in meaning to be kind was the measure of how angry he would be when she refused his choice. As how should she not? And again longed to look towards Francis. Was it possible that—but it was not, and she knew it.

'Well?' the Earl was saying, his expression clouding still further.

'I do not know sir.'

'Why, the answer is that she cannot. How should she? Unless——' He lifted his rheumatic, misshapen finger into the air in emphasis. 'Unless it can be given to her.'

Now he will offer me something she thought in an agony of shame, feeling as if she were growing smaller and smaller, until she was like a small object under a magnifying glass with nothing in the room but great accusing eyes staring down at her, saying in their severity, 'She is poor. She has nothing. Not even a dowry. How can any creature be so wretched?'

'It is fortunate for me that I have not any wish for marriage sir, and therefore have no need of any dowry.'

'Nonsense,' the Earl cried. 'Stuff and nonsense, my dear. Every young woman wishes for marriage. Nay, don't flush, child, of course you do! You should. It is right. It is a woman's business in the world to be married. Eh, Massingham, ain't it so?'

'It is indeed, my lord' Mr. Massingham said. 'Does not Scripture tell us, that the woman shall be subject to the man, and a helpmeet unto him?' He bared his teeth again at Judith, and then rolled up his eyes at the wonder of God's providence.

'There. You see. You wish for marriage, Judith, but you have no dowry, nor means of getting one.' He bent towards her, pointing his bent finger at her face, as well as it would point. Judith half expected the door to open, and some wretched young man to be ushered in and propose to her on the spot.

'Now, child' the Earl was saying. 'We must think seriously for you. What is your future without a dowry? It is nothing. Can your father provide one for you? He cannot. And crippled and ill as he is there is no prospect of his doing so, no way in which he can re-establish Guthrum's into even the semblance of prosperity. Eh, Halliday?'

'I fear so, my Lord. It was never like to be a profitable holding. And now——'

'There, you see? You must take Halliday's opinion on such matters, Judith. He knows such things better than any man. As well as I do myself. It is a wretched sort of land that you have there. Four hundred acres of near waste. Before the Enclosure it was the worst sort of commonage, useless. It was a very short-sighted thing in your father to set even those sixty acres to arable that he did. Was it not, Halliday? You have only to look at the prices Hassett has been getting for your crops these past three years. Nothing. Less than the expenses. Land cannot be run like that you know. No! Guthrum's is not a holding to lie on its own, and never was, and was never intended to be. It was meant at the Enclosure to remain part of the Matcham lands, and had no value apart from them. None.'

He held up his finger again as Judith showed signs of wishing to answer him. 'I do not intend to enter into arguments about the rights and wrongs of your poor father's foolish dispute with me over my grandfather's Will. No indeed. But suppose, Miss. Just suppose. That there was no dispute. No disagreement.'Only your debts. You know your father has debts?'

'I do indeed sir.' This cannot go on, she thought. I shall stand up and leave, run out of this room. I will not stay to be tormented in this way.'

'And do you know how much those debts amount to? Including debts to me? To this Estate?'

'It is my duty to know them sir. I must see to my father's correspondence for him.' Her lips so dry it was hard to speak naturally.

'Now. Suppose. Just suppose, that those debts must be paid at once. Tomorrow. What should you do? What could your father do?'

She tried to answer, and could not. Nor stand up and go. Only sit as she was, her hands clenched together, her eyes held by the Earl's frown. Frowning at her like a mauve and yellow mask of condemnation. To be in debt. Not to be able to answer how those debts should be paid. Like sitting naked there. She was suddenly aware that sweat was running on her skin, under her gown, the room too warm, the fire too directly on her, the humiliation adding to that sense of being burned alive. And the grotesqueness, the vulgarity of the realisation seemed even worse than what was being done to her. Her shift felt suddenly wet with it, clinging to her.

'Well, miss? Well?'

'I—I have hoped—I have had to write to Mr. Halliday, as—as perhaps he has told you—asking that you should—you should be patient with us.' I shall never come to this house again, she swore. Never, never.

'You have wrote indeed in such terms' the Earl was saying. 'And I *have* been patient. Too patient most men would say. It is reproached to me a thousand times by harder men than myself, that I lead tenants and debtors into profligate ways by being soft with them. Is that not so, Halliday?'

'Indeed, my Lord, you have a name for forbearance that does you infinite credit.'

'But I have my duties, Judith. To the land, to right conduct, to the country. Debts cannot be let run on for ever. And the day will come when Guthrum's must pay its debts. And then? Why. You must be sold up, there is no alternative.'

The words were so much the echoes of her own fears that she had not even the temptation to answer. Could only look down at her hands.

'And then, Miss? What will you do? Your father crippled, unable to fend for himself? Not a roof to his head.'

There was a tiny moan of horror from Miss Whittaker, as though all these catastrophes threatened her, or threatened her again. The sound hung in the silence.

'I do not know' Judith whispered at last.

It was evidently the answer for which the Earl was waiting. He clucked in triumph, gobbled his cheeks with mauve-veined pleasure. 'How should you? There is no answer. None. But. But Judith. Your name is Mortimer. You are related to me. I do not mean to see you pay for your father's lack of wisdom. I did not approve of your father's marriage, as how should I have? That is no secret from you. No more than I have approved any of his conduct to me. But I do not mean you shall suffer for any of that. I mean to help you. I have but sketched out the impossibility of your position the more to underline the happy nature of my solution for you.'

'Solution, sir?'

'Yes. And this is it. I shall buy Guthrum's from you. I shall not claim my rights in it under my grandfather's, your great-grand-father's Will. We shall forget our miserable dispute. As if it never was. I shall buy Guthrum's from you at its best price and restore it to the Matcham Estate as it was meant to be at the Enclosure. There is has value. As warren land. Nothing else. And neatness. Rounding off a corner. It has been like a tooth taken out of a mouth, making the whole mouth ugly. I have not been able to bear to look at the map of that part of the Estates for the feeling it has gave me to see it gapped there. Torn out! But we will not talk of that now. Only that your father shall sell to me. You must persuade him to it. Your debts paid. A trifle over. And——' He held up his finger to prevent her. 'And Judith, there is more. More. You shall continue there. In the house. Your father shall not be disturbed. He may live out his days there, in peace and tranquillity. And you with him.'

'But sir——'

'Judith, Judith, do not answer me, do not argue with me. I have thought it all out very carefully. I am not a rich man. I have no great sums of money at my disposal to spend as I might like. These dreadful taxes for the war. This fearsome threatened Income Tax—I am hard put to it to make ends meet. We are not Whig-Johnny-come-latelies with sinecures, and new-made fortunes, and Nabobbery. We are old Tories, and have suffered for it, as no doubt you know, if your father has told you such things.' His expression doubted so much family feeling in his cousin. 'But even so, I mean to do more for you. I mean to give you your dowry. I must rob Claydon to do it, it is a most serious thing, but I shall do it. I shall so set you up with a dowry that you may hope for marriage very soon. Hope for it? Why, expect it. I shall not say how much the dowry shall be. But it shall be as handsome as I can manage, I promise you. Now, now Judith. What do you day to that, eh? Was it not worth your journey to us?'

Again she had the feeling that the doors behind were about to be flung open, and some prisoner brought in, bound and shackled, to be told that he was about to be married to Miss Mortimer of Guthrum's Farm, and the pair of them promptly exiled to Van Diemen's Land. It was not possible to know where to begin to answer such a proposition.

'You—you are too good, sir' she began. Mr. Massingham's eyes on her, as though he knew much more of this business than she yet did, as if he knew who it was the Earl had in mind for her.

'No no!' the Earl said. 'I will not hear myself praised. Only do as you are bid. Persuade your father. I am not sure but what it might be proper to have him declared incapable of making such decisions for himself, and you should be set into Chancery and a guardian appointed who might do such things for you. But that will not be necessary, I know it. Even your father must see reason in this case.'

Chancery? A guardian? Declared incapable? The words seemed like a succession of blows, light but bewildering, and then revealing that they were not light at all, but deep bruising and painful.

'My lord! Sir!'

'Now we shall not have another word upon the subject' the Earl cried happily. 'It must be near dinner time, and we shall have a capital family dinner. No ceremonies. This is a happy day. The end of a wretched dispute that has upset me more than I can tell you. I am not a man for disputes, eh, Halliday? Eh, my lady? I am prodigious pleased that we have thought of this way out, and all to be solved so well and easily.'

'But my Lord! It is unthinkable what you have proposed!'

He stared at her, the jollity, the kindliness, draining away from

[21]

his cheeks, his soft little mouth. 'I have told you we shall not say another word upon the matter, Judith. Do not presume to tell me what is unthinkable. You are scarce more than a child, you cannot know what is thinkable. You cannot know anything, least of all what is your own best interest.' He had begun breathing very fast, his voice sinking to a whisper, his hands grasping at the scrolls carved at the ends of his chair arms. 'I have told you to persuade your father. If you do not, then I must take other steps to persuade him. Other steps. Steps I shall not like to take unless I must. Do you understand me?' His breathing, his look of illness grown almost frightening. 'I am a soft man. A kind man,' he whispered 'but I will not be took advantage of. You will tell your father what I have said. I shall send to you for his answer in a few days. Now, that is an end of it. An end of it, do you hear me, Judith?' His breathing grown irregular, gasping, his cheeks a leaden colour, the veins throbbing at his yellowed, sunken temples. A look that her father had had before his last stroke of apoplexy. She felt that if she answered him again he would grow rigid before her, fall back into his chair in that same paralysis as had gripped her father. She bent her head, allowing him to consider it as submission if he wished.

'Good,' he whispered. His cheeks recovering their usual mauve tint. He managed to smile, to hold out his hand for Claydon to help him to his feet. He seemed to have grown even older in the last minutes, as if the effort of so much kindness and patience had aged him by five years.

Judith looked away from him, and felt her eyes drawn by Mr. Massingham's, standing in solemn obsequiousness behind the Countess's chaise longue. His eyes fastened on hers with the most peculiar of expressions, at once judging, and hungry.

She felt her skin creep as if he was touching it. It is not possible, she thought. They could not, even they could not think—could not imagine that I should—— And knew that they could. That they had already determined on it.

Mr. Massingham widened his hungry mouth, showed all his teeth to her, moistened his chapped lips with his tongue as if he was preparing them.

Chapter 3

'And did you enjoy your day, my dear?' His voice whispering and
slow, the words dragging out like a lame man shuffling heavy feet.
'Were they pleasant to you?'

'Oh, more than pleasant, Father. And you? Did Martha look
after you well?'

'Yes indeed.' His hand lying in hers, gratefully, his eyes urgent
to show love. 'They did not—badger you too much—about—
Guthrum's? About—me?'

'No, not at all. They mean only to be kind.' Keeping her voice
very steady, very light.

'I am glad. When I am gone——'

'Sssh.'

'Let me say it. When I am gone—you will—be in their hands.
His. I have been so afraid for you.'

'Sssh. Let me fasten the shutters. And build up your fire.' She
could not trust her hands touching his. They would betray her.

'No, no. Listen. I have thought—my quarrel with him—would
reflect on you. And yet—it has been for you. To make Guthrum's
yours. For your husband—when——'

'I shall not have a husband Father. You are all I need.'

He tried to smile, his lips moved a little. 'One day—soon—you
will find that you need—more. And you must not be empty-
handed.'

She said nothing, only smoothed a strand of white hair away
from his forehead, so that she might move, do something. Her
hand seemed to burn, his forehead to be ice-cold to her touch.

'What is it?' he breathed. 'Something has troubled you to-day?'

'Nothing! What should trouble me? A fine dinner, and two
drives in a coach! And I have talked with poor Miss Whittaker,

and her maid Annie, and seen a dozen old friends and——' She stopped, making her hands busy now with his coverlid. 'I have had the best of days.'

'You—should have such days—more often' he whispered. And then, his whisper altering, 'And Francis? You do not mention seeing him?'

'Oh yes, he was there.' Making her voice very light. 'In all his new splendour as Lieutenant of the Yeomanry. You cannot imagine how he dazzles.'

'You—still think of him?' His fingers holding her wrist, trying to grasp tight. 'Do not, Judith. I beg you. You will only hurt yourself. He—cannot—marry you.'

'I know. I have not thought of him—like that—since I was ten years old. What a man you are for remembering things to one's disadvantage.'

She had told him on her tenth birthday that she intended to marry her cousin Francis, and he had laughed and then grown grave, and told her that she should not think of it, that Francis must one day marry someone very rich. She had never spoken of it again to her father. Or to anyone.

'Now are you comfortable?' she said, and went quickly away from him to the desk, before she might betray herself any further. All the papers there. The letters to be answered. The bills that could not be paid. Her book. She pulled the sheaf of bills towards her. Mr. Terry, who would be much obl'd if he might trouble Mr. Mortimer for twenty guineas on account, against the costs that had accumulated. Doctor Farquhar, the physician, fifty guineas. Mr. Beauchamp, the surgeon, for eight visits with his assistant, at Doctor Farquhar's instructions, twelve guineas. Miss Frewen, of Frewen's General Providers, of Woodham Claydon, begging to draw Miss Mortimer's kind attention to her account, which now stood at above seventy guineas. A diminution of this amount would be much appreciated. Pargeter's, the stationers in Urnford, to eight reams of second quality white paper, quarto size; two doz. quill pens——

She pushed them away and rested her forehead on her hand. There were, in another pigeon hole, worse accounts than those. The demand for the petty tithes from Mr. Carteret. For the Earl's Great Tithes, that she had had to beg Mr. Halliday about—and not for this one year, but for three years past, until she dare not add the amounts together for fear of what they would tell her. And in the pigeon hole below them, the long, rambling letter of accounting from Mr. Hassett of Moate, explaining to her that despite the war prices and the scarcity of corn and wheat he had got less money for the Guthrum's harvest this year even than last—and with what he had spent on sowing and harrowing and reaping and threshing it, and bringing it to Urnford Market, she might hope for next to nothing in the way of profit. And that the Guthrum's pastures were so poor now, so over-grazed and under-marled, that he could offer only ten shillings an acre for the grazing this coming year.

I am indeed looking at ruin she thought. She had not let herself think it clearly until now. Ruin. Until one day the bailiffs would come in, and that would be the end of everything, as the Earl had said.

She sat thinking of it, very still in her chair, her father's breathing grown easier and deeper behind her. He must be asleep. And if the bailiffs came before—— She made herself think of it. Before he died. What would she do?

An old, sick, helpless man. And herself. Martha thrown onto the parish. Solomon. And the Earl's alternative? Her eyes were looking at her manuscript, without really seeing it. Reading the words without their having any meaning. "A Strengthening Caudle for the Sick."

The words 'Sugar' and then 'honey' came to her. How could they afford sugar, at eight pence a pound? And now Miss Frewen wanted nine pence for it, and a half penny more if she was to give credit. And they did not know how to keep hives, and the Earl's keepers did not like them to.

She thought of Mrs. Locke, with her seven children, and the eighth coming and Mr. Locke earning nine shillings a week when he had work. To tell her to put sugar and honey into a caudle, and Jamaica peppers! What is the use of it? she thought, putting both hands against her cheekbones, covering her eyes against the candlelight, against the image of Mr. Massingham, his smile, his yellow teeth, the sore on his lip; and the lips themselves, thick and discoloured, shaping, shaping to—I would die first!

'And if you do not?' the candle whispered.

She could feel his hands touching her. As if he were standing behind her now, his hands touching her neck, the edge of her gown, her throat. She sat not breathing, not able to move for the vividness, the vileness of the feeling, and could not stop imagining it. Her mind taking control of itself, creating a story, scene by scene, act by act. So that she saw the wedding, the Earl, the Countess, Francis there. Or Francis not there, gone away somewhere to make his fortune, find a rich heiress, a Nabob's daughter. And she—altar—clergyman, gold ring, veil. And the veil lifted, lifted by Mr. Massingham's thick, sweating hands, his eyes turned up in ecstasy, piety. To have and to hold. His mouth. I shall kill myself! But she could not prevent the scenes from following. Until they were in a bedroom, and he was undoing the buttons of her gown, his hands trembling, a bed there, white sheets—white curtains—pillows——

As though when the Earl had talked of marriage, a barrier had broken in her, thoughts that she did not know she could possess had taken hold of her, and with a dreadful sickness of infamy had attached themselves to Mr. Massingham, to his image, because she knew that he wanted her, because he so horrified her. Because—because they meant—intended——

I am gone mad she thought, his presence as real in her mind as if he was in the room, was holding her, touching her breast, and she twisted her head from side to side, the image of his mouth pursuing, pursuing, his breath against her face, warm, stale.

There was a sound, the sharp tap of something striking against the window, and she started fully awake, out of that waking nightmare of marriage. Listened, thought, it is them, they are come again! And did not know whether she was glad or frightened. She went to the window and softly, so that she might not wake her father, opened the casement and leaned out, looked into the dark above the terrace. Two shadows there, horsemen.

'I saw your candlelight' a voice called. 'May we speak with you?'

'Hush! I will come.' She closed the window gently, drew the curtains over it, listened to her father's unaltered breathing. Ran down the stairs to the back door, the stable yard, as they rode in through the gateway. Mr. Robert Barnabas and the man with the wry neck, Slipgibbet, Mr. Cobb.

'Take the horses, Slip. May I come in ma'am, only a moment?'

She had set her candle in the niche, as she opened the back

door, and now she led him by the light of it into the kitchen, set a stool for him by the fire.

'The servants are gone to bed, but I could warm some gin for you. And—and Mr. Cobb? Your own gin.' She smiled at him, glad that he had come, that he had saved her from her nightmare. And to her surprise he smiled at her, his sullenness, if it had been sullenness, quite gone, as though that had been caused by his father's presence, and not hers.

He sat down, and began pulling out his money bag, untying the throat of it, his hair very dark in the candlelight, his face seeming almost pale in contrast, despite his tan; that kind of— what she had imagined as French sallowness about his complexion. His mouth shaped like his father's and his eyebrows almost as heavy and naturally downdrawn, but nothing else of his father in his face. A tenseness about him that also seemed foreign. None of the Essex easiness and slowness of the labourers.

How strange he is she thought, and like an echo of her word he looked up at her, his eyes sharp and quick, and said 'You're a strange one for us to be doing this business with.' He did not smile. It sounded like an accusation. But yet she did not mind it, and sat down opposite to him, the breadth of the scrubbed deal table between them, his hands wrenching at the string as they had done the previous time, nervous and strong and quick and impatient.

'My father does up a bag as if he didn't mean it ever to be untied.' He had a foreign-sounding accent. Essex in it, but not much, not like the labourers or the village people.

He had the gold spilled out, and began to count ten guineas. Eight, nine, ten, in a small separate heap of brightness. He seemed to be waiting for her to reach out her hand, and when she did not he pushed the coins slowly towards her side of the table. She put out her hand then, her fingers resting on the table top. The coins slowly pushed towards her. The edge of one touched her finger, stopped.

'Why're you doing this?' he said. Still that note of accusation. And something about his voice, his face, even his strangeness to her, seemed to touch a locked place in her mind. Like opening a door that has long, long been fast shut on a secret room.

'Because—' she whispered, and could not go on. Her throat

seeming to close up. And to her fury, her utter shame she felt tears coming as if from nowhere, could not prevent them, had to put up her hands to hide her face, could not speak to him, could not do anything. Sat and cried as though all that had happened in these last years had come to her in one overwhelming moment, all her courage had gone. If he touches me I shall break, she thought, I shall die of shame. And wanted him to touch her, or not him, not him, but someone; wanted to be beside her father's bed, kneeling there, feel her father touch her hair, hold her.

I cannot go on being brave she thought, or I shall die of it. In a second she must stop this exhibition of herself. Must pretend it was a fit of illness, anything that would save ultimate humiliation, allow him to pretend to believe her and give her her money and go away. But just now to stay like this, to let the tears come. Go away! her mind cried to him, leave me by myself. Cannot you see?

But he did not touch her and did not move, and slowly she recovered, could take her hands away from her face. He was looking at her with that seriousness, that severity of expression that seemed his habit rather than a mood. And he still said nothing, nothing at all.

'I am sorry' she said.

He stood up, and came round to her side of the table, sat down on the bench by her. She knew that he was going to take hold of her hand, and he did take it, and she did not try to draw it away. As if the lateness of the time, the candlelight, their aloneness in the kitchen, her tears, all these things had conspired to alter the laws of everything. So that it seemed quite natural to sit like that, a stranger holding her hand, listening to her crying.

'I've not stopped thinking of you since I saw you the other night' he said. 'I can't stop thinking of you.'

And that was so far from anything she had expected him to say, that she could only look at him in astonishment. That tenseness in his face.

'What are you saying?' And still she did not try to recover her hand from his.

'This' he said. And put his mouth against hers, his other hand behind her head, holding her. And again it was so unexpected, the sensation was so strange, his mouth so different to anyone else's of the very few, the only two or three who had ever kissed her; so much the opposite of that one horrifying kiss of Mr.

Massingham's, and yet so like an echo of it, and echo of her thoughts, her imaginings upstairs, that she could not draw back, could not protect herself, could only stay as she was, her hand in his, his mouth touching hers, warm, supple, alive. Seeming to draw life out of her, strength out of her, so that she had none left. And they were still enclosed by the silence, by the candlelight, the lateness, by that sense of all the laws turned upside down, of nothing being as it might seem by daylight. His mouth against her eyes, as if he was tasting the tears. His hand unfastening her hair. She felt it fall, the weight of it against her shoulders, the warmth of his hand against her neck, his fingers under the neck of her gown, drawing the front edge of the cloth tight against her throat. His fingers touching the skin of her back, stroking softly. If she said anything it would end, the world would come back, the laws right themselves.

He had put his arm round her shoulders, one hand light against her breast. Against her heart beat. She thought she would give the entire world to let her head lie against his shoulder, to sit like this all night.

There was a knocking at the window, a hoarse whispering. 'Are ye ready, Master Robert? The horses 'ull take cold.'

He had let go of her, was no more than sitting at her side, the gold in front of them. 'Then walk 'em' he said, his voice quite natural.

The man saw us! she thought, and then with redoubled shame, what matter who saw us? I have seen myself! And stood up very carefully, expecting that her knees would give way, that she would not be able to walk to the fire and pretend to bank up the ashes with the shovel. And her knees were shaking, like a driven horse trembling.

He was behind her, taking the shovel from her hand, leaning it carefully against the fireplace so that it should not make a sound. 'I'm not used to your kind of women' he said. 'We don't often meet 'em in our trade.' And then, 'I didn't like to see you crying.' He stood holding both her hands. Their eyes were almost on a level. But he was so much broader than her that he seemed over-whelming.

'You must go now' she breathed.

He held her hands at arms' length, so that he could look at her from head to foot. 'The men who 've seen you about said I'd see something wonderful when I came here. But I didn't believe 'em.'

'Please, please!' I shall fall down, she thought. I am ill, something has happened to me.

He let go of her, and went back to the far side of the table, and the leather sack of gold. Fastened it. 'If this was mine' he said, 'you should have the whole of it. Would that help with what you were crying about?'

She did not understand what he was saying, and could only look to where his voice was coming from, seeing shadows, nothing. She went on standing there. Heard him go, close the door, the outer door. His voice saying something to the man Slipgibbet. Their horses. Silence. Went on standing, seeing nothing, not crying, scarcely breathing, scarcely thinking.

At last she knelt down, beside the fire, began to pray as she used when her mother was alive, as her mother had taught her. 'Our Father'—— But the words would not continue. I am lost, she thought. Could think of nothing but his mouth touching hers, his hand stroking. As if the skin of her back was burning, her breast. She put up one hand to where his had held her, felt her breast. Held it. Her heart beating.

Chapter 4

She slept as if she was dead, as if she had walked twenty miles. Dreamed of what had happened, was shocked awake out of her dream, and Martha was beside her, shaking her, bringing her a cup of chocolate, a lit candle. Old, fat, wheezing about the room, pulling the curtains back, the day still dark. Judith putting one hand out of the covers, feeling the cold of the morning, torn scraps of the dream still in her mind, holding on to the last flavour of it. She realised what she was doing and sat up truly shocked, the cold flowing round her like an icy river.

'An' well you might sit up, miss. Near seven o'clock! It ann't rising at seven as do run a house right. Six o'clock in winter your poor mother did be up, an' five in summer. Up an' dressed and down t'kitchen to see as things started proper.'

'I shall be down soon' she said. What have I done, she thought? She got out of bed, closing the door behind Martha, the question echoing in her mind. And stood looking at the cup of chocolate on the narrow table beside her bed. The boards of the floor icy against her bare feet. Welcoming it, as if the coldness could cleanse away something.

Her hand against her breast, lips parted, looking at the steaming, familiar cup across a great distance.

She went slowly to the glass on her dressing table. Her face shadowy in the candle darkness. Fetched the candle, held it this way, that. Her eyes looked at her, dark with anxiety, and then, as the candlelight touched them, blue as the sky. But no longer innocent. As if they knew things that she herself did not know. God will punish me, she thought. How could I? She looked above the mirror at the portrait, the girl in the blue and yellow head scarf, that her father had bought from a higler because it was like her mother. He had given a shilling for it.

She held the candle closer to the picture. Small and dark, the varnish cracked into spider's webs of still darker lines, so that the girl's oval face, the great eyes, the gently parted lips seemed to be watching her through a brown veil of shadow. There was a signature in the corner, so blackened it was impossible now to make it out. But by strong daylight the name was there. Meer. J. V. Meer. Who had he been? And the girl? His wife, his daughter? Or his lover?

A day ago she would not have thought of that word, it could not have come so smoothly into her mind. Lover. Lover.

But he is not! she cried, not my lover, nor I his. I was mad, mad, as though I was asleep. Like dreaming. There is no wrong in dreaming?

She felt his hand touching her neck, touching the smooth bone at the top of her spine, stroking, felt the neck strings of her gown tight against her throat, pressing the skin. She looked now into the mirror, holding the candle up, as if she expected to see a mark there. Drew down the neck of her shift with her other hand, down until her breast was almost exposed. And there. He had touched her there. And she remembered as if it was now, felt the warmth, against the stuff of her shift, against her skin.

They would be here to-night—to-night! I shall not go down she thought, I should die of shame to meet him, to see him. And in front of others! She stood up, began to wash, slowly, punishing herself with the coldness of the water. Stripping off her shift and letting the sponge run rivulets of ice down her spine, between her breasts, over her stomach. Rubbed herself savagely with the towel, scrubbing at her skin until she was reddened from head to foot, and went to look again in the mirror. A tall naked girl with her hair fallen. Stared at herself, her lips parted like the portrait's, staring, as if she was astonished at what she saw, at her familiar self. Touched her shoulders, the curve of her hips, the flatness of her stomach that had itself the slightest, most imperceptible of curves. What is a young man's body like, she wondered? How does he look naked? She lifted her hair from her neck and shoulders, as if that might help her to know, make her more man-like.

'Miss Judy! Judith, girl! Ann't you dressed yet?'

'I am coming Martha, I am coming!' Flung on her clothes and ran downstairs as if she was escaping from something.

In the kitchen her father's tray, his coffee, hot rolls and butter and a slice of pound cake that she would break up for him.

'That gypsy girl were here an hour back' Martha said. 'The one as danced. Wi' the old father as played the whistle for her. Growed quite big. Saying her daad were sick an' could they stay in the wood a bit.'

'And you told her yes?'

''t 'een't my place to goo saying yes to gypsies an' vagabonds. I towd her t'master was sicker than her daad was like to be, an' to get off wi' theirselves afore the Constable finds 'um an' has 'um whipped.'

'Oh, Martha! Did you give her nothing?'

'An' what would I give her, eh, miss? Eh? Your dinner, mebbe?' Grumbling, banging pots on the shelf, her back to Judith. 'A bit o'bread I give her. An' that were too much. Vagabonds!'

"If she comes again,' Judith said, 'tell me. If her father is ill——' She went out before Martha could argue, and took her father's breakfast up the stairs to him. He was awake, and she drew his curtains back, and lifted him higher against the pillows.

'Do you remember the child and her father who came here, and danced and recited in the kitchen?'

It had been the year after her mother died. An old, bent man like a rusty eagle, with a great hooked nose and one eye, a flapping cloak and a hat that must have been a cavalier's in King Charles's time it looked so strange; old and discoloured and broken-brimmed, and yet with a feather in it, and a kind of swagger. And the child dark as a Hindoo; black, dusty ringlets, bare feet, a ragged red skirt and a tight black bodice like a tiny woman's, tightened and laced. The old man sweeping the ground with his hat as he bowed to the servants in the kitchen, and to her. His voice rolling, magnificent, an extraordinary, extraordinary voice for a tramp, filling the kitchen with richness.

'An actor young mistress, an actor fallen upon hard times for the last while, and on his way to London, to take up an offer. Oddman Dyce, at your service, sir, good people. And my daughter, Evergreen, who if I am not mistaken may one day startle the world with her talents as a dancer, a follower of the great muse Terpsichore. Evergreen, child, the minuet!'

And without preamble, or more than he had given already, he

[33]

had pulled out a flute from a pocket inside his grey, threadbare cloak, and begun to play. And the child to dance, her bare feet on the pudding stone floor of the kitchen, the servants sniggering and staring. And Judith struck to the heart with wretchedness that she did not understand herself. A gypsy child dancing. Only that the dance was so un-gypsy like, so grave and measured, and the thin notes of the flute like a music box. The bare, dusty, child's feet pointing, stepping, turning. And the dance ending, and her curtsy, slow and deep, like wings sinking down. Even Solomon had stopped his sniggering.

'Do you remember them, Father?'

'I remember.'

They had given the child clothes that Judith had grown out of. Had given her shoes. And when they went away, the next morning, Judith had watched them, and a hundred yards down the avenue the child had stopped, and taken off the shoes, and gone on with them in her hand.

'They have come again' Judith said, 'and the old man is ill. They are in the woods, Martha says, and would like to stay there until he is well again. May they stay there?'

'Of course. You must—bring them something. I remember— He told me—wonderful stories, I liked him. He said—he had known Garrick when they were both young. And the little girl. Her mother—was a gypsy, he told me. I remember them.' He began to cough, and she had to hold him up until he was easy again.

'Do not try to talk' she said. 'It tires you so. I do not think you should write to-day. Would you not rest?'

But he looked so downcast that she fetched the writing board and set it out for him, with the paper, and the pencil.

'Not too long' she warned him. 'An hour at the most, and then you must rest.'

She went downstairs and busied herself about the house, still thinking of the child, and the old man, and of what she might give to the child for him if she came again. But she did not come. Dinner time. Afternoon. She went out into the stable yard and looked at the twilight sky that promised an early frost.

I should have gone to her at once, this morning, she thought. Suppose they have nothing to eat, nothing at all?

'I must have broth in a jar!' she cried to Martha. 'And bread and—and some gin, we will make a pint of hot with gin and ale, we have plenty and plenty of gin, and put some nutmeg in, and some sugar and cinnamon. And I must bring them some cheese, and a piece of bacon. Oh Martha, why did not you call me this morning when she came? Why did not I go to her at once? They shall come to the stables to sleep——' And stopped herself, thinking of Mr. Barnabas, of the smugglers coming.

'I shall bring them a blanket' she whispered. 'Two blankets, oh, think how cold they must be in the wood! And he is ill!'

'Blankets!' Martha was crying in indignation. 'Bacon and cheese and broth for they—they *go-by-nights*, are you gone onnsensed Judy child, are you gone wandering? On'y last week you goo givin' your second gown an' half a good ham to that whingeing Mrs. Locke 'cause she come sobbing to you, and now this one is to ha' the rest I suppose?'

'I tell you I must! Oh Martha, please, give me a jar quickly, there is broth left from dinner, I know, I saw.'

'An' what's for our supper, eh? You goo giving away our food to chance comers and we to fare to goo hungry? Oh, that's kindness, that's charity.'

But the old woman gave way in the end, and with Solomon trudging behind her, carrying the basket, his great boots plodding heavy to keep up with her half running steps, Judith set out for the wood as if she would find forgiveness there. A November knife's edge in the air, in the sharpness of the sky's turquoise, a hint of stars already, before the dark.

Far ahead of her, towards the wood, and the sea, there were arrow heads of wild duck, making a wide circle, before heading north to the marshes, or out to the Banks. When she came to the first of the stubble fields that Mr Hassett ploughed and sowed for them, there were more birds feeding, billing at the broken ground for grains of wheat still left there, if there could be any so long after reaping, or simply out of autumn habit. Bittern, and sheldrake, and brent geese, and rooks among them, glossy as clergymen. A hare heard her footsteps, and sat up, twitching his ears, and ran, not fast, but easily lolloping as if he knew she had neither gun nor dog nor evil intentions.

It was a mile and more to the wood's edge and the twilight was settling to a dove grey shadow by the time she came to the last hedge, grown thick and high with neglect, its berries a dark red autumn cloud in it, half-hiding the last of the ploughed fields that ran right to the wood itself. But through the hedge she could see more birds feeding, and she stopped to watch them, and to let Solomon catch up with her. In the middle of the field there was a small cluster of birds ferociously gobbling at the earth. A bittern, a goose, half a dozen wild duck, shelduck and mallard, widgeon mewing like cats as they darted in to feed, rooks, squabbling between themselves over what they had found.

What could it be, she wondered. And as she looked, the bittern seemed to totter and stagger on his long green legs, gathered himself for a moment to fly away. And fell. One of the rooks did fly, craaking. Gained a few feet into the air, and fell to the ground as if he had been shot. But there had been no sound, and who could be shooting here, on their land? One of the widgeon ran a yard, struggled with his wings, and collapsed. A few minutes more, and the ground was littered with fallen birds, a wing fluttering, a rook cawing in despair, falling silent. Like witchcraft. She felt her heart beat uncomfortably, stared at the reasonless massacre. Solomon had come up with her and she held up her hand for him to be quiet, and to look. And he too stared, scratching at his yellow head and shaking it.

The last bird fell, struggled, lay still. There was a flash of colour, of movement, at the far edge of the field, someone coming out of the wood. A red skirt. Black hair. The gypsy. And such a rage of anger caught at Judith that if she had held a gun in her hand she could have shot. Knew suddenly how the keepers felt when they saw the traps set, the nests robbed, found a covert cleared of pheasant they had reared by hand from eggs to splendour. And then saw a poacher running.

'Stop!' she cried. 'Stop!' She ran to the gateway and through it, into the field, the girl already running away from her. 'Catch her!' and before Solomon could break into his obedient, lumbering run, cried 'Come here, girl, I know who you are, I order you to come here.'

And miraculously the girl did stop, hesitate, poised to run again, and then came slowly towards Judith, step by frightened step. Judith stood among the fallen birds, looking about her. They did not look dead. Only wounded, a stir of feathers, the sense that they were still breathing.

'What have you done girl? How dare you do this on my land? When you have asked for help and I am bringing it?' She pointed at the basket Solomon was carrying, at the blankets. 'Have you put poison down?' The girl stood with bent head. Almost grown up in the years since she had danced in the kitchen. Black, dusty-looking ringlets. Her face a narrow oval, swarthy, dirty. What looked like the same rags; red skirt, black bodice laced across her thin, flat breast. Bare feet. Crippled-looking, scarred and scratched. Her head bent as if expecting to be struck.

'Well, have you?'

The girl nodded. Judith picked up the brent goose, its body still warm.

'I have brought you food! And look what you have done! Are they dying?'

The girl shook her head.

'You were going to kill them? Wring their necks?'

The dark, gypsy hair bent forward again, the ringlets hiding the girl's forehead. And Judith grew sick of what she was doing, wished she had not come, not seen, could hear the Earl's voice in hers. She put down the body of the unconscious bird, gently, laying it on its breast in a furrow.

'Will it live? Will they be able to fly again if—if they are left here?'

The girl looked at her from under the tangle of her hair, a wild creature living on the wild, by killing. Nodded.

'Then you must leave them! Every one!' She looked at the twilight sky. There would be foxes, rats and weasels on the hunt, scenting prey. 'How long will it be, before they grow well again?' But the girl did not seem to know. It could not have been a question she had ever asked herself.

'Solomon,' Judith ordered. 'You must stay here with them, see that nothing harms then until—until they fly away. And I come back. Can you carry that basket?' she said to the girl. She remembered her name. Evergreen. It had seemed a beautiful name when she heard it first. It was not beautiful now.

'You may sit down by them' Judith said to Solomon, 'or if you are cold you may walk about. But not far away from them. Do you understand?'

He scratched his head again, screwed up his round, stupid, obedient face in what was meant to be a frown of desperate intelligence. Stamped his feet. Eyed the fallen birds. If he was let, Judith thought, he would kill every one. She felt as though something were reaching towards her out of the dark face of the wood.

The girl had taken the basket and the blankets, bending sideways to ease the weight, her face no longer frightened, as if she knew from long experience the exact moment when danger passed.

'We will go to your father and see what is the matter with him. Have you a fire in the wood?'

'Yes' Evergreen whispered, the fear returning.

'I do not mind that, you may take all the fallen branches you like, but you must not break down any from the trees.' The Earl's tone again. Oh dear God, Judith thought, but one cannot let people break down a wood, and ruin it.

'I will carry the blankets' she said, 'they are too much for you.' There were stone jars in the basket that must weigh like lead. They went into the wood, the girl Evergreen leading, picking her way softly among the fallen tree trunks, the bracken, the trailing brambles and thorn shoots, the branches hanging across what had once been a path through a pleasure wood, leading towards a summer house. The wood was not very great, but Judith needed to go slowly to save her skirts from the thorns, and now and then the girl would stop and wait for her, as Judith herself had had to wait for Solomon. Indeed, it seemed as if the wood was much more the girl's than Judith's. She walked in it so easily, seeming to brush by the thorn branches without their catching at her clothes, nor her hair. It could not be true, but it seemed so. And she made no noise as she went, like a shadow, the colour of her skirt toned down by the twilight, the near dark.

Until they came to the clearing before the mound on which the summer house was built. The mound had been a giant's grave, or a Viking's, and long ago people had dug into it looking for treasure. Judith's grandfather had built the summer house on top of it, like a Greek temple, with pillars at the front, and a bronze statue of a goddess inside, and he had had broad, shallow steps made, so that ladies might go up easily, and rest in the shade of the Greek portico and look out at the sea beyond the sand dunes.

Now the clearing and the steps were overgrown and the white stone of the temple had turned green black with rotted moss and lichen and weathering. There was a smell of woodsmoke that seemed to emphasize the loneliness.

'Where is he?' Judith asked. The girl pointed up at the temple.

[38]

And that too seemed an offence. She had expected them to have camped in the clearing, or by the dunes. But the temple would be shelter for a sick man, was best. What is the matter with me, she thought? Have I lost all sense of charity because of those poor birds?

A voice called from somewhere, from the temple. 'Evergreen? Is it you?' A sick voice. At once feeble and anxious and impatient. They went up the steps. The fire was smouldering between sods of earth the girl must have cut out of the grassy top of the mound. A broad, flat grassy space. The pillars. The ice cold and damp of stone. And it did not seem the best place for a sick man at all. He would be better in the open, under the sky, than in this dankness. And a smell. A strange, sweetish, carrion smell as if an animal had died in the temple and rotted there.

He was lying on a heap of fern and bracken and dead grass, almost invisible in the dark of the building. His old grey cloak covering him except for his face, the eagle hook of his nose. His one eye turned towards them, widening in fright as he saw two figures, growing easy as he saw that the second figure was a woman's, Judith's. Saw the basket.

The smell was worse. How could he lie so near it and not—— She bent down towards him and the stench caught at her mouth, gagging her.

'I have brought you broth' she managed to say. 'And blankets. And something to drink. What is the matter with you?' She had to straighten up, away from the smell.

'God reward you ma'am.' An echo still of the richness his voice had had, that she remembered about him better than his face, his one eye, his great beak of nose, his grey cloak. 'I knew I should find a friend. Fifty miles. Fifty miles walking to find you.' The whisper turning to a gasping for breath, feverish. Fever in the eye. Her own eyes had grown used to the dark, and she could see the shine of sweat, the sick pallor. 'Your father, ma'am? The good gentleman is unwell?' His voice, his whisper, seeming to bow, to sweep an invisible hat towards the ground.

'He is in worse case than you, Mr. Dyce' Judith said. 'He can scarce move himself, and has no hope, like you, of recovering. But he has bid me make you welcome and sends his wishes to you. Will you take some broth now?'

'A trifle, ma'am. I remember your broth.'

[39]

'Give me the basket' Judith said, and began opening the stone jar. If she did not breathe deep the smell was endurable, although only just so, and between his mouthfuls she had to draw back, leaving him supported on his daughter's arm, he himself weak from the effort of eating, of drinking the beef tea she was giving him. Until he turned his head away and said 'no more, ma'am. If—if my daughter might finish it. She has had short commons poor child, the last days.'

Evergreen laid him down, very gently, as Judith herself was used to doing with her own father, and the similarity was painful, she did not know why.

'You must let me cover you properly' she said. 'I have brought blankets.' They would have to be burned afterwards, Martha would remember it against her for ever. 'We can roll up your cloak then as a pillow.' She began to lift the cloak away from him. And the smell was so much worse that she choked, and thought she would vomit. When she could look again she could see what it was that caused his stench. The leg of his breeches had been cut open, half way up the thigh, and knee and thigh were bound round with rags, caked with blood and pus, black, yellowish, the smell of rotted flesh seeming to pulse out of the filthy mass in waves.

'Merciful God' Judith whispered, 'what have you done? What has happened to it?'

'A small accident ma'am. A trifle. But incapacitating for a short while.'

'I must fetch a surgeon! You must be brought to——'

'No! No surgeon ma'am! No workhouse! For God's sake, leave me here quiet, not a word to a soul!' Clutching towards her, his face ghastly, shimmering like moonlight.

'But why? Why? Your leg——'

'A gamekeeper ma'am. A misunderstanding—a full load of shot—I shall be well as ever with a day's—rest. No workhouse ma'am. They'd tell. Bring us up before a magistrate——'

'But you must have medicines, care. Let me see.' She forced herself to touch the blackened flesh above the edge of the rags. It was tight swollen, bluish-black and shining, and there seemed to be red lines running up under the cloth of the breeches. She touched, and the skin burst at the first pressure, an ooze of liquid came from the cracked flesh. It did not seem to have hurt him.

She knelt back, holding her breath. No surgeon had a hope of saving him. She had seen gangrene before, in a labourer who had cut his leg open on a rusty nail and had relied on cobwebs and ointments from Cunning Luke to heal it.

She tried to think what to do, and there was nothing. The surgeon would cut off the leg and kill him quicker, that was all. If he went as the labourer had done he would be dead by morning. Even to bring him clean bandages was worse than useless. It would hurt him to undo the rags, and do no good. She set out the bottle of gin, and wished she had brought more. Evergreen was finishing the broth, small catsounds of supping in the shadows.

Should I tell him? Judith thought. Tell her? She stood up and went out into the cleanness of the air. Over the tops of the fringe of trees that surrounded the clearing on that side she could see the dunes, grass and bent, crouched bushes, already colourless, night-dark. And beyond them, the sea, catching the last of the twilight and a hint of moonrise. Now a shimmer of silver as a wave broke, now only a stirring blackness, quiet after the last week's storms, murmuring.

'Evergreen' she called quietly. 'Come out here to me.' The girl came, wiping her mouth, submissive, frightened. Fear seemed to live with her, like her shadow.

'Your father is very ill' Judith said, not looking at her after the first glance. Looking instead at the darkening sky, the dark sea. 'How old are you?' she said.

The girl whispered something, repeated it as Judith looked round. 'Fifteen? I did not think you so much.' The girl looked guiltily, as if her age was a fault in her. 'Are you a brave girl?' Judith said, making her voice gentle. It was a strange thing, the temptation to be harsh. As though somewhere in her mind, a voice, the Earl's voice, was saying, 'Why cannot they die elsewhere?'

She took the girl's hand then and held it carefully.

'Your father is going to die' she said. 'You must be very brave.'

The girl stared at her, her eyes not altering for a moment, and then seeming to grow not wide but deep. The mouth opened a little.

'Hush' Judith said. 'He must not hear you cry out.'

She stayed holding the girl's hand. The night came closer, emptied the sky of light. Solomon is waiting for me, Judith

[41]

thought. I must go home. Home. And her own father waiting, lying quiet. Fires lit. Candlelight. Supper. Martha. And here? This child. The cold. The dark. And in a few hours, nothing else. Nothing, nothing, nothing. A dead body lying on the bed of bracken. Like a dead fox, and a fox cub whimpering.

'Stay here' she said. She went into the summer house and knelt down by the dying man. The fever had taken its grip of him and he was muttering to himself, making scarcely a sound, a fluttering in the darkness. The bronze statue, Aphrodite rising from the waves, stood in its pale stone niche behind him.

'Lear?' the old man cried suddenly, frighteningly loud. 'Play Lear, sir? Why, as if it were writ for me. I have been much abandoned by people.' He muttered again, his voice lost in a whispering of delirium. And then 'She was a good wife to me. No man had a better.' And again, 'Shuri! Shuri, where are you? Touch my hand!'

Judith touched it. Burning hot. He had pushed his blankets away from his hollowed chest. She drew them up to his throat. His fingers closed on hers, gripped like talons. 'I'll mind her, my love' he whispered. 'She shall be my soul. Never fear for her.' The grip tightening, the eye like a burning-glass. Like water deep in a well shaft, shining. 'Is it a good house, to-night?' he whispered. 'I feel so cold. So cold. Poor Tom's a'cold.'

He began shivering, so violently that the blankets fell again, slipped away. He rolled off the pressed-down heap of bracken, almost pulled Judith with him. Rolled back, grew rigid for a second, and then lay limp, pouring with sweat, the smell stifling, choking her. She did not know what to do, how to leave him. Yet she could not stay longer. Martha would be already angry, needing Solomon for the fires, wondering where she herself had got to.

She had to go outside. The girl was where she had left her, crouched on the steps. 'I must tell my servant man to go home' Judith said. 'I shall come back in a short while.'

The girl nodded, her face blank.

Should I have told her, Judith wondered? 'Go into him' she said. She ran down the steps, made her way through the wood. Solomon was walking in a close circle round and round in the field, swinging his arms about, his teeth chattering. When Judith came up to him he started as if she was a ghost. The birds were

[42]

where they had fallen. Judith stumbled over one, bent down and touched it. Cold. The brent goose. She picked it up. Picked up the bittern. Two of the wild duck. All dead. 'Take these home with you' she said, 'Martha will pluck and scald them. Tell her I may be very late, and then you must come back to me with another blanket. Have your supper, and then come back to me. I shall be in the summer house in the wood. Shall you remember that?'

'Yes ma'am, yes Miss Judy, I 'ull remember.'

'Good. Now run. Run!'

She herself turning back towards the wood, feeling that she had decided wrongly, that she should have gone home with Solomon, left them here. What more could she do? She had no knowledge of healing, they might be much better left alone, without a stranger beside them.

She went into the wood, already dark as midnight. Felt her way slowly, reluctantly.

The girl, she thought. What shall I do with her when he is dead?

Chapter 5

He died in the coldest hour of the morning. He had been in delirium when she came back to the summer house, and did not regain his senses until the last minute of his life. Muttering about plays and players, about his wife, the gypsy woman Shuri, thinking that she was there. About Evergreen. Reciting. Imagining he was playing the flute and Evergreen was dancing. That he was cold. Judith had told Solomon to build a fire inside the summer house, as well as the fire outside, and the smoke and scent of the burning wood had cleansed the air a little, besides warming it.

'Where am I?' the old man whispered suddenly. 'Who are you?' Seeing Solomon there. Hunched over the fire and sleeping.

'We are friends' Judith said.

He looked at her, his face ghastly, death in it. His eye spent.

'I am near gone.' He tried to lift his head. 'Where is she?' The girl was there, creeping to him. He raised himself. 'Your mother—' he said. 'I promised her—I'd mind you. Now—now—' He looked at Judith, his mouth still working, but no words coming. His eye grew frantic with the effort to speak, grew wide, staring. Veiled itself. Like glass misting with breath. He felt the air in front of him. 'Shuri?' His hand open, the palm towards Judith's face, as if he were trying to feel something invisible, there between them. His body shivered, stayed for a second lifted, and fell back. The girl lifted her head, looked up into the darkness of the roof and gave a wailing cry like a dog, an animal despair in it, wildness, until the summer house rang with her pain.

Judith did not touch her. After a moment she went outside, leaving the girl there with her father, her father's body, beckoning Solomon to follow. The girl's grief filled the clearing, and the trees seemed to listen, holding themselves still.

Judith wanted to put her hands over her ears against that wild animal's misery, and was ashamed to. She climbed the dunes between the rough tamarisk bushes and clumps of marram grass, went down the last dune and came to the edge of the sea. The cries died in the distance, gave way to the sea's sullen murmuring.

'What shall I do with her?' she said aloud, Solomon behind her. 'What shall we do with her, Solomon? We cannot leave her here.'

Solomon looking helplessly willing. 'I dunna know, mistress.' Scratching his head with that dry rasping of blunt fingers that set her teeth on edge. 'Tell t'parish? Mr. Carteret?'

'He would have her put in prison.' She looked at the reflections of the sea, the waves breaking far out on the Banks, white as bones in a grave. How can I take her in? she thought. And could hear Martha's voice, rising in outrage, 'A gypsy! A thieving vagabond off t'road, full o' lice an' vermin! In my kitchen?'

It is not rational, she thought, walking by the sea's edge. And when she looked down the old man's face was there, his eye, his mouth trying to shape words. 'Now—' now what? Now what will become of her?

She turned back, began to run, as if by running, by giving herself the least time possible to think, she could turn unreason into reason.

In the summer house the girl had tied a scrap of red cloth round the dead man's bent forefinger. Her cries had finished, and she was sitting crouched in the dark, her knees drawn up, her head down on them, her arms locked round her shins. Her body shook, was still, shook again with sobbing.

'You cannot stay here' Judith said. 'You must come with me.'

The girl did not answer. Judith touched her. The hair dry and matted, like a fox's pelt. 'Listen to me, we must go to my house, you shall lie down and sleep, and we can arrange for your father to be buried. Do you understand?'

There was still no answer. Judith knelt down, made her lift her head. The eyes blind as glass. 'You cannot help him by staying here,' Judith said. 'He is surely in Heaven now, he suffered so much in this life. Do you believe that?'

The girl opened her mouth, gave a low, wrenching cry of loneliness.

'Please' Judith said, 'it is no use to cry, he will hear you crying, and will be miserable in Heaven. He is with the angels now, and

[45]

with your mother. You do not want them to hear you crying, and to be sad for you.' She wondered if the girl knew anything of Heaven, and felt her own hypocrisy in offering such comfort. Like Mr. Carteret preaching Suffer little children. He would make this child suffer well enough if he got hold of her. But he shall not, she determined. Nor the Overseer. Nor anyone. She stood up, and lifted the girl until she too was standing.

When one helps people, Judith thought, it would be much nicer if they were clean. She tried not to think of Martha. 'Come.' And when the girl resisted, Judith called to Solomon to help bring her down the steps into the clearing. Evergreen began to fight then, clawing and spitting and kicking, until Solomon dropped her onto the ground. She ran scrambling back up the steps of the mound, flung herself against her father's body, wrapped her arms round it.

'What shall we do?' Judith said. Half wanted Solomon to say that they must leave her there, that there was nothing else for it.

Solomon held up his thick hand and looked at it. 'I could do give her a dunt' he said.

'No!' She went and picked up the third blanket that Solomon had brought back with him. Carried it into the summer house and wrapped it round the crouched shoulders.

'I shall stay with her, there is nothing else to be done. Go to Mr. Hassett's, to Moate, and wait until someone is about. Then tell them—— Tell them there is a man dead in our wood and beg them to send means to fetch him away for burial. As quick as may be or we shall freeze here.'

When Solomon was gone she built up the two fires, and sat between them. The girl did not seem to feel the cold, nor anything but her loss. When she realised they did not mean to force her away from her father's body she let go of it, and sat quiet.

'I shall see that he has proper burial,' Judith told her. She wondered again at herself for offering such a consolation, she who did not believe in Mr. Carteret, or his prayers, or his religion, any more than her father did. A little more, perhaps. Her mother's teaching having set some kind of roots in her emotions, if not in her mind. And what other consolation could she offer?

She took the girl's hand. Chafed it between hers to warm both. 'You shall stay with us' she said. 'And have your food. Can you do any work? In a kitchen?'

The girl looked at her.

I suppose she cannot, Judith thought wretchedly. She cannot even clean herself. In the past years the girl seemed to have grown dirtier and wilder as she had grown older. Her hair did not bear looking at too close. Even her smell was wild. Foxish. Only her teeth were white and strong, like an animal's, as if she had gnawed bones and roots. And been lucky to find them, probably. How can I criticise, Judith thought guiltily. She looked at the scarlet thread on the dead man's finger, that should ward off witches from his soul. The morning was growing light. A greyness about the wood, the trees taking shape. No dawn.

Lighter still. The cold seemed harsher. She walked about, glad to be away from the smell of the dead man, of the girl. I am stark mad, she thought. Even my father will think me so. What can I do with her? Teach her to scrub floors, wash dishes?

Another hour. There were sounds far off of branches breaking, a clumsy smashing of heavy bodies through the wood. Solomon came, and a man from Moate Farm, leading a plough horse, a coil of rope over his shoulder. Touching of forelock, stupefied looking about for the body. Even more stupefied staring at Judith, to find her there.

'In the summer house' Judith said. The man climbed heavy up the steps, side by side with Solomon. Two such stupid men as it would be hard to find their like in Essex, Judith thought with a sudden bitterness, as if it was their fault that they were so stupid, and a malice of destiny that she should have them for helpers and no one else. There was a sudden scream of fury, of despair from the girl. Judith ran up the steps and found her trying to protect her father's body from being taken up by Solomon and Mr. Hassett's labourer. First Solomon, and then the labourer would push her away, and she would rush in again, claw at their faces, at the body. The leg had burst and become so dreadful Judith felt faint and had to lean against one of the pillars of the summer house. Behind her there was the sound of the labourer's cursing, screams from the girl, and then the smack of an open hand striking hard. The girl fell on the stone floor, half stunned and whimpering. The body was taken down the steps and laid across the broad brown back of the plough horse.

I must comfort her, Judith thought. She began to lift the girl who now seemed to determined not to stand up, and to have no bones in her body. Judith felt the temptation to copy Solomon and give her another dunt to stun her properly.

'Get up!' she said. 'At once.'

After a moment more, to Judith's surprise the girl obeyed, and stood in front of her, sullen, dirty, weeping silently, the tears carving channels of comparative cleanness in the dirt.

'I mean to be kind to you' Judith said, 'and you must obey me in return. If you do not, then you must go to the parish, do you understand what I am saying? There they will put you in prison for being a gypsy. Have you been in prison before?'

The girl nodded, sniffed, wailed again.

She put her arms round the girl in spite of her dirt, her smell. Held her close. 'Now hush. We shall go to my house and you shall have food, and we shall make you clean, and warm. Will you come with me?'

The girl bent her shoulders in submission, allowed Judith to lead her down the steps. The body was already roped across the horse, like a smuggler's bale. It made it impossible to go back through the wood, the paths were too narrow, and they must go to the dunes and plod their way south, then inland again towards the farm and the village. Half way to Guthrum's Judith told Solomon and the labourer Samuel to go direct to the village and to Mr. Carteret, and to ask him in her name that the burial might be in Woodham churchyard, and immediately, with no need to send the corpse to Urnford and the workhouse there.

They plodded away, and the girl tried to follow them. 'No' Judith said. 'They would send you to prison at once if you were with him. Come with me.'

It seemed the last flicker of the girl's resistance, and she walked obediently beside Judith, her head bent. Judith's heart beating faster as they came near the farm, and explanations, and Martha's anger, and everything that would have to be done. The first, first thing to clean her. As they turned into the stable Martha was there, shaking out mats. She stood and stared. Judith put her arm round the girl's bowed shoulders and with her bravest, least guilty face said, 'Look Martha, look what I have brought home for you. She is to be your helper.' And in a low voice, before Martha could speak. 'Her father is dead. Solomon and one of Mr. Hassett's men are taking the body now to Mr. Carteret. I beg you to be kind to her.'

[48]

Chapter 6

It was hard enough to be kind to her. She would not allow herself to be washed, for the first thing, and the tub of warm, soapy water was spilled over the kitchen floor.

'I'll do fare to kill her!' Martha shouted. 'The vagabond, the louse box! Get out o' that corner you thieving witch, get out of it!' Beating at her with the broom where she was crouching between the end of the kitchen dresser and the wall and the hearth.

'Leave her to me' Judith said, 'please, for pity's sake, Martha, she will never trust us.'

'Trust us? Trust *us*? 'tis me as woon't be trusting, I'll fare to tell her that, the black imp of Satan. Look at her eyes, t'wickedness. I woon't ha' her here, I woon't, I woon't. You take her to t'parish an' ha' her locked up, or I woon't sleep a wink.'

'Leave her' Judith begged. She had to take the broom from Martha almost by force, and push her out of the kitchen. Bolt the doors. Get bread, cheese, ham, a piece of cake. A cup of milk. Set them all on a wooden board and push them towards the crouched ferocity in the corner. She was indeed herself almost afraid of her, of the savagery in her eyes. She busied herself about the kitchen, doing anything to seem ordinary and unconcerned. Built up the fire.

She did not look at Evergreen for minutes together. When at last she did the girl was eating, cautiously, her eyes watching Judith. When she saw herself observed she stopped, holding the piece of ham in both hands, delicately, not as Solomon might do, but with a natural neatness.

'Eat everything there' Judith said. 'I am hungry too.' She cut herself some bread and cheese, poured out milk and set it on the table. Lifted the rest of Evergreen's meal from the floor and put that on the table, beckoning. 'Come' she said. 'Martha is not here, she shall not touch you. No one shall touch you.' Slowly the girl came, sitting at the farthest end of the bench away from Judith. Watching her. She put out a cautious hand towards the knife, fork, but did not pick them up. Drank the milk.

'You must be washed at last, you know' Judith said. 'You are very dirty. Have you never learned to wash?'

The girl slowly shook her head.

'When you were little you were not so dirty. At least I do not remember it. It is very nice to be clean, you cannot imagine how nice if you have never washed.'

They finished their meal and Judith took the girl by the hand. Perhaps it had been a mistake to try too much, too quickly. 'Come' she said, 'I shall show you.' There was still water in the sink, and soap by it. She held the girl's wrist and approached her hand to the water. The girl began to struggle, her strength astonishing in someone so small and thin. But made of whale-bone. And terrified. Terrified of the water.

'Look!' Judith cried. Plunged her own hand in the water so deep she wet the sleeve of her gown. 'It is nice. It is not even cold.' With a swift snatch she caught Evergreen's hand and dragged it into the water, began to soap it.

'Look!' she cried again in triumph when she was finished. 'Is not that different?' To tell the truth it was not visibly very changed. Scratched, brown, swarthy by nature, tanned dark by weather, still not truly clean, it was a sad enough looking object. But at least it was five shades cleaner than its fellow. There was a rough line on the narrow sinewy wrist where the cleanness ended and the dirt of a lifetime began. 'Now the other hand.'

It was a long process. Needing now cajoling, now brute force. Rag by rag peeled off. The child clinging to them, her bone-thin arms clasped against them. Judith had already managed to wash both her hands, both her feet, her face, after a fashion. Wet her hair, so that it clung to her cheeks in witch's strands, serpent ringlets of dusty, verminous black. It would need sulphur to clean it and under pretence of fondling her Judith rubbed in great handfuls of suphur ointment mixed with paraffin. The last rags peeled away. Judith was already soaked to the skin. With a swift movement she lifted the girl entire, one arm behind her knees, the other round her shoulders, and plunged her into the wooden bath that on its usual working days was a washtub. There was a desperate struggling of arms, legs, fountains of lukewarm water everywhere. Judith held her down with both hands, all her strength and weight. Like holding an eel. 'God grant me charity! Hold still, hold still!' Water running down her face, inside her clothes. Her own hair falling, the great, pale flaxen mass of it falling like a silk curtain round her. And astonishingly Evergreen grew still, lay in the water looking at Judith's hair, as if in her whole life she had never seen anything so marvellous. Judith began to soap her, the water turning dark grey, black, the body becoming yellow ivory, glistening. Soaped her hair. Soaped and soaped. Until at last everything was done that one bath could do, and the girl stood quiet, knee deep in the filthy, soap-scummed water, and let herself be rubbed dry, her eyes still on Judith's hair. Her own hair dried. It would need to be fine-combed, and sulphured again. But there was at least a remote sense of future cleanness about it. The vermin had been given pause for thought, if not their death-blow.

More sulphur ointment, rubbed deep in. Dressing her in Judith's childhood clothes of years ago, smelling of camphor and lavender. Shift. Chemise. Under skirt. Gown. Stockings. Slippers.

'Why, no one could recognise you" Judith said. 'Martha will think you are a handsome young visitor, and not Evergreen at all. Martha! Martha, where are you—Come and look! Oh Lord, how wet I am, I must go and dry myself.' But she was suddenly afraid to leave Evergreen in the kitchen, in case—— In case she runs away, she thought. Such efforts for someone who probably wanted nothing in the world but to be ten safe miles from here, and to be dirty and ragged as before!

But she could not be anything she had been before. Not alone. If she was not caught by the constable and brought to be imprisoned by the magistrate, the first man that found her——
Of if not the first, or the second, or the third, then some man, some tramp like herself, some drunken labourers reeling home from a tavern, they would find her, and——
Bringing her up the stairs, needing to urge her, force her, as if corridors and stairs were strange to her, and almost as frightening as water. Into Judith's room.

'Now look' Judith said, bringing her before the looking-glass. 'Are not you glad now?'

[51]

Evergreen stared into the grey depths as she had stared at Judith's hair. She put out a finger to touch the surface of the looking glass. Then covered her face with both her hands and knelt down.

'What is the matter?' Judith said. But Evergreen only knelt, and cried. Cried silently, horrifyingly, such a despair as Judith could not bear to look at. She took off her own wet clothes, washed and dried herself at her washstand, dressed again, brushed out her hair, coiled it up and knotted and pinned it, and all the time the girl knelt where Judith had left her, in front of the dressing chest, crouched and wretched.

'That is enough' Judith said. 'I forbid you to cry any more.' Holding her close to show that she did not mean it, was only pretending to be angry. But the girl was not one to pretend with, and Judith had to be gentle with her, stroke her face, sit her down in front of the looking glass, begin to comb out her hair. But that was too painful a business to continue very long, and made Judith think too keenly of what she might be combing out that had survived the sulphur. 'Come' she said, 'we shall go and seek my father. Do you remember him? He was kind to you one day when you were little and has often spoke of you since.'

She brought the girl along the corridor, into her father's room.

'I have brought her to see you, does she not look well and pretty?' He turned his head, smiled.

Evergreen's eye grown wide.

'Give him your hand.'

The hands touched, held.

'Do—you remember—me?'

'He is asking do you remember him.'

Evergreen's head shaking. Judith knelt at the other side of the bed, leaned over him and whispered, 'She is desperate. I think she may run away. What shall I do?'

'Leave her—with me.' And when Judith did not answer immediately he said again, 'Leave her here.'

Judith expected the girl to follow her, to be terrified to be left in that room, with its curtained bed, and closeness. But she did not move. As Judith shut the door she did not so much as turn her head.

In the kitchen Judith found Martha looking at the flood of dirty water and the almost empty tub. 'What else could I have done?'

[52]

she said. 'You could not have left her there yourself, you know it. Nor to have been taken by the constable.'

'I could. An' could now, you give me the chance.' And as she said it, Solomon was at the kitchen door, breathless and alarmed. ''tis Mr. Carteret, 'tis Mr. Carteret, he do ha' come for t'gypsy, he says, an' he do want to put his horse in t'stable.'

'Oh no!' Judith cried, ran on wings. The stables! Full of smuggled goods! 'Take his horse from him, say you must bate it, anything. where is he?'

'On t'terrace, ma'am.'

She found the vicar walking his horse himself, his large face folded into more than its usual grey dyspepsia for his being kept waiting, and perhaps for his mission.

He bowed with the coldest of greetings and surrendered his horse to Solomon without looking at him. 'I am sorry not to have been able to accede to your wish in regard to the tramp's burial' he said. 'But there are regulations in these matters. There is no paupers' burial ground here.'

'It was inconsiderate of him to die here, then' Judith said, unable to prevent herself. 'I am sorry for it.'

Mr. Carteret looked greyer still, his anger showing in the pinched bloodlessness of his nostrils, in the droop of his huge, pendulous lower lip. 'There is another troublesome matter' he said. 'There was a child with him, I understand. Where is she now?'

'She is here' Judith said. She found it hard to control her breathing, not to betray her nervousness.

'Then I shall bring her back with me. She can go to Urnford with the body, and be disposed of there. I have advised the constable.'

'I am glad to be able to save you at least that trouble' Judith said, her heart beating so fast it was uncomfortable. 'I mean her to stay here.' She met his stare of dislike with what she hoped was dignity.

'That is very charitable in you. But quite impossible. Bring her—have her brought out to me, if you please. Since you do not ask me to enter your house.' He said the last with such bitter release of feelings that it was shocking. No one in the parish liked him, and the hostility had carved its way into his soul. Even his wife had abandoned him, running off at the age of thirty-five with

[53]

an East Indiaman's purser, to Gravesend, and then, so far as anyone knew, to Calcutta.

'I did not think you wished to come in' Judith said, ashamed. 'Please, I beg of you, and we may talk of this girl more conveniently.' She led the way in through the front door, that creaked in protest at being so unexpectedly used. Only when someone from Matcham came was it ever opened, in the usual way of things.

'I have no wine to offer you' Judith said. 'But I—Martha will make us tea.'

'Do not disturb her' Mr. Carteret said, sitting heavy and lowering on the edge of what had once been her father's chair. He had brought a chill of the spirit into the room. Even the fire seemed to have lost its brightness. 'The girl cannot stay here with you. She is a vagabond without means and you would be breaking the law to give her shelter. She must be sent to Urnford and brought up before Mr. Percival.'

It was another bitterness to Mr. Carteret that he himself had not been made magistrate.

'But she has means' Judith said, folding her hands tightly in her lap and looking from them to Mr. Carteret's face. 'She has her wages here. She is to be kitchen maid to Martha.'

Mr. Carteret's face seemed actually to swell and take on a leaden darkness. His great hanging lower lip tightened. 'I forbid it! The girl should be taken and whipped! And then set to useful labour. I forbid you to interfere like this!'

'You would have her whipped?' Judith said. She thought that that was not possible now, for a girl who was guilty of nothing but vagrancy, but she was not sure enough to challenge him on grounds of the Law. 'A child? Scarcely more than a child? Who has done nothing wrong except to be born poor and wretched?'

'Do you dare to teach me my task? Mr. Carteret whispered. 'I am the guardian of my flock, and these people—she is a gypsy, she has been described to me. They are evil! Criminal, criminal by birth. They steal and poison. They are like a sickness wherever they go.'

'Nevertheless' Judith said, 'I mean to keep her here.' The Earl's tone in her voice. Mr. Carteret looked at her.

'Do you refuse to give her up to me?'

'I do not consider that you have any rights over her. She is my servant. She has done no wrong.' She was tempted to add, 'and you are not a magistrate.' But she did not wish to provoke him beyond what could not be helped.

'We shall see' Mr. Carteret said. He got to his feet, breathing heavily. She went to the front door with him, called to Solomon who was dreamily leading Mr. Carteret's horse up and down the terrace. The horse looked ill-kept and ill-tempered, an unhealthiness about its eye, and a galled hardness in its mouth. Mr. Carteret mounted as if he disliked the animal, all animals. Rode away with the barest of salutes.

He seemed to leave his shadow behind him, like a threat.

Judith went into the house, trying to feel relieved that he was gone. What could he do? And indeed she had more things to concern her than Mr. Carteret, or even Evergreen. If those were all her concerns! She went through the house to the stable yard, looked in the barn, and the stables. Rows upon rows of casks. Bales, oilskin rolls. If he should have brought his horse straight in! On top of one of the casks nearest the barn doors she saw a piece of white paper. Fastened there with a nail roughly pressed into the wood. Her name on it, on the outside of the fold.

She freed the paper from its fastenings and unfolded it. 'This cask is for you. It has good wine in it for your father. I had hoped to see you. We mean to collect these goods tomorrow night. Not late. Soon after midnight . . .?'

The question mark standing alone, like an initial. It puzzled her for a moment and then she realised that it was an invitation, a question whether she would be there, stay up for them. And she felt the flush climb from her cheeks to her forehead, cover her throat, her breast. She had almost forgotten it, in all that had happened since. Not forgotten, oh no, not that, how should she ever forget it? But put it to the back of her mind, out of her sight. To have been held like that! Kissed like that! And now for him to write this! That anyone, Martha, Solomon, even Mr. Carteret might have found. Although Solomon could not read, and Martha only great print.

She held the letter against her breast. It is a love letter, she thought in horror, and held it away from her again, meant to tear it, and then thought, the fire! The kitchen fire, I shall burn it! Ran in. Martha there, seeing to the dinner at long last, the floor mopped up, something of order back into the kitchen, the wash tub put away. The smell of rags burned.

'I—I will go and see how my father is—is getting on with her' Judith said. She folded the letter, pushed it into her bodice. It did not seem right to burn it. Not with Evergreen's rags. 'Mr. Carteret was very angry.'

'An' no wonder. No wonder. 't'ann't often I do feel as how t'Vicar is in the rights 'bout anything, but he do fare to be in t'right about this. My kitchen maid! You just put her near me, that's all. You just do an' see what 'ull happen.' She banged pots, the shovel, the poker, slammed a dish down on the table. 'Kitchen maid! Oh no, we cain't ha' Peg back, we do ha' no money. But Go-by-nights! Murderers! Thieves! Incomers! Oh, we can ha' they, oh yes. Give me patience! You keep her by you! You do that, Miss. You'll ha' your way, I know that. But I'll ha' mine, and she doon't step her foot in t' this kitchen less you're here wi' her to watch what she does.'

Judith ran, not daring to ask how Martha knew of her imaginary employment for Evergreen.

Upstairs she heard whispering. Evergreen's voice, whispering. She was crouched beside the bed, still holding the sick man's hand. She looked guiltily at Judith, looked away.

'She has been telling me a story' Judith's father whispered, when Judith bent close to him. 'I am glad—you—have brought her—here.'

Chapter 7

She would not wait up for them, she was determined on it. And she was so tired that it would have been impossible. She fell asleep on her chair after dinner, with dinner itself an agony of problems. Martha refusing to have 'that gypsy eat wi' Christians.'

'Let her feed in t'stables where she belongs!'

'Then she must eat with me since you and Solomon are too grand for her.'

'Wi' you? Wi' the best chiny I do imagine?'

'Martha, Martha! Where is your charity?'

'Where it belongs, at home.'

Until dinner became a scrambled thing that no one enjoyed. Evergreen on a stool by the fire in the dining room, with a plate on her knees that she did not know how to balance, and Judith, with all appetite lost, crumbling a piece of bread at the table. To fall asleep suddenly, her head on her arms, as if she had been struck with a hammer. She did not know how long she slept, and woke with her mouth tasting sour and sick and feverish, and then the fear that the girl was gone. But she too had fallen asleep on her stool. Her head on her knees, arms wrapped round her shins, the plate upside down on the faded red and blue turkey hearthrug, crumbs round her.

The evening dragging away, thinking only, almost only, of getting into bed and sinking away from everything. From Matcham, from Mr. Carteret, from Martha, from this creature she seemed to have tied round her neck like a weight. From money, and debts, and the future. From the smugglers. From Robert Barnabas—expecting—how could he think that she would? The Earl's concealed threat. Mr. Massingham. But it was nor really possible, even the Earl could not think such a monstrous thing was possible. It—it would be laughable if it were not so hideous. Round and round.

Looking about the room, the house. At china, furniture. She could sell that, and they did not need that, nor this chair, nor the corner cupboard—surely there were a hundred things? But already they had sold a great deal and got so little that it was like a sacrifice for nothing. Her horse, poor Scipio, to Mr. Gaultrip. Almost all the silver. Things her father had brought home from his Grand Tour when he was young. And from his service in Russia. Even the snuff box the Empress had given him, in memory of it. Gold, with a miniature of the Empress herself, set round with pearls. Mr. Bowen had said that it was not pure gold and had offered twenty guineas. And then twenty-five. She had thought afterwards it must have been worth more, he had put it so carefully into his waistcoat pocket, while he left everything else to be wrapped up by his two porters and packed into a great ugly chest.

By the time she got to bed she was so worn out, and her mind so filled with anxieties, and solutions that fell to pieces as soon as she re-examined them, that she knew she would not sleep at all. She had put Evergreen to bed in what had long ago been an attic bedroom for two kitchen maids, had left a nightlight with her, and had terrors of the house being burned down by it, and gone to take it back; thought of the girl being frightened in the strange dark, and brought it to her again. To find the girl fast asleep on the floor, the blankets round her but the bed abandoned. She left her there, hesitating about the nightlight and at last leaving it, in case the girl should wake, and not know where she was, and cry out.

Her own bed. Dark. Sleep! As if she could! She lay furious with Martha, with herself, with the girl, with the old man for dying, with Mr. Carteret. Round and round and round. Heard the clock in the parlour strike its hours. Ten. Eleven. Twelve. They would be coming soon. The half hour. One. I shall never sleep again, she thought. Twisting, her coverlid sliding, her pillow seeming to be filled with stones.

Sounds.

Outside.

She sat up, listened, threw the covers back, felt for her cloak. They were here. She forgot what she had determined, dismissed it as foolishness. She must go down to them. Must get her money into her hand. Learn when they meant to come again. She went to the door, still listening. Into the dark corridor.

But not completely dark. As if a candle had been left burning somewhere. She stared, not understanding. Crept forward in the familiar passage, came to the corner of it, the step up. Saw the light burning outside her father's room, a shape against the wall. Thought of death. Felt horror for a moment, thought of ghosts, a fetch. And then recognised the nightlight, Evergreen. Her eyes open, shining in the candlelight.

'What are you doing here?' Judith whispered.

The face hid itself behind an edge of blanket. Only the eyes there, shining.

Judith could hear them below. Thought she could hear a soft knocking at a door, a shutter.

She picked up the nightlight. 'Come' she said, not sure whether to be angry or to cry for her. 'Come with me downstairs.' She went along the corridor, heard the rustle of movement behind her.

He was at the back door, waiting, and came in as she opened it. As if he expected to come in. He did not say anything, but took the nightlight from her and went into the kitchen.

'Who is that?' he said, his voice low. Moving the candle-light towards the shadow of Evergreen, against the door, her blanket round her like an awkward cloak.

'Her father died in our wood. I have brought her here.'

She stooped down by the fire and woke the embers, laid on wood. It was as though she had prepared everything. The girl as guardian, as duenna. She almost smiled at him. And he sat opposite her at the table, hefting up the familiar leather bag. Familiar fumbling at the knot.

She watched him counting out her coins. I should be humili-ated she thought. To be paid like this. And unbidden the thought came of women who must be paid like this, across a table, gold coins by candlelight. The thought seemed almost amusing in her tiredness, in that safe secrecy of the kitchen, safe with Evergreen there like a watchman, like a constable of conscience.

'I am thinking how strange it is' she said, 'that we should sit here like this.'

He looked surprised, as if he had expected her to say something

[59]

quite different. To refer to the other night, she wondered? The disappointment spread in her like chill. But how should she have expected him to be different, she wondered. A smuggler's son.

'Your father?' she said.

He nodded towards the window. 'Outside. Not in the yard. With the batmen.'

'The batmen?'

'The clubmen. The guards. We've a ring of 'em round about. In case——' He smiled then, watching her. 'In case the Customs lads should try anything.'

He is trying to frighten me now, she thought. He does not like to see a woman confident in anything. He preferred me crying.

And found herself blushing. That scarlet, burning wave of blood under her skin that she could never control. Like a signal flag. Except that those who saw it were likely to misread the signal, as one of distress instead of anger. She touched the gold, thinking of the debts, the Earl, of Mr. Bowen with the drip on his nose, and his small searching eyes, like a rat's searching out a bird's eggs in a nest, greedy and pitiless. Of Miss Frewen growing cooler and cooler each time she needed to go into the shop. Of Miss Whittaker.

I shall end like her, she thought. If I am lucky. Or like—— She touched the gold, tried to imagine what those women did. Imagining it as one imagines catching the smallpox, going blind. She shivered suddenly, as if her grave was being dug.

'Come to the fire' he said. 'You're cold.' He took her hand, and her hand was cold, his warm, dry, very strong. Square and powerful and certain. She would have liked to ask him what he was so certain of, what made him certain of anything. Stupidity? Bluntness of mind, like his blunt finger-tips?

'Is she a gypsy?' he said. And when she nodded he said 'You've a kind heart.' And without any least show that what he was doing might seem strange, he leaned across to Evergreen and drew down her eyelids with his finger-tips, very gently. Then arranged the fold of her blanket up above her mouth, her nose, hid her eyes. 'Stay like that' he said. And to Judith, 'I've only a few minutes. None to waste.'

She knew what he was going to do, and did not move, not her hand, her head, nothing. He put his arms round her as carefully, as matter-of-factly as he had covered Evergreen's eyes from

[60]

seeing what he did. One arm round her waist, one turning her towards him. Kissed her. And the fact that Evergreen was there, her face hidden, made it impossible to struggle, to prevent him, protest, do anything. As if her safety had imprisoned her. She could only stay still, her body unyielding, mouth unyielding, eyes looking into his. Not even showing anger. Only indifference.

And then there was something in his eyes that changed, became uncertain. His hands loosening, as slowly and carefully as they had taken hold. His head drawing back. He did not say anything. Did not ask if she was angry, say that he was sorry. Not a word. And she thought, wondering at herself, with a kind of distant astonishment, if he had continued another moment I—I should not have stayed indifferent. Felt her breast seem to burn. And he had not touched her breast, not even brushed his arm against it. But I expected it, she thought. And her own eyes must have filled with uncertainties that he could see there.

They sat like that for what seemed a great length of time, not touching, not speaking. Only looking into each other's eyes like looking into dark pictures that one cannot make out without more light. Only that it was not stupidity she was looking at. Not bluntness of mind. And, she could not say anything. If he touched her again? She knew that he would not, and somewhere far in the back of her own mind was desolate because of it. Behind his shoulder she saw Evergreen, the edge of her blanket drawn carefully down, her eyes watching, dark with secrecy and yet bright with reflections from the fire, the candlelight, with wonder at what they two were doing. Sitting like that so silent and unmoving beside her.

'I must go' he breathed. An air as if all his certainties were damaged. Feeling about him for new supports. She would have liked to touch his leather jerkin that he wore under the rough, blue serge coat. Fisherman's coat. Fisherman's jerkin. Grey fustian trousers pushed into sea boots. How roughly he was dressed. Like a disguise? She did touch his jerkin, and the leather was cold to her finger-tip, cold and somehow greasy, her finger slid down it.

He took her hand, held her fingers against his mouth, breathed on them. 'You're too cold' he said. What did he mean? He stood up, still holding her hand prisoner. 'You must go back to your bed.'

With those women, she thought, the man goes with them to their bed. That is the kind of woman that he knows. Counts out the money like that, on a table, and they go up to the woman's bed. And then—— Imagined that he could tell what she was thinking. and that burning came, like fire.

'I've told you' he said. 'I'm not used——'

And she thought, he knows! He knows! If Evergreen had not been there. If—if—— He was waiting for her to try to free her hand and she made herself quite still. He held it then against his jerkin. Near his heart. She thought that she could feel the beat of it.

'You must go' she said. And it sounded in her ears as if they were saying goodbye after a great length of time together.

She went with him into the passage. They were in the dark, she had left the candle in its night chamber stick, burning on the table. What will he do now she wondered. And did not know what she wanted him to do. Heard his hand feeling for the latch. The door opening.

'When will—shall you come again? With more goods?' She had not intended to ask that.

'I don't know. I'm going to Antwerp. Buying.'

She forced herself to say nothing.

He said 'Goodbye.' His shadow hesitating.

'I wish you a safe journey.'

'And—return?'

'Oh, that, of course.'

He closed the door. Was still inside with her. 'I shall think of you' he whispered. 'All the time. Day and night.' He took hold of her, found her mouth. Found her breast. Held her until she could not breathe. and she had put her arms round him, her mouth was soft against his, there were no bones left in her, no strength, like honey melting out of its comb, running sweetness. If he let go of her she would fall.

'If I could stay' he whispered. One hand holding her hair against their faces. He did let go of her with his other hand, took all of her hair that he could hold and drew it round them, wrapped their faces in it, made a silk mask for each of them, thick and soft, here warm, here cold, tightened it until she could not escape from him, was netted there. His hands were under her cloak, on her shift, the warmth of her body. 'Let me touch your skin' he

[62]

breathed against her face. She did not know what he was doing at first, lifting her shift under the cloak, up round her waist, her armpits, uncovering her breasts. She wanted to cry out 'No!' and his mouth would not let her cry anything, she was going to fall. She sank against him, did not know what she was doing. As if she too was drunk, her blood and flesh were drunk. His hand cupping her breast, touching, touching until her body quivered, seemed to shriek under his hand like a horse that is being broken, that does not know what is happening to it.

Gathered her mind, gathered something, pushed him away so that he was against one wall of the passage and she against the other, her shift still caught up round her breasts, her cloak open, only the darkness covering her. The cotton of the shift slowly falling, sliding down like hands touching, waist, hips, down to her knees that shook under her as the horse trembles, shivers.

'For pity's sake go.'

'I'll be back.'

She found the latch of the door, opened it.

'I'll come back for you.'

His shadow. Shadows in the yard. Sounds. The door shut. Pushing the bolt home as if that was safety against herself. She did not think she could walk back to the kitchen, the few steps along the passage to the door, the candlelight, the fire, Evergreen. Her constable.

Her constable asleep, head on her bent knees. The gold shimmering in the candlelight.

Oh God, have mercy on me. She sat down on the far side of the table, touched that gold with her finger. What kind of woman am I? What kind? Outside the sounds of the smugglers grew quiet, vanished. From the parlour, far away in the house, she heard the faint striking of the clock. Two strokes. Two? Only an hour? She went slowly to the fire, and knelt, and held out her hands to warm them. Opened her cloak to warm her body, that was shivering. Looked at Evergreen.

'You shall sleep in my room' she said. Pushing home the bolt of the door.

She caught the stuff of her shift in both hands and stretched it in front of the fire as if she were drying it. Under it her body was still trembling. It is only the cold, she thought.

[63]

Chapter 8

She was in the linen room with Evergreen, when Mr. Massingham came. Counting the linen that was still good, and that could be mended, or mended again, and the frightening quantity of it that was only useful now for tearing up as rags. She had it in mind that Evergreen might learn to sew, and could practise sewing up the sheets they would cut in half, putting the unworn outer edges of the sheets to the centres. Evergreen stood in patient obedience, one pile of sheets and pillow slips and towels in her arms, another at her feet. Ten days had gone by since Robert Barnabas had left for Antwerp, and Judith could think of it now almost calmly, like a crisis of nerves that comes to people who have been under too much strain too long. Nothing else but that. Now it was done with, and she could thank God it had been no worse.

She had been thinking of it as she counted the towels, nine, ten, eleven that—that might be called good if one was generous. Was he in Antwerp still? It did not matter. She would not see him again. His father might pay her, the man Slipgibbet. Any messenger. But Robert Barnabas should not set foot in the house. And that was nothing to regret. She had been weak. Caught in a moment of weakness. And had given to him qualities he did not, could not possess. Seen, imagined things in his eyes—— What nonsense she had been guilty of! To see subtleties and love and—not love, oh no, she had not even looked for that! But—but a kind of gentleness of mind he could not—she could not expect that he should have. How could he? His father's son! No more than a sailor. Worse! A—a sort of criminal, a ruffian used to—used to the kind of women—I shall not so much as think of him again!

That is how it happens to women, she had thought. They have a moment of crisis, of loneliness. A man is tender. Almost any— any personable man. And there is something inside us that answers. Like a traitor in a castle, who longs to let down the drawbridge. It is not wickedness to possess such a traitor. It is only wickedness to let the traitor act. And I did not do that. Not—not for more than a moment. And now I am the stronger for it.

The kind of innocence they all spoke of, that was no more than ignorance. No wonder there were so many fallen women. They stayed innocent only so long as they were held upright by someone else, a father or brothers, or a—a husband. Once that support was taken away, they fell by nature, by incapacity. They had never learned to stand of their own strength. They had never learned, she thought. And tempered the thought with humility, with gratitude that she had been able to learn so safely.

Only sometimes, very briefly, at night, when Evergreen was asleep on her truckle bed in the corner of the room, when her own defences of reason were half asleep, she found herself thinking of what kind that traitor might be she knew now dwelt in her, as she must dwell in every woman. Who had seemed to melt her bones, take her strength, fill her veins with honey, make her breasts long to be touched. And she would find her hand holding her breast, feel almost a stir of her flesh, a swollenness of longing, and all her reason would start awake, cry 'To arms, to arms!', while the traitor crept away into the gutter, into the kennels where she belonged.

Our Father—

She had begun to say her mother's prayers again, fortifying reason with superstition, and ashamed of herself for it, and still doing it, like a homage to her mother, who, if she possessed such a traitor in herself, would have kept her under lock and chain, helpless.

Until as the days went by she came to a sort of tranquillity. All things growing more tranquil. Able to pay Martha's arrears of wages. The Apothecary in Urnford. A part of Miss Frewen's account. She did not allow herself to think of the great debts. The smugglers, old Mr. Barnabas to pay her, came again, and took their goods, and left more, and had taken those last night. Evergreen was growing used to the house, and to living in one.

And Martha was growing if not used to Evergreen, at least more quiet about her. Above all her father liked her. And Evergreen liked him.

They seemed to have understood each other on the instant and Evergreen would spend hours with him, sitting or kneeling on the cushion beside his bed, holding his hand, whispering to him, listening. He was the only person she did talk to.

'What does she say to you?'

'Wonderful things—wonderful.' She did not know whether he was laughing at her or not.

'What kind?'

'About flowers and—animals and—people.'

'She does not tell me such things.'

'She is—afraid—of you.'

'Afraid? Of me?' It was like a small, sudden pain, and she thought, what more can I do to show her that I mean to be kind?

She had told her there had been a burial, there had been prayers, Mr. Forbes in Urnford would have done all that was proper. One day she would bring her to see the grave. In the paupers' plot. And she had to set her mind against thinking how much better it would have been to have buried him as he had lived, in the open. In the wood. But we could not, she cried, it would not have been allowed, Solomon would have told. Mr. Carteret——

Martha was in the doorway, looking sideways at Evergreen. And also looking important, as if she had news to tell, and was vexed at having to tell it in front of Evergreen, instead of with all the invitations to 'guess what do ha' jus' come about' that she would otherwise have employed. She used only one brief gambit of that kind; 'You cain't nivva guess who do fare to be come. An' looking so set up in 'asself!'

It is Robert! Judith thought. And then, it is Francis! And did not know why she was so sure of it, why her heart was beating.

'I cannot guess at all' she said, her voice colder than she intended. 'How should I?'

Martha's look of general vexation concentrated itself. ''tis Mr. Massingham' she said, her old, crumpled face angry and disappointed. 'He's in the parlour waitin' for you.'

'And his horse?' Judith said, fears for the stable attacking her before all else. And then she remembered the stables and the barn were empty again, and felt relief before she could think of why he might have come.

'He do ha' brought that owd Chevell wi' him. He's howdin' both horses an' walkin' about.'

Chevell? Judith thought, her mind catching at the name. The next-to-chief groom at Matcham? With Mr. Massingham? That was a strange thing. It was as though in her own mind she was trying to put off the thought of why Mr. Massingham himself had come. She felt her mouth dry.

'He—he does not say why he is come?'

'How s'uld I know thaat?' Martha cried, delighted to have revenge for her own spoiled surprise. 'Goo an' ax 'em. You woon't find out standin' there like a great musharune howdin' the linen.'

'You finish the counting for me' Judith said, holding out her bundle and list and pencil.

But Martha did not intend to be enclosed in a small space with Evergreen. 'Countin' t'linen! Countin' rags! I do ha' more things to do nor that. An' you best put on your best gown afore you goo down to 'em, an' dolly your hair. That looks like proper thicks the way you do ha' that.'

'For pity's sake, Martha! You make him sound like company. It is a message from the Earl, and he was riding by, that is all.' Felt her heart beat falter as she thought of what the message must be.

And she stood for a long moment at the corner of the stairs, in the darkest place there, letting Martha go down before her, trying to control her breathing.

Mr. Massingham was standing in front of the fire, warming his back, his hands lifting the tails of his riding frock. And he was indeed 'set up in himself'. The coat seemed shining new, of brown Russel worsted with silver buttons; a lilac-coloured waistcoat and the underwaistcoat a darker lilac; white grogram breeches and new short Hessians, showing striped yellow and brown stockings. Everything about him glittering with newness as though he had gone naked into a tailor's shop and come out full-dressed. And scented. She could smell the scent from where she stood in the doorway.

'Why, Mr. Massingham' she said, forcing herself to go forward, curtsy, make her voice sound natural. 'How grand you look. Martha told me you had dazzled her.'

'She speaks too high' Mr. Massingham said, smoothing his finger across his mouth to hide his pleasure. He had abandoned a wig, either to save the tax or because he fancied his own hair for handsomeness. He must have taken great pains to fluff and puff and thicken it out with pomade, so that it gave a hopeful impression of rich chestnut carelessness. His eyes seemed to bulge with the tightness of his white lawn cravat. An amethyst pin buried in its deep folds. A gold chain across his lilac splendour of soft, small paunch. Everything about him, clothes and manner, bow and smile and eyes that seemed to crease with the effort of bowing, expressing the height of satisfaction with how he looked and what he was.

He fluttered his hand. 'I have interrupted your domestic cares, ma'am.'

'Not at all, I assure you.' Begging him to sit, sitting herself, trying not to look at the cold sore on his lower lip.

'Your poor father, ma'am? Poor Mr. Mortimer? How does he do?'

'As well as may be expected, sir.'

'I hear that you have taken on a new responsibility. A vagabond child.'

'I have taken a new servant, yes.'

'Such a soft heart!' He turned up his eyes, showed the yellowish whites to their fullest. 'But you have vexed Mr. Carteret you know.'

'I am sorry for it.'

'And you are not wise my dear. Charity is not always best when it seems kindest.'

She did not answer him, and he plucked at his sore lip, considering her. Thrust out a boot toe and considered that. Turned it to catch the light of the fire. He must have rubbed it over again before he came into the house. It shone.

'You are very young to have so many responsiblities. May I make so bold as to say that to you, Judith?' She raised her eyebrows at such a use of her name, here in her own house where she was mistress. And Mr. Massingham began to blush. A kind of darkening under the thick white skin, giving him a muddy, bilious colouring.

'We are too much old friends for ceremonies, calling each other ma'am, and sir, eh, eh Judith?' Trying to copy the Earl's bluffness of 'Eh, eh?' and failing. His blush darkened. 'And I an *old* friend in more senses than one. I am thirty-five' he said. 'Would you have guessed that if I had not told you?'

She had always imagined him ten years older at least, although it was not the age that mattered. She sat not able to breathe. A drop of blood had appeared on his lip. He licked it away and it appeared again, stained one of his teeth.

He stared at her, leaned forward. 'I have something—something of great import—to say to you. Can you perhaps—guess what it is?'

She wanted to shut her eyes, and was afraid even to look away from him in case he touched her.

She tried to think, of how she might call for Evergreen—for Martha—offer him wine—tea—— And as she thought of that Martha did indeed come in with a tray, wine glasses and biscuits and a decanter of the French wine the smugglers had brought for her father. Mr. Massingham leaning back in his chair like a man checked and momentarily baffled, but not defeated. Sure of victory in the end. He held his wine glass, nibbled his biscuit.

'A pleasant wine, Judith. An extravagance in you——' He shook his head in mock reproof.

'It is for my father. And guests.'

'Ah. Poor, poor Mr. Mortimer. A tragedy.'

'He supports it well.'

He leaned forward again. Dropped his voice to a tone of grave intimacy. 'And his Lorship's plan? That he broached to you the other day? You have considered of it? And—you have attempted to persuade your father? To sell to his Lordship? And to stay here as his Lordship's tenants?'

'It would be a useless attempt. Even if I thought it right to make it.'

He set aside his glass. 'Judith, you are grown into a woman. You are old enough to know that we may not always have in life that which we wish for. But there is the further part of his Lordship's plan' he said, lowering his voice still more. He drew his chair closer to her across the front of the fire. The brasses glistened. The flames burned softly, whispered among the blackness of the burning logs, cracked sharply, blue and yellow, hissing. Grew soft again.

His hand was preparing to reach out, take hers. Hers clenched still tighter, rigid. Unable to look at him, see anything but the colours of the flames, the brightness of brass, blackness of hearthstone, of logs and firegrate. As if all that mattered in the room lay in the hearth.

"All that you would need to do, Judith, would be to marry. Someone—in the Earl's confidence. So that he might know that Guthrum's was in safe, wise hands.'

I shall not speak to him at all, she determined. I could not trust myself.

'Cannot you guess what I am coming at?' he whispered. She heard him moving, wanted to shut her eyes. She heard the heavy fall of his knees onto the coloured rug.

'Judith, I have watched you growing.' His voice hoarse. 'I am not a young man, but not old. It is often good for the husband to be—older. You are very young. You need guidance.'

She tried to stand up, and he caught her hands, enveloped them, his hands damp with sweat, soft as sponges. Yet clinging so fast to hers that she could not free them without violence.

'I beg of you! Let me go! Do not say anything more!'

'Let me finish.' His hands climbing her arms. 'I am not as you have thought of me. You have seen me only as a teacher, someone wise and distant. But I am not only that! Not inside! I can be a lover, Judith! I can wake your heart, wake your feelings, feelings that you do not yet know that you possess!'

Fondling her arms, like a great sponge eating, swallowing.

'Look, I humiliate myself, I am at your feet! The Earl has promised—— Do you know what love is? You cannot, should not, but I shall teach you!' Fastening his mouth against her hands, slobbering her fingers. She managed to free herself, almost to kick him away from her.

'I must call Martha if you do not stop this. I beg of you, get up from your knees, you will be ashamed of this in another moment, you do not know what you have been saying.'

He stayed where he was, holding out his arms towards her. 'I have watched you grow' he whispered. As if that was an appeal to something so deep it must be answered.

'I pray you, not another word. Stand up, we shall both forget what has been said.'

He struggled awkwardly to his feet, supported himself on the mantelpiece. 'You think me ugly. You think I could not be a lover.' He was looking down into the fire.

'I do not think of anyone as a lover' she said.

But at that moment he turned to her with his face transformed again. 'How should you? Almost a child still! You should not! The Earl has said it. But now it is right, it is permitted to you. I have been too sudden, I realise that. I have thought of this so much these past days and nights, ever since the Earl—since before your visit—until—until it seemed to me that you too must know it was arranged—must also be thinking—not as I have thought of you—but—of marriage—of all that belongs to marriage. Of—me.'

She let her feelings show in her face. 'The Earl has no business with my marriage' she said.

He looked at her, and she had the strange impression that a side of Mr. Massingham she had never known had shown itself to her, and was dying in front of her, withering away, like a sea creeping thing that crawls out into the sunlight and becomes nothing but a patch of wetness on the sand. Sickening and pitiable.

Perhaps the pity showed in her face, even before she was aware of feeling it. And the Mr. Massingham she had known and loathed reappeared as though he was slowly drawing back on a mask. He plucked his lip, touched one of his great teeth. 'That is to be seen' he said. 'If you do not care for a romantic proposal, it shall come to you in a different form.'

'I did not mean—did not wish—to hurt your feelings—— ' She felt sickened at herself for what she was saying. She wanted to scream at him, to order him out of her house, tell him her true thoughts of him, and felt afraid. For her father upstairs. For the house. For herself. Sick and afraid, and ashamed. And he saw all of it, his weakness, his moment of romance as dead as the sea anemone in the sun, his old self, real self? In command again.

'Of course you did not' he said. His eyes seemed to have taken possession of her, to be surveying a property. 'You were sur-prised. It was very right and modest in you. I should not want a bride who was not surprised at my proposal.'

'I have told you——' Her mouth so dry she could scarcely shape the words.

'No no. We shall not discuss it now. No more.' He smoothed his lilac waistcoat. Buttoned his riding frock. Caressed his mouth. 'I ask you only to think quietly of the matter. I shall not tell you to think of the alternatives. You have your duty to your father. To the Earl and Countess. To the family. There is the true and only motive for a young woman's entering the married state. Her duty.' He looked covertly down at the floor where he had knelt, and up into her face with such a mixture of confidence and hatred as made her lose her breath.

'We shall often think back to this hour' he said.

Chapter 9

Eight hundred and eleven pounds. Four shillings. Eight and a half pence. No counting, no recounting, would make the debts come to less. She pushed the bills into a heap, made them neat together, rolled them, put them into a pigeon hole. And against them? On the credit side? It did not bear thinking about.

Behind her, by the bed, Evergreen's voice was low and whispering. She caught words here and there, but even when she did hear them they had no meaning. Were not even English. What was she saying? 'Shonuto—lovensa——'

She is saying charms, Judith thought, and shivered, and wanted to turn round and cry 'Be quiet, stop that!' But if her father was amused—— While I sit here and count our debts. *His* debts! And for a second felt rage at his lying there, knowing nothing of what had happened yesterday. Of Mr. Massingham. Of the Earl's plan—his threat. Knowing nothing of anything.

Evergreen saying 'O Del, he made a little cake of dough an' put it into a great oven, an' went away walking.'

What was she talking about?

'An' he forgot the cake an' when he came back it was burned black. That's why there are black people, they were baked too much.' The small voice whispering. Like the soft small flames of a fire in the open air. In the clearing.

'And how—did—there come to be—white people?'

She had not heard her father's voice so strong and happy for a long time. While she——!

'He took the next one out too soon, he was worried it would spoil. And it wasn't cooked at all.'

'But you—your people—you—were made right, just right—a nice—baked brown? Is that—the case?'

'Yes.' A sigh of breath.

She turned round. Evergreen heard her movement, and buried her face against the sheet. Her father met Judith's eyes, the happiness clouded in his as if he could see into her mind.

'My—housekeeper' he said.

She wanted to say 'How shall I keep it? With what?' Made herself smile.

'Is something wrong?' he whispered.

'What should be wrong? There is nothing! I—I have been thinking. I should go to see Mr. Terry again soon. I am sure that by now he must have news for us. And I—I could hasten him a little.' She tried to seem bright about it, and hopeful.

'There is—something—the matter. Tell me.' Fumbling for her arm, her hand. Finding it.

'Father! I have told you——' There was nothing in the world at that moment she wanted so much as to lay her head down, against his hand, and tell him everything. And then? 'I am restless, that is all. I shall leave Evergreen with you and go to see Mr. Terry, and—and tempt myself with a new gown. I shall have a splendid time and you shall be jealous of me and I shall bring you back a new book, and all the newspapers and—that is all I am thinking of—I shall go at once, to-day. If I hurry I shall catch Mr. Walmsley's cart. Or I may hire the gig from Mr. Turton. That is what I shall do, the cart is too slow.'

It did indeed seem to her that that was exactly what she wanted, had planned to do ever since yesterday, and she ran to dress herself for the journey, as though by deciding to go to Urnford, to Mr. Terry, she had taken an important, profitable step. That something good *must* come of it, must.

The feeling stayed with her all the way to Urnford, all the way to Mr. Terry's office, his narrow house caught and squeezed between two others as if it had insinuated itself into a passage-way, and got stuck, and could neither free itself, nor breathe properly. One window beside the door. Grey with dust. His brass plate gone green. The paint faded. The iron bell pull rusty, threatening to come one day away in a client's hand. The old servant. The two clerks downstairs. The smell of ink and parchment, pounce and sealing wax and dust and airlessness. Metal boxes with names painted on them so long ago that the paint had lost all colour and the names were like ghosts, shadows of names, the owners surely dead for a century and their troubles long buried. Mr. Terry's own private room.

'Oh Miss Mortimer, you surprise me, you take me unawares. A seat, Mr. Verreker, a seat for Miss Mortimer. Dust it, man, dust the seat.'

A cloud of dust under old Mr. Verreker's handkerchief. Mr. Terry coughing, grey little face under grey little wig, like a mouse in disguise, wearing silver spectacles to fool the cat. 'Oh huh—huh—ashooooooo! Miss Mortimer—your papa—ah aha ah shoooooo! Oh dear me, oh bless us Mr. Verreker, such dust, stop, man—ah ah ashoo! Oh dear, Miss Mortimer, pray sit, pray sit down, such a pleasure, such an—ashoo!—such an unexpected pleasure.'

His hands already fluttering like little mouse claws among his papers, here and there on his desk among the piles of parchments, rolls of documents; documents with seals hanging, documents whose seals had fallen off, documents waiting to be sealed and engrossed; waiting to be copied; waiting to be read; waiting for some reason to be discovered as to why they were there; waiting to be deciphered, waiting to be signed; or simply waiting for no reason at all but that at some long ago moment Mr. Verreker had laid them down and no reason had ever been found for taking them away again. The very sight of them and their disorder breathed failure and she knew that no matter how she might hurt his feelings she must not, could not allow things to continue as they had done.

And yet that evening, driving home in the early darkness in Mr. Turton's gig, the oil lamp making faint shimmerings of yellow gold on the mare's brown rump, and on the harness brasses and the polished shafts, she realised that that was exactly what she had allowed to happen, and that nothing had been discovered, nor ended, nor decided. She had wasted her day, and a great deal of money, and gained nothing. Indeed, what had there ever been to gain? She had not had the authority, even if she had the strength of mind, to tell Mr. Terry to end his researches.

While suppose—only suppose—that he had actually found something wonderful; a document that proved beyond all question that Guthrum's was theirs in perpetuity and not merely as a tenure for two lives, nor as a servient tenement, nor any of the other things that Mr. Halliday and Mr. Laurence the Earl's attorney said it was, and that accordingly they owed only the Great and Petty Tithes and not any sort of rent or dues or anything else, what real, ultimate good would that do, when they could not so much as pay the tithes? Nor even Mr. Terry's account.

But she was too tired to go on worrying about it, at least for now. And it had been very pleasant to go shopping again, and to look at the fashion plates in Miss Cuthbertson's, and to talk of books and poetry to Mr. Quantock in the Booksellers, and feel the weight of everything lifted from her shoulders, at least for one afternoon. And she clung to that sense of freedom until she had handed back the gig at the Duke of Marlborough's stables, and had walked home in the sharp frost that seemed to fall tangibly from the pale stars like tiny pricks of ice against her face.

'There's a letter do ha' come' Martha said, her tone important, and at the same time accusing, as if for a letter to arrive for Judith and Judith not to be there to open and read it instantly and tell what news was in it was a kind of wrong-doing. 'Tha do ha' come from Matcham' Martha said. 'Young Chevell did bring 'em.'

'From—from Matcham?' Holding the stiff, folded sheet of heavy white paper with its dark red wafer and thick seal. Afraid to look at the direction on it.

'Ann't you gooin' to open 'em?'

'Why, yes—but——' She began to break the seal, her fingers shaking. It would be about Mr. Massingham and his failed embassy. The Earl——

'Dear Judith——'

Looking quickly down the page of sprawled writing to the signature. 'Your affc:te Coz: F. Mortimer.'

Francis? And for a second or two she could not read what he had written, the words seemed to lose their shape on the paper.

'Dear Judith, this in haste to warn you that what you are doing at Guthrum's is begun to be known. I shall not say you are mad to have done it. Such people as the Barnabases and their gang of cut throats! You are truly mad, and now I must betray my solemn duty warning you! Your place has already been searched by a man who has told the Customs Supervisor he found no goods but droppings of horses and donkeys all about. And everyone knows you have not kept any horse for above a year. The Super-

[76]

viser has told us we must stand ready to help his men as soon as more information comes of a run of goods with you. I beg you, put an end to it not tomorrow, but to-day. And do not keep this letter but destroy it instanter. Your affc:te Coz: F. Mortimer.'

'Well? What do that ha' to say?' Martha waiting, ladle poised over the black iron stew pot.

'It—it is from Mr. Francis. He writes only to ask how my father does. I do not know why he took the trouble.' Folding the letter again, trying to keep her hands steady. 'I shall—I must go up and tell my father I am home—and——' Hurrying from the kitchen before she should betray herself. What should she do? Suppose—— Thank God they had not any goods here now! But tomorrow? If they should come to-night? Before she could tell them? Send word they must not come again? And if the searchers——

She had to stand outside her father's door for a full minute before she could control herself enough to go in naturally; control her voice, her expression, seem as if nothing had happened beyond a day in Urnford, shopping and seeing Mr. Terry. Make herself able to smile. At her father. At Evergreen beside him. To say, 'I had the most wonderful time!' While all she wanted was to cry out 'We are discovered! I shall be arrested, taken away to prison! What in Heaven's name shall I do? Laying the *Morning Post,* and the Sunday *London Gazette,* and Mr. Wordsworth's *Lyrical Ballads* on the bed. 'We have reading here for days and days, and Mr Quantock says that the Ballads is even finer than Mr. Wordsworth's first book and there are some good things by a young Mr. Coleridge in it as well. And Mr. Terry has new plans! Oh, it was a very clever idea in me to go off like that, I promise you.'

Kissing him, putting the papers and the books close so that he could reach them. Evergreen half hidden behind the bed curtain. 'And how has she been with you?'

'Splendid. She has—entertained me prodigiously. Such stories! Of her—father and the—places they travelled. You should—write them down one—day. I never heard such—adventures. She is very young to—have seen so much.'

'And I?' Judith thought. 'Am I not——' Tomorrow! What might she not see tomorrow? Forcing her hands to stay quiet, not to twist themselves together in despair. Smile. Talk. Of Mr.

Terry and his hopes of finding another document. 'It is the Commissioners' Report for the Enclosure Bill of 1727. He says the description of our land in it must—oh I did not understand him but he is very hopeful about it.' Put an end to it not tomorrow, but to-day! How? It was late night already. Suppose they came to-night?

Martha brought her a bowl of soup, and she must pretend to eat. And talk. And read a poem from the *Ballads* to her father. She could not understand what she was reading, the words seemed to move about, they had no meaning. 'That blessed mood, in which the burthen of the mystery——' Blessed mood!

'You are too—tired to read any—more' her father whispered. 'Go to bed, my dear. And—Evergreen. I can—read for myself a little.'

And suddenly she was indeed so tired that it was an effort to stand up, to say 'Good night'. Undress. Yet she knew she would not sleep. Sleep! Putting the letter in the fire, watching it burn up and blacken. Too tired even to leave the fire's warmth and get between cold sheets. She knelt, listening to the wind, to the fire burning, to Evergreen's soft breathing. Drew her cloak tighter round her, over her shift, staring into the fire, at the black nothingness of the letter. Half asleep. She did not know how long she stayed there. Heard the clock strike a half hour. And then the hour, but she was too much asleep as she knelt even to count the strokes. Was it eleven? Midnight?

There was a sound. A sharp blow against the shutter, like a stone. She came wide awake, her heart threatening to choke her. They had come! Another pebble struck against the wood. She felt her way to the curtains, opened the casement and the shutters. He was outside, on horseback on the terrace, his head only just below the level of the sill, looking up at her. So close they could have touched hands together. No one else. No sounds.

'Are you—— Have you brought the others?'

'No. I'm alone. Come down to me' he whispered.

She did not know what she felt. Relief? To be able to tell him! Now. At once. That—that they—that he—must not come again. Thank God she could tell him now, in time. And still she did not know what she felt.

'Go round' she breathed, afraid that Evergreen would wake, that—— Not knowing what she was afraid of. 'I must talk to you.

[78]

It is very—I will come down at once.' Almost running along the corridor, down the stairs. The passage. Stood for a second breathing deep. That he should come to-night! And alone. As if he had been brought to her!

'Are you there?' His voice whispering. An inch away, through the timber.

She drew the bolt and he came in and closed the door very quietly. It was so dark she could not see his face. Only hear his breathing. He put his arms round her, and it was as if he had not let go of her since the last time. As if always they had stood here like this, like shadows in the dark, holding one another. And she had thought of nothing since. Nothing else.

'You must not! Let go of me. I have something—something urgent to tell you. I must find a candlestick, I have been half frantic——'

He put his fingers against her mouth. 'Sssh. We don't need candlelight.' He had found their way into the kitchen, to a bench. Drew her down. The fire glowed in the hearth in its bed of ash. So that after a moment they could see one another, she could see his face, the shadows, his eyes shining. As they had done before. Filled with certainties that became uncertainties as he looked at her.

'Have you thought of me?' he breathed. 'I've been thinking of you. A'most of nothing else, no one else. At sea. In Antwerp.'

I must make him let go of me, she thought. She put up her hands to her hair, where she had tried to knot it, and it was threatening to come down. He held her wrists together with one hand, and her hair fell. His one hand holding her prisoner.

'Your gypsy? She's not here to-night?'

'Listen to me. There has been someone——'

'Ssssh.' He took her cloak from her shoulders, tried to draw down her shift.

'No! I must tell you! We are discovered! My cousin——'

He had pulled her shift so far down that her breasts were bare. And she heard her own voice die away as if it belonged to someone else. As if she was still asleep. Was not sure that she had spoken aloud. And wanted nothing in the world but to go on like this, to let him hold her. As if there were no rules. No laws by firelight. He had bent his head and was kissing her, her throat, her naked shoulder, her breast. And she sat pretending to be imprisoned, manacled by his hand. She did not know who she was. What. She bent down her own head, her mouth touching his hair. A taste of salt, of the sea and cold, as if he had just ridden from the sea shore and the spray was frozen there.

His other hand touched her knee, her lap. No more than that. Stroking. Soothing. Finding its way to warmth. And for a second longer she stayed not moving, half asleep, dreaming. And then cried out, with such a shock of horror at what he had done that she was on her feet without knowing it, before he could hold her down. Was three, four steps away.

'Don't move! Don't touch me!'

'Hush! Ssssh! What's the matter? What did I do? Nothing! Come back. Ssssh! I'll not touch you again if you don't want me to, I swear it!'

She could see his face, the glint of his eyes watching her, the dark line of his eyebrows. His mouth. All certainties now. A game he had often played. What was she doing? Here, alone—alone with—— What must he think she was? A woman like—those women. In another second what might he not have—— She must call out, call Evergreen, Martha——

'Ssssh I tell you, I won't move. Look, I'm kneeling quite still. I'm sorry if—I told you, I'm not used to your kind. You'll have to teach me. Come back. Please. Sit quiet there and we'll talk. Just talk.' Was it a game? Only that? The hint of foreignness about his voice. Foreign towns. Foreign women. Candlelight and wine and nakedness. She was crying without knowing it. She did not know what she thought or felt. She should not have come down. What need had there been? She could have whispered her message to him and gone back to bed, been safe.

'Why're you crying?' he breathed. 'Did I frighten you so much? Listen to me, I'll be good, I swear it, I'll not touch you again.' And he was touching her, but not as he had done before, like a possession. Gently. Soothing her. His eyes had changed again. A kind of hurt in them. Ashamedness. At what he had just done? At failing? 'I've never met anyone like you' he whispered against her face, against her mouth. 'A lot of kinds—no, I didn't mean that. Look at me, trust me, let me kiss you just once more, to show you how you can trust me. Like a brother. Just a brother's kiss. Hush, stay like that, lean against me, shsh, I only want to be kind to you, make you happy. In Antwerp I was looking at silks, and I

[80]

thought—how'd she look wearing that? But I knew you couldn't look more beautiful than I'd seen you already. Tell me, have you thought of me? Have you?'

'Yes.' Her voice lost against his shoulder. Wanting to believe. Not think. Only believe.

They sat together, side by side on the wooden bench, the red of the fire dying like a sunset, darker and darker red, black bars of charred and smouldering wood making red tinged clouds. He had taken her hands, to warm them. After a minute he opened his leather jerkin and held them against him so that she could feel the warmth of his body.

'D'you know? I studied to be a doctor' he was whispering. 'In Leyden. Isn't that strange for someone like me? I used to wish I'd stayed there, but not now. My father made me come to him, to help him and if I hadn't come——' He took her hair and made skeins of it across her face, as he had done before, so that when he kissed her all that touched her mouth was her own hair. 'Have you been afraid when I was gone? You've no need to any more. The lads won't be coming here again.'

'Not—?' Sitting very still.

'Not to the barn, nor the stables. It isn't wise to go on in one place too long. We'll use your fields. Some of your hedges are five yards deep, we could hide fifty shiploads in 'em. And there's your wood. You needn't know anything. But I'll still come to you. To bring your money. And—tell you all's well.'

All's well. She let her head rest against his shoulders. She must tell him. Tell him that even the hedges, the wood—that they must not——

'We can begin again?' he whispered. 'As if I'd never——'

I must tell him, she thought again. In a moment. I must.

'Say you forgive me' he was whispering. 'I didn't mean it. I was brought up where girls——'

'You swore!' His mouth brushing her neck, her shoulder. 'You gave your oath!'

'And I'll keep it, what have I done now? Nothing! Only a small kiss behind your ear, where's the harm in that?'

'I am not—a girl in Antwerp.' But she did not move. As if she had lost her reason along with all else.

'D'ye want me to——'

'No! Listen! I have to tell you—tell you something dreadful!

Let go of my hands. Let go of me. You swore! They suspect, listen to me, they know what I—what we—— Listen to me. You cannot use even the hedges, anywhere. They know!'

'Who knows?'

'My cousin. He is in the Yeomanry—he has just wrote to me. A man was here searching. He found the marks of horses and donkeys round the barn, in the stable yard—droppings.'

He laughed so loud it was startling, frightening in the quiet, and she freed her wrists, held her hand to her heart, to her breast, found it bare. And stayed like that. He stopped laughing, felt for her hands again, put one of them against his mouth. 'Let your cousin tell the man he'd best not come back' he said. 'Or he'll find more than droppings.'

And suddenly she was so frightened she could not move nor speak. As if he was a different man. Or she had made a foolish, girl's image of him and it had burned, flared away. Leaving—?' After a long moment she breathed, 'What do you mean?'

'Nothing! Except that there's nought to be afraid of. Lord how your heart's hammering! There's no one'll touch my father's stuff, nor his men. Why, half the customs lads themselves take bribes from him. He's paid old Gaultrip a pension this past ten years to leave him alone. Let me feel your heart. Poor dove.' His voice soft, persuading, laughing at her. 'And let me tell you about the silks I saw. Don't be afraid of shadows.'

'But I am afraid.' Saying it so that he would tell her again, would—— Trying to rebuild the image. Save it. 'You said yourself! You dare not continue using my barn!'

'Dare? Daring's nought to do with it! It's only common sense and the rules of the thing. Old Gaultrip and the others, they don't want to find our stuff. We just make it easy for 'em not to find it. As for the Yeos, a parcel of farmers on plough horses! They couldn't find a cask of Hollands if it fell on 'em. Don't you be afraid, my dear. Sit down by me and stay quiet. Let me kiss you again and show you how good I've grown. No, I promise you all's safe. And once old Gaultrip finds nothing he'll not need to send for the Yeos nor anyone, will he? You see? Give me your mouth, shhh, stay quiet.'

But she could not make herself quiet. Her heart beating as if the Yeomanry was in the yard, she could hear them. As if——As if he—what was he? What kind of man? 'You must go now! You must! Please! If you do not I shall never—you must never come here again——' She had not meant to offer him the least hope that he could come again. He must not. But he had already taken her hands like a pledge.

'And if I go now?'

She could not answer.

'Then that's a promise' he whispered. 'And here's to seal it.' Kissed her. Held her close for a moment. Was gone. Yet his hands still seemed to be touching her, long after he rode away. Her image of him burned up, destroyed, so that she did not know what kind of hands were touching her. Only the strength of them.

Chapter 10

She could settle to nothing in the next days. She expected at every moment something terrible to happen, the Yeomanry to come searching, a letter from the Earl full of new threats. Had he been told already about the smuggling? He must have been. Chevell would have told him first of all. What would he do? Mr. Massingham to be refused and now—— She went about the house and the ruined gardens as if she was looking at them for the last time. Made Solomon bury all traces of the droppings in a deep pit. He had wanted to spread them on their remaining patch of vegetables, and was stupefied at being forbidden. What would happen, when? And Robert promising, threatening, to come back!

She thought at moments that she was more afraid of that than of all else. She had been mad, wicked, what would become of her? To have such a traitor in herself, and to give her another chance of treachery! I did not deserve to escape, she thought.

She lay awake at nights listening and waiting for a stone to strike up against the shutters. Lay holding Evergreen like a protection. She had taken her into her own bed now, as if by such a small sacrifice of comfort she could pay her debt to conscience. And she would lie awake, afraid of his coming, and yet wondering why he did not come, where he was, what he might be doing, now, this moment, midnight. Was he abroad again? In Antwerp? And if he was? What kind of man was he? What kind? That image of candlelight and bare flesh and laughter. As if she was there with him. Standing by a fire, letting her gown fall round her feet, her shift. Standing naked, watching him stoop down, his brown head, hair smooth and thick, chestnut glistening, tied in a club behind his neck with a black ribbon. Felt him touching, kissing,

[84]

shivered in horror, waking Evergreen with her shocked movement. And she must make her sleep again, tell her stories, as if
Evergreen was her child.

Indeed, it was during that time of waiting, and fearing, not
knowing from one hour to the next when the storm might break,
that Evergreen became real for her. Not simply an added burden,
but a living person, close to her. She began to draw an odd sort of
comfort from her, and to understand what her father had
already found in her. Like a deep well of—what? Companionship?
Friendship? If one could call anything so quiet, so undemanding
by such a title. Without her, if there had been only Solomon and
Martha, her father to be deceived that everything was as it always
had been, or even better, she thought she would have run mad.

Not that one could talk to Evergreen as one would to a real
friend, or expect her to answer sensibly. But merely to have her
there, not to feel completely alone, as her father made her feel, or
Martha. To be able to hold her, watch her moving about so quietly
and gently; to teach her to sew, scold her if need be and then
comfort her and make her smile. She did really smile now, sometimes, almost as if there was a small, secret spring of gaiety
hidden somewhere behind the dark, anxious eyes.

A companion. Someone to walk with in the fields. Not to be
alone. And about the third or fourth day of waiting, that terrible
waiting for something to happen without knowing what it might
be or when it might come, she felt that she could not endure the
house another moment, and told Evergreen that they must go
out, for the whole day, they should go as far as they could walk,
and bring bread and cheese with them and stay out until it was
twilight. Like a holiday. And walking beside Evergreen in the
winter sunlight, swinging their bundled luncheon by its knotted
corners, feeling now the warmth of the sun on her upturned face,
now the cold, sharp as ice in the air, promising frost; and warmth
again as they ran, it was truly a kind of holiday.

She had not run like that since she could remember. Without a
purpose. For the sake of running. Evergreen running just behind
her, like a young fox, her tongue lolling. Yet when they stopped
Evergreen was breathing no faster than when they began.

They ran again. Lay on the hard ground to recover, staring up
at the silvered sky. Found a dormouse asleep, wrapped in his
nest. And came at last to the sea, far to the north of Guthrum's

wood. They walked on the storm-littered beach until they found a sheltered place between two sand dunes to eat their bread and cheese, and drink their buttermilk. Lying back against the warm sand. The sun bright and strong and no wind there. Like an hour of summer in the winter's heart.

They scarcely talked. There seemed to be no need for it. And afterwards, when they were home again, Martha gone to bed, and they were alone in the kitchen, making a second supper for themselves, Evergreen had stood up and put off her slippers and begun to dance.

She did it so gravely, so beautifully, that Judith held her breath as she watched. Could almost hear the music. But it was only the wind outside. And Evergreen's shadow kept time with her, curtsying as she curtsyed, moving forward, moving back. Child and shadow dancing their minuet.

Only for the length of a dance, a few minutes at the most. Yet it seemed to Judith as if the dance was as important as all the remainder of their day.

They went to bed immediately after, and Evergreen fell asleep before she had undressed herself. Judith had to put her into the bed, rolling her over to one side to make room for herself. Why had she danced like that? For gratitude? Or happiness? It was not possible to know. Like holding something in one's hand and not knowing in the least what it is, except that it is beautiful, and mysterious, and contains secrets that must have a great value if only one could find them out. Know what they meant. But she could not guess. Or at least, not until long, long afterwards, when so much else had happened that to look back on this day was like holding a lock of someone's hair when the owner has died years ago, and there is nothing else of her that remains.

But for the moment all that mattered was to have companionship. Like becoming young again. And not the next day, but the day after that, they went for another expedition.

'There will be ice on the marsh very soon' Judith said, 'and I shall teach you to skate. You cannot imagine how wonderful it is. Like being a bird! I have another pair of skates somewhere and I shall tell Solomon to clean the rust from them and sharpen them. Oh, I am so glad that I have you for a friend!' She gave her a squeeze that for a moment Evergreen answered, with a timid pressure of her thin arm round Judith's waist.

[86]

I do truly have a friend in her! Judith thought wonderingly. What a great thing that is! And she must hug Evergreen again as if to make sure of her reality. And then run, to race her to the hedge, and beyond it, and beyond. Until they were far off their own land and it was truly another expedition, truly an adventure. Perhaps nothing would happen at all? Nothing terrible at least! It was almost possible to be sure of it, walking along the sea shore, following the edge of the marsh as they turned for home. Ice was already forming like thin glass among the clumps of reeds. It would soon be thick enough to skate on. A few more frosts. They ran, their faces glowing, the air sharp as a knife edge. To reach Guthrum's hungry as wolves, in the twilight. Nothing would happen! Nothing! Running in by the stable yard. And there, in his once familiar stable, was Scipio, her grey, tied up to his own manger, stamping his feathery grey heels with pleasure.

'Why, Scipio!' Judith cried. Fondling his black muzzle, letting him kiss her, blow against her cheek and ear, nuzzle her hair, and then her cloak, searching for sugar lumps or a carrot.

'And I have none by me! Oh Evergreen, come and meet Scipio my darling horse, I could cry to see him again. What are you doing here, is Mr. Gaultrip come—?' She stood stock still, like the manger's pillar, while the heavy, bony grey head blew its affection and disappointment against her breast. Why had he come? Solomon was shambling towards her from the kitchen doorway, making shows of secrecy and anxiety.

''tis the Customs Rider, ma'am, Miss Judy, ooh, in a terrible taking, looking for 'a. Ooh, ma'am, what do that mean?'

'Nothing, where is he? in the kitchen? Find carrots for Scipio, I will go in at once.' Surely it meant nothing? How could it mean anything?

Mr Gaultrip was sitting by the fire, his broken-brimmed old hat unlaced from under his chin and pushed back on his wig, his face as rosy-wrinkled as an old, old apple that has lain in a loft for a year. He had loosened his stock, and thrown off his shabby grey riding coat for the heat of the kitchen fire, and he was sitting in his old-fashioned, long-sleeved waistcoat, sipping a glass of hot. The scent of the saucepan filled the kitchen with odours of simmered gin and ale, and nutmeg and cinnamon.

'Miss Mortimer!' he cried, seeing her come in, 'thank God you've come at last!' Clambering to his feet as if the fire had brought out all his rheumatism and locked him with bent knees. 'Here's terrible news. All the goods are discovered! I could not help it, I swear!'

'What do you mean, what is discovered?' Her breath seemed to have turned solid in her chest, like a stone.

'I had no help for it! Mr. Mason from Shoreham was sent up to me, and he wanted to search your wood. There weren't no way of stopping him. And—there everything was. Such a run of goods as'll cost Mr. Barnabas a fortune, and he'll kill me, I know. Oh Miss Judith, why did you have ought to do wi' this business? It ann't for such as you, I knew ruin 'd come of it.' His hand shaking so much that his liquor spilled.

She sat down, her legs threatening to give way beneath her.

He came to sit opposite to her, his face seamed and riven with wretchedness. As if, she thought, what had happened was his ruin and not hers.

'Is—is Mr. Mason there now? In the wood?'

'He ha' gone to Urnford' Mr. Gaultrip said, 'to fetch help.' The Yeos. So I took the chance to come here and—for God's sake, ma'am, speak for me to Mr. Barnabas, get him word somehow. I daren't be seen looking for a messenger, Mr. Mason'd hear of it, but you can, or else if you don't help me I'm a dead man.'

'You?'

'He'll ha' me shot. A whole run! He'll never believe I knew nowt of it, he'll not wait to hear me.' He put his face in his hands.

'But how can I get a message to them? Shotton is seven miles.'

'Send her to Mr. Turton, at the Duke,' he whispered, his thumb jerking towards Evergreen. 'The lad's too thick to send, I tried 'em afore you came. Send her.' Dragging out his fat silver turnip watch on its brass chain. 'For God's sake, ma'am!' he cried, 'send her to warn Turton afore all chance is gone. I ha' waited already above an hour for you. They'll be back on top o' us afore——'

'But——'

'Send her!'

'I will, I will, but——' Wondering should she go herself. But for her to go to the inn at dark? Be seen there? It would cause so much talk as—— But would Evergreen understand, would Mr. Turton listen to her, would—— Giving Evergreen the message, impressing on her the need for hurry, for secrecy, not to be seen if

[88]

she could help it. But how could she not be seen? 'I must send Solomon with her, I cannot send her alone, someone might——'

'Send anyone!' Mr. Gaultrip cried, 'only be quick about it or I'm a dead man afore tomorrow! A dead man' he repeated, sitting down again, seeming to lose hope just as she was gaining it, thinking that indeed if Mr. Turton was in the smugglers' confidence he must be willing to warn them at all costs, if he had to ride to Shotton himself. And he had men to send, grooms, Tom the ostler—— But when he had warned them, what then?

'Mr. Mason—' she said, pushing Evergreen out of the kitchen door, pushing Solomon after her, urging them both to hurry, run, tell no one but Mr. Turton, not be seen— 'Your Mr. Mason' she said again, coming back into the kitchen. 'How long may he be?'

'How can I tell that?' Mr. Gaultrip muttered, staring into his empty glass. She pointed towards the saucepan on the fire, and he shook his head impatiently. 'Nay, nay ma'am, I do ha' had enough. Too much, waiting for ye.' He stood up, fumbling his hat onto his old greasy wig, tightening his stock. 'I'd best go. Altho' the De'il knows what it matters now. Mr. Barnabas——'

'But he cannot be angry with you for such a thing. How could you help it?'

He barely glanced at her, as if she was a child badgering him about grown-up troubles. His face so grey with despair that it seemed cruel to ask him about her own safety. But she must, she must know. 'Will he—Mr. Mason—what will he do when—will he seek to have me arrested?' Almost losing her voice on the word 'arrested.'

'You?' He tried to laugh, and sounded like a man dying. 'Why did you have to get a'self mixed up in this?' he said, almost shouting. 'You do ha' brought all o' this down on us because of the Earl!'

'The Earl? Has he—?'

But he waved her away like a child. 'I must go' he said.

She followed him into the stable yard, still trying to frame questions, about her danger, about the Earl and what he had done, might still do. About her being arrested and whether it would serve to claim that she knew nothing. And she had not known! She had known nothing! Had told Robert Barnabas that he must not—— 'I told them they must not come again!'

But he was not listening. Struggling into the saddle, Scipio

[89]

wanting to turn his head and nuzzle against her. The cold seemed to have struck Mr. Gaultrip half tipsy, coming from the heat of the kitchen fire. 'Please!' she cried. 'I have tried to help you. Tell me what may happen to me.' He was trying to tie the laces of his hat under his chin and they kept escaping from his old, rheumatic fingers. 'Let me! Bend down and I will tie them. Only tell me I cannot be arrested! My father—he would die of it!'

He did not bend down. Only looked at her, his eyes watering with the cold, and the liquor. As if he was crying with despair.

'Tell me! Please!'

'They'll not touch you' he said at last, his voice filled with contempt. 'T'Earl's cousin? I wish to God I were half as safe.'

He swung Scipio's head away from her, banged his heels into the grey sides. Scipio walked his slow, grave pace out of the stable yard. The heels banged again, and Scipio began a reluctant trot, the old short-barrelled musket lurching in its leather bucket. He had not gone twenty yards before his hat fell off.

'Your hat! Mr. Gaultrip! Your hat!' But he did not notice it was gone, nor hear her calling, and rode on, to become lost among other shadows, until he was no more than the distant sound of hoofbeats in a field.

She went and picked up his hat, and brought it back to the kitchen. Martha was rocking herself on her stool, her own glass refilled, and the saucepan empty. 'He—he says that I am quite safe' Judith whispered, frightened of contradiction, wanting to hear someone, anyone, tell her again, 'You are safe, you cannot be arrested, there is nothing any one can do to you.'

'Aye, aye' Martha said, waving her glass in the air. ''tain't nought against a body if people do leave stuff about anywheres, your wood or not. How could 'a fare to help what folks do an' you not there? But him! She jerked her thumb and cackled, her eyes suddenly wicked. 'That spy! Kneeling down afore owd Mr. Barnabas an' pocketing his gold, an' then robbing poor folks o' their bit o' gin an' tea as cain't afford to bribe 'em. Let 'em sweat a bit! Did a' ivva see any 'un so sweating frighted?' Cackling with laughter.

'But they cannot touch him! For what? Mr. Barnabas could not—what should he do to him when he could not help himself from finding—when this Mr. Mason——'

'Shoot 'em!' Martha cried. She had drained off her glass and her cap had slid to one side of her grey topknot, giving her an air of rakish cunning and villainy, like a pirate. 'That's what owd Barnabas can do to 'em! Shoot 'em dead!'

'Shoot him? Martha! You are making a joke of it, tell me you are only joking!'

But there was no comfort to be got from the old woman in the condition she was in, and Judith could only wring her hands together, and sit waiting for Evergreen and Solomon. One moment certain that she would be arrested before morning, and the next that Mr. Gaultrip and the soldiers would be murdered, and the next again that all Mr. Barnabas's men would be shot as they tried to seize back their goods. And Robert—God prevent his being there, she prayed. God keep him safe from—— Until Evergreen and Solomon came back, the message delivered. And there was no more to wait for, nothing else she could do. Except to go on waiting.

Chapter 11

She could not sleep, and determined to get up as soon as it struck five, and dress herself, and go to the wood to spy out what had happened. She would have gone at midnight if she had not been afraid of what she might find there. Once in the night she thought she heard shots, and went to the window that she had left un-shuttered, to listen. But there was nothing more.

Two o'clock. Three. At five she would get up. And she fell so deep asleep that she was only woken by the sounds of shouting, of horses and men. And started up in terror, thinking there was fighting, that he was being killed below her window.

It was not yet daylight, but when she looked out she could see the shapes of the horsemen, the shine of harness and brass scabbards. Soldiers.

Dressing, her fingers shaking, whispering to Evergreen to make haste, the buttons did not matter. But they did, they did, oh make haste, where are my slippers, my brush, a spencer. And Evergreen to dress herself, hurry, hurry!

Martha was calling her, panic in her voice; 'Judy, Miss Judith, ma'am, 'tis Master Francis wi' a regiment o' sojers, oh Judy child, we're lost.' All her drunken bravery gone. She looked dazed with drink and sleep, her topknot askew, her bare feet pushed into a pair of unlaced boots.

'Be quiet!' Judith ordered her. 'We know nothing, do you hear me?" She ran down, and found Francis standing in the hall, a sergeant behind him like a scarlet and pipe-clayed ramrod.

'Francis!' Judith said, her heart not beating so much as hammering, and then seeming to falter and stop altogether before racing again, so that it was impossible to speak.

Francis turning to the statue-sergeant, ordering him outside.

He waited until the echoes of the stamping heels had died, the door closed behind them, before he came to the foot of the stairs, his face drawn, an expression on it she had never seen. 'Judith! This is murder, nothing can cover it.'

She put her hand against her side, held herself upright by will-power. Her own face drained white. 'Murder?' Her lips were not shaping properly. 'I—do not understand you. Who—?'

'Mr. Gaultrip!' he cried, between despair and fury. Nothing of his familiar self about him.

She was going to fall, felt herself going. He caught her, half carried, half dragged her to the settle, Evergreen on her other side.

'Go and fetch your mistress something! Hartshorn, wine!' He held Judith up, shook her, slapped his glove across her face to bring her round.

'They have—shot him?' she whispered, hardly daring to look at him, to look at anything.

'Shot him?' he echoed her. 'God knows how they killed him. Shot. Drowned. I only know he must be dead. There is not a trace of him. Nor of the goods, nor anything.' He put the heel of his hand against his forehead, the effort of not shouting at her making his voice unsteady. 'And he was here! He was seen riding towards you!' He gripped her by the shoulders. 'He is not still here? His—body?' Such a beginning of horror in his eyes as made her own fears worse. She tried to gather herself, to think, to keep the truth from showing. As if it mattered, as if there was anything left that mattered.

'He cannot be dead! If you have not found—not found him—how can you be certain that—?' Evergreen had brought her the wine and she sipped it without tasting it, or even knowing what she was doing. He had gone to the fireplace and was grasping the stone mantelpiece.

'For Heaven's sake!' he shouted, 'what else would they do with him?' He swung round on her, his face as grey as Mr. Gaultrip's had been. As haggard. 'We have been to Shotton' he said, 'and they are all in hiding somewhere. We found only women and children there. But they must come back, and when they do——'

She tried to put down her wine glass on the edge of the settle and it fell, and broke. He started at the sound. There were dark shadows of sleeplessness under his eyes, a faint glisten of gold along his

[93]

jawbones where he had not been shaved since yesterday. 'When they do' he whispered, 'they may inform against you to try and save themselves. Or bring you down with them. I warned you, Judith!'

'I know nothing' she said. 'Nothing! And there is nothing they can tell. I took your warning. I swear it. I told them they must not——' She thought of her father, lying upstairs, listening, hearing the sounds of the horsemen outside, hearing Francis's raised voice. 'Keep your voice low' she breathed. 'Please. I swear to you I know nothing. Nothing of—of anything that has happened. If he is dead—— But he cannot be! He cannot!'

She did not know what she was going to say, what she wanted to say. Except to throw herself on her knees, cry out to him 'I knew! I let him go back! Oh God how can he be dead? It cannot have happened!'

But Francis was already shouting again. 'If? *If?* Of course he is dead! D'you think they would leave him alive as a witness to what they've done? They can be hanged for taking back the goods by violence. Do you think they'd keep from murdering one old man? What would they have to lose? You ought to know! They are your friends!'

His voice echoing against the roof beams, high above their heads. One of the bats that lived up there woke and flew round in panic.

'My father will hear you! Please, I beg of you!'

'He must know soon enough' he said, his voice still harsh, but quieter. And then, bending over her, gripping her by the shoulder again, he said in an altered whisper, 'Judith, if they say—if when they're arrested and questioned these people say you knew of this, nothing on earth can save you. Unless——'

'They can say nothing about me.' It was almost as if she was asking him a question. She felt herself breaking.

'But if they do? Judith, your life may depend on this. Tell me the truth, the whole of it, and then—and then perhaps—perhaps I can make some bargain with them——' He put the heels of both hands to his forehead, and shut his eyes. He looked so worn and tired that she felt almost sorry for him.

'You mean to be kind' she said, 'I know it.'

'Kind? I am your cousin! What else should I be in a case like this?'

If he had said, 'you are my friend', she thought, she would have broken down. She seemed to be looking at him across a distance.

'I have told you' she said, in a low voice, 'I know nothing of—— Why do not you go and search for him instead of tormenting me? Can you think that I—?' She raised her voice on the last words in a kind of hysteria, and began crying in earnest, not able to keep from it any longer. Evergreen with her arms round her, her face so frightened that Judith needed to comfort her in the moment of being comforted. Both of them crying, Francis standing helplessly in front of them. 'I am sorry' he said. 'But others may treat you worse than this, I warn you. Unless you help me to help you.' He looked down at her, as if he was waiting for a confession. Lifted his hands in frustration, his fists clenched, dropped them to his sides. 'Have you nothing else to say to me but that you know nothing? I tell you, he was seen riding towards you. Do you deny that he was here?'

'What else can I say? What else——'

He hesitated, his face with a grey sheen of exhaustion on it. Turned away. Outside she heard him shouting for the sergeant, the men mounting, riding. Silence at last. And then the soft, slow shuffling of Martha's slippers. 'God rot 'um' the old woman said, her voice rising as she reassured herself that the hall was empty of everyone but Judith and Evergreen. 'God rot their sowls! Questioning an' questioning! But I towd 'um nowt.'

'They questioned you?' Judith whispered. 'And Solomon?'

A wheezing of contempt. The fat old cheeks seamed with cunning. 'Him? I sent 'em off to Moate to fetch us a cheese, soon as I catched my wits togither. I were fast asleep when they came, and stricken frighted for a minute, but it dunna take me long to sense myself up. Doon't you worrit, precious. No 'un 'll touch you, my moppe. Not if owd Martha can do owt to help it.'

The day dragged forward. Telling lies to her father, who tried to look as if he believed them, while his hand shook. He knows, she thought. She would have given her hopes of salvation to be able to take the shadow from his eyes as he looked at her. And Evergreen. Not quieting her fears, they were already as silent as fears could be. But trying to do away with them while all she wanted was to be able to lay her head down and have her own fears smoothed away. Trying to keep Martha from getting drunk again, out of triumph, that was really a kind of hysterics after being so afraid. Trying to make sure that Solomon would say nothing, if they came back to question him. Listening for every sound. Francis returning. Or someone worse.

Until when the sounds did come she could not move, could not trust herself to walk down the stairs.

They have come to take me away with them, she thought. And then, I should say goodbye to him, to my father—tell him——

Francis was already in the hall. And another man, in a plain blue uniform, a tricorn hat. A great sheet of paper in his hand. Shaking it at her as she came down towards him, his face contorted, livid.

'You knew of this!' he shouted at her, while she was still on the stairs, her hand gripping the banisters to support herself. 'You think you have made fools of us! But by God——'

'Mr. Mason!' Francis said, his face grown even more haggard. 'Control yourself, man. Judith, he wishes to question you about this paper. We found it nailed to the church door here in Woodham.'

'You—you have found—' She could not make herself say 'his body?' What had the man said? A paper? She took it from Mr. Mason's shaking fingers. Could not focus her eyes on it. Large, printed letters. 'TO THOSE——' She still could not make her eyes obey her, and she held the paper towards Francis, her lips so numb that she could not even ask him to take it from her. But he took it, and read in a voice without any inflection, as if he was reading in his sleep; 'To those who may be concerned: I Mr. Philip Gaultrip, Riding Officer of this district, do declare and state that I am going to the Low Countries because of my debts and to avoid imprisonment for them. A friend is taking me safe across. I do ask pardon of my employers, and creditors, and hope that I may one day come back to pay all I owe and make amends. In the meantime let no one trouble to search for me as I shall be across the sea and well hid, before this is seen and read. Signed, Philip Gaultrip, Riding Officer of the Customs Service. Post Scriptum: To Mr. Mason, do not fear for my safety. I am among good friends. P. G.'

'It is lies!' Mr. Mason shouted, almost before Francis had finished reading. 'He is dead! Drowned, buried in the marshes, this is a monstrous lie, and you know it! Where is he? Who thought of this villainy? Where are the goods we seized?' He was black-haired, and the stubble on his cheeks was charcoal dark against the livid pallor of his face, his eyes circled with black and sunk into deep hollows, his skin shining, like melting wax.

'Francis' Judith whispered, 'please tell me. Is he safe? Is this true?' Putting out her hand for the paper as if she meant now to read it herself, get assurance from it. Her knees shaking.

'Mr. Mason has recognised the signature' Francis said. He sounded as if he did not care for him. Judith held the paper in both her hands. The print wavered in front of her eyes. Mr. Mason snatched it away from her.

'What do you know of this?' he shouted. 'How was it got from him?'

'I know nothing about it' Judith said. She seemed to herself to have spent all day saying 'I know nothing.' Strangely enough the words sounded more of a lie now than when she had been really lying.

'You persuaded him to write it!' Mr. Mason cried furiously, 'I know it!'

'I told you she knew nothing' Francis said in a tone of weary dislike. 'She gave me her word for it.' He looked away from her.

'Then—you will not—go back to Shotton now?' Her voice whispering. Looking down.

'I am returning to Urnford with my men,' Francis said flatly. 'There is nothing more to do here. Mr. Mason must do as he thinks fit.'

'If you had come quicker!' Mr. Mason's voice trembling with anger.

'If we had done as you wished the horses would have been finished by the time we arrived. You have no more questions for my cousin?'

And quite suddenly they were gone, ridden away again, the house was empty of them. She sat down by the fire in the hall and shut her eyes. He is safe, she thought. And realised she was not thinking of Mr. Gaultrip but of Robert. As if from the beginning her real care had been for him. She had not even the strength to go upstairs, to tell her father that all was well.

Chapter 12

She woke in the night thinking, it is not true! That man was right, it is all a trick, and he is dead! As if she could see his dead body in the dark, in front of her. She lay listening to the clock, to the scurries of wind, rain and sleet driving against the shutters, down the chimney, spitting like a cat in the fire. Slept again, and woke with her arm gone to sleep under Evergreen's head.

She dreamed of Francis. That she had driven him away from her for ever. As if the last of her childhood was gone. And she lay cold and quiet for a moment. And only then thought, Mr. Gaultrip! I must get news—oh, please, please God he is all right, that it is true!

Still dark. Was it five o'clock? Six? How long before she could send to Mr. Turton? She got up and began coaxing life into the ashes of the fire. They could not have killed him. They—not Robert—but the others—might have thought it a great joke to take the old man across to the Netherlands, make him sign that paper. Even that was a dreadful thing, to tear him away from his home, his work. But they could not have murdered him.

The fire began to burn. If he is alive, she thought, I will never again in my life tell a lie, do anything wrong.

And if he is dead?

She shivered in spite of the fire, shut her eyes, bent her head down until her forehead touched her knees. He cannot be dead!

She would have gone herself into Woodham, to Mr. Turton, to ask for news, but she was afraid of being seen, and causing worse gossip. It was bad enough to send Evergreen and Solomon again. But she would not send them until it could look as if they were on an errand to the shop or—or anything. Not until eight o'clock. At least eight.

She sent them at a quarter to. What did it matter if they were noticed? What did anything matter so long as—only hurry! Hurry!

Watching them go. It should take them no more than half an hour, there and back. She forced herself to go inside. And then to be busy, in the storeroom, counting preserves, candles, bars of soap. Forcing herself not to go into the hall to look at the clock. Not yet. But the half hour must have gone by, it must. She went and looked at the clock and twenty-five minutes were gone. Went away. Came back. Thirty. Three quarters of an hour. An hour. What could have happened to them? She went out into the yard, and to the top of the avenue. What were they doing? Trying not to think, he is dead! They have been told he is dead and are afraid to come back to tell it to me! Or they had been seen by the Customs man, Mr. Mason. He was questioning Solomon, prising everything out of him. She went back into the yard, pushing her fingers into her hair, trying to think of anything that could have kept them an hour, more than an hour. Mr. Turton had not been there! They were waiting for him! But he was always there.

She thought of sending Martha, of going herself. What could they be doing? What had happened? She could see the old man's body, could see men dragging it out of the marsh, drowned. Could see the Shotton men arrested. Could see the gallows, see them hung in chains, tarred and gibbeted and shrivelled, their eyes pecked out. Robert!

She flung on her cloak and ran like a lunatic towards the avenue, and saw them. At last! And then saw how they were coming. Solomon staggering, falling, held up miraculously by Evergreen, like a tree leaning against a sapling for support. He was waving his arms and singing, and then as he began to fall again he flung his arms round Evergreen's thin shoulders and sagged against her, almost on his knees beside her, giggling. When he saw Judith he clutched at Evergreen so lovingly that he brought her down with him, in a heap on the ground, his long ungainly legs straddling out as if they were double-jointed.

'What are you doing? What have you done?' Running, lifting Evergreen to her feet, catching Solomon by the hair as he sat in a patch of half frozen mud, shaking him until his teeth rattled. 'Get up! Where have you been!'

'I do ha' bin drinking, mistress.' He thought his answer so funny that he fell over backwards and Judith had to let go of him.

'Evergreen! How could you! Were you mad?' She caught hold of her and shook her in her turn. 'Tell me! Tell me what news!'

Evergreen cringed away, throwing up one arm to defend herself. 'Tell me!' Judith shouted, and had to turn away to control herself, take a deep breath before she could say more quietly, 'You have been two hours gone. Tell me what has happened, before I lose my reason.'

'There's men there' Evergreen whispered. 'They gave him brandy.'

'Men? The Customs men?'

'T'hell wi' the Customs men' Solomon shouted. 'The whoresons! Damn their blood an' let 'um drink it! Shotton hurray, mis'ress, hip hip hurray fur Shotton an' Mas'er Barnabas, God save t'owlers as loves poor folk! Damn t' Gov'ment!' He fell back again as if he was in a fit, his eyes bulging out of his head.

'Who gave him brandy?' Judith cried. 'Who?'

'T'owlers gi't to me' Solomon said, his voice thick as if his tongue had swollen to fill his mouth. 'I want t' be an owler, they ha' promised—promised—half guinea a night—carry ten gallon—God save——' He rolled onto his side and clutched helplessly at the mud. After a moment more he began to spew up liquid, as if he was a pump.

'Who has done this to him?'

'There were so many of them,' Evergreen whispered, 'they wouldn't let go of us, I tried to run away.'

'Oh why did I send you, why?' She turned back towards Solomon again. He was still vomiting, but now he was on his hands and knees, a great yellow stain under him on the grass and the mud. He looked as if he was dying.

'You wretched creature!' she shouted at him. 'How could you? Even you!'

'Queen o' t'owlers. Miss Judy for ever. God save Miss Judy, t'owlers' lady. Tha' wha' they do be singin'. God save Silver Tail, tha's wha' they do call you, ma'am, save y'r presence, Go' f'rbid disr'spec'. Silver Tail, 'count o' y'r hair.' He was taken with a seizure of laughter, a paroxysm that threw him onto his side, onto his back, legs and arms in the air kicking and waving. 'Sil' Tail!' he whimpered. 'God save ye, ma'am.' Lay still. Kicked once more and was unconscious on the ground like a log, like a corpse, his head and shoulders haloed in yellow puke.

'Let him lie there!' Judith said between her teeth. If she had had a club in her hands she would have beaten him with it. 'And Mr. Gaultrip?' Turning on Evergreen. 'For pity's sake! Tell me!'

Evergreen staring at her, as if she had forgotten why she had gone. Judith caught her by the shoulders, began to shake her. 'Tell me' she whispered. 'Is he—is he alive?' She shut her eyes in case she should see the answer in Evergreen's face before she heard what she would say.

'Mr. Turton—said——' The words whispering, dragging out, 'Yes. He is safe.'

She thought she would fall. She felt round her for something to hold her up. The gatepost. The oak wet, cold. Clung to it, hung against it. Thank God! I will spend my whole life being thankful. I will ask nothing else, ever. Felt sick with relief. She wanted to forgive Solomon, to tell him that she forgave him. Wanted to laugh, and then to cry; to tell someone the news; Martha, her father, anyone. It is all right, he is alive.

A long way off there was the sound of a horse galloping, wheels striking against a stone, rattling. She looked up and saw a gig driving furiously up the avenue, swinging out into the field to avoid the fallen elm tree, back into the avenue again. Mr. Turton's gig. Thomas the ostler driving it, standing up in his urgency to drive faster. He almost ran over Solomon's legs, and came to a halt beside her, beside the yard gates, the horse panting and steaming, shaking his head and making his harness ring.

'Ma'am! Miss Mort'mer, ma'am, come quick, come to the Duke, there's murder doing, they ha' young Chevell there an' are beating 'em wicked. Come quick a' mercy's sake, stop 'um afore they fare to kill 'em dead!' Dragging at the horse's mouth as he started to turn the gig.

'What are you saying? What do you want?'

'T'owlers!' Thomas shouted, the horse growing frantic, threatening to kick the gig to pieces as Thomas dragged him round. 'Ben Cobb an' t'others, murderin' drunk, an' they do believe as young Chevell do ha' peached on 'um. T'bloody spy they a' callin' 'em. Come, I tell you, they do claim you as their lady, they'll listen to you if you tell 'um stop.'

'But how? What can I—?' Only half understanding him, what

he had told her, what it meant. 'What do you want me to do?'

'I tell you they're fare to murderin' 'em, young Chevell, t'groom at Matcham's son. They do ha' caught 'em ten minutes back an' ha' 'em half killed dead a'ready. Dunna jus' stan' there dawzled girl, come up wi' you, come up an' stop 'um!'

And as she still stared at him he bent down and tugged at her arm. 'Come wi' me, dam' an' blast! The lad's dying! You're t' last chance we do ha' o' saving 'em!'

She let herself be pulled up, was half-lifted by him, half-lifted herself into the gig. Was standing beside him for a moment, and then as the horse bolted with them she lost her footing, falling against Thomas, finding herself crushed down on the seat, swaying and jolting, the gig bounding over the ruts and hummocks of the field, back into the avenue.

'How can I—?'

'They'll listen to ye. Ann't they singin' 'bout you, their queen o' t'owlers, their Silver Tail?' Hatred in his voice behind the terror, as if it was she who had caused it. All respect gone. She clung to the side of the gig, still not understanding what he wanted her to do, what she could do. She tried to ask him if Mr. Gaultrip was truly safe, and he shouted in contempt; 'Him? Owd Gaultrip? 'tis young Chevell they're murdering, beating 'em wi' whips an' cudgels, an' t' screams o' 'em! God send he ann't dead afore we gets to 'em.'

Tearing into the village, down the street, into the yard of the Duke of Marlborough. She heard the shouting even above the noise of the wheels and the horse's galloping, a crowd of people in the yard, looking towards them as they came careering in through the gates, scattering to make way, someone crying out 'here she come, he do ha' brought her! 'tis Miss Mortimer come!'

A crash of breaking glass, a bottle smashing on stone, and a scream of agony, long and high and then whimpering. Thomas lifted her down, her legs trembling so much that she would have fallen if someone else had not held her up. Mr. Turton, his face grey-white with terror, his stomach fallen away as if it had shrunk into itself with fear.

'Thank God ye're come. Go into 'um, ma'am, stop 'um afore they ha' him killed.'

'Where is the constable? Mr. Furness?' Clinging to Mr. Turton.

'T'constable?' Thomas cried behind her, catching hold of her and tearing her away from his master. 'What in Hell 'uld he fare to do wi' 'um, t'way they are? D'you want 'em killed as well? Go into 'um!'

She looked round. Faces staring at her. And again that high-pitched screaming. No longer like a man dying; like an animal.

'What can I—? Why had none of you—?' A dozen, twenty men there, labourers, the ostlers, tapsters, John Rayner the wheelwright and his son—and they had stood listening, waiting for her, for her! While they heard that screaming! 'Cowards!' she shouted at them, 'You vile cowards!' And they only looked at her, Thomas shoving at her, pushing her through the doorway into the emptied downstairs room, the bar of the inn.

'Go up to 'um, damn you!'

The stairs, pulling herself up by the banisters, looking back, Thomas's fat round face twisted into threats. Thomas who had touched his forelock to her all her life, since she could walk. 'Thomas!'

'Goo up!'

She was sick with fear. She could not walk with it. She had never thought that she would be afraid. That men might—— Men of this kind might—— Another scream, ear-splitting, horrifying. She flung herself up the last stairs, not knowing what she was doing, what she could do.

There was a crowd of men at the far end of the room, their backs to her, shouting, pushing one another, as if they were trying to see something by the fire. Smoke and a stink of liquor. And of burned flesh. Someone whimpering. She tore at the men's shoulders, trying to drag them aside, and from the unexpectedness of her attack three or four of them went staggering and falling. Only Slipgibbet stood facing her, lolling drunk and slobbering, a bottle in his hand. And tied in a wooden chair beside him there was a boy, no more than a boy, sunk down in his ropes, his feet and legs stripped bare, a man gripping his ankles, still trying to force the burned feet down into the fire again.

'STOP IT! STOP!' She was fainting, she was going to fall into the fire herself. Pulling at the man holding the boy's legs, half falling on him, while the men round gathered their wits, shouted in astonishment, anger, saw who it was and cried out ''tis her, Mast'r Robert's girl, Silv'r Tail!' Someone caught her by the sleeve. Slipgibbet swaying in front of her. She was dragging at the chair, the boy hanging against his ropes, and the chair fell backwards, the burned feet lifting, the boy crying. A red-haired boy she had seen at Matcham. Crying in agony and terror, his feet blackened, the blood itself turned black as it ran. She knelt where she fell, sprawled over him. Someone was pulling her away and she clung to the boy, the chair, and they were both dragged.

'Silver Tail! Robert's lady, God save her, gi' her a drink, bor! Turton ye sow's get, gi' us more liquor, drink to' Sil'r Tail, SEND UP MORE LIQUOR CURSE YE!'

The smashing of glass, of a window. Shouting. Singing. And then, like a door slamming, the sound of a shot. She knelt where she was, her hands on the fallen chair, the boy. Silence. The shot still echoing.

'If any o' you has touched her——'

Robert. Her eyes shut. She was falling.

His hands gripped hold of her, lifted her. 'Who touched her?'

Silence.

Leaning against him, his arm round her. A thread of smoke still curling up from the barrel of his pistol.

'The boy' she whispered. 'His feet.' She looked down at them, and did faint. Came to herself again sitting on a bench, a glass held to her mouth, the taste of brandy. 'Drink' he said. Burning her throat. They were carrying the boy away. Labourers from the yard below, frightened as sheep. Mr. Turton. Grease white, like melting tallow, his apron shrunk over fallen stomach. Thomas. Touching his forelock. 'God save ye, Mistress, no harm took? She do fare to ha' coom round, eh master?'

'His feet' she said. She wanted to get sick.

'Don't worry about him. He's all right. I'll dress his feet and they can bring him to Urnford. Now drink a sip more, you need it. What in Hell's name did you think you were doing, coming here?'

'Thomas——' she whispered, and Thomas was gabbling, ''tweren't me, Master Barnabas, 'twere t'guv'nor sent me for her. Doon't hold it against me, ma'am, master. We thought as they'd kill 'em dead, an'—an' Mistress Mortimer could—could——'

'Get out o' my sight before I kill you.' He was helping her down the stairs. The people still in the yard, crowding, staring, hanging back as he brought her into the air. Giving orders about looking after the boy until he could come back to see to him, after he had taken Miss Mortimer home.

'No!' she whispered. 'Look after him now. Now!' She would not let him put her into the gig. He had to give way to her and she stood leaning against the wheel, feeling sick and faint, listening to the boy's whimpering, and then his scream as his feet were lifted up while Robert dressed them, with cold tea leaves and torn linen. A scream as if he was being tortured again, while the crowd stayed quiet, only the sounds of jostling and whispering as they pushed close to look. No one came near Judith. And she kept her eyes shut so that she should not see any of them, nor what Robert was doing. She would have liked to stop her ears against the boy's crying, only she was ashamed, and she needed her hands to support herself, clinging to the iron rim of the wheel. She was so weak that when Robert came back to her he had to lift her bodily into the gig. More whispering. Driving out of the yard. She did get sick then, leaning over the side. He pulled her back onto the seat, close to him.

'I'll kill them' he said. 'And you! To have gone down there! What got into you? If anything had happened to you!'

Leaning against his shoulder, her eyes still shut. The avenue. Driving into the stable yard. Lifted down. Martha, and Evergreen. Helping her, carrying her up the stairs. 'No noise!' she whispered. 'My father, don't let him hear!'

Her room. Laying her on her bed, very gently, very carefully as if it was she who had been injured, and not the boy. 'Hot milk and brandy' he was saying. 'Go on and get it quick, old woman, d'ye think I'll harm her? Go on—hurry. An' you child, undress your mistress, take off her gown and get her between sheets. I'll not look, for heaven's sake.'

She felt sick again, and tried to sit up. He sat on the bed and held her, laid the back of his fingers against her forehead. And it seemed at one and the same time extraordinary and quite natural for him to be there, and she tried to smile at him and was crying, shivering with fever and weakness.

'Hush, don't cry, you're safe now, it's over. Don't cry my dear.' The rough, tar smell of his coat. The roughness of his hand as he smoothed back her hair. 'Try and sleep.' Making her lie back against the pillow. Drawing up the covers. Martha bringing the hot milk and brandy, wanting to make him go away, out of the room.

'Let him stay' she whispered. 'Please.' Or perhaps she was already asleep, and only dreamed that she had said it.

Chapter 13

She slept for twelve hours. And woke with a headache and the feeling that something was desperately, frighteningly wrong. Like waking from a nightmare, and then remembering. She lay very still, her heart beating again as if the danger was still there, as if she was still climbing the stairs of the inn, still hearing—— She clenched her hands against her breasts, and stared into the pitch dark. The fire had died, and the room was cold as ice. Silence. Only the softness of Evergreen's breathing. And—another sound? Someone else's breathing? She lay rigid, her own heart-beat making it impossible to listen. Someone—he was still there! Still there!

'Are you—is that—?' Her voice so low that it would have been difficult to hear her even if—Evergreen stirring, muttering in her sleep. There was no one. 'Robert?' No sound. No answer. Slowly her heart grew quieter. He was gone. When had he left? She lay remembering, trying to remember. As if his hand was still there, touching hers.

A pistol shot. Sharp as breaking glass in the silence. Outside. She could not move, could not breathe. They were there! Outside on the terrace! Someone—— They have come to—— A minute. Two minutes. What were they doing? Was it—? But she had heard it! It had been—— 'Evergreen!'

'Yes?' Her voice full of sleep. Then wide awake, frightened. 'Yes?'

'There is—I think that——' Needing already to be the stronger, not to show fear. 'It is all right. Only—I heard something. Outside. I must——' Forcing herself out of the bed, while Evergreen sat up, not even her eyes showing in the darkness.

The floor like ice. Curtains. Window. Shutters, her hand shaking as she felt for the iron latch. Coward! she told herself. Coward, coward! Do you think they mean to shoot at you? Easing one leaf of the shutters open. There was starlight. A quarter moon. The night black and silver. Nothing. Not a stirring in the air, frost bound like iron. There was a white glittering of frost from the ground, like silver dust. The trees black. No one. Not a living creature moving. And the sound came again, sharp as a gunshot, from the avenue. An elm branch fell, snapped clean by the cold. Tore its way down through twigs and smaller branches. Hit the ground softly.

Dear God.

She closed the shutters and the window, and drew the curtains again. 'It is all right' she whispered. 'It was only a branch breaking. Go back to sleep.' She felt about her for her cloak, and her slippers. She was already cold, and yet she could not think of going back to bed, of lying awake in the dark. And although she knew that there was no one there, the feeling of it remained and she knew that she would lie hearing movements, imagining——

'I—I shall go down and make myself a tisane. I have slept so long. Go to sleep. I shall be back directly.' The candlestick. She took it to the fire and stirred the embers until they glowed again and she could light the wick. Candlelight. And already she felt better, the room familiar, safer, safe. Evergreen's eyes shining as she lifted the candlestick and looked towards her. 'Go to sleep at once. When—when did Mr. Robert go? Was it—immediately after I fell asleep?'

'He stayed a bit. A long time.'

'What did he say when he left? Did he—give you a message for me?'

'He said he'd be back. Next week. He can't come before, he said. He was very sorry for it but he can't.'

He had been in this room. Sitting there, on the bed, while she—— She felt herself flushing, her face, her throat, burning as if the fever had come back. And she—but he was gone. 'Go to sleep at once!' Suppose—suppose he was down there, in the kitchen, waiting? And she stood shielding the candle-flame with her hand. I am mad, she thought. Wicked mad! What am I thinking? I would not go down to him, I would not, I swear it!

She went out into the corridor. I shall make a strong tisane, she thought, and then I can sleep again, and when I wake in the morning everything will—— But nothing would be as it had been. As if till now, till yesterday, she had been surrounded by—by safety, like a locked and bolted house. And now the safety was gone. She stood for a moment outside her father's door. The shadows moved on the panelling, on the door frame. A timber creaked in the roof. A mouse scratched. As if the night was trying to get in.

And I have done it! she thought. I have—— She put her forehead against the door, her eyes shut. If she could tell him what she had done, all that had happened. Hear him tell her that it did not matter, that everything would still be safe. Beyond the door her father cried out in his sleep, not loud, only a kind of muttering. She was afraid that she had woken him by standing there, and went quickly away, on tiptoe. The stairs were a well of dark. She stood and listened.

Coward! she told herself again. In her own house, her own familiar stairs! They were all back in Shotton now, lying drunk asleep. There was nothing. Not a sound. The doors were bolted. Never, never, never again. Francis had been right, she had been stark mad to let them—— She made herself go down. The passage. The kitchen. Stirring the fire, until it burned up and she could let down the kettle on its chain and settle it among the flames. Stark mad. But now—— She collected the herbs she wanted, rosemary and endive and wild thyme and mint. A mug. Powdered cinnamon. She would make it so strong that she must sleep again. Familiar kitchen. Except that—— He had sat there. There. And she——

She sat trying to think, and could think of nothing. Except that he——

She must not see him again.

The kettle simmered, boiled. She tilted it, filled the mug, and the scents of the herbs, of the rosemary, spread and grew stronger. She would write to him and—— As if he was kneeling there, beside her, his head resting on her knees. How could she write and say—I will not see you again because—— Because you are your father's son. Because—— And suddenly it was not Robert beside her but the boy, roped into his chair, his feet—— Because I have let in the dark! Because I am frightened! Terrified of——

'Hush, you're safe now, it's over. Don't cry, my dear.' The smell of tar, of the sea. Holding her. What was he? One of—of them? No! His hands holding—holding her up. She shut her eyes, gripped her own hands round the china mug until it burned her palms. I must not think of him—like that. I must not! He will not be back until next week, and by then—— By then she would know what she—— But I know now, it is impossible, it is like—it is like doing again what I have already done, and Mr. Gaultrip kidnapped, and the boy tortured, and—I have been saved by miracles, and I am thinking already—Francis was right, a thousand times right, and I deserve to be——

I cannot write to him though, she decided. That would be truly cowardice. And ingratitude. Worse than ingratitude. I must see him once again. To tell him—— But she had a week—days in which to decide what she must tell him, decide how she could—— What mattered now was to make all things right, as they had been, before—— Make herself right. Learn from this dreadful time and become wiser for it, and stronger. To-morrow—tomorrow she would—— They should clear the weeds from the vegetable garden. And Solomon must cut the fallen elm tree into manageable logs and—— There were ten thousand things to be done. Her mother had always said it, when one was in any doubt about things the only remedy was work, and everything would solve itself if one worked hard enough.

She finished her tisane and pulled the kettle up into its place, high in the chimney. They would plant vegetables and flowers. It would soon be as if nothing had happened at all. Except that—— But they could not leave the old man too long across in the Netherlands, they must soon bring him back. And the boy's feet would heal up, and—— And she would be wiser. The next time she saw him she would be astonished at her folly. She would know exactly what to say. What did matter what kind of man he was? What mattered was——

Only as she went up the stairs again, the shadows wavering in front of her, the certainties began to dissolve, become as full of shadows as the candlelight. Evergreen was still awake, and she knelt beside her and held her close, like a protection. 'Hush, go to sleep I told you, everything is all right.' And the echoes of his voice seemed to be there as she was whispering to Evergreen. 'Go to sleep.'

But when they woke it was daylight, and all the shadows were gone. And immediately after breakfast she found a spade in the stables and began trying to clear away the weeds from what had once been a cabbage bed. And she had been the one who was going to teach the Riggs and the other cottagers how to grow cabbages and cook them! She should be ashamed!

'Evergreen! Come and pull up these weeds. I cannot get the spade into the ground they are so thick and strong.'

But Evergreen was worse than useless. She became more interested in the weeds themselves than in pulling them up by the roots and she did not know even how to hold the spade, let alone get it into the ground. And when Judith tried to begin a bonfire so that they might burn the weeds away instead of having to dig them up, the smoke choked them and they had to abandon everything until it died down. They went instead to see what progress Solomon was making with the elm tree, but he was doing no better than they had done with the weeds.

''a do fare to need two on us, mistress, a job like this 'un. An' a big saw an' wedges an' a smith's hammer to drive 'um. I'll not never do split 'um t'way I'm gooing.' That seemed true. Indeed he had made things slightly worse by cutting off some of the heaviest branches and leaving them scattered.

'You had best come and help us with the bonfire, and we must ask Mr. Hassett to lend us someone, and the saw and the hammer. Oh, there is so much to be done!'

They choked themselves again with the bonfire, and Solomon burned his eyebrows off, trying to make amends for yesterday. But at least she was tired enough by the evening to persuade herself that they had begun very well. And during the days that followed she did seem to be achieving something in the kitchen garden, or a corner of it, and she could almost imagine as the earth grew neat and ready for planting that her own life, and her thoughts and anxieties, were growing neat and ordered too, and that when—when he came back—she would be able—she would know exactly what—— And she would push the spade into the ground and call for Solomon to continue digging the row, because she had blistered her palms.

'And we must prune the fruit trees. Look at that apple tree, covered in lichen, it is a sin! And there is not a flower bed left. There is so much to do!'

[111]

In the evenings she read to her father. *The Ancient Mariner.* *Tintern Abbey.* But although he tried to seem glad to listen she saw that there was a restlessness about his eyes, and the shadows under them had grown darker.

The evening of the day that they had pruned the trees, and she was telling him about it, she saw his eyes wandering, searching the corners of the room, behind her, as if he was looking for someone.

'Is anything the matter?' she whispered. He had not asked for his writing board and paper for days—since—since what had happened at the inn. As if he knew of it. She came and knelt on the other side of the bed from Evergreen, and felt his pulse. 'You are not worried about anything? Tell me.'

'What—should I—worry about?' he said, his voice hoarse with effort. She took his hand and kissed it.

'I am glad. I should be very cross with you if I thought you were keeping secrets from me. It will soon be Christmas and after that in no time it will be spring, and there will be flowers for your room. We have the walled garden almost ready, you cannot imagine how much we have done.'

'That was—a famous garden—in its day.'

'And shall be again! We shall plan it together you and I. You shall remind me of all the flowers that Mother liked to have growing there. All her herbs are turned into bushes, and there is a young tree of rosemary. Did you smell the herbs I have been drying? The whole house is scented with them! I am storing them in sealed jars.'

'You will be just like—your mother. You—are like her.'

'If only that was true! I have thought of her so often these past—days.' She had been going to say 'nights'.

'I—dreamed of her—to-day' he whispered. His eyes feverish. 'She was standing—behind your chair. Looking down at—the desk. I—am not sure even—that it was a dream. And she turned round and—looked at me. As if she was——'

'Sssh. You must not talk any more. You know you must not get excited. Do you promise me you have not been worrying about anything? You have not—been imagining things?'

'Imagining?' He looked at her, his smile strange, more drawn down at the one side than usual. He shook his head slowly. 'No. I have not—been imagining—I promise you.'

'You must go to sleep again. And no dreams. Is that another promise?'

'I—like to dream.'

'Then no bad dreams.'

'It was not—a bad dream. I think—she came to tell me—to get ready. It cannot—be very long—now.'

'Hush! I will not have you say such things! I shall not let you go for—years and years and years, do you hear me?' Tried to smile, to make it into a joke. Kissed him. Smoothed his covers. Beckoned Evergreen and took the candlestick from the desk where she had been reading.

'Good night. Sleep well.'

'Sleep—well, my dear. And—you, Evergreen.'

Closing his door. An odd foreboding as she closed it. But that was nonsense. She was growing worse than Martha; she would be looking for omens in the tea leaves next. 'Quickly into bed' she said to Evergreen. 'We have lots to do tomorrow. We have all the vegetable seeds to plant and cover. And there is the soap to cut. And if it is fine we must spread out the linen to bleach.' As if she was persuading herself of how ordinary things were.

She woke a few hours later as though someone had shaken her awake. Could feel a hand on her shoulder. She sat up, not afraid, too startled to be afraid, the sense that someone had touched her so real that she thought at first it had been Evergreen. But Evergreen was asleep beside her.

She did not even need to think of it, that something had happened to him, was happening. She found her slippers, her cloak. Lit the candle at the fire. Felt her way to the door, and along the passage. The step. His door. And she stood with her forehead against the wood, listening, holding her breath, trying to make her heartbeat quieten. She could hear the rattle of his breath. Like—like the last time. But it was not the same! No! She touched the door handle and was afraid to turn it. It is only a dream, he is breathing fast in a nightmare, that is all. And did not want to go in, to see——

As if he was struggling for life. The sound terrible in the quiet. She went in, the flame of the candle guttering, steadying as she shut the door behind her, and stood for another second of hesitation with her back to it. Inside the drawn bed curtains that gasping, tormented breathing. She pulled the curtain aside. He was lying on his back his face sheathed in sweat. And as she looked at him his body twisted away and his head jerked towards her, all in the one wrenching cruel movement, like trying to free himself from bonds; a savage, unnatural twisting. And the next second his body shuddered, became rigid for a moment that was like an hour, and went slack.

'Father! FATHER!' Wanting to fling herself forward, catch hold of him, keep him alive. And at the same time she dared not move, as if her moving might kill him, like a candleflame blown out. His breathing grew quicker and shallower by the instant. His cheek fell outwards, slack and lifeless with each breath, to be sucked in again with the next in-dragging of air. She stood frozen, as if she too had suffered that stroke of paralysis, and was on the point of falling.

She did not know how she was freed from it. She found herself outside the room, running, the candle gone out. Crying 'Martha! Solomon! The master, the master is dying, come quickly!'

Up the narrow, twisting stairs to the attic room where Solomon slept, the blankets wrapped round his head against ghosts and the night air; shook him awake. 'The master! The master is dying!' Endless moments before he could understand, while he was trying to wake, to shake the sleep out of his head.

'Get dressed! Get up! Hurry! You must go to Urnford. Hurry!'

Running to Martha's room, and the same fury of waking her, making her understand. 'He is dying! Oh, hurry, help me!' Down to the kitchen, to the fire, to set water to heat, find stone jars to warm the bed, keep death away. Run back up the stairs to him. Still that shallow, rasping breathing. His flesh cold. Wet with fever sweat and at the same time cold. Where was Solomon, what was he doing? She must write a note to Mr. Turton for his gig. Another to Doctor Farquhar. More candles. More light. Wrapping cloths round the jars so that they should not burn him. Set them against his back, his stomach. His body like an emptied sack.

Then the waiting.

Evergreen had come creeping in. She crouched now on the far side of the bed, holding his hand as if she was trying to warm it. Her face hidden. They had had to change all the linen of the bed, and the smell still hung in the room. Excrement. Part of the smell of death. Was death always like this? Filth? Indignity? She sat stiffly upright on the chair she used for writing, as if to sit like that, hands folded, not to let go, bend forward, cry, would give him strength. Evergreen was crying. Silently, her shoulders hunched. Shadow tears.

He will be dead tomorrow. To-day. She had heard them say it the last time, the doctor and the surgeon. The third seizure kills. She changed the jars. Tried to make the slack mouth react enough to take sips of brandy. He was sweating again. And then ice-cold. His cheeks had turned leaden-blue, were sunk away from his nose and teeth. Five in the morning. Six.

Martha brought her tea, and toasted bread. She even brought some for Evergreen. 'Take a bit my moppe' she whispered to Judith, 'You do need heat in you as much as he do, poor soul.'

But she could not eat. She sipped the scalding tea. Laid it aside. Seven o'clock. She could not think beyond the minutes, the sound of his breathing. As if she would pass the rest of her life in this room, listening to that rustling of breath. Now and then he fought harder for air, and that was worse. She was not aware of tiredness, of closing her eyes, but her head nodded forward, jerked, and she was awake again. She heard voices, heavy foot-steps. Doctor Farquhar? Solomon? Robert's voice. Robert!

He came in, too big for the room, for the still, heavy atmosphere that was not used to health. Filling the doorway. Martha behind him. He looked at Judith, but went direct to the bedside, as if he were truly a doctor. Stood looking down. He took her father's wrist and felt the pulse.

'Give me the candle' he said. He held the candle flame close to the open right eye, and then the left, moved it sideways, back again. Held it closer.

'Is he—?' she breathed. Afraid that her father might still be able to hear; to understand the word 'dying'.

He did not answer her. He set down the candle and took the empty glass from the table, Evergreen shrinking away from him, hiding herself in what had been her favourite hiding place, behind the bed curtain. Robert held the glass to his nose. 'You've given him brandy?'

'Yes. Was that wrong?'

He nodded. 'But it doesn't matter.' He looked down at Evergreen. 'Leave me with your mistress a bit.' And when she did not move he lifted her, putting his hands under her elbows and setting her on her feet, turning her towards the door. 'Go on out, my dear.'

He wants to comfort me, Judith thought distantly. As she had once, with Evergreen. How easy she had thought that was! And yet it was a kind of comfort that he was there. She had not thought that anything could—give her comfort. 'He is dying?'

'Yes.'

She was glad that he did not try and tell lies to her. He was looking round for a chair, and she gave him hers, and went herself to Evergreen's place and knelt down. She took her father's right hand, and then his left, and held them against her. 'Can he hear anything?' Whispering.

Robert shook his head.

'How long?'

'A few hours. To-night. But I'm not a doctor. When Dr. Farquhar comes——'

They stayed silent after that. Now and then she looked sideways, not at his face, but at his knee, close beside her as she knelt on the flattened cushion by the bed; rough blue serge, the top of his boot, the black leather salt-whitened, stained by sea water. His hand resting on his thigh, the nails blunt and rimmed under with tar that washing would not remove. A square, powerful hand, for ropes and timbers, and heavy weights. Not for a sick room. The smell of leather, of sea-salt.

Once he leaned forward and took her father's left wrist from her, held it up, let it fall. It fell disjointedly, and she felt as if her heart was being torn. Robert put his hand on her shoulders.

'If I was a full-trained doctor' he said, his voice low, 'I could do nothing for him.' And after another silence, a long silence; 'I'm going back to Leyden.' He seemed to be waiting for her to answer, to say something, and when she said nothing, he went on, 'To finish my studies. The other day. That made up my mind.'

It took her a moment to think of what he meant. The inn. He was looking at her. His eyes searching hers. 'I'll be three years gone. If I come back at all.'

He is going, she thought. And she must say something, answer him. Not let her silence answer. What should she say? I am glad for you? I am sorry?

How could he expect her to think of anything except that her father lay there dying? As if he was already dead. Three years. I must be glad of that, she told herself. I must.

She took a handkerchief and wiped away the film of sweat from her father's temple. The skin had turned darker blue, and his breathing had become even faster, and shallower. She gripped Robert's arm. 'Tell me! Is it—now?' She felt for a second that she could not endure it any longer, that she wanted it to happen, be finished. He put his hand over hers.

'It'll be a few hours yet' he said. 'You've got to be brave.' Like an echo. Had she said that to—?'

Waiting.

I must not lean against him, she thought. I must not touch him. Must kneel upright. As if she was learning to be alone. I must not let him touch me. But his hand was on her shoulder, behind her neck. His wrist against her neck, under the mass of her hair that had fallen and covered it. She thought she could feel his pulse, or was it hers, the beat of it? She wanted to put her head down on his leg, rest it there. Shut her eyes. I must not! Even the thought of it! And as her head had nodded before he came, without knowing it, she felt it dropping now. Half asleep. Starting into wakefulness. Nodding again. Lying on the warm serge. His hand on her cheek, holding her. She could feel the roughness of his palm. Of his fingers. No sound in the room except that shallow, hurried breathing, hurrying to the end.

Chapter 14

There were only three funeral coaches. The Earl's and the Countess's coach going empty behind the hearse. Black plumes, and the servants in mourning-livery, for a cousin of the house. The Earl had arranged everything. As though death had reclaimed her father into the family, erasing everything about him but his name. To become no more than a marble tablet in the family vault at Matcham, beside all the other Mortimers. But the Earl not there, nor the Countess. Only the empty coach to represent their empty grief for a dead cousin they had disliked. Behind their coach, Lord Claydon and Francis, riding together.

Francis at least felt real sorrow, she had seen it in his face, felt it in the grip of his hand. But only breeding and good manners held Claydon back from saying all he was longing to say to her. About young Chevell's injuries, the men from Shotton, everything that had happened, and every moment of the half hour they had been together he had had to turn away from her to hide or try to hide his feelings. It had made a wretched time almost unendurable, until she would have preferred him to shout at her, anything rather than that ill-concealed fury. While she tried to be courteous to Mr. Massingham, who had not been content with coming to represent the Countess and ride in the first coach, but must have a coach to himself. 'It makes a third' he had whispered to her confidentially. 'Even three coaches, you know, are scarce enough—why far far less than enough. For such a gentleman! Such a profound scholar!' Rolling up his eyes, clasping her hands that she could not refuse to him on such an occasion. As if already he was himself a member of the family. 'And soon!' his eyes said, 'soon there may be a happier occasion, to make me truly one of the family.' The hatred at the back of his eyes made her shiver. 'You are alone now,' it seemed to whisper. 'Wait. Just wait.'

Until at last they were leaving, were outside, Claydon saying in a furious undertone to Francis, when he thought that she was out of hearing, 'She cannot even have the avenue cleared! The damned hearse will be overset, I know it!'

But it did not turn over, and they were gone. She could go back into the dining room and sit down on a chair and shut her eyes. Thank God that she did not have to go to the funeral itself. Thank God. She took a glass and filled it with wine, thinking it might calm her, but as soon as she held it near her mouth the smell sickened her and she put it down again.

'Evergreen?'

Evergreen came sidling in as if she had been outside the door, hidden and waiting. 'You must eat something' Judith said. 'You have had no breakfast.' She put her hands against her eyes to ease them. She had not slept since he died, or so it seemed to her. Had scarcely eaten.

'I am very sad for you' Evergreen whispered.

Judith put her forehead against Evergreen's cheek, that was not much above the level of hers, even though she herself was sitting down. 'I wish I had been kinder to you' she said. 'I wish I had been gentle. When—when your father—— Can you forgive me?'

'Forgive you?' Evergreen said wonderingly, touching Judith's hair, the scrap of black silk she wore on it for a mourning cap. 'You were so good to me.'

'If I could believe that' Judith whispered. 'You must stay with me always. For ever and ever. We will be like sisters. I shall always look after you, I promise.'

After a moment she said, 'I want to go up to his room' and they went together, Evergreen hanging back a little. Stood in the emptiness by his bed, that was no longer his bed. No longer his room. 'I am lighting a candle' he had said to her once. Not here, but on a walk in the fields, when he could still walk, and when she had really been too young to understand. She was not even sure that she understood it now. Candles are blown out, burn down, gutter. If no one sees them?

She picked up the untidy pile of his manuscript from her desk and held it against her heart. Perhaps—perhaps one day—— She laid it down again, and went out of the room with Evergreen. And by an association of ideas of death, perhaps, went to her mother's room. The very day before she died, Judith's mother had come into this small dressing room of hers, leaning on Judith's shoulder, and on Martha.

Had insisted on coming, although she had almost fainted at every two or three steps. Why had she wanted to come here? Not to the parlour. Not to her husband's study. Here, where she kept her sewing box. And a shelf of books that she had brought from Paston in Suffolk. Almost the only things she had brought, except her basket of clothes, and a pet hen, and two horn spoons, and a silver porringer. The porringer was in her father's desk now, locked away. He had told Judith it was from Charles the First's time, and a rare piece. But that was not why it was locked away.

Judith went to the bookshelf. *The History of Valentine and Orson. The Seven Champions of Christendom. The History of the London 'Prentice.* Judith took that down and held it between her palms, not needing to open it to know what was inside.

It had been the first whole book she had read. How proud she had been. And how proud her mother had been. Not only that her daughter had learned to read, but from her book!

'We are wasting time' Judith said, keeping her voice strong. 'We must strip my father's bed, and put the linen to be washed, and—— There is a great deal to do, and we are standing here not doing it.' This afternoon she must go to see Mr. Carteret, and arrange for a memorial service. The village would expect it, and if she did not ask for one Mr. Carteret might find more cause for offence in that. But perhaps she would not go this afternoon. Tomorrow. Tomorrow morning. 'Come' she said to Evergreen. 'We must make ourselves busy again. It is the best way to overcome sorrow.'

And the next day she did feel, not better perhaps, but at least able to think of his death as something that had had to come, and to accept that she herself must go on living. And living as—as wisely as before. More wisely even, not that—— And at the same time she could not creep away into a corner and hide herself. Nor—nor do any other stupid, frightened thing. She must go on as one should.

She had her mind made up to it, and even the day seemed given especially to help her. It was like a spring day come by marvellous chance into December. The sky was a pale blue silk above the black of the elm trees, and the birds sang to them, as they walked down the avenue, picking their way among the ruts.

I must not be afraid, she told herself, and was not really certain what she was afraid of. Of speaking to Mr. Carteret? Of the village? But that was madness! Afraid of seeing people—people she had known all her life? Afraid of remembering—what? Drunken ruffians she need never see again. Would never see again. They had not been Woodham men, and the villagers here—they would be more ashamed now to see her than she could possibly be at seeing them. And well they might be ashamed, she thought. And Mr. Carteret too! More than any. Where had he been that day? Hiding in the vicarage? Pretending he knew nothing of what was happening?

She held Evergreen by the hand, drawing companionship from her. A cock pheasant flew up from the middle of the field beside them, with a hard rattle of coloured wings. And for a second it was as though the sun had gone in. The birds lying in the frozen furrows, where Evergreen had poisoned them. Dying. Dead. Had she known that they would die, that they could not recover? She wanted to ask her, and was afraid of the answer. Afraid even to look down at her, at the dark head, the still secret eyes. What does one know of anyone, she thought. And shivered slightly, and wanted to say 'Let us run.' Do anything to drive such thoughts away. But they might be seen running, and cause scandal, running together the very day after her father's burial. They were almost at the village. She could see the vicarage gate, the thick, overgrown laurel hedge that had formed an archway above it. She saw a man crossing the road ahead of her, and felt her heart-beat quicken and then hesitate.

Do not be such a fool, she commanded herself. Such a coward!

'Stay there' she said to Evergreen. And that too was a kind of cowardice, leaving her by the gate for fear of Mr. Carteret seeing her and shouting. But it was best not to look for trouble. She knocked at the door, and waited. Felt as if eyes were on her from windows. From beyond the hedge and the trees of the large, unkempt, uncared for vicarage garden, that had turned into a near wilderness since Mrs. Carteret ran away with her East India lover.

But the vicar was not there, the servant told her, he was in the church. Looking at Judith with an expression that seemed half insolent, half inquisitive, as if Judith was something to be stared at at a Fair, like a peepshow. Even her conventional word of respectful regret for Mr. Mortimer's death sounded false and almost impudent.

I am imagining things, Judith told herself. The girl is an ill-mannered sloven, that is all, the kind of servant he always has, no others will stay with him. Yet she was very glad that the village street was empty. Although it was strange that it should be so empty, even on a weekday morning. No one. Not even children playing.

'Stay here' she said again to Evergreen. 'I shall not be more than a few minutes.' She pushed open the heavy oak leaf of the church door. Mr. Gaultrip's message had been nailed here. I will not think of that, she told herself. It was done with, nothing could alter it. Robert would see to it that he was kindly treated, until—until he could safely be brought home. Pushing open the door. The cold like an ice-house, dank and clinging. Her footsteps echoing. 'Mr. Carteret? It is Judith Mortimer.'

The sunlight giving way to shadows. Oak pews. Benches. Stone. The faded mural of St. Christopher, yellow and blue and dulled reds. 'Mr. Carteret?'

He came out from the vestry behind the altar, and she felt her heart check again. Went up the aisle, her hands clasped together against her cloak. 'I have come to speak to you—about —about a memorial service for my father.' He was above her, standing on the altar steps, staring down at her with his lip pushed out like a threat, his face dark with its habitual anger. Anger at the world, held ready always to concentrate on anyone who came near him.

'Memorial service? What should that be? For an unbeliever?'

'It is expected' Judith said, forcing her voice to stay quiet and even. 'The people will expect it. It does not matter what you and I——'

'Does not matter?' His voice rising. 'Does not matter that he was an unbeliever, and you are worse than he?'

'I—my beliefs—his—they do not enter into the question. It is out of respect to his memory.'

'This is not a House of worldly respect!' he shouted. 'It is the House of God! Here there is no respecting of persons, even of

Mortimers! Here God dwells, and I am His servant, and I shall not allow His House to be profaned! I shall not!' His voice echoing, echoing from the hammer beams of the roof, and the thick Saxon walls that held them up. The echoes crying 'house—house—profaned—profaned.'

'I did not come to quarrel with you' she whispered, afraid to trust her voice louder. 'Can not we preserve appearances at least?'

'You? You to say that? YOU!' He came down the steps of the altar towards her, and she must step back or be driven back by his bulk and fury. Driving her down the aisle, away from the altar, as if her presence there was a sacrilege, a profanation. 'You who have brought wickedness into this parish! WICKEDNESS! To dare speak of appearances! Appearances! An old man kidnapped, a boy burned because of you! Crippled!'

'He will get well again!' she cried. 'Mr. Barnabas told me——'

'That villain! That murderer! Your lover! He is your lover! You shameless creature! You vile thing! OUT! OUT OF GOD'S HOUSE!' Driving her before him, flapping his arms, his face filled with madness, with a mad religion, his spittle like rain against her face. She wanted to run from him and was half afraid to turn her back. The doorway. 'OUT OF MY SIGHT! JEZEBEL!'

'You are mad' she cried at him. 'Mad and cruel. What kind of God can you believe in?'

'Out of this House' he whispered. 'I know what you do. You lie with him, fornicate in the darkness. Vileness and evil, the Devil's work. Get out of God's presence.'

She turned away shuddering, into the porch. And saw women gathered across the street. Whispering as they saw her come out, one of them bending down, picking up a stone from the ground. Evergreen shrinking against the wall. The woman lifted her arm, threw. The stone struck the church steps and rolled away, harmless.

'What are you doing?' Judith cried. 'Are you all gone mad?'

They did not answer her. Seven or eight of them. Women who all her life had curtsyed to her. As Tom the ostler had used to greet her.

'Take that witch girl out o' the village!'

'An' you goo with her!'

[123]

Their courage fostered by hearing the first shout of enmity. 'Bringing trouble, bringing the Shotton men! A lad near dead for you!'

'For me?' Judith cried. 'Did I not try to help him? While your men——'

'An' Mr. Gaultrip, where's he? Dead an' drowned, murdered for you, an' you takin' his murderer for lover!'

'That is a lie! Two lies!' Judith cried.

Another of the women picked up a stone, flung it, her aim wide, but no less frightening for that; the hatred more frightening than any injury. More women coming up the street, hurrying. Curtains moving, the sense of eyes staring, of something planned, waiting for the first time that she should come here, be at their mercy. Not a man in sight, not a child. All taken into their houses, indoors, so that—so that this could happen. Evergreen close to her, gripping on to her cloak.

She turned to go back inside the church, but Mr. Carteret was there. He pushed her out, slammed the massive door behind her. Bolts ground into sockets. A stone struck against the oak. She held Evergreen by the arm, went down the steps towards them. Still could not believe it, that poor village women—— They faced her like geese against an enemy, ten, twelve of them now. Still held by the remains of respect. More than half afraid of what they had already done. And if Judith had been alone she could have faced them down. But Evergreen crippled her authority. That dark skin, that witch-gypsy hair, the kind of creature these women shouted away from their kitchen doors, set their dogs on, called for the constable to arrest and imprison; Evergreen destroyed Judith's authority simply by being there beside her.

'Child o' Satan!' a woman cried from behind the others. More stones. One of them struck Judith on the arm. She began to back away, pulling Evergreen with her, protecting Evergreen's face with her cloak. It was the worst thing to do, and she knew it, but her fear for Evergreen overwhelmed all else.

'Run!' she whispered to her. 'Run home as quick as you can.' Pushed her, but Evergreen would not let go, would not leave her, or dare not. They backed further, round the corner of the church, along the church yard wall. A woman ran forward, carrying a stone in both hands, lifting it, flinging it with all her strength into Judith's face. It hit her forehead, stunned her for a second. She heard herself cry out with the shock; and then the pain, the blood running, so that she could not see anything. She fell against the wall. More stones. Evergreen sheltering her with her own body, crying with terror.

The blood like a scarlet curtain. She tried to get back onto her feet, knowing by instinct that if she lay there they would kill her, they would not be able to stop. And stood swaying, like a Guy Fawkes image, her face a mask of blood. She could not see where the women were, but she heard them, gabbling hatred, heard a man's voice shouting. 'Leave her be now, 'tis enough.' Heard, sensed that they were running away, that she and Evergreen were alone. She tried to clear her eyes, but the blood came again. She felt for her handkerchief to staunch the bleeding, and the scrap of cambric turned sodden in her fingers, horrifying. She heard the ripping of cloth, Evergreen tearing something, pressing it against her forehead.

'Quick!' Evergreen was whispering, 'Run! I'll hold you up.'

'I'll not run' Judith said. 'Guide me, I can't see properly. But walk, don't try to run.'

After twenty yards she had to stop, no matter who was following, or what might happen. Had to sit on the ground. They rested, walked, rested. She tried not to think of getting to Guthrum's, of Martha, of lying down in her room. Only of the next few steps. Her head had begun to throb and she felt sick and faint. She leaned on Evergreen, Evergreen's arm round her, astonishingly strong. The next step. The next. They were in the avenue. She could begin to see again. The trees like shadows. The stable yard. Solomon. Staring, opening his mouth, crying out in fright at the blood, her face. Martha coming out of the kitchen, waddling, horror-stricken. Holding her, bringing her to the fire. Everything seeming as if it had happened before. Like a nightmare that comes back. The sound of Martha's voice, scolding, soothing, frantic by turns. The smell of the hot brandy, the taste of it, burning her throat. The feeling of sickness, her legs not able to support her. But this time—— He was not here—not here. Martha sponging away the blood and the pain was so shocking that she almost fainted again.

'Goo f'r the surgeon!' Martha was crying to Solomon, 'an t'doctor! They do must bleed or else she'll take a fever!'

'No!' Judith said, and then again and again in case they should not listen to her the first time. 'I'll not be bled, no!' The shine of the blade against her father's temple, the grey, swollen artery. The jet of blood. She had wanted to vomit then, and she wanted to now.

'I will not have the doctor. No one! I will not!'

'Hush my dove, hush there, shhhh, Martha's moppe. Martha's holding her pet, she 'oon't do nowt you dunna want, my darling, but we must fetch summ'un. Hush there, stay quiet an' still, Martha 'ull make you well again. Take another sip now.' Held the brandy and hot milk to her mouth.

'Fetch Robert' she whispered. And wanted to say 'No' as soon as she had said it. 'But I do not—need anyone. No one. Just—I will lie down. For a little time. Only not the surgeon nor Doctor Farquhar. Promise me!'

They brought her up the stairs and put her to bed, and she lay in the quiet darkness, the shutters closed and the curtains drawn tight. Firelight and shadows, and the thought that perhaps they had indeed sent for him, Solomon might have gone to Shotton. He would not dare to go to Mr. Turton again to beg the loan of the gig, or a riding horse. Not after what had just happened. He would have to walk, and that would take two hours and more. And then for Robert to ride back. If Robert was there. Or Solomon might not have gone.

She lay not knowing what she wanted, half asleep with the brandy and hot milk, and the shock, and then full awake, wanting to get up, do something, she scarcely knew what. Her head throbbing. Evergreen bathing her face, her wrists, quiet and gentle and frightened. She felt feverish. Began to dream. That he was here, bending over her. But it was Evergreen. Martha came to look at her, held her forehead, kissed her.

'Where is Solomon?' Judith whispered.

''a 'll not fare to be long, dunna fret my dove.'

They made her drink more brandy and milk and put hot water jars into her bed to stop the shivering. She must have slept then and woke to find he was there, bending over her, lifting the make-shift bandages away, touching the wound.

'It seems to have become a habit' she whispered. 'For me to be—in bed like this and you—to come to me.'

He did not smile in return. He was smearing salve onto a pad of cotton, and laying it against her forehead. Cold, soothing. Tying the bandage, lifting her hair to secure it behind her head.

'Who did it?' he said, his voice carefully quiet.

She caught hold of his sleeve. 'You are not to—they were only women. Stupid creatures who think that—' Even the effort of that much determination made her head hurt again. '—that it was my fault that the boy Chevell—— You are not to touch them!' Raising her voice in near panic as he did not answer her. 'Promise me!'

'I might not touch them' he said. 'But they'll have husbands. Or brothers.'

'I beg of you, please! If you do not promise me——' She put both hands to her forehead, to the bandage. The thought of revenge, of more cruelty, of—— 'Promise me!' Tears coming.

'Hush' he said. 'Don't get frightened. Nought'll be done that you don't want. Although God knows I've—hush, I promise, ann't that enough?'

'Truly? You swear?'

'I swear. Don't take on, it'll only harm you. Sssh.'

He was so big, so broad and strong-made, that it was almost something to smile at to see him in her small bed-chamber, trying to make himself neat and gentle, fit for a sickroom. His clothes too rough, his boots too heavy, his hands too square and calloused as they held hers between them. His face tanned and full of health, wind-burned and stung by sea spray. That air of the sea and salt air about him as if he had stepped straight from the deck of a ship to her bedside.

'You make me feel ashamed of being ill just to look at you' she said, trying to smile again.

'You're good practice for me.'

'You are very kind to come. I am grateful.' She wanted to say 'I shall miss you when you are gone away' but she dared not say that. 'I am glad you are to be a doctor' she said.

He leaned closer above her, so broad and powerful that it was frightening, as if she could not breath.

'You're glad I'm going away?' he said.

'Please' she breathed, 'my head is hurting me so, I cannot talk of anything.' And then wanted to hold his arm for fear of the images that came when she closed her eyes, and thought of his being gone, and of the village, and the women's faces. 'Please,' she whispered, 'promise me again you will do nothing? Nor your men. There has been enough.'

'I promise.' And then with sudden harshness, 'They're not my men!'

He took her hand and held it, and she lay with her eyes closed, thinking that she no longer minded anything. And then not thinking, only drifting, because she was half asleep. Was asleep. She woke in terror from a nightmare of being buried alive, to find that he was still there, he had not moved from the bedside. Slept. And woke to candlelight, and the fire, and Evergreen's shadow beside her.

'Where is he?'

'He's coming back. Tomorrow. To-day.' Her voice like a shadow's.

'What time is it?'

'Two o'clock in the morning. You're to drink this, he said.' She held a cup for Judith. 'It's to make you sleep more.' Whispering. Her whisper losing itself among the shadows, the soft hissing of the burning wood in the fireplace, the quietness of the room.

'I do not want——' But she was already drinking it. Already drifting away.

Chapter 15

He came again that next day. And the day after. And would be here soon this fourth day of her illness, that was no longer anything like an illness, and only an excuse for keeping to the house, and her bed chamber. For hiding. And beyond that an excuse—to let him come to her.

I must not, she thought. It is wrong. It is weak and wrong, everything that I must not be. Must not do. To lie here thinking that drawn curtains and hushed voices and pretence would keep away life. Would keep away the Earl, and Claydon, and their Mr. Laurence who must see her at all costs, they wrote. If she would not, positively would not come to Matcham, then please to appoint a day when they might come to Guthrum's. And let it be soon.

They did not refer to the stoning. Nor even why they must see her. But they did not need to do that. To hear her father's Will, and tell her that they objected to it. And wanted the debts paid. She had written to Mr. Terry, and had only the most evasive of replies; that she was not to hesitate to call upon his services which were always at her disposal in every pertinent matter; and his deep regrets—and trusting that she——

When she had wanted solid help, solid assurances that she need not be afraid of anything.

But who could give her any such assurance? Certainly not Mr. Terry. And so she had stayed in bed, like a child covering her head against the noises in the night. Or she sat by the fire reading her mother's books, crying over memories, and out of weakness, and more than willing to let Evergreen lead her back to bed, and spoil her, and worry over her and bring her milk caudles and beef tea and possets. And to let Robert come visiting like a real doctor, to change her bandages and dress her forehead, he himself very happy to join in the pretence that she was still weak from the wound and the shock, and needed his daily attention. Or nightly, rather, for he came after dark, before whatever business of the dark took him way again.

I should not let him come to my bedroom, she thought. She should stay up to-night, and see him in the parlour. With Evergreen there. She was determined on it, and got herself dressed, and downstairs, and was ashamed that she had not done this yesterday and even the day before. There was nothing wrong with her that a walk in the fresh air would not have cured. To be afraid of going out! As if it would happen again so soon as she should meet half a dozen of the villagers. It was done and over, and they were now probably more afraid than she was; lying awake in terror that she might have them arrested and taken to Urnford gaol; that the Earl would see to it that their husbands lost their employment, or their customers. If she met them now they would probably go on their knees to her, begging forgiveness and swearing it was not they who had wanted to hurt her, and that they had tried to hold the others back.

I am a fool, she thought. And sat by the fire downstairs until seven o'clock, in the fullest determination of waiting there until he should come. And she would tell him that he need not, must not come again. Like this! After dark, almost in secret! Truly in secret. And at the thought of that she became frightened once more, not of any particular thing, but like illness coming back, a feeling of weakness, starting at sounds, her nerves raw. They would know of it in Matcham. That he was coming to see her every night. Someone would have seen, would tell. And they would think——They would think the worst. When they came to see her next week——She had put it off so long as that, and would have put it off for ever if she could. She had known that the sooner it was over the better, the better she would feel that it was over; and yet she had written, 'To-day week, if that is convenient to Lord Claydon and Mr. Laurence.' When they came they would know of it. And of the stoning. Of Mr. Carteret's refusal even to—— What would they say——

It did not matter what they said. And yet it seemed to matter, to be of vast importance. She put her hands to her head, felt the bandage. Half past seven. Perhaps he would not come to-day. To-night. He had been called away. Or had already gone to Leyden! She sat still at that. He would not have gone—without—without saying—— But perhaps—— Perhaps he had had no choice. Had sent a message that—that would only reach her tomorrow? That would be best. Much the best. She felt cold, and slowly held down her hands towards the fire, shivered a little. It would be the best thing by far. Not to say goodbye. In the past days he had——

Grown too much of a friend? That was a strange thing to think of. How could anyone be too much of a friend? And yet in these last days, visits of only half an hour, an hour; only of talk, of holding her hand, dressing her forehead; there had grown—— She shrank away from the word intimacy. There had grown a kind of—friendship that had nothing to do with that other—with his kissing her as he had done, holding her as he had done, touching her nakedness. And while that had been dreadful, dreadfully wrong and frightening, like getting drunk and not knowing quite what one was doing, or was going to do, or what might happen; in a strange fashion this new friendship was more frightening still. Because she did not understand it, or him. Did not know where it was leading her—might lead—if—if she allowed it to. She found herself looking back on that first simplicity of their meetings as—almost a kind of safety. That she could understand. Wrong, desperately wrong, but even because of that so easy to decide on. While now——

She had thought at first that it was only that he was two kinds of men in one. His father's son, and his mother's. The one rough, and hard, careless of everything. The other French, and subtle, loverlike, not to be trusted in a promise and yet very dear to listen to. While now—? Both those things indeed, very like, although he had not broken any promises. But behind them again? A kind of man she did not know, could not have imagined. His wanting to be a doctor, for one example, not in the way that one thought of doctors, of Doctor Farquhar, but as if to be a doctor was the most important and mysterious thing in life.

'We know nothing!' he had said, growing passionate and almost fluent. 'Nothing! It's like a book of which we've read only the first page. And as for the mind! We've not opened the covers of that book.'

'The mind? Doctor Farquhar said once——'

'That fool! If he knew where the mind was he'd put leeches to it. In Leyden there are men who——' He had turned silent again as if he had said all that was to be said. Staring into the corner of

[131]

the room as if the closed book was there and he meant to open it by will power. And yet he still did not seem a man of books. Not as her father was—had been. And it seemed to her for a moment as if it was treachery to her father's memory to think of the very word friendship in this man's connection. Or books, or learning. And she would look at his hands, square, powerful, tar-stained, and try to imagine them opening the covers of a book. But they would do it neatly. Although not as her father had used to do, with a sort of love, of union. Robert would open a book as he would open a box, to take things out of it, and set them in patterns.

'There was a man called Mesmer' he said again. 'A sort of charlatan with conjuring tricks. But behind the tricks he knew something. Still does. And I mean to find him, and find out what it is.'

Then, as if he sensed that she was growing uncomfortable with such distant things, he had turned and taken her hands again, and been the lover of before, although much gentler, less frightening. And in a perverse way she had been almost angry at such complications, as if she would have preferred that earlier dangerousness so that she should have known where she was. Was it still there? And the real self of him, while this was a pretence? When he was not in her room with her she was quite certain what he was. Although one day she was certain he was one thing, and the next day another. But when he was there she could be certain of nothing.

She had thought him long ago sullen and French, and then bear-like and Essex rough. And then handsome. And then savage. And now? She did not know. She would look away from him, and not know how he looked, and must glance back at him to be sure what way his mouth was shaped, and his eyes, and his dark hair, and his eyebrows, and the way his cheekbone caught the firelight, now bronze-gold, now almost red, that dark rose red that should belong to women only, his skin was so fine. She would long to touch it, and be afraid. Until he turned round and looked at her and touched her, his eyes unreadable for a moment as if his thoughts were still in the heart of the fire. Then full of things she dare not interpret. His finger tips against her cheek, the nape of her neck, her throat. She would feel herself quivering and was afraid that he would know it, feel it in those blunt, rough fingertips that were like his inheritance from his father, and his father's father. And that yet contrived to touch her as if she was made of silk.

'What are you thinking?'

Had she asked that of him? Or had he asked it? And neither answered. Until she must close her eyes against his, against her thoughts that might show themselves to him. Draw back into being an invalid.

'My head is hurting' she would whisper. 'You must go now.' And he would go, and it would be minutes, a quarter of an hour before she was still again, could think of him quietly, could think what she should think, and dismiss all the complications, all the subtleties for what they were. A traitor's deceptions, self-deception, nonsense. If she allowed it to go on very long like this——

I shall not allow it, she told herself. It is worse than nonsense. It is wrong. It could never, never come to—a true friendship. How could it? Our lives are completely apart. No matter what kind of man he may exactly be. The way we think, the way we were brought up. We could not be more than acquaintances and I have been very, very wrong not to be clear in my mind about that, and not to let him understand it too. It was my place to do that, and I failed. He is not to come again. He cannot. And then he will be gone. And—— Three years away!

It is a life time. By then—— By then he would be married to—to a young Dutch woman or a French girl, and would have a son to take his mind from everything else except his work.

And I——What shall I have in three years' time?

Eight o'clock.

'I think I shall go back to bed' she told Evergreen. 'You need not come up just yet. If you would finish those hems? You are doing them very nicely, you will become a great needlewoman, I can see it.' That was not even approximately true, but it made Evergreen smile with pleasure over her ill-made stitches, along the borders of the old, halved and remade sheets.

Up the stairs. She could not so much as pull herself up the stairs without remembering the inn. It is not my body that is ill, she thought, it is my mind. As though the scar was there, and not on her forehead, where the broken skin was already healing over and the bruise had turned to an ugly rainbow of dark blues, and yellows, and sullen black.

[133]

Undressing. Suddenly so tired, so weak, that she could believe in her illness as a real thing, and was very glad to sit down on the bed, and then to lie in it, lie back against the heaped pillows, close her eyes to the candlelight and the fire's flickering, listen to the wind sighing overhead and rattling softly at the shutters.

She was almost asleep when she heard the sounds of his horse, of his coming into the house. Voices. Doors. Footsteps. She came properly awake, and for a moment felt a swift excitement, relief, joy—she did not know which was uppermost. And behind them a sense of guilt, of betraying her new-made resolutions of wisdom. What should she say to him? How could she tell him that he must not—— Must not think of her as—— But there was no need to tell him anything. He was coming to say 'Goodbye', nothing more. And if he should think that there might be something more, then time would take care of that and solve all problems of—— She must not, need not hurt him. How cruel, how selfish that would be, to hurt him so that she herself might feel wise and virtuous!

She sat up in the bed, drawing the sheets close round her. She should get up, put on her cloak. But she might be in the midst of finding her cloak as he—— And he was already there, shown in by Evergreen, coming in with a quick confidence of the right to enter, a doctor's right, a friend's. Taking her hand, sitting on the bed's edge, looking at her in a questioning way as if he had detected something in her own expression. So that she must smile at him whole-heartedly, to banish any suspicions that she had changed towards him. She had changed, but he must not be allowed to see it. For a hundred reasons. Kindness. And not to let him think that her feelings of yesterday were more than they should have been. And—— She felt that her own thoughts were growing too tangled to be safe, and said quickly 'I am glad to see you.'

Sounded in her own ears too glad, too quick to say it. Oh heavens, she thought, how desperately hard I am making a simple thing. Talk to him kindly, nicely, a quarter hour of friendly gratitude, and then goodbye, and that is the end of it. She held his hand, and could not think of what to say next. Say something, her mind begged him. Do not let there be a silence. But he said nothing. Sat and held her hand and looked at her, his smile fading, gone; the look of gravity deepening.

'What is it?' she said at last, trying to sound light and pleasant.

'You are looking so serious and I was hoping—you would tell me that——' Her voice lost itself in a whisper of uncertainty.

'Tell you what?'

He must let go of my hand, she thought. If I allow him to hold it much longer he will think—— 'You would tell me that I looked quite recovered' she said, her voice still uncertain. 'I thought that you would. And instead—you look as if—as if you found me quite—altered for the worse.'

He shook his head, and drew her hand closer to him. 'I don't find that at all. Only——'

'Only?'

'Come with me to Leyden,' he said.

She had known he would say it. Had known all night. Since—since she had sent for him to come to her. She had known then. When they sat watching by her father's bed. Before that. Long before. 'What are you saying?' All the blood gone from her face. From her heart. It seemed to lie still in her.

'I'm saying marry me. Hush, don't answer me, not yet.' He put his heavy, rough finger-tip against her mouth. 'I'm not what you've dreamed of, I know that. But I'll keep you safe against harm, I'll care for you, I'll love you. More than you can imagine looking at me, maybe.' He had taken both her hands now, and made them lie in the palms of his. He closed them all together, his hands covering hers. 'Like this.'

'You must not! My father——'

'It's that as makes me say it now, an' not wait. An' there's not time for waiting. I'm going, and how can you stay here alone, after what happened you in Woodham? How could I leave you here, thinking of it?'

'But——' She could not think where to begin answering him. The madness of it. To leave Guthrum's, Woodham, Essex! Everything that was—everything. *Come with me to Leyden!* Was he mad? And she could not answer him, could not speak for the rush of thoughts in her mind. The impossibilities, the madness of it! She scarcely knew where Leyden was, what kind of—— But what did that matter, it was not the place that mattered, it was him! How could he think——

'I said don't answer me.' As if she had been answering. 'Just listen a bit. You can't tell me anything against it that I haven't thought of your saying. I know what I am, and how I must seem to you. But you can teach me, and I can learn. I said that to you down below, remember?'

'I remember' she whispered, and her face burned remembering. Send him away, her conscience cried to her. Now! Do not so much as let him hold your hands like this, like a pledge, like a weakness!

He leaned forward, and then went down on both knees by the bedside. Not clumsily, not even heavily. And yet something bearlike in the movement. She clung to that image, as if she was trying to frighten herself away from him, keep hold of her fear of him, of his bigness, of—of the things that—that down in the kitchen—he still held her hands, against his leather jerkin, that coldness of leather, and her face flamed and burned again. All these past days, these visits to her in her sick bed, she had sworn to herself that if—the first moment, the first suspicion that he might——

'Let me tell you where we'd be going' he whispered. 'To my grandmother's. She has a big old house, like this one, and there's a garden with fruit trees and she keeps tame ducks and a goose—you'd like her, I know it. She's always hated the trade.'

'Robert! It is not possible!'

'I said, don't answer me. There's nothing that's not possible. The first time I saw you, I thought, how'd it be possible for me ever to kiss that girl? Take hold of her hand? And here I'm knelt down beside you, holding your two hands while you lie in your bed, and——'

'Robert!'

'Hush. I'll not try and kiss you again if you don't want. Only your hands. Only like this. We'd bring your girl Evergreen with you, to be your maid, you'd not be lonely then for someone from home. Hush, I said, hear me out. And we'd send money back to Martha, and one day we'd come back here, and I'd be Doctor Barnabas, and you'd be my wife and——'

'*It is not possible!* Please!' Trying to free her hands. How can you torment me like this when you know I am ill?'

'I'm trying to save you from being tormented. What'll your family do to you if you stay here? What have they tried to do already? Look at me. I have to make one more trip for my father, he's made me promise him, and I owe him that much. I have to buy for him, and find someone, there's a cousin of mine I have to

[136]

find, to take my place. It'll take maybe ten days. And then back here for a last time. I was going to leave it till I came back to say all this to you but——' He caught her two hands again, held them like prisoners on the coverlid. 'I have to go tomorrow night. I couldn't leave without——'

'Tomorrow night?' Could see the darkness, the boat. She let her hand rest in his, and thought, he will lift them up, hold them against his heart.

'What's the matter?' he whispered. He did lift her hands then, brought them close to his face. She felt the harshness of beard not shaven since the morning, scraping at her palms, her finger tips. Her mouth was dry.

'Nothing,' she said, her voice not seeming to belong to her. He is going to touch me, she thought. He will hold both my wrists in one hand, and then he will—— He laid her hands down on the covers of the bed. 'Come with me tomorrow night' he said. 'Don't wait to think. Trust me.'

Trust him? She clenched her hands, freed them, pushed them deep in her hair. 'How can you ask me? My head is hurting me so much! You must go away.' And somewhere in her mind that traitor's voice was crying out 'Yes, yes, I will come with you! Ask me again, take hold of me!'

'You must go now' she said. 'You must!' And thought, he will not go. He can hear it in my voice, he can hear the treachery. He knows! He was moving, she felt the weight of his hand bearing down on the edge of the bed, tightening the covers over her, holding her still and helpless.

'Then I must leave it until I come back' he said, his tone as heavy as his hand. The words seemed to take a great time to reach her. 'God keep you till then' he said. 'I've been too sudden, but there's not much time for being thoughtful. Ten days. Will you wait up for me? Ten nights from now?' Smiling. Trying to make it sound lighter-hearted than it was, than he really meant it to be.

She tried to say 'no'. Her mind grown cold and tired. He was going. Ten days? Ten nights? If she told him not to come then? Would he listen? He must not come, there was no sense in it, only—only to give him a false hope—torment herself. But she did not say anything.

He bent down and kissed her. Lifting her chin. So suddenly, and yet so quietly she did not know what he was doing until it was done and over. Not like his other kisses. This time it was as if he had never kissed her before and was afraid of what she might do, afraid of her anger. A young man's kiss. Holding her a moment longer. At the door. She must look round, say 'Goodbye', 'Godspeed'. But she could not move, could not look at him.

'Ten nights from now' he said again, a flatness of disappointment in his voice. That she had not looked at him? Said 'Goodbye'? She knew it, she wanted to cry out to him, and could not, and he would be gone, and he would not come back, ever.

'Robert?' she whispered. As if to make any sound was painful, like lifting too heavy a weight, like a nightmare in which one cannot move. 'Robert?'

Silence. He was gone, she thought. But the door had not closed. Look round. You must. You must!

He was standing there. His face serious, considering. What was he thinking, to look like that, so withdrawn into thoughts? As if he had not heard her whisper, and yet was still there, making up his mind to something.

'Robert?'

Looking at her now. Her heart beating, her breath seeming to struggle for its life. Like a rope twisted tight round her breast. Coming towards her, slowly. Still with that considering, thinking look. He must not. Must not! She must cry out, call Evergreen! If——

Beside her. Bending over her. She could not move. could not cry out, nor breathe. Only look at him. He put out his hand to the covers by her shoulder, gathered them in his fist. She lay quiet, no strength left in her. As if it had happened already, and she was seeing it again, in slow, dream movements, silent. If it was really happening she would cry out, fight against him. But in a dream one cannot—cannot——

Pulling the covers back. And she lay and looked at him, and waited. Still held, and helpless. He took hold of her arms and lifted her, and she came up, boneless, unresisting, sitting up, and then as he continued lifting, kneeling face to face with him, kneeling in the stripped hollow of the bed. Knew what he would do, and could not move, could not say anything.

'I was too sudden' he whispered.

Too—sudden? When had—he said that before? The way a dream repeats itself, over and over.

[138]

'You must get dressed' he said unsteadily. His hands unsteady as they held her. 'Get dressed and come downstairs with me.'

She stared at him, hearing the words, understanding nothing of what they meant. Knelt staring into his eyes. Get dressed? Downstairs? With me?

'Where's your gown?'

She did not answer him and he found it for her, while she continued kneeling, sitting back now on her heels. A feeling of lostness, of bewilderment. He began bundling up the skirt as he must have—done before?

'Put up your arms' he whispered. She put them up, pointing her hands as children do. The gown falling, soft folds, cold wool. Grown cold. Against her ankles as she knelt. He smoothed the bodice down and she wanted to lie against him, be like a child who is being dressed and is still half asleep. 'Hold up' he breathed. 'All right then, lie against me and I'll fasten the buttons up your back. God A'mighty, so many of 'em!' Only that unsteadiness in his voice, a trembling in his hands to belie the lightness of what he said.

'Robert' she whispered at last. 'What—are you doing?' He was so solid as she lay against him. And yet his hands gentle. She had thought that the first time she saw him, she remembered. Hands that were used to manipulating small, neat things. She lay and let him do up the buttons, no longer trying to think, expect. Let him—do what he—what he wanted to do. To go downstairs. He does not mean to harm me, she thought. And had that flatness of emotion that comes after dangers passed. It was surprisingly pleasant to be dressed like this, like a child. He lifted her up and sat her on the edge of the bed. Put on her slippers, holding each foot in turn in the palm of his hand, fitting her toes into the narrow opening, the smooth, cold leather.

He even brushed her hair, and she began to smile at that, and then suddenly, in a weak, foolish way, to laugh. He was so big, and so clumsy neat, like a bear brushing her hair with the ivory brush almost lost inside his hand. He stopped his brushing, and looked at her in astonishment.

'What are you looking at?' she whispered. Their eyes meeting in the dark shadows of the mirror. 'What is—what is the matter?'

'Nothing' he said. The brush touching her hair, drawing down its flaxen, silvery length. Down her back.

'You cannot knot it' she whispered. 'That at least you cannot do.'

'Are you sure?' And he was gathering it, gathering the whole mass of it into his cupped hands, lifting, parting, drawing it out again in two thick skeins. Laying one forward across her shoulders so that it hung down into her lap. Plaiting the other with swift, practised fingers. Like a flaxen rope. Shining in the candlelight, the firelight. Silver-gold. Making three heavy strands, twisting them in and out, one between two, over and under, as sailors plait a rope for splicing. 'All I need now is ribbon to tie it with' he said. He found that, on her dressing table, secured the end of his long rope, and made the other skein into its twin. When they were both done he brought them forward, over her breasts, held her by them.

'There's fairy tales' he said, 'of girls with hair like this.' He pulled her gently up until she stood facing him, and he still held her prisoner. 'D'you understand?' he breathed, his voice so low she was not sure what he had said. Understand? She shook her head very slowly. Smiled at him. It did not matter about understanding. He drew her towards the door. 'Come down to the kitchen with me. Come and sit by the fire.'

'Martha will be there. And Solomon. And—and Evergreen is somewhere.'

'It doesn't matter. Come down and give me a glass of wine. And a bite to eat. And—and sit looking at me. And let me look at you.'

'With—Martha there?'

'Yes. I don't want you to be afraid.'

For a second she held back. Almost as if she was clinging to her fears, did not want to be reassured. And then let him lead her out of the bedroom. Outside in the corridor he let go of one of her plaits of hair and put his arm round her waist. 'You need holding up' he whispered. Almost lifted her as they went along the corridor, up the step, were outside what had been her father's room. He did not go by the doorway quickly, but he held her firm, his other hand with her roped hair twisted round his fingers, round his wrist. 'I have you made fast' he said. 'I'll not leave you free again.'

She did not answer him. Down the stairs. Evergreen sitting in the dining room, she could see her through the doorway. Candlelight, dark eyes staring at nothing above her neglected sewing, and then coming wakeful and looking at Judith and Robert, standing like that outside in the passage.

'Come' Robert said. 'We're going to have another supper, and a glass of wine. Come with us.'

He is making—he is making a betrothal supper of it, Judith thought, her mind seeming to drift, no more in control of its drifting than she seemed to be of her body, held and supported and imprisoned by his arm. She wanted to say that he must not think of such a thing, that she had not said—could not say yes, could never say it, think of it—that it was all a kind of gentle madness—not frightening as their other madness had been, not dangerous, but still folly. Self-deception. She must tell him soon. Now. But she did not say anything, and they were in the kitchen. Martha and Solomon looking their surprise. Solomon only astonished as he was astonished at everything that was not the most humdrum incident of every day. Getting up and touching his forelock. While Martha sat down after a moment's respect, and stared at them with small, cunning eyes that seemed to know a thousand things that had not happened. To be saying 'I know, *I* know!' Until Judith wanted to cry out at her 'You do not, you stupid, stupid old creature! There is nothing to know, it is the most innocent of things!' She felt her cheeks turn crimson, her throat burn. While the little, blackcurrant eyes stared their cunning. I know, *I* know.

'Wine and food!' Robert said, his voice grown loud and happy. As if he was sure of something now. 'Come old mawther, let's drink to the future. I'm off to Leyden to become an honest man, what d'ye think o' that?'

'Where's Leyden?' Martha said.

'Far away. Far away, old dear. Bring out some wine an' we'll drink to safe journeys, aye? An' happiness at the end of 'em.' His arm round Judith's waist, unashamed, unconcealed. Solomon staring. Evergreen come in behind them like a shadow. Taking a stool far away from the fire, far away from Martha. Martha standing up, looking at Robert with a new watchfulness.

'I dunna fare to howd wi' far off places' she said. And Robert's arm stayed very still round Judith's waist, as if he realised suddenly that here was an enemy.

'Dunna fear me, owd one' he said, the dialect sounding strange in his half, his quarter foreign voice. 'I'll be back safe in Essex once I'm set up as Doctor Barnabas. Ye'll drink to that? To my coming back?'

They drank, and Robert ate, but the old woman was not comfortable with them, with that thought of Leyden, that fear of losing Judith, losing everything. And Judith put out her hand and took Martha's, and held it, tried to say by the pressure of her fingers, 'Do not be afraid. I shall never leave you, this is only a dream, only playing! But let me play for an evening, let me imagine. Tomorrow we can be wise again.'

But in the end she had to say 'Go off with you to your bed, Martha. I have slept so much these past days I shall sit up a half hour longer. I want to say 'Goodbye' to Mister Robert. And you, Solomon, you are asleep already, sitting there.'

They went, Solomon unsteady on his feet with sleep, and the glass of wine, and an extra mug of ale, and Martha spreading uneasiness round her like a marsh fog, tightening her lips at Evergreen who sat mouse-still and quiet in her corner. But the old woman said nothing about Evergreen's staying, when she herself must leave. Perhaps she took comfort from Evergreen being there, to protect her mistress against being carried off to Leyden.

Yet in spite of that, it had been a pleasant time. Like an old, old time, family and servants sitting round one fire and talking. Nodding with sleep. Like the times one heard of, that her mother had told her of, before farmers grew too grand to sit with their labourers and maids.

He refilled her glass, and Evergreen's, and made Evergreen come and sit close by the fire. The silence drew out, and settled, filling the spaces left by Solomon and Martha, recreating tranquillity.

'Doctor Barnabas' Judith whispered, letting the sounds fall into the silence. 'Doctor—Barnabas.'

He looked at her, was on the point of saying something, asking a question, and she shook her head, and smiled at him, and miraculously he understood that he must not ask her why she had said that. And in that moment she could have cried, 'Yes, yes I will come with you—to Leyden, anywhere, I am ready now!' But one cannot say such things, even though one can say 'Doctor Barnabas.' Like touching. She wanted to reach out and touch him, but Evergreen was there, and it was best to do nothing, say nothing more, sit still and quiet. Listen. To the fire, their breathing, the stirring of the wind outside, her own heart beating. Beating softly. No longer trying to escape.

'Tell me about the sea' she whispered, staring into the fire. Sea journeys there in the heart of it, and distant towns.

'About the sea?' he said reflectively. 'The sea's why I've kept on. Kept on with the trade so long as I have done. It wasn't for the profit, nor anything else about it. Except to help my father. Only the sea.'

He did not say any more, and yet he seemed to have said everything, and she imagined she could feel the spray against her face, could hear the timbers creaking. She wondered if Evergreen could feel it, the sea's wildness. I have been closed in, in a small space, she thought. Trapped by walls. And duties. And the sea was all about them, like a cry of freedom; a black rush of water. And then in the next instant all of it was still. The northern dawn threw up its flames of jewelled fire and she thought that to go on and on towards the north, towards the ice floes and the silence would be to find the oldest paradise. The ship sailing so quietly, so evenly, prow rustling through drifts of ice. And he would hold her warm.

Until her own image made her shiver, and draw closer to the fire, and they were in bright seas with coral reefs, and undiscovered islands. I will go with you, she wanted to cry to him. Bring me away now, bring me to freedom. Wished that he would take her hand, and he was holding it, her hand lying in his. Wished that he would kiss her, not frighteningly, but gently, quietly, and he was kissing her, and she did not know if it was reality or her imagining. While Evergreen sat staring into the fire like a wise duenna who sees nothing that she should not see.

I cannot be in love, she thought. It is the wine. It is the lateness. Love cannot come like this. But for the moment it was enough to sit there, their hands touching. And suddenly Evergreen was gone from her place beside them. She had not seen her go, had not heard her. Until the smallest of sounds behind her made her look round, very quietly, not to disturb Robert from his quietness. And Evergreen was dancing. As she had that other time. But not for them. For herself. As if she did not wish to be seen, and it was like eavesdropping to watch her dance.

Very slowly Judith turned back towards the fire, until all that she could see of Evergreen was her shadow, on the wall. And then the shadow was gone. When she looked round again Evergreen was standing by the window, staring out into the darkness of the stable yard. What was she looking for? Dreaming of? Not love, not yet? But even to think the word was wonderful, and she held his hand, and it seemed wonderful to hold it, to feel the strength of it, the warmth and roughness, and gentleness. He does not want me to be afraid. And part of her longed for the fear to come back, so that it might be quieted again.

She wanted to lay her head against his shoulder, and it was lying there, and he did not move. Is this truly how love is, she wondered. To be quiet together? Not need to talk, not need to do anything? But I should like to do something, if this was love. I should like to give him a gift, a keepsake, so that we might—— And she searched in her half asleep mind for something precious enough to give him. To take with him to Leyden. Because she could not go with him herself. And she imagined having jewels to give, a ring, a miniature, a box like the Empress's box that they had sold to Mr. Bowen. If she still had it that would have been perfect. To hold her love in, so that now and then he might open it and look inside, and say 'There is her heart.'

How stupid one's imaginings are, beside the fire at night.

He stirred himself, broke the silence, and the dreams vanished. How late it must be, and yet she did not want it to end, she could have sat like this till morning. But he must leave, and she and Evergreen must go up to bed, and she must think of sensible things tomorrow.

'I must go' he whispered. Echoing her thought. And even that was wonderful. She wanted to say his name, but did not, for fear of sounding—sounding foolish. I shall be truly sensible tomorrow, she promised herself. I am in great need of it. He seemed to be waiting for her to say something, and she looked at him, and perhaps that was enough. At least for now. 'I'll be back in—not more 'n ten days. Say ten. Ten nights from now.' As he had said upstairs. But not as he had said it then. As if now he—expected something? In ten nights' time? And she grew afraid. Yet in a strange way it was a pleasant kind of fear. A—kind of breathlessness.

'Ten nights from now?' she whispered. When the time came

she would be sensible once more, recovered from—from to-night. But just for this moment—to imagine—if—— They were standing up. Evergreen still by the window, not looking round at them. 'I'll have your answer then?' he whispered. 'Promise me?'

'I promise.' What did he take her to mean by that? She should tell him, now, that she could not, could never go with him. But—— He held both her hands, both of them in one of his, and with his other hand drew her head forward by her ropes of hair and kissed her bruised and bandaged forehead, and then her eyelids as she closed them against seeing his eyes, letting him see hers, and all that was in them for him to see. He put his arms round her, held her pressed against him for a moment, and another moment, and then let go. She stood still, her eyes still closed. What would he do now? Heard his footsteps. Heard the door shut behind him. And felt in that second as if she could run after him, go with him then, never leave him.

Running, seeing his shadow in the dark, crying 'Robert! Robert! I will come with you!' How many follies one can dream at midnight.

'Come to bed' she whispered to Evergreen. 'How late it is! Come.'

Tomorrow she would be wise again.

Chapter 16

Four of them. Lord Claydon, getting down stiffly from the coach as if he was frozen by the journey, although there was a brazier inside it, and fur rugs and foot warmers. He hunched himself together like an old man, his nose bluish, his eyes furious, scarcely answering her greeting at the front door. Going past her into the hall of Guthrum's with no more than the curtest of nods. Behind him, Mr. Laurence, the Earl's country attorney; who lived indeed mostly in London, but was the country attorney in the sense that he dealt with the Essex and Devonshire estates and not with any London matters. He gave Judith a grave and cautious inclination of his head, that committed him to nothing beyond acknowledging her existence.

He was an elderly, grey, paunchy man, with sagging cheeks and eyelids and an attorney's wig, grey and neat, with a rather mean-looking queue under an old fashioned tricorn hat, and he wore a long rusty black coat and rusty black breeches and black silk stockings, and black, square-toed shoes with large plain silver buckles, as though he dressed to be always ready for sad news and fatalities and the reading of Wills. Mr. Massingham stepped cautiously down on to the grass-grown gravel, and then Mr. Halliday. Mr Halliday as gravely non-committal as Mr. Laurence, his mouth Scotch-pursed, his eyes not meeting Judith's, his ordinary clothes as suitable for mourning as Mr. Laurence's.

But Mr. Massingham was in full, formal mourning, a true splendour of black. Even his shoe buckles had been blackened, and the lace at his cuffs and the handkerchief in his sleeve had a rich blackness that seemed to cry 'He's dead, thank God! Now let her try and refuse me!' He jutted his yellow teeth at her as he bowed, clasped his hand agaist his stomach and creased himself in half.

'A sad tragedy, tsk tsk tsk. But in its way a release. One must put a Stoic face on these natural losses.'

'What are you doing?' Lord Claydon cried from the hall. 'Massingham, Halliday, are we to stand all day in the cold?' He turned to Judith. 'Well, where are we to sit, eh? Eh?' He had adopted his father's habit of a petulant 'Eh? Eh?' at the end of questions, like part of his Coat of Arms. He stripped off his gloves and held out bone-white hands to the fire. Smoke eddied as a draught came from the open door and he coughed, searched for a handkerchief and coughed again, angry reproach in the sound of it, that she should have a fire that smoked, and have required him to make a journey in the cold instead of her coming to Matcham as she had been bid.

She felt the necessity of apologising for that and explained again that she had been ill; implied that she was still very weak from the wound, touching her bandage with an apologetic hand, although in truth the pain was almost entirely gone and the bandage was quite unnecessary. But it was a mistake to remind him of the cause. He swung on her.

'By God, and well might you be ill! With shame if nothing else! To be stoned in your own village, by the village women! Like a—like a—I'll not put a name to it, but we both know what it is. Let's get on with this business.'

'Yes, yes indeed. I—I thought—the dining room?' She led the way, walking too fast as if she was running, and then holding back, so that Claydon almost knocked against her. She had not meant to be nervous, had sworn to herself that she would not be, that there was nothing to be nervous of, nothing that they could do beyond what they had already done or tried to do. She was her own mistress, entire and complete. It was even a proof of it, that they had summoned her to Matcham, like a naughty child or a servant, and she had refused to go, and they had now come here.

'An affecting ceremony' Mr. Massingham whispered as he passed into the dining room in front of her. 'Funerals touch a deep chord in me.' He turned up his eyes to show how deep. Parted his coat tails with care and sat beside Mr. Halliday. Lord Claydon at the head of the dining table. Mr. Laurence on his right, Mr. Halliday on his left. Judith facing him. Like judge and prisoner she thought, with Claydon for judge and the others for jury. Well, let them try to judge. Or rather, make any sentence effective. But in spite of her confidence her heart was beating so that it was difficult to breathe or speak naturally, and she was afraid that they would see her hands trembling. She hid them in her lap.

Mr. Laurence had already taken up the copy of her father's Will that she had laid out for him, and was scanning it with professional slowness through a gold lorgnon on a black ribbon. Lord Claydon drummed his finger tips on the table, stared at the Will, at the ceiling, at the window, at anything in sight but Judith. His pale eyebrows drawn together in ill-temper, his lips tightened, an astonishing likeness to his father in him.

'Your father is well, I hope?' Judith said, unable to prevent herself from breaking the silence. And again it was a mistake, giving him the chance to turn on her with a new accusation.

'Well? How should he be well with the kind of news he has of you? I had thought we should have two funerals! Gaultrip taken like that and sent to France—goods seized back by those villains, seized back from the customs, here, on this land! With your connivance! And young Chevell half murdered and like to be crippled, and you ask is my father well?'

'Did you say it is my fault that—?'

'Say? I know! I know it and half Essex knows it! My mother cannot bear to hear your name spoke, my father took to his bed for it, and you sit there pretending to be ill! You make me come to you when if you had an ounce of shame you would come to us on foot, on your knees, to beg forgiveness! And 'pon honour, if it lay with me you should have no more forgiveness than—than——'

'My Lord!' Mr. Laurence was saying. 'Pray, do not give way to your feelings, however natural. Let us stick fast to your main object here. Which is to settle Miss Mortimer's immediate future. Let us not quarrel before we begin.' He sounded as though this was an argument he had been using in the coach on the way from Matcham, and he was a trifle tired of repeating it.

'I am ready to forgive' Mr. Massingham said. He rolled his eyes upwards again, and steepled his fingers, as if he was praying for Judith's salvation. 'A young person—without guidance—we must show understanding, my Lord.'

He truly believes that now my father is dead I shall want to marry him, Judith thought wonderingly. There was no mistaking the bridegroom air behind Mr. Massingham's mourning, as if the lining of his black coat was white and he would suddenly turn it inside out and be prepared for orange blossom and nuptial bliss. She hid her hands again and waited. She ought to offer them the wine that was set out in decanters, and the sweetmeats and the cakes on the side table. But she could not trust her voice, and was half afraid that even offering them might set Claydon off again.

Mr. Laurence coughed, and looked first at her, and then in their turns at the others, over the tops of his lorgnon. 'I must say that the late Mr. Mortimer's Will seems to me, ahem, without having had the proper time to examine it thoroughly, a—shall I say a somewhat imperfect instrument?'

'It was made by an attorney' Judith said, commanding herself to sound assured. 'By Mr. Terry of Urnford. He has corresponded with you about—about my father's—about Guthrum's. Has he not?' The mere remembrance of Mr. Terry, of his office, his mouselike scurryings about that impossible desk of his, robbed her voice of anything resembling assurance. She sounded in her own ears as if she was apologising.

'Damn the Will!' Lord Claydon said. 'What the devil does it matter who drew it? What matters is what we have decided on, and to have her agreement to it. And by heaven if she don't agree——' He made to bang his fist on the table and reconsidered, bringing the heel of his hand down with a self-preserving slowness that had indeed more emphasis and threat about it than if he had crashed it on to the mahogany. The gesture gave Judith a sudden chill of warning. What had they decided on? And to have her agreement? To what? She wanted to ask, and was afraid, and found herself staring at his small, ineffective fist as it lay on the table, a pale reflection of it in the depths of the polished wood. The lace of his shirt sleeve was white, and the only sign of mourning he carried was his black cravat.

'My father has undertook to be your guardian,' he said, 'and as your guardian he requires you to do certain things immediately. Are you listening to me?'

She lifted her eyes from his hand to his face. 'But I do not need any guardian' she said, 'nor want one. I am quite content as I am.'

She spoke so gently that she thought it could not make him angry. Instead he seemed to have been struck dumb for a moment, and to be struggling for breath. He had to pull at his cravat to loosen it, and his sallow cheeks took on his father's colour, a pale mauve, as if he was threatened with a seizure, in spite of his being not yet thirty. He could have been already near fifty, from his appearance.

'Content?' he whispered at last. 'Content as you are? The talk, the shame of the county? To have blackguarded your name—our name? To be mixed up with murderers! And you're content? My oath, ma'am, if you are content you're alone in it. I am telling you what my father has decided for you and you had best listen and agree to it! Or it'll be so much the worse for you as you can't easy imagine.' His voice had risen to a shout.

'Lord Claydon' she said, her voice still quiet, but growing very cold, her nerves set aside by anger. 'I will not be shouted at in my own house.'

'Damnation! It is not your house, and never shall be! That Will!' He seized it out of Mr. Laurence's grasp and seemed on the point of tearing it in halves. Instead he slammed it down on the table, making the glasses dance and ring. 'That thing is not worth its parchment and ink. You have nothing! Nothing but debts, and the reputation you've been busy making for yourself, although, upon my soul, that's enough to be going on with. Now listen. My father still has a partiality for you, God knows why, but he has, in spite of all. He's still prepared to forgive you. And so is Massingham here.'

'Indeed, my Lord, that is so. To err is human, to forgive——' The eyes turning upwards again, like hard-boiled eggs peeled out of their shells and dipped in oyster sauce.

'He'll still marry you. And I pray he knows how to treat you when he does.'

'I have already told Mr. Massingham——'

'Be quiet! I don't care a blade of grass whether you marry him or not——'

'My Lord!'

'You be quiet too, Massingham. What I do care about is that she's out of this house, and parish and county, as soon as possible. And that I never have to hear of her again.' He wiped his mouth with his handkerchief and looked at the white cambric as if he suspected there might be blood on it. 'You'll go to Devonshire, to Oldhampton, d'you hear me? Lady Partington has said she'll look after you down there and Massingham shall join you and you'll do well to accept him. No one else is likely to have you after what's passed. If you marry him——' He dabbed his mouth again. 'Tell her, Laurence, you have it jargoned down there, tell her what my father says.'

Mr. Laurence shuffled one paper for another, coughed, lifted his lorgnon, scrutinised, coughed again, his loose cheeks like grey wattles. 'These are his Lordship's express wishes, Miss Mortimer——'

'I have every respect for his Lordship' Judith said. 'So much so that I prefer not to hear his wishes since I cannot agree to any of them. I know I cannot before I hear them.'

'JUDITH!'

'Claydon, please do not shout. May I offer you wine, all of you? I am very remiss. And some cakes? Martha has baked them especially for you, in your honour. She will be very disappointed if——'

'This is beyond bounds' Lord Claydon whispered, his voice choked. 'I tell you, you shall be made sorry for it. Even my father's kindness has an end, and then—oh then, you'll learn a lesson. Such a lesson as——'

'You have come here to read my father's Will. I could have had copies sent to you, but you insisted——'

'Miss Mortimer' Mr. Laurence said, lifting a restraining finger. 'We have come here to tell you certain facts. The first is that in the Law's eyes you are not an adult. You are an infant, in need of care and protection. It is the Law's business to ensure that you have both, and to that end it provides for you to have a guardian. Your natural guardian is the Earl of Matcham, your father's cousin, your closest kinsman on your father's side, and the head of the family to which you have the honour of belonging. He will apply to the Lord Chancellor to have you made a Ward of the Court of Chancery, and for himself to be appointed guardian. No, no, Miss Mortimer, I must insist that you hear me out. This has a great importance for you, and must happen with or without your consent.

'You may object, of course, but in such circumstances as yours, I do assure you that your objections will carry small weight with the Lord Chancellor. And once the Earl of Matcham has been appointed your guardian, he will have all the rights over you, and the duties towards you, of a parent towards a child. You yourself will have the duty to obey him as if he was your true parent. Your refusal so to obey him would be treated by the Law as if you was a child rebelling against a natural parent. In addition to which you would risk being held guilty of contempt of the Lord Chancellor's authority. I need not underline for you how gravely such a contempt might be regarded.

This Will——' He held it up as if he shared Lord Claydon's opinion of it, 'requires before all else an Administrator to be appointed by your guardian, when he himself has been appointed. So that you see, all these things hang together, one depending from the other. It is quite useless for you to say that you do not wish for a guardian, nor wish to hear Lord Matcham's terms for you. You must hear them, and you must have a guardian, and you must do what you are told. I regret having to speak so firmly to a young gentlewoman, but I am no more than stating facts, however unpalatable to you.'

'You hear?' Lord Claydon cried. 'You hear Mr. Laurence? Eh? Eh? Now will you listen?'

'I will listen' Judith said, 'out of politeness to Mr. Laurence, who has come a great way to tell me these things, and does so only because he is paid to.' Mr. Laurence looked down, a faint flush of pink on his cheeks indicating that he did not care for such reasoning.

'But I must repeat to you' she went on, 'that I will not, I cannot, agree to anything that suggests I am not my own mistress.'

'You are not! And cannot be!' Claydon cried, his voice rising to a falsetto. 'And thank God for it! How have you behaved when your father was still living? What can we expect of you now that he is dead? Give me patience, Laurence! I am sorry to have brought you to hear such wicked obstinacy.' He seemed to be gathering himself together. Once again he brought his small, strengthless fist down very softly onto the mahogany, and let it lie there. 'I tell you, Judith, if you do not learn some humility within the next few minutes, it will taught to you and damned unpleasantly.'

'I will not be threatened' she whispered. And again the fist held her eyes, the reflection of it. Less strength in it than there was in her own, and yet she found herself frightened, not by it, but by what lay behind it, as if its very lack of strength carried a conviction that shouting could not. And thought of Robert, and his hand, and the strength of it. And yet——

'I am past threatening' Lord Claydon said. 'So is my father. This is a plain fact, like Laurence's. You have disgraced us, and we do not mean you to have the opportunity of doing it again. You will go to Devonshire as my father's ward. Or you will be locked up.' His control broke, and he shouted at her; 'locked up, you wretched girl! As a lunatic! Locked up in Bedlam! There's not a doctor in the kingdom as 'd not say you were mad. And then by God, let you tell us you'll not listen!' He lay back in his chair and wiped his mouth, shut his eyes against the sight of her.

She stared at him, began to say something, and the words did not come. 'You cannot' she said at last. She looked at Mr. Laurence, as if appealing to him as the representative of reason. But Mr. Laurence was making himself very intent on the document in front of him, frowning.

Locked up? In Bedlam? She almost laughed with helplessness, with the sheer unreason of it, the hopelessness of arguing with such unreason. Looked from Mr. Laurence's face to Lord Claydon's to Mr. Massingham's, to Mr. Halliday's.

Mr. Massingham had found a shred of fingernail that he could worry with his great teeth, and his eyes were caressing her body like a scholar looking at a book he has been given and that he means soon to open. As much as to say, what reading I shall find inside such covers!

She caught the tail end of his glance and began to flush, must have shown her feelings, the shiver of disgust that she could not control.

The chewing at the finger-end stopped, and the hatred she had seen in his face before came back, tried to mask itself, and failed. 'I will not be threatened' she said again, her voice very low, her eyes still on Mr. Massingham.

'Is that your answer?'

Lord Claydon raised both his hands, made to slam them down, let them drop softly on the arms of his chair. 'You see, Laurence? You see now?'

'There can be no compulsion on an infant in such a case to

marry against her rational disinclination, my Lord. But I take your point, I do indeed. You do seem to show, if I may presume to say it, Miss Mortimer, a—— Shall I term it a lack of due and proper submissiveness to those whose whole concern with you is your true welfare? You have not yet permitted us to disclose the terms of this proposed marriage with Mr. Massingham. They are very advantageous to you.'

'I do not want to hear them!' she cried, standing up, needing to support herself against the table's edge. 'I shall never marry him! Never, never, never! I would go to Bedlam first!'

Mr. Laurence pursed his lips, raised his grey, tufted eyebrows as high as they would go, still without looking at her direct. Mr. Massingham's cheeks turned crimson, and then drained of colour.

'Did not I tell you?' Lord Claydon said. 'She is lunatic! She needs cold baths and a whipping, not arguments. We are wasting our time. I told my father so, and I was right.' His voice rose again. 'What happens now is on your own head! If Laurence——'

He gathered himself, stood up, his hands shaking with anger. 'Mr. Laurence sir, I am sorry you have been subjected to this display of folly. But it will have its value if evidence of her state of mind is ever called for. If you wish to stay longer and try to read the marriage conditions to her, you are welcome. And so is Massingham. Halliday, shall we go outside?'

He moved round the table, and she stayed where she was, not knowing what to do. She made a gesture towards opening the door, but Lord Claydon had already brushed by her. Mr. Halliday inclined his head. In all the time they had been there he had not spoken one word. Why had he come? As—as a witness? But of what? What had she done, what had she said that they could claim—?

She sat down again, Mr. Laurence looking at her as if he had already been called on to judge her state of mind.

'You are being unwise, Miss Mortimer' he said. Mr. Massingham had begun on another fingernail, but this time with a different air; of slow malice, the nail a substitute for what he dreamed of doing to her in their eventual bedchamber. You will not enjoy it, his look told her. But I shall. Oh yes, oh yes.

'I understand nothing of this' Judith said. And the words seemed like an admission. 'Mr. Laurence, I thought that you were to come here to read my father's Will, and nothing else. And perhaps to tell me some objections to it. I was prepared for that. I have wrote to tell Mr. Terry so, and to—to ask—his advices if—— But all this! And—and to threaten—to threaten me with——'

'Not Bedlam' Mr. Massingham said. 'Not the Bethlehem Hospital that the paupers go to. His Lordship would never consider that. A private madhouse. Where you could be treated in accordance with Science. And cured.' He smiled at her.

'You have no right' she whispered, 'no one would believe——'

'From the account I have had of it' Mr. Laurence said, 'your behaviour has not seemed that of a reasonable young gentlewoman. It has not, Miss Mortimer. And just now, here, with your debts to be paid, a marriage portion offered you, this gentleman willing to overlook all past—shall we say indiscretions? And you say that you will not so much as listen? That is indeed such conduct as must——'

'The dowry is to be two thousand pounds' Mr. Massingham said comfortably. 'And we are to have a house on the Oldhampton estate, rent free, in virtue of my becoming steward there. Almost as if it was our very own.' How I shall make you suffer there, his eyes smiled at her. How you shall pay me for the way you have spoke, and looked, and sneered!

'If you do not accept these terms' Mr. Laurence said, 'then I am instructed to contest your father's Will. I need not trouble you with the grounds. I need only tell you that his Lordship's claim is a very strong one, and must, in my opinion as an attorney, succeed.'

She sought about for an answer, wanted to scream 'Look at him! Look at that—that creature! Am I mad to shudder at him?' But she could not say such things aloud, had already said too much. She felt exhausted, as if she was walking through heavy mud, and it was an immense effort to lift her feet one before the other.

Mr. Laurence looked at her, his eyebrows raised like grey caterpillars trying to climb up to his grey wig. 'I see that you are not yet prepared to agree with me, Miss Mortimer. Let us put it down for the moment to your still very recent sad bereavement. I shall certainly speak to his Lordship in those terms, and beg him to give you more time for reflection. But that time cannot be unlimited. Quite soon, within a day or so, you must be summoned to London to appear before the Lord Chancellor, and you must obey the summons. If you do not, then I am afraid you must be fetched to London, will you, nill you. Should you still prove recalcitrant there, why——' He shook his head sadly. He had stood up, and was putting his documents together like a judge leaving the bench. 'Mr. Massingham, sir? Shall we leave Miss Mortimer to reflect upon what has been said?'

Mr. Massingham seemed to wake out of some ugly reverie of his own, that had not much to do with the Law. He stood up in his turn, smoothing the wrinkles of his coat and outer waistcoat, adjusting the black lace at his cuffs, touching his black cravat with gentle care to reset its folds. He came very close to her, and standing on tiptoe so that he was at her exact level he whispered '*O mulier pulcherrima. Di tibi formam dederunt.* What a shame if such beauty must be shut away in a madhouse!' He laughed silently, showing her all his teeth and tongue, creased his eyes with his laughter. 'You will say "Yes" on reflection. Will you not, my dear?'

Before she could answer him he was making his stiff, thick-bodied bow to her and was going out of the door. Mr. Laurence bowing, a different sort of stiffness, a legal instrument of a bow. Making for the door also, while she still stood transfixed at the foot of the table. They are no more than trying to hoodwink me, she thought. It is not possible. And looked at Mr. Laurence's severe indifference and knew past question that it was.

'I shall see you to the coach' she whispered, her mouth too dry to do more than whisper.

'Pray do not trouble yourself' he said, but he allowed her to hold the door aside for him, bowed again, and went on into the hall as if she no longer existed for him. As if she and all her concerns had been folded away with his documents. She stood in the doorway while the coach drove down the avenue. No one saluted her from inside it, and only the footman on the dickey seat looked back for a moment.

As it had had to do for the funeral, the coach left the avenue to skirt round the fallen elm tree, and again it lurched dangerously as the coachman drove into the field, the wheels bumping over tussocks of grass and old, overgrown plough furrows. Then it was back between the lines of unkempt, winter-naked trees, the glasses winking as they were now hidden, now revealed between the trunks. It came to the avenue's farthest end, turned towards Woodham Claydon. Was gone.

She stood in the doorway, looking at nothing. At the winter clouds. Then down into the moat beyond the terrace.

The next time someone, a coach, comes up the avenue, she thought, it will be to take me away from here. Against my will. To London. To Devonshire. And if she resisted them? A lunatic fighting against her well-wishers. She turned her head very slightly from side to side, seeing it happen, remembering a print she had seen of Bedlam, of the naked madmen, screaming with dreadful laughter, their chained hands playing with straws.

They cannot, she thought. They cannot. Thought of Robert. Who would not be back in Shotton, would not come here for six more days. Nights. Before that they—they might—would have come. And if he—should come first? Before they—they came? If? What would she—— What could she do? Staring at the avenue as if the coach was already there, returning.

Chapter 17

'Martha, please, please understand. You *cannot* come with me. I am running away, running away to London. How should I look after you there?'

'Look arter me? An' who'll fare to look arter you? Make your broth an' air your bed an'—an'—' Martha glancing sideways at Evergreen as if to say, Her? D'you think she'll do owt for you?

Judith interpreted the glance and wanted to wring her hands for frustration.

'I must take her with me!' she cried. 'What should she do here, and you do not want her here, nor like her, and she is afraid of you—Oh Martha, I beg of you, try to understand, I am so miserable and frightened I do not know which way to turn. And someone—you, who else have I?—someone must look after this house. I have wrote again to Mr. Terry to say what I am doing, to tell him that I am going away. But not where, I have told no one that except you, and you must pretend not to know, do you understand? Except to Mr. Barnabas, Mr. Robert Barnabas. He is to have the letter I have left for him with you, and you may tell him everything—oh what shall I do, the coach will be gone and it is miles and miles and late already, and there is so much for Solomon to carry——'

She looked round the kitchen, the brasses, the china on the shelves, the fire, the benches, the table where Robert had counted out her gold; of which almost none was left. Coach fare, and a guinea for Martha's urgent needs, and two guineas for themselves in London.

'I shall send you money as soon as—as Mr. Richardson——'

But Martha would not listen about money, nor about anything. Looking sideways again at Evergreen, her eyes sullen and angry and betrayed. Even when Judith threw her arms round her fat, bowed shoulders, her tortoise back, squeezed her close, she would not relax her anger.

'Lunnon!' she grumbled. 'Running off like a bad creature as is shamed afore her own folks. I do fare to believe in facing folk out, an' staring 'um down.'

'But they threaten to have me locked away as a lunatic! If I do not do what they say! I would die first, I would die if he touched me, that toad, that—Oh Martha! I am all tears and wretchedness and you are making it worse!'

Trembling to be gone, and terrified of going, of walking out of that door behind her knowing that she might never see this kitchen, or Martha again. She had not known how dear she was, how much she loved her, how much her second mother she had been. She held her close and closer, until the old woman softened at last, and hugged her and cried too and blessed her journey, and then flung herself down on her chair by the fire, and covered her head with her apron.

They were out of the door and almost at the stable yard gates before she ran after them. 'Your bread an' meat, an' cake, you do ha' forgot your wittles.' A bottle of wine sticking its neck out between the knotted corners of the napkin.

'An' there's a corkpull inside an'—an' glasses—dunna you break that nor drop 'em Solomon lad, or you'll answer to me for that agen you come home to me. And you wait an' see 'um all safe an' into t'coach, dunna be leavin' till they do well and safe along t'road.'

They had gone another thirty yards, when Martha was calling after them again, waving a carving knife.

'You best take this wi' you' she said, when she could speak for her panting. 'Suppose there do come a highwayman and want your val'ables, you can fare to stab 'em wi' that.'

"But I do not have any valuables!'

'You do ha' one that every girl do ha' got, an' that's the one as he'll want. You take 'em.' She held the knife out to Evergreen, who obediently reached out her own uncertain hand for the black wooden handle and long, triangled blade. 'You take 'em, girl, and you mind you use 'em to save your mistress, or I'll fare to come arter you wi' another an' chop you in bits.'

'Martha! We are going to London, not to Africa! What should the other passengers think if they saw such a thing with us? Take it back at once, she will cut off her fingers with it. You silly, silly old thing, we are going to make our fortunes, and we shall bring you back a silk apron and a silk cap and——' She had to fling her arms round Martha again, almost spearing herself on the knife blade. 'Oh my dear, I do love you so, it will not be long. I promise, I swear it, I shall get the greatest lawyer in London to protect us and I shall sell my book and my father's book, and come back on horseback with new clothes and a negro page. You must just sit and wait a little while and imagine us coming, and we shall be so fine you will not recognise us.' More tears, more hugs, walking quickly away, looking back to see the fat, dumpy figure still watching after her, like a dark sack of barley set down on the path.

They had to make their way north towards Itchen, which they would skirt round on foot, and west from there to Grayling, where they would take the London coach on its way to Ipswich and Norwich. Two or three coaches along they would get down and take the Ipswich coach to London. It was roundabout and desperately expensive, but it was the best way she could think of to throw any possible enquirers off their scent. And once they were in London, who should ever find them in such a vast city, with so many people? Almost a million! It was past imagining.

She tried to think as they hurried in the twilight, I shall make our fortune there. I shall. I shall! But her footsteps seemed to be saying, never, never. She looked to her right to where the wood, her wood, lay like a grey shadow. The ground they were on was rising towards a low ridge, and from the top of it she could see not only the wood, but the dunes, and beyond the dunes the dull, dove shadow of the sea. And beyond it?

He will follow us, Judith thought. Six days. Nights. She had written him the briefest of letters. Nothing of love, not asking him to follow them. When she wrote it she did not want him to follow. When she sealed it up, gave it to Martha to keep always by her, in her bosom, under her hand, to give to no one on earth, no living soul except Robert, she did not know what she wanted. Only afterwards she thought, he must follow us. If words, if looks, if hands touching mean anything, he must follow. And I do want him to! I do! Had known then, and had had half a mind to take back her letter, make it clear and open that she wanted him to come to her. And had been ashamed.

Will he follow me? Will he? She would not think of it. She must depend upon herself. And began to think instead of Mr. Richardson, who must at the very least direct her to safe lodgings, and advise her, and give her a few guineas, advance against her own book, and perhaps much more against her father's, once he had read the manuscript. He had said he could not publish it, with the war, and the government so strong against the radicals, and the public so—but he had not read it, how could he know what it was really like, and whether it might not be that great, great success her father had dreamed of? It could be, it could. And so might hers. Every one wanted receipts, and her mother had such receipts as people nowadays did not know of, and she herself had gathered all kinds of herb lore and—people read the most foolish sorts of books, it would be very strange if for once someone could not persuade them to read two sensible ones, instead of novels about love.

Until by the time they came to Grayling, and the coaching inn there, with its torchlight and lanterns, and the smell of horses, and of mulled ale and wine, and the crush of ostlers and passengers and onlookers and passers by; by that time she had passed from hopes of success and fortune to a certainty, and was returning to Guthrum's in her own coach and four, with a page in livery, as she had promised Martha. And Robert—she would not think of Robert. Would not.

It was only when they were in the coach, and the coach was already moving, their luggage piled on the roof with the other passengers' portmanteaux and boxes and tied bundles and baskets, or else on Evergreen's lap, holding their supper in its napkin that looked ridiculous now, the other passengers eyeing it with curiosity; it was only then, Solomon waving his hand from the roadway outside the inn yard, looking more foolish than ever, his hair more standing on end, more dandelion yellow and furze bushy than ever; and suddenly more dear; it was only then that her frail-built pretence of confidence fell like a house of cards and she sat in terror, listening to the wheels, the horses' hooves, the harness jingling and creaking; never come back, never come back, never come back. And she would have got down from the coach if it had not been travelling so fast, so breakneck towards

Ipswich. Would have run back to Martha and to Guthrum's, and the kitchen fire and her room, and bed. And hidden herself there like a child beneath the blankets.

But she could not even lean out of the window to see if Solomon was still waving to them, because she was pressed into the middle of the leather seat, between two farmers' wives. Evergreen facing her, wedged between the women's husbands. Evergreen looking frightened, but only as she always looked if anything strange was happening. Not as if she knew how fearful, how tremendous their journey truly was. And Judith sat listening to the sounds of the coach, feeling it sway on its huge springs and leather straps; the iron tyres grinding against gravel where the ruts of the road had been filled with stones.

You will fail. You will fail. You will fail.

She tried to think against that threatening of the wheels, of the horses' hooves, the harness; he will come to me, he will follow. But if he did? What must she do then? To go to Leyden! Because she was frightened to be alone? Because her blood ran quicker when he touched her, when she thought of his touching her? Was that a reason for marrying, for giving oneself to a man, to a stranger? A smuggler, smuggler's son, master of men like——

He is not like them. He is not like them. But who was he like? How could she tell? And the wheels ground, 'locked away, locked away. Bedlam. Bedlam.'

Chapter 18

It was five o'clock before they reached London. Already dark, the street lamps flaring. The inn. The shouting. Other coaches. Passengers. Porters. Beggar children running under the horses, under the wheels, shouting for pennies, for parcels to carry, trying to tug her portmanteau away from her, and Evergreen's basket, and the parcel of manuscript, as they stood stunned at the noise and the rush and the lights and the living darkness, the roar of the city, the smell of smoke, of a hundred thousand fires burning beneath a hundred thousand chimneys. The breath from the horses' nostrils clouded into the sharp air like steam from kettles. A smell of cooking from the inn kitchens. Men in green baize aprons, in shirt sleeves running here and there. Country women almost as stunned as they were themselves at all the tumult, standing dazed and staring. City women going by, ignoring the stage coach and the mill of passengers and ostlers, horses unharnessing, beggars shouting, waiters running; as if they saw such things a dozen times a day and no longer noticed them.

Urnford High Street and the market place were nothing, nothing compared to it. A footman in livery with a heavy, silver-topped six-foot staff trotting ahead of a sedan chair, the chairmen crying in an almost incomprehensible sing song, 'make way ye divils, Jasus an' Mary an Joseph shrivel ye ye imps, make way for us damn ye' as little boys ran at them and tried to trip them up and threw horse dung at their legs.

Shops upon shops upon shops. Milliners and saddlers, drapers and umbrella makers, butchers and grocers and apothecaries. Glimpses of coloured silks in a window, lit by the yellow street lights, bright globes of lamps at every corner. A dray going by loaded with huge oval barrels, wine tuns piled in a dangerous pyramid and the vast shire horses straining at their collars, planting their heavy feet on the cobbles. The carter swinging his whip, his cry of 'Huh, hup, hew op, Daisy girl, hew on Sergeant' rising and lost again in the crash of wheels, the shouts and rushing of the street, the cracking of their own hackney coachman's whip, his own cries to his spavined Rosinante, that was a kind of four-legged skeleton in harness. The coachman himself covered against the frost by a worn and cracked and patched black oil cloth like the aprons sailors wear, his face yellow-white, corpse-like..As if neither he nor the horse had eaten anything for a month.

"'arf a crown, Paternoster Row, 'arf a crown that'll be. An' a tanner fer the luggage.' Only his nose red in the white face, his eyes showing red rims under them, his teeth black.

'A—a tanner?' Judith said, uncertain, and he wheezed compassion for country ignorance.

'Sixpence. Three bob altogether. 's an awful weight in that there stuff for my pore 'orse.'

Indeed Judith wondered if it would not be too much for it to bring them to Paternoster Row at all. But they came there at last, the street quiet after the shopping streets and the evening crowds, and the traffic. Still passers-by hurrying and a coach going by, and another hackney coach, crying 'Wotcher Jem!' to their coachman. And a man with a barrow loaded with boxes, and a woman and a child carrying a washing basket so large that the child seemed to vanish under it rather than to be carrying one side of it.

All this, and yet it was quieter than what they had already seen and passed through. There was an air of haven, of backwater and safety here. The very name Paternoster Row had a sanctuary sound about it. Raising her hand to the knocker, her heart unsteady, her breath catching. But a feeling that this was a welcoming place, a friend, that they were not lost. Mr. Richardson might even insist that they stay in his house. He must have a housekeeper since he was a widower, who would preserve the conventions, and he might be glad of their company for a day or two until she could find good lodgings. How lucky she was that she had someone to turn to, somewhere to come. To have landed in such a place, knowing no one! How would she have managed, how would they have survived?

Knocking. Knocking again. It looked as if no one had polished the knocker for a hundred years. Had he a housekeeper? But perhaps in London, they could not keep brasses clean because of the air? The sound of footsteps behind the faded, scuffed door, slippers flapping against bare boards. A bolt, a chain unfastened. At this hour of the evening? Bolts, chains? The door opening, not wide, but a bare crack, a few inches, to show a woman's face; the eyes suspicious, the mouth unsmiling, an impression of dirt, slovenliness, unwashed skin and unkempt hair under a brown holland cap.

'I—' Judith began, thinking, this is the wrong house, surely this is not his servant, I have made a mistake?

'Well? Wotcher want, 'urry up an' tell us.'

'I—I am looking for Mr. Richardson. Perhaps—'

'Per'aps wot?'

'Perhaps this is not his house? I thought—the sign——'

'Per'aps it is an' per'aps it ain't. Wotcher want wiv 'im?' It was difficult to understand what she was saying. She had almost reclosed the door, rather than opening it wider, so that only the narrowest strip of her face showed now, one eye, and her nose, and half her thin mouth.

'I am Miss Mortimer' Judith said. 'A—friend—I have written often to Mr. Richardson—on my father's behalf. I want to see him if you please.' Beginning to lose patience with such discourtesy and allowing her voice to grow firm. Behind her the wretched horse stamped its hooves, the coachman grumbling at being kept standing.

'I'll see if 'e'll see yer' the woman was saying, and before Judith could say anything more she had shut the door in her face, and run one of the bolts across, as if she imagined Judith was going to burst in and murder her. What kind of woman could she be? How could Mr. Richardson endure to keep her? But then, she thought, someone seeing Martha for the first time might get a strange impression of Guthrum's. One must not judge too harshly by first impressions.

She waited, and the horse stamped again, and then again.

'I'll 'ave ter charge yer waiting money' the coachman said. 'I carn't stan' 'ere all night. That's another tanner I'll 'ave ter arsk yer.'

'I cannot understand it——' Judith was beginning, when she heard more footsteps, dragging this time, the woman's voice saying urgently, in a hoarse whisper, 'tell 'er to bugger 'orff, I'd tell 'er for yer, wot yer want to see 'er for? Yer a disgrace, look at yer, showin' yerself!'

The bolt was dragged back again, the door opened, wider this time, a man, Mr. Richardson?——The ruin of Mr. Richardson, hanging onto it with both hands. In a dirty night cap and a dirty dressing gown that might once have been grey velvet. His eyes peering, bloodshot and weeping. A stench of liquor. His mouth opened as he looked at her, three or four teeth seeming ready to fall out of their shrunken, discoloured gums. He tried to bow, and his night cap fell off. The servant—was she even a servant?—picked it up and jammed it on his grey wisps of hair as if it was a candle snuffer and she wanted to extinguish him.

'Miss Mor'mer' Mr. Richardson said, attempting another bow. 'Y'r father? Wi' you? Fin' me—inn—isposed—in-di-sposed. Not well' he said, clinging to the door, peering at her, peering beyond her as if for her father to be standing there. 'Boo-bus'ness—gonner dogs—printing——All gone.' He waved one hand in dismissal of hope. The woman supported him, glared at Judith.

'Well,' she said fiercely, ''ere 'e is. Wotcher want wiv 'im now?' Somewhere in her voice an ugly satisfaction in displaying this drunken refuse to a visitor.

'I—I am sorry you are not well' Judith whispered. 'We—I—must call another—another day.' And her mind cried, what shall I do? What shall I do now? Oh dear God, how could this happen, why did not I write first? But there had been no time to write and receive an answer, and how could this poor swaying thing have answered her to any purpose? Yet only a few months ago she had had a letter from him.

The door was already closing, the woman pushing it shut as Mr. Richardson tried to keep it open. 'Not well' he was saying, the spittle running in a long streamer from his mouth. 'Inni—in-nispo'—not well.' The door almost shut. 'Y'r father—books—gonner dogs——'

'He is dead! Judith cried to the last inch of opening. 'I—I must find lodgings—an hotel—I have brought manuscripts—my book of receipts——'

The door opened violently, full open this time, and it was the woman who had flung it wide, showing herself in her slut's dirtiness, the old man leaning against the grimy wall where she had pushed him, propping him there like a corpse for burial.

Judith saw a length of naked passage, darkness. There was a smell of dirt, of burned cooking and old grease, and a faint glow of candlelight from a stair head. 'Go to 'ell an' don't come back' the woman shouted. 'Look at 'im! Wotcher want wiv 'im? Wot's anyone want wiv 'im? Leave us alone, bugger orff. Mannerscrips! Bloody books! I burns 'em, I lights the fire wiv 'em, it's all we got to burn! Books 'as ruined 'im. Now yer've seen 'im, shag orff an' leave us alone.'

The door slammed. Bolts. Chains. The old man's voice protesting, the woman's rising to shrieks, half triumph, half rage. Fading. Another door slamming. Only the traffic sounds behind her. The hackney coachman cleared his choked throat of phlegm, spat heavily. 'That wosn't ezackly a welcome, wos it?' he said. 'So yer lookin' fer lodgings eh?'

'Why yes. Or—I had thought first—an hotel—and then—then to look for——'

'Somewheres nice an' quiet an' respeckable, eh? A respeckable widder lady per'aps as keeps rooms?'

'Oh yes!' she cried, 'you do not know any one of that sort?' How she had misjudged him, his kind, good face! He could not help his eyes watering, nor his nose being red, nor his face being so yellow-white nor his horse so thin. 'I should be so grateful!'

'I summed yer up the first minnit' the coachman said, growing animated. 'There, says I, there's a young leddy, a pair o' young leddies, as don't know their ways roun' Lunnon an' might get took in, an' wot a shame that's be, them so pretty an' young an' innocent, as could be done dreadful wrong to if they wosn't took care of.'

'You say you——' She was not sure what he had said, the accent was so difficult, and the voice so hoarse. '*Do* you know any one?'

''smatter o'fack' he said, the animation growing more marked, 'I does. A widder lady. Widder o' a harmy orficer. A Mrs. Ware. Wot keeps a very seleck academy for young leddies an' 'as a couple of rooms above for respeckable lodgers jus' like yerselves.'

'An army officer's widow? That would be perfect! Oh, please ——!'

'It ain't just *any* young leddies wot I'd bring to Mrs. Ware an' reckermen' 'em to 'er. But you! I on'y 'ad to look at yer, an' I thought, there's a young leddy wot——'

'Oh let us hurry! Quickly! Can we go there now?' Climbing

back into the coach to hold Evergreen's hand, reassure her. The widow of an army officer! Who knew what troubles they might have found themselves led into but for this good, kind coachman? How wrong it was to judge by appearances! The streets seemed like fairy-land; the lights, the traffic, the people, all with homes, and now she too, she and Evergreen! An Academy for young ladies! If one tried to design a guarantee of respectability and safety one could not think of a better! Oh, please let her have a vacant room for them! Please!

She lay back in her corner imagining a thousand hackney coaches from all over London converging on Mrs. Ware's Academy, each carrying a potential lodger eager to take the last of Mrs. Ware's vacancies. Oh hurry, hurry! And at the same time trying to seem confident in front of Evergreen, and behave as if her reception by Mr. Richardson was quite ordinary, and just what she had expected.

' 'ere we are,' the coachman cried, 'King Street. Mrs. Ware's!'

Such a handsome, well kept looking street! So quiet and genteel and—and *safe* looking!

The coachman got down himself this time, and tugged at the neat, bright bell pull beside the door. Fresh cream paint, glistening windows, a brass plate announcing the Academy, for Dancing and Deportment. Bright light of candles and lamps behind the downstairs curtains of two of the tall windows, the sounds of a violin. They must be dancing now, how happy it sounded! A maid in the lit doorway, curtsying to the coachman and the almost invisible coach passengers; a maid with a bright young face and a brown silk cap and a brown silk apron over a neat, dark red dress. More lights. A house of life and handsomeness.

The coachman came back to the coach door and opened it for Judith, helped her down. 'Wot a stroke o' luck!' he said. 'There wos a werry elegant young gentlewoman lodging upstairs as 'as just gorn orf to marry a wiscount's eldest son. You can 'ave 'er rooms the girl says, an' welcome, an' she'll jus' fetch Mrs. Ware to greet yer, she won't be a minnit.'

'But—' Judith said, hesitating now that the house was in front of her, in all its elegance, its air of quiet prosperity. 'I only wonder if——It must be very expensive?'

'My 'eavens' the coachman cried, a trifle of impatience in his hoarseness. 'Mrs. Ware ain't one to screw a young leddy wot 'asn't got much blunt at this werry instant. She'll put it on the slate for yer.'

'On the slate?'

'On tick. Pay when yer can. Oh, she ain't a one to Shylock any 'un as pretty as you are. An' 'ere she comes! Get down wiv yer now an' yer little frien' inside, an' I'll introduce yer.'

A stout, active woman, with piled russet curls under a widow's cap, a black silk dress and a black silk apron of the kind that one might wear for sewing, with pockets for threads and needle cases and thimbles. White lace at her neck and cuffs, a liveliness to her walk despite her widowhood and plump middle age, her face lighting up with interest and kindly welcome at the sight of Judith and Evergreen beside the coachman, so grotesque a Charon for two such ferry passengers.

'Well I never!' she cried, her voice light and trilling and still somehow youthful. 'Jem Hughes, is it you? And bringing me two young ladies! Well, I never did in all my days! What a pleasant surprise! And such young ladies! Come in my dears, come inside out of this freezing cold night and tell me all about yourselves, where you've come from and what you're doing in London. A warm fire and some Negus and a tray of supper and we shall have time to become friends. No no no, don't worry about your bags and bits, Jem Hughes and my lad Harry can see to all that. Harry! Harry, you young devil, where have you hid yourself now? Quick, boy, give a hand, carry in the young ladies' luggage and up to the top rooms, and look sharp about it, d'you want me to lose my patience with you? Such a rascal!'

A boy of fourteen or fifteen in page's uniform, with curly brown hair and an impudent eye, and his cheek swollen out with something he was eating, ducking his way under Mrs. Ware's raised hand and mock threat of chastisement, glancing at Judith and Evergreen as if he knew them already for five years and was not much impressed. Jumping down the front steps and calling 'Hey, Jem, yer 'orse not dead yet?'

'That boy, that boy!' Mrs. Ware cried. 'But what can one do, boys will be boys till the world ends, I suppose. Now here is my small sitting room where you shall have supper, but first you can see your own rooms and wash off the journey and leave down your cloaks.'

[169]

It was difficult to interrupt her. They were on the second landing before Judith managed to say something about the coach fare. 'Oh that? Harry can pay it and we'll talk of it later, but it's nothing to worry about, what is a shilling between friends? And I know we shall be the greatest friends, I can see it in your faces. One of you so fair and tall, and one so dark and quite small, such a charming contrast!'

'A shilling? But we are to pay him three and six, and I wished to give him——'

There was a table with two chairs set to it, and two armchairs How lucky you've left it to me to pay him! Now, here are your rooms, they're nothing so fine as you've been used to, I'm sure of that, but poor as they are they'll keep out the rain, and there's at least a fire, and a bed for each of you.'

There was a great deal more than that, from the crisp, red and white print-cotton curtains to the turkey rugs on the polished floor and the sea coal fire set in the grate, with the maid already there, bent down beside it and lighting it. Such a pretty maid, with her neat dark hair as smooth as velvet, and her neat red slippers to match her red gown, their soles turned up as she knelt with the bellows, briskly encouraging the fire.

There was a table with two chairs set to it, and two armchairs and another table, and a cabinet with china ornaments, and more ornaments and silver candlesticks on the mantelpiece, and Chinese wallpaper with pictures of Chinese scenes and flowers and trees. It seemed at that moment the prettiest room that Judith had ever seen in her life.

And when Mrs. Ware opened another door beyond the fireplace, there was the most comfortable and welcoming of bedrooms with two prettily curtained beds, one with white muslin and one with blue; and another fireplace, the fire already burning and blazing up, while Mrs. Ware apologised for the simplicity and untidiness of everything, and the fires not being ready lit, and Harry being so noisy and so impudent as he tugged and puffed and lugged the portmanteau and the basket and the parcel of manuscripts into the sitting room and dumped them in a pile on the carpet behind the maid's heels.

'Not there you stupid, wicked boy! Not like that! What *shall* I do with you?'

'But ma'am' Judith said, when at last she could say anything against the torrent of kindliness. 'I beg of you to listen to me. I do not think we could possibly take these rooms! Not—oh please, please listen, not because they are not fine enough, they are splendid, I never saw such rooms, but they will be so expensive! And we have, I have—so little money, and I do not yet know where I shall get more.'

But it seemed useless trying to be sensible about such things with Mrs. Ware. She looked almost delighted that her new lodgers, as she already called them, had no money, and positively laughed at the idea of not being paid.

'Lud lud lud' she cried, 'let us not talk about such dreadful things as money, at least not now, nor for ages after I hope. Come straight downstairs and we shall have supper, if you can possibly bear to eat anything while they are playing that dreadful music across the hall. And afterwards you shall meet the dancing master if you like, a French Marquis although he does not use his title, he is quite ashamed of his poverty the creature; the Marquis de Beaulieu. Such estates as he had, such a fortune! And now because of those dreadful Jacobins he has not a shilling left and must scrape his fiddle and teach young ladies not to fall over their own toes when they are dancing. Poor fellow, he is so grateful to me, and no cause for it in the world, it is a positive pleasure to help a gentleman in distress. My dear, dear, dear Major Ware was the most lovable gentlemanlike man you ever could wish to meet and I have such a fondness for the sex because of him my heart positively melts when I see one of 'em in need of anything. But what was I going to tell you? It does not matter, I shall think of it again. Albertine? Albertine? What are you at, girl? Run down to cook and tell her if the finest supper she ever prepared for two starving young ladies is not on my parlour table within one minute she must look for another situation tomorrow if not tonight. Vite, vite, vite! Albertine is French too, poor thing, her mother was housekeeper to a Duke and really it is the most dreadful come-down in the world for her, she was quite a playmate to the Duchess's children and spoiled to death as you must have seen already but what can one do, one cannot spend one's life shouting at young creatures because they are young creatures.'

Supper and more talk. Oysters and champagne, and game pie and claret, with cold beef and burgundy to follow, and fruit pies

[171]

and sweet cakes after that, until the room was a warm nest of exhausted contentment. The marquis coming in like a rather shabby old crow with his violin case under his arm, and the most charming manners imaginable, to take coffee and a liqueur and sweet biscuits, and blink hooded old eyes first at Judith and then at Evergreen, complimenting each in turn upon possessing every conceivable virtue of appearance and deportment, in a slow and stilted English that gave a last touch of pleasure and cultivation to the evening, without in the least impeding the waterfall flow of Mrs. Ware's talking.

Reminiscences of Major Ware, loving complaints about the servants, the pupils, past lodgers who all seemed to have married handsome gentlemen of fortune, ranging from Nabobs up to a near Royal Duke, however it might be possible to be near but not quite in such a rank. It did cross Judith's tired mind that so much good fortune for so many lodgers was a shade surprising, but it would have been a bitter meanness of spirit to criticise anything after such a welcome, and when at last she and Evergreen dragged themselves up to their rooms, accompanied by Mrs. Ware still talking, and Albertine carrying hot jars to replace the ones already in their beds, and Harry carrying a tray of biscuits and cake and candied fruit and a great jug of hot chocolate in case they should feel overcome by hunger in the middle of the night; when at last they were in their bedroom, and alone, and lying in their beds, and in the three seconds before Judith fell like a stone into a well of sleep that seemed to have no bottom; she thought that it must have been her mother's spirit that guided her to such a wonderful place, and such a wonderful woman.

'God bless my mother' she said, as if she was a child again. 'God bless Mrs. Ware and Evergreen, and me.' Was already half asleep. 'And God bless Robert,' fading into dreams.

Chapter 19

She tried to make herself work. Tried to put all thought of his coming, all dependence on it, quite out of her mind. She must not depend on—on anything but herself. Her own efforts. Suppose he did not come? Did not so much as write? Because her new letter—but she had been right to make it as cool as the first. Simply to give him Mrs. Ware's direction, and the plain statement of their journey, and of Mr. Richardson's condition, and their coming by such a wonderful accident of fortune to this house.

She could not have made it a love letter! Nor even have shown anxiety. Unless to say 'I do not know what exactly we shall do' had been to show it. But that had been no more than fact. How could she know? And in the meantime she must think exactly of that, of their future, of money, of every rational thing. Not—not of sitting by firelight, holding hands.

She had bought ink and paper and was fair copying her father's manuscript. But the very act of copying it out was helping to convince her that it was a waste of time, and had been a waste of precious, precious shillings for the paper and ink and pens. The book was very wise, about the nature of Government, and Justice between men. It must prove to any rational being that the whole idea of Kingship was the grossest of superstitions. But how many people would want to read such a thing in this modern day? It was like Grotius, or Melancthon, while what people wanted was Mr. Wordsworth, or Miss Burney, or Mrs. Radcliffe.

And as for her own book! Who in the name of reason would buy a book of receipts by Miss Noone of nowhere? They would want it by a Duchess's housekeeper at the very least, if not by the Duchess herself. And she sat staring at the sprawled, barely legible pages of her father's writing, and the neat folder of her own receipts, and felt despair at the very sight of them. What had the woman shouted at her? She flushed even at the memory of her vulgarity. But there seemed a horrible truth contained in its ugliness. 'Bloody books! I burns them!'

She sat at the window, staring down into the street and wondering again, when—if—if he would come. If three carriages went by while she held her breath, then he would surely come. But only one went by, and a running footman, and a man with a handcart. She held her breath again and nothing went by at all. Not even anyone on foot.

It was a ridiculous, stupid thing to do, worse than stupid, utterly irrational. He would come, or would not come, and there was an end to it. And if he did? What should she do? I cannot marry him! It is not—not thinkable! Not in cool reason, not in daylight. To marry him—anyone—like that! Between one day and the next? And go—in time—perhaps—when—they could have got to know one another properly—but he was going to Leyden and——And if he did not come at all?

One way or the other she must find work, must find some truly practical way to earn money. She should have tried already, instead of wasting days copying unreadable chapters from an unreadable book, and useless advice for women who either would not read it because they knew it already, or could not read it because they could not read anything, and did not know anything, and had no means nor intelligence to put any advice into practice. What point was there in telling Mr. Rigg how to plant cabbages or Mrs. Rigg how to cook them?

To find work. She must. But what work could she do? She might have been able to be a secretary to some one if that was work that was ever done by women, but it was not. An amanuensis. A woman amanuensis! It sounded as absurd as a woman driving a coach. Yet if one thought of it there was no real reason on earth why there should not be female secretaries to men-of-letters, and men-of-business. To copy out documents and keep accounts and write letters. There was surely nothing that Mr. Terry's clerks could do that she could not do at least as well? But who would believe that?

Or she could be a cook, or a housekeeper. Except that she was much too young, and no one would trust her with a house, or a kitchen. And she had no references, and would not dare even to use her own name for fear of being discovered by the Earl and Mr. Massingham. When she went more than two streets away from Mrs. Ware's front door her terrors were not only of being lost in London, but of being seen by someone from Matcham.

That was an added reason to look for Robert's coming, to have news of Guthrum's, and Martha, and what the Earl might be doing to find her. And if he did not come himself he must at least write. She had begun to look for the post, to count up the days. Four. Five. He could not be here before tomorrow, or it might be Saturday, or Sunday. Even a letter from him could not arrive until——

They must truly and really find some way of earning money. She could not sit here at a window day after day, with Evergreen trying to sew handkerchiefs beside her, and succeeding in nothing but pricking her fingers, and spoiling the cotton. They must earn money. Find work. They must!

But the very comfort of the house, and Mrs. Ware's kindness, seemed to make the task even more difficult. And frightening. How much must all this cost? And how impossible it seemed to earn enough for their daily keep here, let alone for every other thing they must soon need. Mrs. Ware had simply laughed away her anxious questions about payment, as if they were ridiculous. 'Lud, child! Time enough! We can talk of all that when you've found a—oh dear, oh lud, what a trouble money is! I hates even to think of it!' And she would be off down to the kitchens, or into the music room, or somewhere; or else she began talking about something else a hundred to the dozen, and it was impossible to get any sensible answer from her.

She was, Judith thought, a most extraordinary woman for a landlady, and indeed it was an extraordinary household, and seemed more so with each day that they remained there. The first puzzle was to imagine where the money came from to provide the luxury of everything. The wages alone, the salary to Monsieur de Beaulieu, to a Mr. Featherstonehaugh who came to teach the pupils elocution, and a Mrs. Harcourt who came to teach them fine sewing. And then the Italian, Signor Baccharelli, who came to dress their hair, he must also be paid, and probably a great deal, from the way he conducted himself and the air of consequence he had.

And yet there were only seven pupils! Their fees must be

enormous to justify so much expense on their behalf, not to speak of Mrs. Ware's own household expenses. She had already confided that her husband had left her penniless. The dearest, sweetest, most understanding creature in the world, but lud! Money! Money and Major Ware had never been friends, nor even frequent companions. He had only to look at a guinea but it disappeared. And Mrs. Ware had given a fat, fond laugh as if it had been the delight of her life to provide him with guineas to squander and she would do it again in the morning if she had the opportunity.

She herself, she said, taught the pupils conversation and the uses of polite society, which however broadly that might be interpreted, seemed a very limited sort of education, Judith thought, even combined with fine sewing and dancing. Perhaps they had all finished their real, book education, and this was only a sort of finishing off and polishing? And yet they were all still very young, the eldest of them no older than Evergreen, and the youngest no more than twelve, at the very most. And how extraordinarily various they seemed to be in background! Two, Mrs. Ware said, were the daughters of a French Vicomte. They had velvet eyes and chestnut hair, and a hint of demure malice behind their smiles that would be almost shocking to see in anyone—and in young girls!—although Mrs. Ware regarded them as her stars, and was continually holding them up as models to the other five pupils.

Another was, Mrs. Ware had told them, the daughter of a very well-connected clergyman in Northumberland, and another again, she had whispered, looking roguish, was the daughter of someone she positively dare not name, or Lud! what a scandal there might be if she was to tell it round!

But the youngest girl had the most surprising history of all. Nearly as fair as Judith, fine boned and with a skin like porcelain, and already learning to walk and dance like a fairy, she had a cockney accent that Judith could not begin to understand unless the child repeated something four or five times, and even then Mrs. Ware must interpret for her.

'Oh lud lud, my dear, such language! We'll have to pretend you're mute unless you can learn better than that! don't dare to open your beautiful little mouth until I give you leave, d'you hear me, child?'

[176]

She was scarcely twelve, with eyes like drowned violets and golden curls that fell to her shoulders when Signor Baccharelli dressed them. A child to pick up and cuddle and cherish like a wonderful kitten, until the rosebud mouth opened and the appalling accent revealed itself, and the ferocious, incomprehensible words.

'One of my little self-indulgences' Mrs. Ware said, visibly embarrassed. 'A beggar child I found one day in Soho, guiding her poor blind father along on a leash. Oh lud, I thought my heart'd break to see such beauty so downtrodden, and croaking for charity. Dear oh dear, I'm a foolish woman, but I cannot bear to see beauty and poverty allied, I have to do something about it, it's my failing, I know it, my dear Major always chided me for it. Look after number one, Fanny, he always told me, although that was only his talk, he had the kindest heart, and not a beggar could pass him by but he'd empty his pockets for him. And I'm the same. Oh lud, it'll be the ruin of me, I know it, but what can one do, one can't go against one's nature.'

She had proved that the first day of their staying there, if more proof was necessary, by offering to allow Judith and Evergreen to attend the pupil's lessons, as an amusement, to pass the morning, and have 'a mouthful of luncheon afterwards' with herself and the pupils, and 'the dear, dear old marquis. Not that I think we could teach *you* anything, you great beautiful creature, oh lud, I ain't such a vain old merry-legs as that I promise you. And I'm sure you've taught Miss Evergreen all *she* needs to know, the pretty sweet thing, but lud, it's raining outside, and you can't possibly be dreaming of going out in such weather and getting yourselves drenched, so why not come and laugh at my little creatures' awkwardness and oddities, and amuse yourselves, instead of moping upstairs in that dreadful little garret I've put you in? And we shall all have our déjeuner together and you shall tell us all your gossip and what the world is like where you come from. Eh? Will you give an old woman the pleasure of trying to while away your morning for you?'

She looked so kindly, and so anxious that they should not be dull upstairs nor drenched outside, that it would have been very hard to refuse even if Judith had had other and better plans. But indeed she had none. What was there else to do? Where could she go in the rain to look for anything that might earn her some money? And as for the manuscripts, which she had already looked at for an unpromising hour, they must wait until she had bought ink and quills and pounce and all that was necessary. The thought of sitting in a pleasant room, listening to music and watching pretty children dance was suddenly a most attractive one, and the thought of not having to be alone with her thoughts for the rest of the morning was quite wonderful.

And the dancing room *was* pleasant. As unlike the usual idea of a schoolroom in an Academy for Young Ladies as one could well imagine. The floor was polished brown parquet, and the fireplace was marble, with carved nymphs in marble draperies to either side of it, holding up garlands of flowers and fruits. There was the jolliest of coal fires making the brass firedogs wink like constellations of stars. The gilt Louis Quinze chairs scattered round the walls were upholstered in mulberry velvet with a great, flowing W A in gold thread worked into the heart-shaped back of each of them, to remind one of Mrs. Ware's Academy, if one needed reminding. There were little tables with cards scattered on them, and comfit dishes, and cut crystal decanters, and vases of flowers, and a group of handsome velvet-covered arm chairs at one end of the room to which Mrs. Ware conducted Judith and Evergreen, sitting them down as if they were the most honoured of guests, and pressing them to take a glass of Madeira, and Bath biscuits, or else a sweetmeat.

'O lud, comme tu es comme il faut! That bend of the wrist as you took your comfit! Oh deary me, blood will tell, blood will tell! As my dear, dear Major always said, you can tell the whole of a girl's breeding in the turn of her wrist, and he was right, as always. And you, you sweet little creature, *you've* not been spoiled with too many sugar plums, *that* I can tell. Don't be afraid of it. Open those pretty lips and just *pop* it in. Like this!' And to match her words she pursed her own pretty red mouth as if she was about to kiss someone, and then opened her lips quite slightly, and put the sweetmeat between them as if she was about to kiss *it*. It was a quite extraordinary thing to watch, and gave Judith a moment's feeling almost of discomfort, until Mrs. Ware dissolved it all with a peal of laughter, and a pat on Judith's knee. 'Lud, oh lud, you'd think you never saw a lady eat a sugared almond before. Now, watch my little school of comfit eaters show you their paces!' She clapped her hands imperiously, and the cluster

[178]

of young girls who had been whispering at the far side of the fire came obediently forward, and formed a line, the tallest to the left, and the smallest to the right, that being the ex-beggar child with the fair hair and the drowned violet eyes. 'Viens, chérie, make your curtsy to my new guests, and then take a sweetmeat and show them how prettily you have learned to be greedy in company.'

It was indeed a good description of how the girl ate her crystallised cherry. A kind of languorous greed, but with the prettiest, most delicate way of taking the cherry from the dish, a drooping of her eyelashes before she tasted it, that made of the episode something remarkable, and half pathetic, as if the child was remembering times when she had not a dirty crust to put to her mouth, and was half afraid the sweetmeat would dissolve into dream if she tried to taste it.

'Bien, mais pas trop bien, my little one. You must not look at the sweetmeat, you must look at the gentleman who is nearby and who has given it to you, for it will always be a gentleman who offers you a comfit, you will never, *never* commit the bêtise of helping yourself unasked. *That* would be to condemn yourself as a petite gourmande who thinks only of food instead of—instead of the things that young ladies *should* think of in a gentleman's company.' She snapped her fingers. 'Justine, viens ici. You shall show us all how it must be done.'

The elder of the Vicomte's two daughters came rustling forward. Like all the children she was dressed more for a ballroom than for a schoolroom, at least in Judith's eyes, and her green satin skirts brushed the parquet floor as her red morocco slippers now peeped from under them and now vanished, like scarlet mice. The demure malice that Judith had already noticed when they were first introduced had become entire demureness. The dark eyelashes were lowered, the curtsy had a swan's grace to it. The skirts spread out, the shining chestnut hair glowed like the fire, and the child drifted up again, a swan's neck lifting. A flower. The almost slanting eyes looked at Mrs. Ware not as a pupil looks at a teacher, but as a young woman might look at a man if she wished to flatter him. The white hand went out, the lips, thin but bow-curved upper lip; pouted, bee-stung underlip, shaped themselves, not towards the bowl of sweetmeats, but towards that imaginary gentleman who stood where Mrs. Ware was sitting with concentrated interest and guidance. The thin, childish fingers took a sweetmeat as if that was the least of the girl's concerns, the man everything, and the sugared violet was eaten like an unspoken word in a silent conversation of the eyes and lips. Only at the very last the eyelashes fell in a demure, oh! how demure veil of modesty, and the sweetmeat was gone, and the tiny, brilliant scene of acting was over.

Mrs. Ware clapped her hands in delight. 'Comme tu es belle! Brava, brava! Is she not the dearest, cleverest thing you ever saw my dear?'

She was indeed the cleverest, without doubt, but whether she was the dearest Judith allowed herself to wonder, silently. There had been something—something almost immodest about such cleverness, such an ability to transform the trivial action into—into who knew what. Certainly the child herself could not know. Perhaps, Judith thought, it was her French parentage, and felt ashamed of criticising her for what she could not help. But surely Mrs. Wade could see that—that *no one* should look at a young man like that, even if the young man was imaginary, and the girl was still a child? But Mrs. Ware obviously felt no such thing, and the lesson continued, as if the eating of sweetmeats in company was as important as algebra, and just as difficult.

After that lesson they must perform their curtsys, as one does to one's hostess, and then to one's host. As one does to Royalty—for 'Lud!' as Mrs. Ware cried, 'Who knows where'll they reach to, such pretty loves as they are? Look high, as my Major always used to say, and you'll find the best apples.' How to curtsy in a way that tells a gentleman he is de trop, for as Mrs. Ware declared again, 'there is such things as gentlemen who gets under one's feet and is no good for anything, an' the sooner you learn how to rout 'em out of your way the better, and make room for the right 'uns.' And finally how to curtsy to a gentleman who seems indeed to be a possible rightest 'un, the kind of gentleman whom one would like to see again and as soon as might be, while remaining utterly and completely within the bounds of the *strictest* modesty.

It was for Judith, the most astonishing of mornings. And not the least, in fact the most astonishing part of it, was Mrs. Ware herself. Like a great actress teaching pupils who are too slow for her, and unable to prevent herself from jumping up and demonstrating, not so much because a demonstration is really necessary, but for the sheer love of doing it. And she did everything with such zest, such humour and such art, that what she was doing seemed far less important than the way she did it. In the middle of a minuet she would leap up on her light small feet and contrive in spite of her generous figure to be now a slim young girl, and now a tall gentleman. To bow, to curtsy, to use a lorgnon with a killing air of nonchalance or arrogance, to use an opera glass as if she was surveying dancers on a stage, to sweep her cheek with her fan and slaughter an admirer with a look above the curl of feathers and painted chicken skin.

She would suddenly turn her armchair into a hard bench in an Assembly Rooms, and make room for a gentleman with the sweetest modesty, so that everything was there in a flash, from the gentleman to the tenor singing his Bel Canto to the several hundred other people of the audience to the Master of Ceremonies. Or she would look up in a reprise of the same charade with the most icy surprise, warning off the attempted invasion of her bench as if she was the white cliffs of Dover warning away a rascally French privateer. 'For' she said, 'the greatest gift a gal can have is Judgement. The gal as can sum up a gentleman the first glance, is the girl who's going to end up as Her Grace, with a Duke's coronet on her writing paper, and a couple of hundred thou per annum in rents. Oh, it can happen, I promise. But you've got to have Judgement. You've got to tell the gentleman with blunt, the *real* gentleman, from some poxy little jumped up attorney's clerk with nothing in the world but a good tailor. I could smell the sealing wax at twenty yards, and the Duke's coronet at fifty, in a room full of people, and you've got to learn it too.'

It was astonishing advice, but given with such earnestness, that it made Judith wonder if perhaps it really was as important as Mrs. Ware thought, and if she herself had been at fault in not learning it. Indeed it was almost impossible to listen to Mrs. Ware without being carried away by her flow of talk and vitality, and by the end of the morning Judith felt as if she herself had learned nothing in all her life that was of any real value, and began to wonder how she had ever dared to hope to make her living in London without the sort of intellectual and moral equipment that Mrs. Ware was providing for her small flock of pupils.

And the splendour with which it was done! Apart from the pupils' gowns which must have cost someone, presumably their parents, a very great deal, between their silks and their taffetas, their lace shawls and their cashmeres, their fans and their slippers and their reticules—but who, for example, except Mrs. Ware herself, could have provided the ex-beggar child with her satin gown, and her gold bracelet, and the little gold locket on its black velvet ribbon that set off her narrow white throat so beautifully?—apart from all that, what Mrs. Ware called indifferently their déjeuner and their luncheon, was a feast for honoured guests, rather than anything one might associate with school. Pâté de foie gras and cold stuffed trout. Fieldfares in aspic. Orange salads and boned ducklings stuffed with roasted chestnuts. Fricassées of sweatbreads in a veal gravy sauce that tasted of white wine and mace and nutmeg, each taste delicately blending into another. Glacéd fruits and jellies and flummeries with steeple cream that trembled gently as one touched them, and that seemed too beautifully shaped to be eaten at all. How in the name of economy and reason could all this be provided by a school unless the school fees were *out* of all reason, and paid by Nabobs who counted their money by the lakh rather than by the guinea?

But once again Mrs. Ware waved away Judith's tentative curiosity with her fat jolly laugh and an invitation for more pie and some claret.

'At this hour of the day?' cried Judith, for whom wine was a solemn evening event, and that not often. 'And your pupils—they drink *wine?*'

'Just a sip' Mrs. Ware said carelessly, filling her own glass to the brim. 'Justine, accept as I drink your health my child, show the others.' And turning back to Judith when the momentary lesson was done, 'you see my dear, I'm teaching 'em about *life*. You spend half your life in your bedroom, and the other half in company and what the deuce do most schools teach their gals about? Neither the one nor the t'other, so that the poor dears totter out from their schoolrooms like day-old chicks, to be knocked over by the first real rascal as sets his eye at 'em. No no no, I teaches 'em what counts. If you haven't never sipped a glass of claret till you leave school what's going to happen to you the first time you dines in company? The best is you'll get sick, and the worst is you'll get tipsy foolish and make a performing show of yourself. I could tell you stories of gals as had done *that!* An' worse after. And food. Now, take that flummery, if you've never seen one before, you'll look surprised at it, and a gal shouldn't never look surprised at anything, unless she means to. It shows her up for a bumpkin within a second. So I gives my little dears the things they'll get in company.'

'But do not their parents——'

'Lud my dear!' Mrs. Ware whispered behind her glass, 'Parents! The stories I could tell you about them! They leaves it all to nursery maids, and then they're surprised what their Goldilocks gets up to. Oh my stars, parents is often the worst handicap a girl can have.' And then summoning the beggar girl's attention with a lift of her finger, 'Juliet, my pet, that accent! Don't *talk! Listen!* That's your gambit. Any girl in the world can say something clever, but who wants to hear it? While a *listener!* That's a different kettle of fish. The gentlemen as I've seen led to the altar by a listener! And you can mark this too, Justine and you Marie. Cleverness has its places, and a *bon mot* at the right time is worth a lot, but you can overdo it, and the minute a gentleman *sees* that you're clever, you have overdone it. There's nothing a gentleman hates like a clever woman, she frightens the stockings off him. While the girl as can listen to him tell her about how he plans to improve his Estate and how he means to have his people dig a ha ha across the grounds, and can make him think he's being brilliant, that girl can practically be one-eyed and lame in both legs, and she's got him.'

It was an extraordinary morning, and followed by others, because Mrs. Ware renewed her invitations every day, and it was almost impossible to refuse her without seeming rude, or critical. And although the criticisms mounted in Judith's mind as she listened to such a torrent of worldliness and cynicism that she seemed at times to have stumbled into the parlour of an English Voltaire rather than a girl's schoolroom, it was difficult to lay her finger on any precise moment when realism became immoral. It was indeed true, as Mrs. Ware said, that a girl's business in life was to get married, and to get married as prosperously and respectably as possible, and that to treat girls in the schoolroom as if this was not so, and that they were going out into a world where money did not signify and marriage was a matter of waiting for a knight errant, was the real hypocrisy. 'I teach 'em what's what' Mrs. Ware said roundly, and more than once. 'Not what it ought to be, or what I'd like it to be. But what it is. So—now my little Evergreen, are you going to show me a curtsy? D'you think you can copy t'others?'

Judith had an instant desire to prevent it, so strong that she had already lifted her hand to Evergreen's shoulder, to hold her in her place. But why? And what would Mrs. Ware think if she did? And the pupils, and the old marquis, who was there for the dancing lesson, and already tuning his shabby violin? Evergreen stood up obediently, moved to the front of Mrs. Ware's arm-chair, and made her the curtsy she had learned from her father. Compared to the other children's precocious grace it had immediately a strange appearance about it, and Mrs. Ware cried in a kind of professional horror, 'Lud child, where did you ever learn such an antique thing as that? Why, it is demodé by fifty years' if not a hundred! Look child, look at Justine's curtsy. Justine, ma chère, demonstrate to this poor antiquity here how it must be done!' But Judith noticed that she had sat forward in her chair and was obviously intrigued by something about Evergreen, beyond the pleasure of teaching a new pupil. And again she had the desire to prevent this going further, and was astonished at herself. Was she—she could not be jealous? Of Mrs. Ware with Evergreen? And tried to laugh at herself and rebuke herself at the same time for such a nonsensical possibility.

Justine dropped her bending, lovely, too-adult curtsy, floated upright. Evergreen stood mute, watching.

'Now. Vite! Vite! Do the same.'

But once again Evergreen made her father's curtsy, seemed even to underline its strangeness, that had not seemed strange when Judith had previously seen it.

'Lud, lud, lud! Oh, we shall have to work hard with you, little dark one. Can she dance?'

Judith wanted to say no, but Evergreen had already bent her head in acknowledgement. The marquis had come forward to watch, and now he tucked his violin under his chin and drew the bow across it, shaping his old soft lips in a smile, not at Mrs.

Ware or Evergreen, or the schoolroom and its flower pupils, but at some distant memory of his own, as if only when he played music he belonged to his own past. By a chance, or perhaps it was natural enough given his age, he began to play an antique minuet, as old-fashioned as Evergreen's curtsy, not unlike the tunes that Evergreen's father had played long ago.

And Evergreen began to dance. She did not drift like a swan on the water, as Justine and her sister did, nor with the flower beauty of Juliet the beggar girl. She carved her dance in the air. Drew it with brush strokes of her small feet on the shimmering parquet, that reflected her like a shadow. Everything about her dance was old. And tragic. It caught even the pupils' childish minds for a moment, and they stared as the servants and Judith had stared long ago in the kitchen. Then indeed they began to titter, hiding their pretty mouths with their hands in an elegant, learned mimicry of how the bon ton behaves in the face of anything strange and outlandish. They whispered to each other and cast glances at Mrs. Ware for her approval of their contempt for this newcomer's ignorance. Judith's face flamed with anger, but before she could say anything, the tittering died away. Mrs. Ware had not approved of it. She was leaning forward, watching, her face quite changed. Intent. Drawn.

As for Evergreen, she might have been alone. Might have been in the moonlight in a wood for all she noticed of her surroundings. There was moonlight. There was a wood. Dark shadows. The sighing of the wind in branches, the cry of owls. Silence. Leaves rustling under her feet. She is dancing her freedom, Judith thought, the image coming from nowhere. And felt her heart tighten. I have taken her freedom away, she thought in despair. And what can I give her in exchange for it? This? The music came to an end, faded. The schoolroom was a schoolroom again, one of the pupils giggled uneasily, fell silent.

Judith wanted to seize hold of Evergreen and run out of the room. Mrs. Ware drew in a long sighing breath and let it out. She seemed to shake herself awake from whatever thoughts had held her and her face changed back from its absorption to its usual eager vitality of instruction and good humoured disapproval of ignorance.

'Oh my stars what an exhibition! If one was to dance like that one would frighten every gentleman in miles into thinking fits.

That is not dancing, that is—I do not know what to call it! Oh lud, child, who has been teaching you such dreadful feelings? Not you, I hope my dear Miss Mortimer?'

'No indeed' Judith said coldly. 'It was her father who taught her.'

'What a strange man he must have been.' Mrs. Ware seemed to shiver for a second, and need to rally herself again. 'What we all need after that is a good déjeuner and a sup of claret to put the hearts back into us. Gaiety, ma chère! Gaiety and bubbles, that's what gentlemen likes in a gal, not depths and moping and thoughts and such rubbish. Heavens above, imagine a gentleman taking to a gal with depths! It's like giving him a horse as could answer him back. No, no, no, I can see it's a providence as has brought you to me, my sweet little creature. Oh how I long to begin to teach you what's what!'

'I do not think that will be——' Judith began, but Mrs. Ware flowed over her protest like honey onto dry bread.

'Now, now, not another serious word till we've all sat down to table, and then there'll be no need for seriousness. Come Marquis my dear, give Miss Mortimer your arm, and show our gals how a gentleman takes a lady into a dining room.'

The déjeuner, or luncheon, a meal that Judith had scarcely heard of until now, even Matcham being content with dinner at four o'clock of the afternoon, and supper at eight or nine, the luncheon was served in the back room, the table as elegantly furnished as in any dining parlour in a gentleman's house. Silver and lace and crystal, the covers already set out in a formal pattern on the long mahogany table by Albertine and Harry. Hare soup to-day for a centre dish, in a massive silver tureen, flanked by boiled lobsters garnished with shrimp and wine sauce, and roast buck venison, with corner dishes of goose paté and Scotch collops of veal, rubbed in egg yolks and nutmeg and served with truffles and hard boiled eggs. Matcham itself did not eat as well as this except on days of ceremony, and once more Judith wondered who and what could possibly pay for such a profligacy of comforts.

But it was not possible to think of anything in Mrs. Ware's company except what Mrs. Ware wanted one to think of. She told stories, made jokes, corrected, offered, corrected again. Demonstrated how a lady does this and that. Holds her glass. Eats an

[186]

orange. Drinks soup. 'Lud, you think there's only one way to drink it? Open your pretty mouth and swallow? Oh my stars! There's a hundred ways! Now suppose you're with a gentleman as is of a delicate stomach, and picks at his own platter. He's not likely to want a trencherwoman for company as downs her two dozen oysters with a gulp and calls for another dozen before he's emptied a shell. No, with him you pick, and you sigh how vulgar food is, and how you wish we could live like the angels on air and love, and so on. Or say you're with a grand fellow with lots of bottom, as likes his dish and his glass and damn the heel taps. He likes a trencherwoman as can can keep him company and not make great eyes at his appetite. So there you match him mouthful for mouthful and cry for more pudding, and slap his knee and tell him he's the kind of fellow as made England what she is.

'But then, take care, there's another kind of gentleman as likes to eat himself but thinks it desperate common in a gal to do the same, and yet he don't want sighs and vapours, he just likes to see you satisfied with a wing of partridge and half an orange, and the rest of the time you must listen to him chomp his chops as if it was music. You have to judge. Judge, judge, judge, that's your biggest task in life. Men is half children and half monsters, mixed up in different ways, and you've got to work out what ways this one beside you is mixed up. Is he child in this part, and a monster in that, or t'other way round, or mixed quite different like a marble cake, with squares of monster and squares of child one next t'other, or what? Judge, my loves, and judge quick, or you'll lose him afore you've got him.'

Or else she was telling stories about her Major, and a voyage to India they had made together, and each story led to a lesson. For example how to know whether to be seasick in order to get sympathy, or to be as well as a sailor in the roughest storm in order to be a good companion, and a nurse at need. 'You think it can't be done, or you will if you ever get to feeling seasick, which God forbid for you my dears. But it can. You've got to have a will of iron and a stomach as is copper-bottomed and teak-lined if you're to get on in the world, and a little thing like seasickness as flattens a gentleman into a pea-green bit of wreckage for days on end has got to have no more effect on you than a headache. Less. You've got to pretend to yourself that you've got no stomach, and you must bring him dishes of gruel and wet flannels to lay on his forehead while he thinks he's dying, and you know you are, and you've got to smile and hold his hand and tell him he's wonderful and you can't think how he's so brave. And when he gets up again, you have to let him persuade himself that it was t'other way round, and it was him as looked after you. Oh lud, my ducks, gentlemen! I could write books about the darling creatures as would curl the hairs on a wig.' And she would drain her glass and flush faintly as if she felt Judith's concealed astonishment and was embarrassed by it. Then she would laugh, and fondle Judith's knee. 'Don't mind me, my dear. I'm an old woman as has seen life, and I likes to pass on what I've learned to these little buds before the frost has a chance to nip 'em. Oh, I do love young creatures, and pretty young creatures above all things.'

It certainly seemed an odd sort of learning.

But it was not until the Thursday evening that the accumulation of oddities about the household began to seem more than merely extraordinary. About seven o'clock, as Judith was looking at her manuscripts in despair, and thinking how pleasant it might be to go downstairs and forget them, and find company again, Mrs. Ware came tapping at the door, full of smiles and breathlessness, to beg them if they would not mind, if they would promise not to be the least, the teeniest bit offended, would they—just for an hour or two—would they very much mind keeping to their rooms? Some visitors—parents—grand-parents—were coming to see their darling children—and might be alarmed at finding young ladies—such grown up young ladies! Such worldly examples!—You do, do understand my dear, dear beautiful creatures? They want 'em to live like oysters and yet be prepared for the world! Lud, oh lud protect me from parents! But you *do* understand? Just until I come and release you! Oh deary me, I hear a carriage already! I must fly!'

Judith did not understand at all, but she certainly had no wish to intrude on parents visiting their daughters, and she and Evergreen contented their curiosity by looking down from their sitting room window, to see the carriages arrive.

There were not many of them, and each time, surprisingly, it seemed to be only the father, or else the grandfather who arrived. Not a single mother, nor elder sister. And then, about ten o'clock, the carriages came back, and in three instances an elderly gentleman got back into his coach accompanied by a pupil and her box. Exactly as if they had had some grave faults to find, and were taking their granddaughters home with them!

Poor, poor Mrs. Ware! Judith thought, astonished. What ever could be wrong? Perhaps the parents—or grandparents—had found out that Mrs. Ware's teaching was more worldly than they had bargained for? Which if they had heard the least sample of a lesson could hardly have been avoided. And then a few minutes later Mrs. Ware came up the stairs to knock on Judith's door and reveal herself in floods of happy tears, patting her bosom with a lace handkerchief, and crying, 'Lud, lud what an old fool I am to be so sentimental, but how I hate to see my darlings take wing and leave me! But what can one do? It's the way of the world and nothing'll ever change it, certainly not crying over it. And now you must come downstairs and celebrate with me and the dear, dear poor marquis. When you're sad, there's only one medicine, and that's a good bumper of champagne. And then we'll have some supper, an' talk about your futures. Oh my dears! Such a future as I can see for you!'

She was so flushed it seemed very clear that she had had more than enough champagne already to lift her spirits, and Judith felt the gravest of hesitations about accompanying her downstairs. But Mrs. Ware was so joyfully and tearfully insistent, and so obviously meant to be kind, and to make up for what she called their 'imprisonment', that it was impossible to refuse.

Downstairs the marquis was waiting for them in the little parlour, bowing to them as they came in with a Versailles elegance that did not completely conceal that he too had been at the champagne for quite some time. 'Quel plaisir' he said, and began to reel off compliments until Mrs. Ware grasped him by the elbows and sat him down again.

Both the servants seemed almost as elevated as their mistress and the marquis, Albertine's eyes snapping, black as black cherries, Harry with his page's cap tilted to one side, bringing in more champagne in ice buckets, and a great silver dish of oysters. Albertine positively hiccupping as she filled Judith's tumbler, while Judith tried not to allow her astonished disapproval to show itself too openly.

'Here's to love!' Mrs. Ware cried. 'I mean—Here's to

marriage! And love along with it! An' may our three darlings who've just left us never forget the dear, dear Academy where they learned to be worthy of their futures! To love! To handsome gentlemen of fortune! To happiness!' And, when the two servants were gone, 'What wouldn't I give to be fifteen again! Eh, monsieur?'

'You are fifteen in your heart, madame' the marquis said, 'and that is the important place to be still youthful.'

'There are other places too, you wicked old creature, and well you know it, but oh dear, one's as young as one feels I always say, and I do declare tonight I feel so young I could—what am I saying, what will Miss Mortimer think of us? So stern looking, you quite frighten me, you'd frighten any poor gentleman to death if you looked at him like that!'

Her genteel accent had frayed at the edges, and her face was taking on an increasingly vulgar colouring, pale red patches beginning to appear on her cheeks like ill-applied rouge. The marquis, by contrast, looked as if he would remain gentleman-like in manner and appearance even if he was stretched speechless on the carpet.

'I'll tell you about life' Mrs. Ware said, her widow's cap slipping forward and threatening to fall off. ''s a battle. An' I know how to win it.' She winked and squinnied and emptied her tumbler. 'This is the stuff f'r living! Puts blood in you. Pu's bubbles in you! Makes you float, eh, y'old rip?' Giving the marquis a tremendous nudge that threatened to stretch him flat then and there. He bowed his compliments and simpered, only his glazed eyes showing that he was no longer truly part of the conversation. 'He don't eat enough, that's his trouble. Eggs and chickens and muck like that's all he eats. Beefsteak an' claret, tha's what a body wants. Good bloody beef, an' two-three bottles a night.' She refilled her tumbler and emptied it almost at a swallow. 'I was a three-bottle girl in my day, you wou'n't think it to see me now, sipping an' tasting. But in my day! Lord save us I could put it down. An' *hold* it down, which is more'n my poor major could do. No more bottom than a schoolgirl, he ha'nt. But me! I could tell you stories, 'bout me an' Crispin, that was a dear, dear frien' o' mine—Crispin's Eve they called her—' She seemed to recollect herself for a moment, perhaps at the sight of

Judith's face. 'Bu' what you want to think about's the future. *I* know! What young thing wants to hear 'bout twenty years ago, the times of Methusalem? Now, what a won'erful future you two can have if you'll listen to me and be guided by an old woman as knows life. The girls as have gone through my hands! An' the fortunes they've come to! An' I can do the same for you, no matter you're turned eighteen. That look o' yours, oh lud, how it'd turn some old fellows' knees to water! They'd kneel down in front of you an' if you kicked 'em they'd beg for more.'

'Mrs. Ware! What are you saying?' It could not be true! She wanted to run from the room, with Evergreen. And could not, as if she was turned to stone by the old woman's dreadful jollity. Mrs. Ware winked and laid her finger against her pink nose and looked unutterably cunning and rakish.

'An' then, our li'l Evergreen here, oh my stars an' garters, there's a different story al'ogether. Dress her up like a dolly, chase her round the house, Lord save us the games an old chap could play with her! An' its games old fellows need, that's the secret, that's—' She hauled herself up all standing. 'There's my tongue running 'way with me, an' the marquis snoring with his eyes open an' his mouth shut, lud knows how he does it, learned it in court he says, an' never go lavatory neither, fear o' missing something. The stories he cou' tell you!' Waving her tumbler about, refilling it, the champagne spilling and bubbling like a drunken fountain. 'Jus'—just you pu' yourselves in my hands, an' you'll bless the day ol' Jem Hughes brough' you here, I promise you.' Giggling, holding the last of the magnums upside down over the marquis's unconscious head, while Judith sat rigid with horror, grasping Evergreen by the arm.

'Go—must go—up t' bed' Mrs. Ware said. Staring down at the marquis with a fond contempt. 'Frenchies! No bottom! But I do like a gen—gent'manlike man about the place, no marrer how wore out.' She peered about her as if she was searching for Judith and Evergreen. 'Help me to bed, girls. Cripsin's—Crispin's Eve! There was a girl cou' tell you 'bout life. Hold me steady. ducks! Bloody Frenchies.'

Supporting her up the stairs.

'Lud, wha' strong girls you are. Whoops! G'night, g'night my pretties, Go' save the King!' Clambering into her room as if the floor was sloping upwards at a steep incline. Falling onto her pretty bed with its daffodil yellow flowers and snowy curtains. Her mouth sagging open. She began to snore.

'We must leave here tomorrow!' Judith whispered, as soon as they were safe in their own rooms, the door double locked. 'This is—I do not know what kind of house it is, but we cannot stay here another day!' And yet it was not possible, not thinkable! No matter what kind of woman Mrs. Ware might be, the pupils could not—They were only children! The beautiful, thin child with the dreadful voice—she was not yet twelve! And she had been one of the three who had been taken away tonight! A beggar child——What grandfather could she have had? Yet how could—how could anyone? Standing in the middle of their sitting room, afraid to undress, to go to bed. And as for sleeping! They must stay awake until tomorrow—she must stay awake, watch over——Where would they go? Where? And the money to pay this—this *woman?* How much would she ask? And Robert—how should she let him know? In case—in case he——What would they do?

She went to bed at last, holding Evergreen tight in her arms, and woke to hear knocking at the outer door of their sitting room. Albertine's voice calling 'Madame! Madame! There is a Monsieur Barnabas arrived. He is waiting down in the parlour with Madame Ware.'

Robert! And the morning sun shining through the curtains. Robert come! All the nightmares of last night already fading, faded, gone into nonsense. An old woman who drank too much——

'Help me!' she cried to Evergreen. 'Cannot you do up my buttons faster? And my hair brush!' Snatching it from Evergreen, only to drive her hair into such tangles that she must sit quiet again and let Evergreen brush and knot it for her, her own hands trembling as she held them tight clasped together in her lap. She would be ill. She would not be able to speak sensibly to him. What would she—what would he——She would not be able to walk down the stairs. 'Stay here' she whispered. 'Do not move from this room until I come back for you.'

Running down the stairs. And then, the last flight, walking, very soberly. Rationally. Her heart beating as if the next moments were to settle all her future.

Chapter 20

'That woman's a whore mistress!' Robert said furiously, as soon
as she was safely beside him in the hackney coach. 'What in
heaven's name—couldn't you see it?'

'I—I guessed—'

'You guessed? And you're staying there? Have you no sense at
all? You're not fit—'

'If you have come all this way to be rude to me——'

'Judith! Let me feel you're really there! I've been half frantic.
I've had such a journey up to find you as I don't want repeated.'

'And I—' she whispered. 'I have——'

She would have liked to touch his hair. But he had her hands
imprisoned, holding them tight against his coat; a heavy, green
cloth coat for travelling that yet managed to have something
about it of the sea. She would have liked to lay her head against
it.

'I—we—we must leave that house, I know' she said. 'It was
only last night that—that I suspected—and I am still not sure.
She is very kind. She—she does drink a great deal, I know that.'

'She does more than drink. Let me see you, let me open your
cloak, touch you. Judith, you're coming with me. To Leyden. No,
don't answer, don't try to think. You are. And to-night—I've a
friend here, my father's friend who'll give us a room—and we'll
get married, lord knows how you get married in a day, but we'll
do it. I have the ring, look.' Taking it from an inner pocket,
holding it up in the light from the glasses. 'What do they say?
With this ring——' He took her hand, pushed the ring onto her
third finger. It did not fit, and he had to change it to her
fore-finger. For a moment she resisted, as if it was an omen of
ill-fortune, to change like that. And then he was kissing her. The

coachman's grey cloth coat in front of her eyes, the glasses on either side of them as if to permit all London to see that she was loved. 'You must not! In a hackney coach!'

'What do we care? Lord above, the fuss you left behind in Woodham, disappearing like that! Like a hornets' nest. They'd been to Martha already and badgered her sick, the poor old wretch. Threatening her with gaol and the devil knows what for helping you.'

'She did not tell where I am?'

'She swears she didn't, and what the deuce does it matter if she did? We'll be out of England in two more days. My grandmother's waiting for you. I told her I'd be carrying you off if you wouldn't come willing.'

'Like Mr. Gaultrip?' Smiling, touching his sleeve, It could not be true, she was only imagining, dreaming. It was not possible that she should leave England, live in a strange country with this man. But to dream of it, just for these minutes. 'You were going to carry me off as you carried him away? Poor, poor old man!'

'No!' His face suddenly greyish in the dull winter light, a stranger's face. 'Don't——' Trying to cover his strangeness, lifting her hand, putting it against his cheek. 'We'll not think of anyone else but ourselves, not be like anyone else. Don't talk, don't say anything, let me kiss you again, shhh.'

I am going to faint, she thought. No one can be so happy! She tried to free herself, to say 'Evergreen—we cannot—I cannot—two days!—it is impossible——' But he did not allow her to finish any word. The post-chaise drew up in a strange, empty street, the kind that no one seems to live in, the houses abandoned. A smell like the sea, although the sea must be miles and miles away. Smell of mud and fish and rotted things driven ashore by the wind. And yet also of distance, of distant cleanness. All that in a breath of air in a grey, muddy street, sloping down towards nothing. And then she realised that, that nothingness was the river. They were in a lane running down to some kind of wharf. The houses leaning against one another with age, and decay. Like old sailors on wooden legs. She stood waiting, while Robert told the hackney driver to come back for them, she did not hear exactly when. Thought, I should not allow the coach to be sent away at all, it can only take five minutes to look at lodgings surely? I should not allow it. And Evergreen—I have left her there. I should not—not even for an hour. Not even by daylight.

But she said nothing, and felt a stillness inside herself. As if she knew already what must happen, and was glad, prepared and calm about it. She looked back up the lane, and a coach, black painted, blinds drawn, crossed the top of it, seemed to hesitate. One of the blinds was moved aside, a face peered, and for an absurd second it looked to her like Mr. Massingham, as if she was being haunted by him. Then the coach was gone, and she was left shivering, and half laughing at herself, and still shivering.

'You can turn at the bottom' Robert was saying. The coachman lifted his whip handle in salute, and drove on down the slope, his braked wheels grinding their iron tyres on the cobbles.

'It doesn't look much from outside but its a safe spot. What's the matter? Have you seen a ghost?' Putting his arm round her, whispering against her hood, 'Are you afraid?' And as he said it she was afraid, so frightened that she could not stand without his holding her.

'We cannot stay here! You must give me time to think! And Evergreen—she is—we have left her there!' But the door had already opened on a heavy chain. A man staring at them, recognising Robert, greeting him in what she imagined must be Dutch.

'Captain Schalk' Robert said. 'This is his house.' And to the Captain, 'We need a couple of rooms for two-three days. I'm bringing her to Leyden, Captain. And a young girl with us.'

Captain Schalk as low built as an ale cask. Yellow beard, fat, pale cheeks, blue eyes sunk deep as though someone had dug two fingers into unbaked dough and set a blue glass bead at the bottom of each hole. He did not seem a likely host for lovers. Nor his house a likely haven. And if its outside had looked unpromising the inside seemed worse. A smell of decay, of wet-rot and sewers, like a sweetish fog. But Robert did not appear to notice it, and he was already guiding her after Captain Schalk who walked like a barrel rolling, his fat round shoulders brushing first the left hand wall and then the right.

Up two flights of stairs and along a corridor, down another flight. No daylight from anywhere. A corridor that twisted, turned. More stairs, until she was as lost as if she was in a maze. And no one else there. No sounds, no light until without any

[195]

warning the Captain stopped short and she had run into him, like running into a barrel.

'Staa vast. Hier ist de kamer,' he said, rattling at a lock. Grey daylight. Furniture. She made out a bed with posts and curtains, a hearth and iron grate with no fire. She shivered again. The Captain struck flint and steel, and after a few moments had a candle lit, and then busied himself at the fire place, a huge blue rump in worn serge stuck up in the air, and the soles of his thick woollen socks. Like a caricature of the neat, pretty Albertine, lighting the fire in Judith's sitting room at Mrs. Ware's. Growling at the damp wood, the tinder.

'Godverdomme! De pikken moet me schennen!'

'We'll be snug here as sailors,' Robert said, his arm round her again, squeezing her waist. The fire began to burn, flung a throatful of smoke into the room. The Captain sat back on his heels, to gather breath, leaned forward again and blew like a gale. More smoke came in gusts. 'Agh! Dat vermaledijde vuur! Light, you devil!'

Robert pressed her into one of the chairs. It creaked with loose joints. 'It isn't luxury, but it's safe and warm.' Safe? He broke off to talk again in Dutch to the Captain. She thought she heard 'wein' among the other words and wanted to say no, no wine.

'If I could have some tea?'

'Ja, ja, immediate.' Even when the Captain was standing still he rolled by habit, from one foot to the other. Why did he wear only socks and no shoes or boots? What was he doing here in this empty house? He went, and Robert put back her hood.

I must not let him kiss me, not here, not now. But it did not seem possible to prevent him.

It was a long time before the Captain came back. He brought a tray, with a jug of something that might be tea and two cups, and a bottle of wine and glasses. But she was no longer thirsty. The Captain went again and Robert lifted her and laid her down on the bed.

'We cannot! You must not!'

'We're married' he said, 'it's all right, this is our marriage, trust me, love me.' She could not hear what he was saying, his mouth against her throat. Undressing her. He must not, must not——And she had waited for this as she had waited for him. He had drawn the blind across the skylight window, and there was only the candle flame and the fire, giving the room a semblance of comfort and secrecy and warmth. The bed smelt of damp, the curtains were heavy with it, seemed to breathe out a damp greyness. But she no longer cared, no longer thought of anything. Except that he was touching her, holding her, undressing her. Until she lay naked, and she was shivering, not with cold, but with something else, an expectation, a longing; oh, not for that act that must be suffered, that she knew of, from descriptions, from maidservants' long ago sniggerings and stories. But beyond that, as if the act was fire to go through, and beyond the fire lay—everything.

He kissed her breast, and she lay still, waiting, her eyes shut. He took her hair, laid it between her breasts like unravelled silk, kissed that, bathed his face in it, in her body, in her lap. And she lay still, and waited.

He will hurt me, she thought. I know that he will hurt me. And beyond the hurt? She felt herself trembling, felt such a beginning of sweetness as made her arch her back, clench her teeth against it. Lie still, wait. Be hurt.

'You must not' she whispered. Tried to fend him away, and her arms had no power in them, her hands would not obey her. She began to twist herself from side to side, like a hare driven towards the net, crying out 'no, no!' until she could not think or see, only try to roll face downwards, protect herself. And a last cry of resistance, a long shuddering, as her body lost itself, lost its identity. Then pain. The pain unbearable, unending. Ended.

She lay as if she had run a race. The pain dying. Until at last she could lie still, his arms round her, his face against her hair. Asleep. One part of her mind still shocked and puritan. And the other, the traitor, lying in a warm, moist hollow of tenderness, like a child in the womb, safe, loved, held. All questions gone, melted away. Who he was. What kind of man. Her kind. This kind.

This is love, she thought. This quiet. Now. And for him? What a strange, strange way of taking pleasure. Is it always like that? But it cannot be, or no woman would endure it twice. But that other——She grew ashamed as she thought of it, and felt her body stirring again.

'Robert?' she whispered, 'are you asleep?' Stroked his face, his shoulders, felt the warmth and hollows of his back, the deep valley of the spine between his shoulder blades, the nape of his neck, drawing his head down so that he could kiss her throat, her breasts, felt her mind grow dizzy with wanting. And the pain still there, so that it would not be possible to feel the pleasure, find it again. But only to be kissed, fondled, touched, loved, to feel her body, feel it like something not entirely hers, yet part of her, like riding bare back—like——

Like nothing but itself, that quivering, trembling, melting of one's flesh, twist and arch and stretch and cry out, gasp with the impossibility of surviving, enduring such pleasure. Something must end, break, it cannot go on, and does, and does. Her body bent like a bow, like a bridge, crying out, oh no, no! no more, I cannot, oh I cannot! And one can.

She lay still again, face down, driven, dead. One's skin sweats pleasure she thought, and tasted it, her own soft, smooth flesh against her mouth. Drowned with pleasure. His arm across her shoulders, warm and heavy on her.

'I knew' he whispered. 'That first night I knew.'

'How could you tell?' Whispering against her own flesh, tasting it, stretching down her legs, moulding her nakedness against his naked side. To lie naked by candlelight and talk of love, whisper of meeting, thoughts, dreams.

'Your mouth. That's what tells. And under your eyes, the underlids, they tell. The way they swell a bit. Take her, they said to me. Don't listen to what she says, or what way she looks at you. Just take her. You were made for loving, d'you know that? Lift your arm.' Kissing the side of her breast, down her ribs, the softness of her waist, the curve of her hip, down the back of her leg to the hollow behind her knee. Smoothing, stroking, lifting one leg, the other, lifting her body by the hips as if she was a lay figure, had no will or life of her own.

'Is this really what marriage is?'

'This an' more. So much more as you can't imagine yet.'

My puritan is dead, she thought, my traitor is become Queen.

What can a new Queen do to celebrate her coronation? Let everyone be happy! No one sad, nor cold, nor hungry, nor lost! How I shall love Evergreen! And Martha, and Solomon, and Mrs. Rigg and——

But I shall not be here to make them happy! I shall be in

Leyden! She sat up, heard him protest between sleep and drowsing.

'We cannot go to Leyden! Martha——'

'Lie down. Be quiet. Damn Martha.'

'But——'

His arm pulled her down, his hand silenced her. Like this? In Leyden? In that house, with the good grandmother, and Evergreen? Nothing but this all night? In the days she would dream of him, and wait, and listen for his feet, the door opening.

And Mr. Gaultrip! She would be able to——

She sat up again, quick with excitement. 'Where is Mr. Gaultrip? Is he near Leyden? We must help him, we must go to see him and arrange——'

'Don't think about him' Robert said, his voice muffled against arm and pillow, drowsed and muzzy. 'He's——'. He lifted his head to face her as if he had spoken without knowing what he was saying, and knew now. The word he had not said echoing in the room. The word she had known already. Known ever since——

'Dead?' She stared at him, still not believing, not wanting to believe. 'He—cannot be!'

'I said don't think about him! Lie down' He whispered. 'Please.'

'Don't touch me! *Is* he dead?' Looking at him. At the shadows in his eyes. 'He *is!*' No longer needed to look at him to know it. Had known it from the first day. 'How did he die?' she whispered. 'Tell me! How?' She had gripped the quilt of the bed, dragged it between them. 'You drowned him!' As if she could see it happening. They would have tied chains to him, rolled him overboard, still alive. She knew it, knew it. From old stories that they told. Of the chop-backs, of all the murders. And I have done this! her mind screamed. I have murdered him, and lain with his murderer!

She crept backwards from him, the quilt still held against her. Her mouth numb. And she had sent to call his murderers! Come and kill! She looked at the bed as if the hollow of it was a pool of blood. And there was blood there, bright crimson on the grey sheet. She thought she would faint. Caught at her clothes, dragged her gown round her, her other clothes bundled in her hands. Back towards the door.

'Don't move! Don't touch me!' Murderer! She had seen from the beginning what he was, and still had——

'I didn't know!' he shouted. 'Judith, I swear it, I didn't know! Only yesterday, I only knew for certain yesterday!'

Throwing himself towards her. She began to slam the door against him, and the edge of it caught his forehead. As if she had hit him with an axe. She saw him falling as the door closed, stayed for half a second listening, her heart pounding. Ran. Along the dark corridor in her bare feet. Down flights of stairs, feeling her way, hand against cold, damp-oozing walls. No sound of his following. Doorways. More stairs. Trying to remember. Corners, passages, light from a window, dark again. Until there was a sort of daylight growing, she was in a passage ending in a door, a fan-light. Drawing the bolts, unfastening the chain. A voice called 'Gegroet, juffer!' The heavy softness of stockinged feet. 'Wat doe je daar?' And in the far distance Robert's voice, muffled by the turns and twists of corridors, flights of stairs; crying "Judith! JUDITH! *Come back!*' But the door was open, she was in the lane. Turn right, uphill. Running. Into the street above. A carriage. Black. A hackney? If it was! If it would take her home! To Mrs. Ware, Evergreen, oh please God!

Someone gripped hold of her. She began struggling; Robert, the Captain, come behind her. Managed to turn her head, and it was the groom Chevell, William's father. Two, three others.

'Please, please, what are you doing? Let go of me! Help me, someone is following me!'

She did not know whether she cried aloud, or not. And the groom was smiling, lifting his hand. 'That's for my son' he said and hit her so hard that the world turned crimson, her knees sagged, they were carrying her towards the coach. Pushing her in, lifting her like a sack.

And in the coach, Mr. Massingham.

'Why, Judith!' he said, in mock surprise. 'Running in the street half naked, in broad day? This is truly sad. But we shall have you cured. In the end. It was kindly in your lover to lead us to you.'

The others climbing in. Hands gripped her head, thumbs pressed into her cheeks so that her teeth must open. Mr. Massingham held a bottle against her mouth, a sweetish, sickly liquid flowing over her tongue. She choked, gasped for air, had to swallow. The groom Chevell hit her again. 'Bedlam whore!' he shouted. 'And my son crippled for ye!'

'No, no' Mr. Massingham said, 'there's no need for that. Leave it to the madhouse keepers. They'll see to her.'

Cold leather against her back where her gown was undone. Mr. Massingham holding her shift against his mouth, looking at her over the white folds of cloth. His eyes seeming to grow larger, and then far away.

'They'll take good care of you, my dear. And then we shall see which you prefer. Them. Or me.'

Chapter 21

She could not move her head.

Nor her arms. She seemed to be sitting on the floor of an empty room. Her back against the wall. A stench of urine. Why? Where was it? She could not remember anything, except the nightmare. A coach, Mr. Massingham, William Chevell's father. A vile taste in her throat as if she had been sick. She wanted to get sick again.

An empty room. Stinking.

Evergreen! She tried to sit up, and she could not. Something hurt her neck, as though there was a collar there, an iron ring. Nothing else in the room but herself, the vile smell, a twilight that seemed to filter down to the floor like pallid dust. And a blanket. Dull grey and threadbare. Covering her legs. Straw. Straw under her. She could feel the prick of it against bare flesh.

I am naked! she thought. And the nightmare came back. Held upright. Someone lifting her gown over her head. Struggling, almost falling out of their grasp. Then nothing. She moved one leg, trying to push it from under the blanket, to look at it. But she could only raise her knee, she could not move her foot sideways. Something was fastened round her ankle. Like an iron cuff. When she tried harder to move her leg there was the sound of iron. She managed to turn her head, at least enough to look down at her hands. One hand. Three or four links of chain, fastening a handcuff to an iron bar that ran an inch or so above the bare boards and the straw.

The skin of her wrist looked raw as if she had fought against the handcuff and torn herself. The sickness faded, and she felt only the torn skin. And then her throat. If she tried to turn her head sharply the pain grew worse. She was awake! Chained up in a room! In Bedlam! She began to scream.

After a few moments there were screams that answered. A knocking against the wall behind her head. A voice calling 'Who's there? I'm Jenny Wren, Jenny Wren. Save me. Save me!'

Feet running, clattering on wooden stairs, doors kicked open, the sounds of blows. Without knowing it she stopped her own screaming and lay quiet, like an animal that hears the hunter. Her door was grinding open, heavy timber crashing back against the wall. A woman standing there, panting. Thick with fat. Carrying a heavy wooden club. She came waddling in. Black greasy skirts. White face like suet. Grey strings of hair under a black cotton cap.

'So yer starting?' She came close, leaned down. Judith opened her mouth. Said nothing, held by the woman's eyes. Slate grey, flat in the fat white roundness of her face like an insect's eyes. Nothing human in them except hatred. 'I'll learn yer to scream.' She pushed her club into Judith's blanket, jerked it away. Left her naked, lying on the straw.

'For God's pity! What is this place! I am not mad, someone has brought me here, told lies about me! Let me——'

'I 'ates loonies' the woman said. 'I 'ates the look of 'em.'

'I am not mad! Let me——'

'But I breaks 'em.'

'Let me up, I tell you!'

The woman caught her by the hair, wrenched her head. 'I got my methods. Now let's 'ave this off of yer afore it gets filthied up.' She took something from a pocket inside her skirt and began to cut. The sounds of a razor hacking at thick skeins of hair.

Crying 'No No! Fetch someone, you are mad, I tell you, listen to me!'

''old still yer 'ore's get! I'll lady yer!'

The air cold against her scalp, horrifying. 'I am not mad! Stop!'

The woman did stop her cutting. She picked up her club and brought it down across Judith's shins. Judith heard herself screaming. The pain sickening, as if her legs were broken. Her knees jerking up, trying to save herself, the leg cuffs tearing her ankles. 'I told yer to cut yer bloody row. A couple o' days and I'll 'ave yer licking the floor.' She finished shaving Judith's head. When she had gathered up the hair, and stuffed it into a cotton bag hanging at her waist, she said, 'Now we knows one another.

[203]

So don't let's 'ave no trouble. Else yer knows what's coming, don't yer? Yer ain't such a loony as yer don't know that.'

Still sobbing with the pain. The woman was going out. She tried to call after her. 'Tell someone, tell——' And then as she saw the door closing, heard it grind shut, 'Cover me up! Don't leave me naked! Send someone——'

Bolts. Lock.

Still the nightmare, it must be. Could not——'Evergreen!'

Losing consciousness.

She thought that Mr. Massingham was there. Where the woman had stood. Looking down at her, holding a lace handkerchief to his nose. His eyes creased with satisfaction. Smiling.

'I am going away' he said. 'Into Devonshire. Do you remember? We were to get married there.' He held his hand in front of her, opened it, the fingers holding the lace handkerchief, a gold ring lying in the palm. 'What is this?'

'I—I—' As if there were curtains of mist drawing across her mind. 'Where is Evergreen?'

'Did you lie with him? In that house? Become his whore?' The drink they had given her, the laudanum. Like mist curling up from the ground, white, milky thick, hiding everything.

She woke in the dark, shivering. Like going from one nightmare to another. She began to cry out, and stopped herself. Her whole body was shaking with the cold. She had slipped down the wall, the ring fastening her neck had slipped down whatever held it, and she lay stretched out, only her head bent up and cramped.

There was a knocking on the wall behind her head. She thought it had been going on for a long time, a voice calling. 'I'm Jenny, Jenny Wren. Pretty Jenny. Who are you? Please tell me, who are you?'

I am dying, she thought.

She was so cold she was no longer shivering. Far away in the house someone was shouting. After a long time she heard footsteps, climbing the stairs. A door crashing. Silence. Dark. 'Pretty Jenny. Pretty Jenny!'

She did not know if she slept or was awake. But it had been dark, and was now light. The same naked room. Her body naked. The walls were leper grey. Like the floor. The way her head was lying she could see her breast, the details of the skin. Blue, rough with cold. It seemed not to belong to her. Beyond it, the grey wooden floor boards. The door. Spy hole. Iron. The sound of bolts grinding. She tried to concentrate, to see what was happening.

A man was standing over her, enormously, impossibly tall from where she lay, the way her head was held. White silk stockings, black kneebreeches. The skirts of a blue frock coat. And a flowered waistcoat, a gold chain. A blue satin stock. Above that, infinitely high up, a small round face, eye glasses winking, the edge of a curled wig, a black tricorn hat. The man bent down, his nose like a birds' thin beak, dipping towards her.

'Well, well, well, and how are we to-day? HOW ARE WE TO-DAY?' Raising his voice as if he believed her to be deaf. 'Bad, bad girl! Exposing yourself! And such a hectic look! D'you mark it, Poll? She has too much blood in her. There's the problem. But we'll soon set that to rights. Lift her up, Poll. Dear me what a mess. But we must not be angry, no, no. Purity. PURITY!' He cried, 'That's what you've come to me for. PURITY!' The fat woman grasped her under the arms, lifted her. Iron against iron behind her neck, iron dragging at her wrists and ankles.

'I am not mad! Are you a doctor? Listen to me, I am not mad, I was brought here——'

'Dear, oh dear, were you brought here? And you're not mad?' Snapping his fingers. Spectacles glinting, bending over her. 'You hear, Poll? Is that not terrible?'

'Terrible' Poll said, wrenching Judith's head straight.

'We must fetch the constable and tell him. Should you like us to do that?' the doctor said.

'Please, fetch someone! I am not mad, I can prove——I can show you——'

'Fetch the constable at once, Poll. Oh dear, oh dear. Open your mouth.'

Poll digging her thumbs into Judith's cheeks as they had done in the carriage. The man whipped out a bottle, a spoon, poured drops. The spoon choking her, far back in her throat. A bitter, oily taste. 'And now the laudanum. Oh, what teeth she has! Mind your thumbs, Poll.' Another bottle. The same sweetish taste, thick and sickening. 'There. That'll quiet you. And then you'll empty out. Clean bowels are half the battle. Mens sana in corpore sano. Nothing like a purged body for a troubled mind. You'll see.

Now cover her up, Poll. Never uncover yourself girl. And she'll need bleeding. Oh, how much blood she has! A sad case. AREN'T YOU A SAD CASE?' Raising his voice on the question, shouting down to her, twinkling. 'Morbid, nymphomanic tendencies from birth' he said, lowering his voice again. 'Not a doubt of it. You see the eye, Poll? We must have Mr. Barforth in, he'll like to see this one. That mouth, that eye! There's the key. Sensuality. Sensuality in a woman, there's the path to madness. First lust. Then madness. The true Dementia Femina. A case for Nymphotomy if ever I saw one. But she might die of it, it's always a risk unhappily, at her age. But we'll wash it out of her. Aqua purificans.'

'I beg of you, listen to me, I am not mad, I am quite sane, as sane as you are. It is only—you have——I am so——YOU HAVE DRUGGED ME AGAIN!'

'There, there! The constable is coming, isn't he, Poll? Oh, you're a lucky young woman to have been brought to me. Isn't she fortunate?'

'Oh yus, doctor, that she is. Werry fort'nit.'

Their voices fading. Dreams. And then such a stab of pain as made her scream, wake, half wake out of her drugged sleep, try to clench her body together, bring up her knees, twist herself. Her stomach on fire. Gripe on gripe, muscles contracting, burning, her ankles held fast. Tearing at them, wrenching her legs against the iron, twisting her head, trying to scream 'I am dying, help me!'

Someone was there. Kicking her. A flood of water, ice-cold, drenching.

'Shut yer gob or I'll kill yer!'

'Jenny Wren, I'm Jenny, I can sing, I'll sing for you. Cherry Ripe, Cherry Ripe.'

'I am dying.'

'Then die, sod yer. Empty yer gut, that's all it is, yer bloody purge. Empty yourself.'

'For God's sake, help me.'

The woman was gone.

The griping came again.

Chapter 22

She lost count of time. Days. Weeks. Only light and dark. Now dark. Now greyish light. Sometimes she was fed. Gruel out of a bowl, Poll feeding her. How long had gone by? She tried to think. Of how long she had been there, of where she was, of whether they meant to kill her. But it was very difficult to think of anything. Sleep. Darkness. Dreams. Griping.

A man there with a kind of board resting on his knees. A drawing board. Sitting on a stool in front of her. A long, gaunt face, a black jaw. Squinting at her. Scratch of pencil, squinting, scratching, tilting the long, bony, blacksheep face to one side. Tilting it to one side and then the other.

'Oh capital, capital!' he said. A sheep's voice. 'Caapital, caaapital.'

'Didn't I tell you, Barforth? Such a head, such an eye. And the mouth, mind you capture the mouth. And look at the body, you see it?' Lifting her blanket away. 'Tsk, tsk, tsk, how they bruise themselves, they injure themselves with their chains, you cannot prevent 'em. But count the ribs, see the flesh begin to lose its terrene heaviness, its female exuberance, and reveal the skeletal purity. ADAM'S RIB, THAT'S WHAT WE WANT TO SEE! Not flesh. Not soft sensuality. Not traps for man's weakness. The bone! A bone harp for the Etheric Air to play upon, the Etheric Substance to reclothe.'

Dark.

She became too weak to lift her head. The tall, thin man feeling her pulse, her ribs. Undoing one of the cuffs that held her wrists, lifting her hand, dropping it.

'Lift your arm!'

She could not.

The same unfastening for her left ankle. She could not move that, either. Could only bend her knee a little.

They unfastened all the chains, the collar, lifted her up, carried her out of the room, down a corridor. Her foot banged against the wall, but she did not feel it. Into another room, her shin scraping against the doorway.

'In with her Poll.'

Water, ice cold, deep. Hands pulling her upright, sitting. Fastening straps round her. Water up to her throat. A great wooden tub. They fastened a lid over it that left only her head uncovered. Wooden lid. She could see the cracks between the planks that formed it. Blackish wood. Rust brown nail heads. I am in a bath, she thought. Remembered something, long ago. Evergreen. Bath. She had fought against it. How foolish she had been. Clean bath. Cold. But she was always cold. It did not matter.

They were going away. Gone.

It grew so cold that she felt it. Became aware of her body. She began to shiver.

She tried to get out of the water. But she could not move. Only bruised her knees against the underside of the timber cover.

Ice cold. Her body lost all feeling again. Had she died?

'There's a nice clean girl! Look at her, Poll! Even the smell's gone! That's your water for you, Aqua Pura. The basis of life. We shall only need her collar from this on. What a cleansed and mortified body! Who'd recognise it that knew it in its garb of arrogance? No lover would paddle it now, eh, Poll? Bone and spirit, there's the goal of our striving. Easy. Here we are.'

Laying her down.

'Jenny Wren, Jenny Wren, pretty Jenny, good Jenny.'

Gruel. Purge. But the purges no longer served, there was nothing to purge out. Another bath. Was it the next day? Next week? There was no way of telling. Dreams. Robert. Francis. Mr. Gaultrip. The Dutch Captain leading her to an altar, she was being married. But Mr. Carteret would not marry her. 'WHORE!' he shouted, 'Lustful whore!' And the congregation took up the cry, began to stone her, fling filth and stones and mud at her. 'Whore, whore, whore!'

Running from them. Evergreen with her. And then no one.

They took off her collar, and she lay on the floor under her blanket. She could move her head. Roll it from side to side. But it was a great effort.

'Who's there, who's there? I'm Jenny Wren, I can sing, shall I sing for you? Cherry Ripe, Cherry Ripe, ripe I cry.'

She thought Evergreen was there. Holding out her hands towards her, crying 'Help me! Save me!' But when she tried to touch her Evergreen faded, grew smaller, seemed to be drawn further and further away. 'Evergreen!' Searching the corners of the cell, feeling the walls for a crack where she might have slipped through. Trying to climb up to the window, to see if Evergreen was outside. But she could not reach the bars.

Sometimes Robert came to her. She did not know if he was really there, or if she was only thinking of him. There did not seem to be any difference. Things, people, moved in and out of her mind. Perhaps there was nothing else but what was inside her head. Even the cell, the doctor, Poll. Perhaps she had imagined them all? Imagined herself. Her whole existence. How could one know? Her knees seemed real, her hands. The chains, lying empty by the far wall. When Robert came again she asked him if he was real, but he did not answer her.

She crawled into a corner, where her mother was, curled herself up against her, clung to her hand. But it turned to bone, she was lying against bones. The smell of the room had become a smell of corpses, a charnel house.

One day, it must be daytime, there was light from the barred window, they brought in Jenny Wren. Dressed in a blanket, her head pushed through a hole in it. Like me, Judith thought, she is dressed like me. And she crouched into her corner, afraid of what they were going to do. But they did nothing. They left Jenny in the middle of the floor and went away. Except that they were spying through a hole in the door. She could hear them. Hear their whispering and laughter. Soft, hidden laughter, but not quite hidden.

Jenny had arms like sticks. She was small, and bald, her eyes sunk into great hollows. Her head like a skull. She lifted up her blanket and showed herself, her nakedness. 'I'm Jenny Wren' she whispered. 'Pretty Jenny. Good Jenny. Jenny's quiet. Jenny can sing.'

She began to sing *Cherry Ripe*, her voice cracked like an old, small bell, cheap metal. Came closer to Judith. Judith made herself as small as possible. Jenny put out a stick arm, her hand like a twig, and touched Judith's head. Scratched at it. 'Angel's feathers' she said. She rubbed and scratched. 'Who are you?'

Judith did not answer her. Hid her eyes. Jenny sat down on the floor and took Judith's hand. 'I'm not really a woman' she whispered. 'I'm an angel, like you. You mustn't believe I'm a woman because I'm pretty. He wouldn't like that.'

'Poll is too fat' Jenny whispered again. 'Sssssshhh, she mustn't hear, she'd fetch the constable. Doctor thinks the constable is good and kind, but he isn't, he's horrid, he beats my shins, look!' Her shins were dark with bruises. 'He doesn't like me singing. He doesn't like me at all.' She made herself closer, wormed her way in between Judith's body and her upraised knees, like a child. 'But I like you. You're quiet. Oh, I was a wicked one, I was fat, I used to lie in my husband's arm and he'd fondle me. But he liked my sister better, he liked to fondle her too and I was angry with her. I was very wicked. I clawed her face. Poor Jenny, poor Jenny, no one loves poor Jenny. Shall I sing?'

They are spying on us, Judith thought. Listening. But I shall not say anything.

'God hates us' Jenny whispered, 'did you know? We smell of flesh, that's why he hates us. We're fallen angels.'

After an hour or two they took her away. But they brought her back the next day. Some time—when was it?—they brought in her straw and said she was to share the room with Judith.

'Two guineas a week!' Poll shouted. 'Yer don't think yer can 'ave a 'ole room to yerself for that, do yer? Kiss the floor yer bitch. KISS IT!'

Jenny knelt down and kissed the floorboards, licked them.

'Now you, you 'ore!'

Judith crouched where she was, hugged her knees. The woman Poll did not have her club with her. She came and kicked Judith in the side, knocked her over. 'KISS IT!'

No, Judith thought. Not angry, not frightened. Not even puzzled. Only saying 'no' in her mind. God hates us, she thought. Jenny is right. It is God's doing, all of this. The woman gave up kicking her, shouted 'FILTHY 'ORE!' Went away.

Jenny bent down beside her and tried to click her fingers like the doctor. 'There's a naughty bad girl' she said.

In a way it was better to be with someone. They had two

blankets and somehow warmed one another when they slept. She watched Jenny for days and days before she spoke to her. Watched her when Jenny did not know it. When they were lying down holding one another for warmth. When Jenny was singing. She seemed to know only the one song.

I could teach her other songs, Judith thought, but I shall not, she might make use of them, you could not tell what people might use against one. It was more frightening now that she knew that she herself had not invented everything. One could not tell what would happen.

The baths were terrible, and yet after them one was clean. When she was dry, had dried herself with the scrap of cloth that Poll gave her, or with the straw of her bed; when the soddenness had worked its way out of her skin and the skin stretched tight again over her bones, it seemed to shine with cleanness. She was very fond of it, and when Jenny was not looking, when she was sure that no one was spying through the small hole in the door she stroked her skin, kissed it. I love you, she told it. God hates you but I love you.

She thought about it in the cold baths, to take her mind from the pain of the coldness. If one hated God enough one got warm, felt warm. The branch of the tree outside the window had put on leaves. Birds sat on the branch and sang. And in the cell the light seemed to last much longer, and the dark much less. Jenny had stopped singing and spent most of her days sitting against the wall. She was always coughing, although there was colour in her cheeks now, not much, but a little; patches of pale, pale pink, as if she was flowering with the spring. A dry, small cough that went on all day and all night.

Sometimes the doctor came in to remake their minds from the Etheric Substances surrounding them.

'What is woman?'
'Carnality and lust.'
'Good, oh good! Marvellous! What must a woman become?'
'Cleansed and humble.'
'Better and better! What is sanity?'
'A purified mind.'
'What is health?'
'A purified body.'
'Wonderful! You have overtaken Jenny, you are on the Path,

you are beginning to creep, soon we shall have you totter upright, one day you shall walk in the pure light of sanity and goodness, a rectified mind. JENNY, SHE IS OVERTAKING YOU! PAY ATTENTION!' Clicking and springing, bouncing up and down with joy, blue coat and black breeches, silver buckles, black tricorn hat that he never took off, as if his visits to the house were too fleeting for that. She would hear his voice in other rooms, crying 'Purity! Aqua pura! Oh, marvellous!'

The next time Poll brought Jenny in from her bath she could not speak, and lay coughing blood. Her body was so cold during the night that Judith shrank away from it. Like ice. It seemed to pulse cold out of it. She is dead, Judith thought. God has killed her at last.

In the morning they took Jenny away. Like a bundle of sticks. The doctor and Poll carrying her out in a blanket, one at each end, the doctor crying 'Tsk, tsk, tsk, just when she was recovering, and there's two guineas a week gone. I am disappointed in her.'

'AND I AM DISAPPOINTED IN YOU!' he cried when they came back, and she would not answer him. 'But Science does not become angry, does it Poll? Oh dear, oh dear!'

Poll kicked her when he was gone. With each kick it seemed as if there was a flash of light, of clarity, in Judith's mind.

'If you kill me' Judith whispered, between the spasms of trying to vomit, 'you will lose another two guineas.'

It seemed to astonish Poll so much that she stopped kicking her, and never kicked or beat her again. She even seemed afraid of her, backing out of the room, never taking her eyes off her while she was in it, to bring food, or bring out the bucket, or occasionally fling water on the floor and sweep it out of the doorway.

I will not die like Jenny, Judith promised herself. I shall not let Him kill me so easily.

They did not bring anyone else to share the room with her and she was glad of that. It was still cold, but not so bitterly cold, except when she must lie fastened in the bath. After a bath it took the night and the next day to get warm again. A kind of warmth. The light that came from the dirty, barred window was still grey as dust, but there was warmth in it and for an hour or so she could sit in the pallid remembrance of sunlight, creeping along the wall as it moved. God did not know that it came to her, or He would have prevented it. She would lift up her blanket and let the light fall on her skin. She was still fond of her skin in a distant way, but it was not hers any more. She lived inside, and only looked out of the holes in her head.

Inside, where she hid, she was very small, and had long beautiful hair. And her own beautiful smooth skin. This skin that she was looking at was filthy, stretched over bones. There were sores on her legs. Poor body, she thought. She would play with the chains and the handcuffs when she could no longer sit in the light. How little she had known then, when she was chained up.

She was playing with the chains when he came in. Mr. Massingham. Holding something to his nose. Licking his mouth. He stood still and his mouth opened wider and his hand that held the vinaigrette came away from his face. He seemd to change colour, or rather to lose all colour. And then he smiled.

'What a time we must have had' he said in a soft voice. 'Did you hear that I was married? A lady of some small fortune, a widow lady. And do you know, I have regretted it at times, thinking of you? But not now, my dear.' He licked his teeth and bent down. Lifted her blanket away. 'I think we have both learned a lesson. And there's no need to go on wasting money. You're cured Judith. And so am I. So you can go out into the world again, a cured woman. As sane as everyone. Is not he a fine doctor, our friend who has looked after you?' He held the vinaigrette to his nose, pushed a finger into her ribs. 'I used to dream of that breast, these flanks, this mount of love.' Pushing his finger here, there, against skin and bone. Touching bruises, pressing them. She did not answer, or move.

He thinks that he has done this, she thought. What a fool he is.

'And now, where is all the beauty gone? The hair, the smooth flesh? The thighs and buttocks that I thought should give me so much joy? Such a playground I meant our bed to be. But you could scare crows now, if you were set out in a field. Shall you like to be free again?'

She did not answer and he poked his finger deep into her side. 'Fresh air? No screams or shouts in the night? Shall not you like that? But where will you find food? Who will look after you? Or do you think Robert Barnabas would feed you? Would still like to take this into his bed? But he is gone away, gone out of the country.'

The doctor was there behind him, looking displeased.

'Do not go near Matcham, nor any one there' Mr. Massingham said, 'or they will have you locked up again, in prison this time. Or in Bedlam. You have never been here, do you know that? You have been wandering the streets, a poor lunatic beggar, that is what you have been doing. So do not try to tell about anyone bringing you here. It would be held to be only your lies and madness, do you understand?'

'She understands nothing' the doctor said. 'She is a wretched, obstinate case. And once she has gone from here she may come back as much as she likes, I shall not waste time on her, they may take her to the Bethlehem if she causes trouble. It is a sad, disappointing case, sir. But the path of Science is strewn with disappointments.'

'It must be. But I should prefer she did not find her way back here. There are reasons. I have no personal apprehensions but there are reasons. She has never been told your name, I trust? Nor where this house is?' He drew the doctor out of the room with him. She heard them whispering. Heard Mr. Massingham's voice rising, saying 'Very well, sir! Four guineas for the bedding, and another for bringing her away, five then. And this present week. It is a monstrous sum! But there's an end of it. We have never met one another, never heard of one another——' His voice whispering again.

What a fool he is, she thought again. Imagining he has done all this.

Chapter 23

She stood in the doorway on the corner, where the doctor had lifted her down from the hackney coach. He had asked her if there was any dictrict she had a fancy for, or any address she wanted to be put down beside. But she had not answered him, she was not going to be caught so easily as that. And the doctor had set her down here, and the coach had driven him away.

She had been quite confident until then that she would know what to do, but now she could not think of anything except to stand here and wait. She had had plans. She was certain of that, but she could no longer remember what they were. They seemed to have faded, dissolved away into a kind of mist inside her head, as she rode in the coach with the doctor. All that she could remember was that she must find Evergreen. But she could not quite remember why. And Mrs. Ware. In King Street. Robert had called her—what had it been? A whore mistress! That was it. A whore mistress! What a strange thing to be called. In King Street. But how should she find it? Without telling anyone where she was going? At least it was not cold, here on the corner, in the doorway.

It seemed to be summer although she could not see any trees, nor anything at all that was growing. Only the crossroads in front of her. Four streets. Houses with railings before them, and steps, and areas. A boy was sweeping the crossing. It had rained, and there was mud in the gutters, and a light grease of mud filmed the pavement beside her, drying slowly in the sunshine. The sky was hazy overhead. She wondered what month it was, but it did not really matter. The boy had come to her soon after she was set down from the coach, and had said something, and then looked at her skirts and laughed in a jeering way, and gone back to the other side of the road. Whenever someone well dressed came by he made a great fuss of sweeping with a broom as tall as himself. The women always gave him something, lifting their skirts to show their slippers as they followed him across where he had swept for them.

It would have been interesting to watch if she was not so frightened. She was not really afraid of him, but she was afraid of everything else. Even to stand like this in a doorway, with the open roadway in front of her, instead of being closed round by walls, and with the door locked; that was frightening. She could not tell what was going to happen. Had the doctor really meant to leave her here? Would he come back? Be angry to find her still here?

The sounds of the traffic from nearby, busier streets frightened her. The smell of freshness in the air. Everything. And most of all, the passers-by. Whenever one came close to her doorway she turned her back to him and hid her face against the door-jamb.

Why did they look at her like that? If she should ask them the way—but she did not dare. And they might follow her. Tell Mr. Massingham. She could not remember why he should want to find her again, but the idea frightened her so much that she stayed minutes together with her face turned to the door. It was painted yellow, and the paint had faded, and cracked, and begun to flake away from the greenish, older paint underneath. As if the house was abandoned, and the door had not been used for a long time.

She was glad of that. It gave her a feeling of safety to look at a locked door. To touch it with her hands. She imagined being on the other side of it. Locked in. Hidden. She would stay there for ever and no one would be able to find her. She would be completely safe.

Except that she must find——? Must find Evergreen. Must.

Two people went by, and looked at her and looked away, and began whispering. The man laughed and the woman looked back and shook her head.

Judith turned her face to the door again. They wanted to see her twitch. And they were telling each other how she smelt. She had not been aware of that before, not for a long time. But here in the street she had begun to notice it, in that strange openness of the air. She thought it was the gown they had given her. It might have been a very old one of Poll's, it was so large, and so tattered, and polished with grease. But if it had not been too wide for her it would have been much too short. As it was it hung round her in greasy folds, touching the pavement. They had given her a chemise as well, and wooden pattens.

'I am disappointed in you' the doctor had said, his voice rising. 'I AM DISAPPOINTED!' And then he had told the coachman to drive on.

A man with a gaunt, severe face and severe clothes and a black hat with a crape band round it and a crape rosette came slowly towards her, black mittens on his hands in spite of the sunshine. He peered into her face when he was close to her. She shrank away from him, hid.

'Wretched creature' he said, 'what has brought you to this state?'

She did not answer him and pressed herself into the doorway.

'But God is all merciful!' the man said. 'No one falls so low but He can stoop to pick them up, and set them on the Path. Are you hungry? Are you thirsty?'

She nodded, realising that she was both, but without showing him her twitch. Would he tell her the way to King Street?

'God has finer viands than meat and bread!' he said. 'A finer drink than the choicest vintage. Take, my child, eat of the Bread of Life! Drink of the Waters of Paradise!' There was a rustling of paper and he pushed something into her hand. She looked down at it and it was a leaflet. The man was already walking away.

'THE WAGES OF SIN. Being the True and Dreadful Story of Eliza Goodbody and how she came to be Hanged but found Salvation upon the Gallows. PRAISE BE TO OUR BLESSED SAVIOUR JESUS CHRIST.'

She could not read any more because the printing was very small, and her eyes did not seem to work as they should. The crossing sweeper boy had come up to her.

'What'd 'e give yer?'

She showed him the leaflet. She was not so afraid of him because he was small, and seemed more interested in his broom than in her. He had no shoes and stood squeezing the mud with his toes. His only clothes were a man's breeches. The knees hung down round his dirty, knobbed ankles. The waist band came up to his arm pits and was fastened over his shoulders with string. His head stuck up from the opening as if he had been stuffed into a brown jug.

'What's it say?'

She told him, and he snorted. 'I don't 'ave no time for any o' that lark. I got me crossing to look after and me fambly to keep. *I* can't go gaddin' about to 'angings.'

She wondered if he knew the way to Mrs. Ware's and if she could trust him. He had given her back the leaflet. 'If yer on the beggin' lay yer'd better not let Nosey Grimes catch yer, she'll stove yer box in. This is 'er pitch. Although you ain't done much yet. You ain't right in the attics are yer?' He made some practice sweeps in the gutter, as if to keep his hand in. A young man was walking towards them, surveying the dirty pavement through a lorgnon and wrinkling his mouth at what he saw.

'Boy' he cried. 'Is there a chair anywheres about?'

'I'll getcher a chair, Capting, 'arf a jiff there. Mind me broom' he said to Judith, and ran away like a sparrow taking wing.

'Hey by damme' the young man said to Judith, 'You look prodigious sickly.' She was holding the broom in one hand and the leaflet in the other, so that it was difficult to hide from him. She tried to hide her face with the leaflet. 'Ah! One o' those, are ye?' He took a handkerchief out of his tight sleeve and waved it gently under his nose. There was a scent of flowers from it. 'An' pretty ripe, too.' He had moved away. ' 'od rot the child, will he be all evening?' The boy came running back, two chairmen trotting after him with a sedan chair. 'Thank God! Almacks, my fine fellows, and look sharp. Wait.' He felt in the dove grey waist-coat, one pocket and then another. Threw a coin to the boy, and as an afterthought felt again and threw a coin at Judith's feet. The chairmen heaved up their poles, trotted away, their great calves bulging their dirty stockings, their thick shoulders bowed. The shilling lay in the mud like a tiny reflection of the moon. The boy came close.

'Aintcher going to pick it up?' When she did not answer he made a tentative movement, bending down, stretching his hand, and watching her at the same time, a sparrow tilt to his head, and a sparrow sharpness in his eye. The hand darted, and the shilling was gone. 'You're a queer one.' He looked at her. She could not

[218]

prevent herself from twitching. He swept thoughtfully round her feet when he had repossessed himself of the broom. 'I'll keep it for yer, it'll be safer wiv me. All right?'

She made up her mind. 'I live at Mrs. Ware's' she whispered. 'In King Street.'

'Do yer?' He had backed gently out of her reach.

'Would you take me there? You can keep the shilling if you do.'

'I got it already' he said, backing still further. He tilted his head, and pursed his lips, whistling.

'You can have this too.' She held out the leaflet.

He snorted contemptuously. 'What King Street is it, anyways? I can't go leaving me crossing. Not for long I can't.'

A carriage went by, spraying them lightly with mud, the horses glistening, the coachman glossy in green and black, with a white cockade in his hat, and two footmen behind, splendid in black and gold, and white silk, and powdered hair. Arms painted on the shining door. She thought it might be Mr. Massingham and hid herself, her face to the doorpost.

' 'ave yer done a bunk out o' somewhere?' the boy said.

'I live at Mrs. Ware's, King Street. She's a whore mistress.'

'Well, she ain't going to 'ave much use for you, if she is. Yer mean, you used to live there? Afore you got put away?'

She nodded. The boy began sweeping for a lady and a gentleman. Came back. 'Bloody 'afpenny token! So yer wants to go back to 'er? I wouldn't waste yer time if I was you.'

'What do you mean?'

'Look at yer! 'oo'd want yer back in a 'ore 'ouse, the way you are? Twitching like that! An' yer 'air! Yer'd frighten 'em.'

'Evergreen is there' she said. 'I must look after her.'

The boy snorted again, and had to spit to express his contempt. 'You? Look arter anyone? It's you as needs lookin' arter.'

'You think so? That's what they said—where I have been.'

'An' they was dead right. Gawd alive, Nosey's a bag o' brains compared to you, an' she ain't much. Watch out, you better dive off, 'ere she comes.' He backed away, making a pantomine of running, jerking his thumb to where a creature was shuffling towards them. Judith stayed in her doorway, not out of defiance, but more afraid of leaving this much familiarity than of any danger that might be coming. And where could she run?

The creature was already crying out ' 'oo's that, 'oo's on me

pitch? Get orff wiv yer, get away from me pitch yer 'ore's get.'
Running towards Judith, or stumbling rather, rags fluttering, her
skirts like the torn sails of a wreck. Brandishing her fists, shouting
curses. When she came close she stopped, seeming surprised that
Judith did not run away, and was so tall. She had no nose, Judith
saw. Nothing but two holes in her face above the mouth. Nose
holes and mouth crusted with scabs, yellowish. One eye
bandaged over. Her fist had no fingers, only stumps. She did not
seem half so frightening as the passers-by in their clean, bright
clothes.

'I'll murder yer' the woman shouted, but she stayed clear of
any possible reach of Judith's arm. 'Wotcher mean by it?'

She is afraid of me, Judith thought, surprised.

The boy leaned on his broom handle, 'She's a big un, Nosey.
Mind she don't belt yer one.'

Nosey began to snivel, lifting her useless hands in the air. 'It's
me pitch, it's mine, 'e'll tell yer, every 'un knows me, ain't it
mine, Jacky?' Judith wondered distantly why she was crying; if
she too was lost.

She herself felt so weak that she sat down on the step. The
woman seemed to take that as a gesture of contempt. She danced
about on the pavement, waving her arms. 'If I 'ad me fingers I'd
claw yer face, you 'ore, you dung bottle.'

'She's just outer Bedlam' Jacky said. 'Don't make 'er violent or
she'll carve yer, Nosey.' He seemed to be enjoying the scene, and
already to have changed sides. Nosey came closer to the doorway,
dragged up her skirts, threatened to kick. But she had no boots
on. Judith knew that no one can kick properly without their boots
on. She watched the woman over the tops of her knees, her mouth
and her twitch hidden.

'Mind she don't strop 'er chiv acrosst yer gob' Jacky said, his
voice mocking. 'She done a woman down the 'aymarket, Nosey,
that's why they locked 'er up. Cut 'er ears orff. Yer don't want to
lose yer ears too, do yer?'

The woman knelt down in the mud and clasped her stumps
together. 'Gawd strike yer both dead. Gawd give yer the plague.'
Judith watched her, not sure if she was really there, or if she had
imagined her. But how could she have imagined a woman with
no nose?

The boy was shouting, jeering the beggar woman. 'Garn out of it, yer met yer match eh, yer old pox bag? Look' he said. 'I'll give yer a shilling for yer pitch an' you move up the Square, 'ow's that? Bet's afraid of yer, she'll let yer share.'

'A shilling? For me pitch? A shilling yer dirty little villain! Me living!'

'Yer can get drunk now. Yer can go orff an' get drunk this minnit, soon as yer gets to a crib. And then tomorrow you can move in wiv Bet. On'y don't try an' come back 'ere, or she'll chive yer. I seed 'er knife, Lord, yer won't 'ave no 'ead left, let alone yer ears!' He held out the shilling. The woman tried to snatch it, but without fingers it was impossible, and he danced away and tripped her with his broom. When she had clambered upright he made her cup her palms, and led her away to the far side of the crossing, tempting her with the shilling like a carrot in front of a crippled donkey.

'Bet'll pick up for yer. You go an' tell 'er. An' don't come back 'ere or we'll both do yer.'

He watched her shuffling away, and came back to Judith, using his broom as a kind of vaulting stick. ' 'oo'd a thought it, eh? A few munfs back she'd 'ave runned you out of it like frowing stones at a cat. It's losing the last of 'er fingers as must 'ave done it, she can't pick up. If they frows a copper at 'er or anythink an' she don't catch it, she can't pick nothink up orff the pavement.' He did a pirouette round the broom. 'So now yer got a pitch all yer own. What yer going to give me for it? We'll go 'alves, eh?'

'I want to go to Mrs. Ware. In King Street. She's a——'

'I knows, I knows yer do. But she don't want yer there. Yer going to stay wiv me now. 'old out yer 'and and when they goes by, like this. Yer don't know nothink, do yer?' He took her hand, pulled at it, opened her fingers and turned them palm upwards. 'Then you 'as to 'ave a bit o' cant. Tell 'em yer starving, yer looks it right enough. I'm starving yer says. An' me little sister at 'ome is dying fer want o' medicine. Can yer remember that?'

'I want to go to Mrs. Ware. In King Street. She——'

'If yer don't belt that up I'll give yer a bang wiv me broom.'

'I must go to Evergreen.'

'Sod Evergreen! She don't want yer! No one wants yer! Get that into yer skull! No one wants yer, 'cept me. I'm starving! Garn! Say it! Or I'll bang yer!' He made a bayonet of his broom handle, and threatened her as Poll did. He was a quarter the size of Poll but the broom handle was nearly as big as Poll's club. And what was the harm in saying it? It was not like kissing the floor or licking it, as Jenny used to.

'I'm starving' she said obediently. It was true, in a way. 'I am very hungry' she said. 'Have you got anything to eat?'

'No, no. no, *nao!*' he cried. 'I thought yer 'ad it for a moment. I'm starving. An' me little sister's at 'ome dying for want o' medicine. I gives yer one more chanst before I bangs yer.'

She said it perfectly this time, and he did another pirouette round his broom. 'There yer are. There yer are! Yer see? Yer can do anything when yer tries. Say it again.' She said it again. 'Look, 'ere's a cove, the old geyser in the white 'at. Try 'im. An' there's a woman comin' up t'other way, give it 'er next. Show yer twitch to 'em.'

She let them both go by, hiding in her doorway, face to the door jamb. The boy danced with anger and came and gave her a dig in the back with his broom handle. She lay against the door and cried.

'If yer lets another one go by I'll go an' fetch Nosey back.' An old man and a young girl came towards them, and Jacky hissed ''ere's yer real last chanst. I'll spill yer guts if yer don't do it right. Out on the step wiv yer.' He gave her a dig in the side that made her cough and bend forward. She was still coughing when the old man came level with her.

'My poor woman!' he said, 'What is the matter? Are you ill?'

'Oh grandpapa, look at her hair, it has been cut off!'

'She's starving guv'nor, that's what she is' Jacky said from the gutter. And added in a threatening voice 'Ain't yer?'

'I am starving' Judith whispered. 'I want to go to Mrs.——'

'An' 'er little sister at 'ome is dying for want of medicine, that's what she's doing.'

'Grandpapa, give her something, please! May I give her my guinea? Oh grandpapa!'

'Adèle, child! That is far too much! And perhaps——'

'She is telling the truth, I know it, can not you see it, how hungry she is? And she is ill. Here, oh, you poor creature.' Pressing something into Judith's hand.

'You are not drunk?' the old man said. He came forward to smell if there was any liquor on her breath, and then drew back, shivering. Judith looked at the guinea, at the old man, at the young girl. She held out the guinea towards them.

'No' she said. Her face twitching.

The young girl caught her hand and closed her fingers over the gold coin, her eyes bright with tears under the pink frame of her bonnet. Her grandfather drew her away. 'Did not you hear her voice, grandpapa, she speaks like a lady, oh, what can have happened to her?'

The couple went further off, she could not hear them. She looked at the guinea in her hand. Jacky came and took it from her. Garn away! A quid! A blessed quid!' He jumped and vaulted about with his broom, swept mud over Judith's skirts in a delirium of joy, made a couple of dashes into the roadway and back again. 'Yer a winner! D'you 'ear what the young 'un said? Like a lady? That's yer lay! That's yer cant. I'm a lady what's 'ard up an' come down in the world. Misfortchings 'ave ruined me, me Lord. There's your cant. Can yer say it? Go on, try.'

'I am very hungry.'

'Nao nao *nao!* I'm a lady what's—oh Gawd, anyways, yer done it. I tell yer what, we'll go an' get a pair o' meat pies an' a pint o' porter, and then we'll go 'ome and I'll show yer to me fambly. Oh won't they be pleased! An' 'ole quid!' He had to dance again, looking rather as if a pair of patched and dirty knee breeches had taken a life of their own, and were jumping about the roadway in company with a bewitched broom. He came back and gave her a friendly dig with the handle. 'Yer a loony, but yer lucky, an' that's what counts. Come along wiv yer, we're going to knock off. 'alfpenny tokens! I 'opes they gets their slippers filthy. We'll get the pies first, an' then some bangers an' pease pud for me fambly. Oh won't they be pleased? Not 'arf.' He took a firm grip of her skirts as if suspecting her of trying to escape and began to lead her away.

'Where are you taking me? I want to go to Mrs. Ware's.'

'Yus o' course, we'll find Mrs. Ware, not 'arf we won't. But first you come along wiv' me nice an' quiet, and if we sees another soppy lookin' old geyser wiv a young 'un we'll try yer new cant again.' They went down one respectable looking road, and then a busier street, with shops and traffic. She hid her face with the leaflet and let herself be drawn along. She knew they were talking about her. She tried to make herself smaller, hunching herself down and creeping. Now and then she tried to turn into a

[223]

doorway, but he would not allow it. 'Come on wiv yer! Don't yer want a pie?'

'I want to find Evergreen.'

'We'll find 'er, don't you worrit, just you come along nice an' quiet. 's a born lady, sir, what's come down in the world an' I'm lookin' arter 'er. She's 'ad misfortchings an' can't talk. Gawd bless yer, me lord.' Dancing five steps, hissing up at her, 'a shilling, cut me throat, this is the lay. Me own beggar! Yer better nor any crossing. I'll tell yer that. Let 'em look in yer face, see yer twitch, that's what catches 'em.'

'I have to find her.'

She thought for a moment that she could remember everything. Almost. Except that some of it seemed very far away. There was Guthrum's, and her father. And Robert. Were they dead? Jenny had died. And she had been going to be married, she could not quite remember why she had not been. Or was she married? She tried to think. If she could stand in that doorway quietly and hide her face, she would remember. She had not invented it. It was true. All of it. If she could only be quiet for a moment. But the boy would not let her. Perhaps he was taking her back to the doctor's?

She began to resist. There were people, and they stopped to look, at the tall, ruined girl in rags, and the small, ridiculous figure with the broom, trying to drag her along. 'It's me sister, she's touched in the 'ead, she don't want to come 'ome wiv me.' People began to talk at her, to shout, to laugh, someone pushed her. She had to go on walking, let herself be pulled along. People followed them, jeering and laughing. Perhaps it would be better to go back to the doctor and Poll, at least she could be quiet there, there was no one in the room with her since Jenny died. And Poll did not let the others scream too long.

'I want to go back to the doctor' she said.

'That's right, that's where we're going. On'y we'll 'ave the pies an' porter first, eh? Lord bless yer ma'am, she's touched in the 'ead, I 'as to look arter 'er, she's me big sister, ma'am, an' me muvver an' farver's dead o' the consumption, ma'am.' He gave a savage hike at Judith's skirts, and tore them. 'A penny, Gawd rot 'er! 'ow does she think I can look arter a mad loony sister wiv a penny? I 'ope she breaks 'er leg in a gutter. Down 'ere.'

A narrow alley between two shops. Suddenly dark and quiet

and nice. A kind of tunnel, a smell of food, a wide space filled with stalls, and people, a slither of trodden vegetables and mud underfoot, a smell of bad meat and rotten fish, of bruised apples filling the air with a sharp sweetness. Women selling fish, their sacking aprons fish-silvery, their arms crimsoned and sequin-silvered with blood and fish scales, shouting in hoarse, rasping voices; 'Prime cuts o' cod, a penny, fine cuts o' turbot tuppence!' Smacking down their knives on the trays as children tried to steal from them. Women customers with baskets, women in shawls, women in rags, women with babies on one arm and two and three more toddling children hanging onto their skirts.

'Luvly toffee apples a 'alfpenny! 'ere y'are my ducks, lemon fizz a penny a pint! Root beer, an a'penny!'

'Lobsters tuppence each, tuppence each me fresh lobsters!' Blackish-greenish, decayed-looking lobsters spreading their dead claws towards the pale herrings and the dark blue mackerel, lying with slack eyes and faded scales, not even their smell remembering the sea, putrid as sewage. A man with a kind of metal oven on wheels was crying ' 'ot pies for tuppence, full o' best meat, bursting wiv gravy, 'ot pies just baked. On'y tuppence, threepence the big 'uns.'

' 'ere we are' Jacky cried, tugging her towards the pieman. Her pattens slipped on rotted cabbage leaves, and she was so faint with hunger that she wanted to fall down. She found that she was sitting on a pile of filth, sweepings of vegetable refuse, mud, torn sacking, her back against soot-smelling, soot-coloured greasy brickwork. The boy put a pie into her hands. She held it for a time, not knowing what it was. Half remembering, waiting for someone to give her a spoon, thinking of gruel, of Poll, of food.

'Eat it! Garn, take a bite! Yer said you was 'ungry!'

She bit the crust. Gravy flowed down her chin, warm and sticky. There was a suddenly familiar, long ago familiar smell of meat, of baked pastry. She was so hungry that she could not taste anything. Only the warmth, her own saliva. The pie was gone and she began to search for crumbs in her lap, among the rags. The boy gave her a tin mug of blackish, creamy-foamed liquid. He said it was porter. She drank it and choked on the first mouthful, thick and gritty and bitter tasting. But it was liquid. She suddenly felt better. Sick but better. I'll vomit soon, she thought. He'll be pleased then. She sat on the heap of filth while the boy talked to the pieman and drank his own porter.

She had another moment of almost clarity. She knew who she was, what had happened. 'You are a dreadful boy' she said in a clear, strong voice. The boy stared at her in amazement, his can held in both hands, tilted, as if he meant to pour the contents into the top of his gaping breeches.

'I'm wot?'

The clouds had closed over again. She shut her eyes. She had a feeling of being nearly arrived somewhere, of having almost found her way. But it was no good, everything was shifting, had lost its sharp edges. The boy gave her a kick. 'Don't you go speaking ill o' me in front o' people, nor anywheres, 'cause I won't 'ave it, d'yer 'ear me? I'm your keeper, I am, an' if you don't do as I tells yer I'll bust yer ribs in. *Dreadful boy!* Me givin' you fripenny meat pies an' takin' yer 'ome to me fambly to look arter yer, an' yer goes an' calls me that! I'll dreadful yer! Get up, an' don't 'ave me draggin' yer all the way 'ome, I'm near wore out wiv yer already.'

He made her get up. Pushed and dragged her through the crowd of women. The close-jammed stalls and wheelbarrows, two-wheeled carts, broken boxes, piles of refuse, scavenging dogs and cats, scavenging children; barrels set up on trestles with rows of tin mugs hanging from nails hammered into a wooden beam overhead; women drinking, two women arguing with a man behind a meat stall, his arms mottled purplish with dried blood, his apron like a dirty red flag, his knife dripping. The boy draggin' yer all the way 'ome, I'm near wore out wiv yer the smells fading. Other smells, sewers and soot. A grey rat was crouched behind a fallen brick, staring at them, its eyes red and fierce. As big as a large kitten, its tail naked and grey and shiny. She went stumbling past it, behind her keeper, wanting to get sick, to vomit up the leaden weight of the pie, and the porter. Corners, laneways, a low arch leading into a blind court. Half a dozen houses crouched and crushed together.

Doors hanging open, windows broken, piled filth drifted like dirty snow against one side of the courtyard. Children were digging in the drift with bits of wood, fighting one another for something. A woman was sitting on a stone with folded bare arms, and a woollen cap, and a pipe. A dog with no tail and not much hair crouched at her feet, nibbling under its hind leg.

[226]

' 'ow are yer, Slops? Look what I brought 'ome! Me own beggar! She's a loony, done a bunk out o' Bedlam. I found 'er on me crossing. Down 'ere, you.' He dragged her towards an opening in the ground. Black wooden steps led down into darkness. 'Down yer goes, mind the pig, 'e 'ates to be trod on.'

He pushed her and she almost fell headlong into the cellar.

' 'elp 'er, yer little varmint' the woman shouted. 'You'll break 'er neck. 'elp 'er get down.'

'Watch it!' the boy cried, flung his broom down into the hole, and began to manoeuvre Judith as if she was a tall thin sack of coals to be tipped down the ladder. A man appeared from below, cursing, preventing Judith from being pushed on top of him.

' 'old 'ard, damn yer, 'oo's this, what the flaming 'ell d'yer think she's going to do down 'ere?'

'She's come to live wiv me, she's me beggar.' And to Judith, by way of introduction, 'Me landlord, 'e's Sam what owns the pig.'

'An' the bloody cellar too, I owns the cellar, an' you don't bring no one more in unless you pays me more rent. Threepence a week, she'll cost yer.' He seemed to be measuring Judith's height. 'Fourpence. Where'd yer find 'er?'

'On me crossing. She druv out old Nosey. Just sat down on 'er pitch an' wouldn't move, so I gives Nosey a bob an' makes 'er slope off wiv 'erself.'

They stood arguing about the extra rent until it reduced itself back to threepence a week.

Children had gathered round them. And behind the children, women, men, until the court was crowded. But not noisy. Only the children made a noise and not a great deal of it. She was glad of that. She sat down on the ground, her feet dangling into the hole. The people stared at her. White, sickly faces, rags. Only the man who owned the cellar, and the woman with the pipe and the dog, and Jacky himself, seemed to have any life in them. The others appeared to be dying, and she felt a kinship with them at once, as if they were like Jenny. She tried to smile at one of the children, and the child hid itself behind another child. She liked that too.

And she liked the cellar, when at last she got down into it. There was a familiar smell. Urine and excrement, and something else that must be the pig. It lay in the middle of the earth floor, in such light as came down through the entrance hole. Pallid, gaunt, its great chops working. There was a thick mulch of straw under it, like a dark brown, sodden bed. There was straw everywhere, piled into the corners in particular, like the drifted filth in the courtyard overhead. A woman lay against one wall coughing, her breath whistling when she was able to breathe between the spasms. Her face was no more than a shadow, and two burning eyes.

'Me missus' Sam said. 'She's poorly.' And to the woman, 'Jacky's brought a loony to live wiv us. Threepence a week.' The woman did not answer. The pig rolled its eye. ' 'e won't get fat, curse 'is lights. I don't know, 'e gets everything, 'e don't 'ave to do nothing 'cept get fat, an' 'e won't do it.' He kicked the animal in its stomach. The pig grunted and tried to roll on its other side.

The boy brought Judith to a corner and made her sit down. 'Mary! Come 'ere wiv yer.' A small girl in the remains of someone's chemise. Tufts of hair on her head like a moulting sparrow. ' 'ere's a shilling. Run an' get some bangers an' pease pud. Take Tom wiv yer, an' make it quick, an' don't drop nothing in the mud.' He sat down beside Judith and stretched his short legs, wriggling his toes, his hands behind his head, a straw sticking out of the corner of his mouth.

'What yer fink of it? We 'as this arf o' the cellar. Me and Mary and Tom an' them two little 'uns, 'enery an' Annie. Them's me fambly what I told you I 'ad.' As he pointed, two babies, the same size as one another, came crawling out of a heap of straw that had covered them, and began to clamber onto Jacky's lap. 'Pease pud yer going to get, what yer fink o' that, eh? An' I'll give yer each a banger to suck.' He stuck a finger in one of their mouths. 'They ain't got no teeth' he said. One of the babies noticed Judith and began to crawl onto her. It was a girl, naked, her stomach swollen, her eyes crusted round, a kind of polish of dirt on her skin, brownish and iridescent in the shadows, and the half light from above them. The hands began to fumble at the front of Judith's torn and greasy gown, as if somewhere in the baby's mind it had remembrances of its mother, of being fed at her breast.

Judith let her. After a time the baby gave up the search, whimpering for a moment and then settling down in Judith's lap. She was not very heavy, and Judith did not mind.

'She likes yer' Jacky said. He had the other baby by the ankles and was dancing him up and down, his head bouncing off Jacky's knees. The two middle-sized children came back with the pease pudding wrapped in dirty cabbage leaves, and a bundle of reeking hot sausages parcelled in more leaves. Every one ate. The babies covered their faces with a green mud of pudding. Mary and Tom were sent off again for a jug of ale, and some milk. When they came back Jacky took a long pull from the jug and passed it to Judith. She made a pretence of drinking and gave it into Tom's small, impatient hands. She wished she might have some of the milk, but she was afraid to ask, and the babies were already fighting over it. Jacky gave the cabbage leaves to the pig and the pig ate them languidly. The woman coughed. It grew dark. The landlord who had been gone a long time came back drunk and cursing, and fell down the ladder.

'Where's me pig?' he shouted. He lay on top of it and went to sleep. Judith slept.

Chapter 24

She woke in terror. Pitch dark. Something on her legs. She screamed, kicked. The thing scurried, claws scratching, light, furry body, a squeaking, chittering sound. She lay trembling. Nothing familiar except the straw, the stench. She did not know where she was.

'Jenny?' And when there was no answer, 'Evergreen?'

Coughing. A strange grunting, snores. People? The cellar. The boy. Things rustled in the straw. Whimpering. She was afraid to move. Something else touched her, but flesh, not fur, not claws. Like a hand. Tiny. The baby crawled close to her, felt at her rags, at her non-existent breast. She put her arm round the small, naked body. The head nestled under her arm pit, stopped its whimpering.

She lay trying to think. At moments everything seemed clear. She was in a cellar. The boy had brought her here. He had a broom. Her name was Judith Mortimer. She lived at Guthrum's Farm, in the County of Essex, in the Kingdom of England. She had written that in her books.

'I am Judith Mortimer' she said aloud, as if she expected to be contradicted, her voice uncertain. They called me Silver Tail, she thought. Is that my name? I live with Mrs. Ware in King Street. She is a whore mistress. She had a swift picture in her mind of young girls, with beautiful, malicious faces, and old gentlemen in coaches come to take them away. Then of candlelight and naked breasts, and Robert.

Had that been her? She tried to hold on to Judith, and Guthrum's Farm. But the shadows from the candlelight blotted it out, and there was only Silver Tail. Long bright hair and naked breasts, and being kissed. He had undressed her. Robert! Robert!

A sense of loss, as if her arm had been cut off, but was still hurting her.

'Is that why You hate me?' she asked aloud. The woman in the far corner wrenched herself with coughing. 'Something to drink' she whispered. 'Love o' God, I'm burning.'

She would die soon, Judith thought. Then she would be all right.

'Gimme something.'

The pig snored. And its owner. The rats chittered in the straw, feasting.

She had married Robert? Had she? She was not sure, but the pictures came to her. And always that one of naked breasts, of being kissed. It must be true. No wonder it had made Him angry. She wondered if He could see her here, in the cellar. She held the child closer. 'He hates you too' she told her, 'but I shall hide you.' She put her other arm round her, turning on her side so that she might protect the child better.

'Robert?' she whispered. The rats squeaked and rustled. One ran over her feet. The vermin bit deep and deeper. But she was used to those. She no longer itched, except now and then.

'Robert?'

She went to sleep again. Dreams of nakedness, of Poll, of the children in the courtyard, Poll beating them. And they came to Judith for protection. In her dreams she was not afraid of them. A woman stared into her face, said 'Whore!'

'Yes! Yes! I was called Silver Tail!' In her dream her hair had grown long, fell down between her naked breasts. The woman turned into a man, gave her a golden coin, laid it on her skin, and it burned like fire. She woke with the shock of the pain, crying out, pressing her hand against her ribs, and the rat that had bitten her squeaked away in the darkness.

A grey square overhead. Dawn. Day.

The boy took her back to the crossing, and set her in her doorway, which no one seemed ever to use, the door locked, the window shuttered inside. A dead house. Nosey came back, drunk and weeping, saying that Bet had driven her away. She tried all day to get into the doorway beside Judith, but the boy kept digging at her with the broom handle, until at last she shuffled off, weeping, leprous and dreadful.

She came back again and again in the days and weeks that

followed. But each time more shadowlike and crouched and shuffling. Then she did not come any more and Judith forgot her, or pushed her memory into an attic of her mind. She had forgotten almost everything except the immediate things. But sometimes she would dream of Robert, or of Evergreen. She was searching for them in the darkness. Underground. Rats with shining eyes were the only light there was, and her voice would lose itself in echoes. 'Robert? Robert? Evergreen?' The syllables of their names echoing and re-echoing farther and farther off in the darkness. Or she would hear their voices. But never see them. Crying 'Judith? Where are you?'

'Here! Here!'

But the echoes melted together, became meaningless, and she would be enclosed in silence, not even her own running footsteps making a sound that she could hear. She would know that she was crying, could feel the tears, but could not hear herself. Knew that Evergreen was crying, and could not even call out to comfort her.

In the times she was awake, lying listening to the cellar's half-life in the dark; or when she was dully standing in her doorway, she tried to bring them to her as she had sometimes done in her cell. To bring Evergreen from the shadows, talk to her, tell her stories. Or she would look for Robert, be sure that this figure, the next one, or the next, must be his. Must. That one now! But it would be an old gentleman, or an errand-boy. And in the cellar, in the dark, or the grey beginnings of dawn, it was not Robert, but Mr. Gaultrip who climbed down the ladder, his clothes dripping, seaweed wound round his throat, tangled about his hands. And she would lie in terror as he came searching for her, feeling about in the stinking, rotten straw, his eyes blind, eaten long ago and yet still searching. She would cry out 'I ran away from him! Because of you! You must forgive me, I do not want him back, I promise you!'

But the lie could not deceive the old, drowned man, and he would come still searching, touching, until she held the baby against her flat, vanished breast, like a last hold on reality, and she would gather up all her strength to drive her imaginings away, recognise them as imaginary. Sometimes, instead of imagining she tried to think things out, without giving them shapes and bodies that took on lives of their own.

[232]

She would think, I must look for Evergreen. Tomorrow. I must. But then the thinking would dissolve, drift, and she was not sure what she had decided, or whether it was possible to decide anything.

Another time she would think about Robert. Dragging her mind into a clear space as the pig dragged itself into the shaft of daylight, to warm itself. Was she married to him? Sometimes she was quite certain about that, and sometimes not. Where was it he had gone? And Mr. Gaultrip? Had Robert murdered him? If he had——

And almost by her own wish the small clear space in her mind would begin to close, like an eyelid dropping slowly. And there were only shadows.

Even those efforts at thinking were rare, and grew rarer. For most of the time there was only the cellar, the children; begging; the boy; being hit with the broom handle; the pig; the landlord Sam.

The landlord tried to rape her and she bit his wrist so deep that his hand became paralysed; she must have bitten through the sinews. He had screamed all that night with the pain and had wanted to put her out of the cellar the next day. But he could not use his hand and Jacky defended her with his broom. He had given Sam two shillings in the end, to go and get drunk. When he came back he fell down the ladder and hurt himself. He lay in the corner beside his wife, crying and cursing Jacky, and his wife, and Judith. The next day he could barely drag himself about. He seemed to have hurt his back very badly, his legs no longer worked properly, but trailed behind him as he drew himself across the floor to his pig.

Sometimes the pig got up and moved about, and they would find it lying in their half of the cellar when they came home at night. It would be eating their straw, or wallowing in it, and Jacky would have to drive it off. It moved about at night as well, and once it came and lay on top of Judith and almost crushed her legs. Its bones had begun to stick out of its skin, now that Sam could not get up the ladder to fetch food for it. He had used to collect the sweepings from the rotten food market, getting them for nothing. But now he had to pay Jacky, or Mary, or Tom, to go and fetch them for him, and sometimes they forgot, or could not be bothered, and simply stole the penny. Judith felt very sorry for the pig. When she tried to comfort it, it would gnash its bony, emaciated jaws and seem pleased. And when they came back through the market from her day's begging and Jacky's sweeping, she would gather up armfuls of cabbage stalks to bring home for it. Some days Jacky would allow that, and some days not. It depended on how the day had gone.

She never received another guinea, and in fact never tried to get anything. She would stand in the doorway until she was too tired and too hungry to stay upright, and then she would sit down. When people came by she would hide her face. Jacky had given up beating her for not trying to beg. He told people that she was his sister, and touched in the head, and that there were eight little ones at home that they had to feed. The passers by dropped pennies into her lap, or halfpennies, or very occasionally a sixpence or a shilling, and Jacky would wait until they were gone before he took the money.

If they did well he would be good humoured, and give her pease pudding and sausages, or a mutton pie, for her supper, and a pint of ale or porter. Or sometimes milk. There was an Irishman near the court who kept four cows in a stable and his wife went round with two buckets selling the milk. It had a pale blue colour because they put in so much water from the pump by the stable. And there were cow hairs and straws, and bits of cow dung and dead flies in it as well as water, and it did not taste very nice. But neither did the porter, nor the ale, nor the mutton pies nor the pease pudding. And the milk reminded Judith of something. Of trees. Of a house. She liked it for that reason, even longed for it. Only the sausages were enjoyable for themselves alone and she did not get them very often.

On poor days they had mouldy bread and anything Mary and Tom could steal, which was not much because they were too small to run fast. She began to forget that she had ever lived anywhere but the cellar. Poll and the doctor and Jenny retreated into the nightmares and mixed themselves up with a man whose teeth stuck out like yellow fangs. And a man undressing her. Hurting her. Robert? She knew that she had known him somewhere but it was difficult to remember where or when. Pictures drifted through her mind like cards being dealt onto a table, now slow, now fast.

Fields, and a wood, and an old man lying in bed, in a shadowy room. She knew that it was her father, and yet she could not be sure she was not dreaming that. And another old man lying in the wood, in a stone summer house, and Evergreen was there, and she could hear the sea. And Jenny dying, turning so cold.

It had grown colder. It rained, and when it was not raining the wind blew through her rags like knives. It was very cold in the cellar. It stayed dark longer. It was dark when they woke in the morning, and went to the crossing. Dark when they came back. The landlord could not move at all and depended on Jacky or on the neighbours for everything. He lay all the time beside his wife, not even cursing. The woman who smoked a pipe came down into the cellar every day to look after him and it was agreed that she should have half the pig when it came time to kill it.

It seemed to Judith, somewhere in the far back of her mind, where it was still sometimes almost clear, although very distant, and no use for ordinary thinking, like a patch of sunlight breaking through a sky of clouds, and lighting a patch of hillside far away towards the horizon, that the time for killing the pig was long gone. She was half glad and half sorry. She did not want to think of the pig being killed, and yet she knew it would be happier when it was dead. And she would kneel down at its back and scratch its mangy skull, and it would flap its ragged, rat-chewed ears in gratitude, and grunt at her.

The baby, the girl baby, Annie, was her other pleasure. She was not too afraid of any of the children, but the baby Annie she loved. She would pretend to feed it at her flat breast, at the bones of her ribs, and croon over it until Jacky made her stop. She would steep pieces of bread in the milk, or the porter, and feel the gums in which teeth were growing suck and chew at her finger ends. The child could not see very well, perhaps from living in the dark, and yet it always knew her, and crawled towards her. The boy was beginning to walk, stumbling about in the straw on bowed, stick legs, his stomach thrust out like a blown up bladder in front of him. But Annie still crawled. Every night she lay in Judith's arms, or nestled under her side as if she was hiding.

'I shall not let Him find you' Judith would whisper.

But He did find her. They came back one night and the pig was lying on their side of the cellar and Judith could not find the child anywhere in the straw. Until they drove the pig away. When it had rolled and staggered to its feet the baby was underneath. Still warm from the pig's body, but not moving. Judith held her all night but she did not move. She grew cold and stiffened as Jenny had.

After that Judith shrank into herself completely. The last moments of clarity disappeared, and there was nothing in the world but the cellar, and the crossing, and the streets and lanes between, and shadows. The cold turned savage. God's breath. Ice. Her fingers swelled with huge, plum-coloured chilblains, and burst, and ran matter. And her feet. She had long ago lost her pattens, and Jacky wanted her barefoot so that people should see how poor they were. Her rags had begun to disintegrate, and were tied together with string, like Jacky's knee breeches.

Jacky himself seemed to flourish, and grow bigger and stronger between one day and the next. When he hit her with the broom she took a long time to recover. She could not sleep at all because of the cold, and the dreams. She dreamed of warmth, of white beds, of fires, of food on plates, of a man who kissed her and gave her a glass of wine. She dreamed of God, preaching in a pulpit, His huge, purple lower lip thrust out, His voice echoing into huge silences and darkness. Of the child Annie. Of all the dead. When she was in the doorway and hid her face behind her knees she would fall asleep for a minute or two, until the dead woke her, or someone would drop a coin beside her, or Jacky would dig the broom handle into her side, or hit her with it.

One day she decided she would stay in the doorway for always. It was dark. It had been dark for a long time and Jacky told her to stand up, it was time to go home. She would not move. He tugged at her and she sat down again, like an empty sack. He hit her, and she sank into the corner of the doorway and looked at him.

'No' she said.

'Wotcher mean, no? I'll kill yer, yer flaming loony.'

She said nothing. He began to jab at her systematically. She cried. She could not help crying, but she would not move. He tried to kick her out of the corner, dragged her out. She lay on the pavement and he stamped on her. Hit her with the broom until he was exhausted. She lay crouched, not even trying to protect herself.

'I'll give yer a toffee apple' he wheedled. 'I'll give yer some luvly bangers, and a glass o' gin. Hot gin.'

She did not answer and he began thumping her again. 'Gawd

above, what's got into yer?' He kicked her face with his bare feet. 'Ain't I bin kind to yer? Ain't I bin like a bruvver to yer? Where's yer gratitude? I'll kill yer, I'll knock yer eyes out. What's wrong wiv yer? Don't yer want to go 'ome, 'ave yer supper?'

'No' she whispered to the wet mud of the pavement. There were lights in the mud. Like gold and silver. Shifting and moving. Rivers of gold and silver. They were beautiful. The sound of a carriage, horses, the carriage lamps throwing reflections onto the roadway and the pavement, showing the boy with the upraised broom, the shape lying at his feet.

The carriage halting, a girl's voice crying 'What are you doing? Boy, stop! Stop!'

Footsteps running. Heavy. Light. There were silk stockings, buckled shoes, great calves swelling. Hands. She could see dark skirts, slippers.

'Lift her up! John, Frederick, lift her! Carefully! Boy, what have you done?' A girl's voice. And then 'It is her! It is the same one, the poor creature, look at her face! Be gentle with her!'

Jacky crying 'It's me sister, me loony sister, what yer doing wiv 'er, leave her down, leave 'er alone. I'm trying to get 'er to go 'ome wiv me, she ain't right in the 'ead.'

'You were hitting her! With your broom! you wicked, wicked boy. Oh, what shall we do? Coachman, what can we do for her?'

They had lifted her. She was standing. The girl in front of her, dark mauve bonnet, dark brown eyes, an expression of horror in them. Judith tried to hide herself.

'What is the matter with you? What can we do for you?'

'Yer can't do nuffink for 'er, on'y leave 'er alone and give 'er somefink. Leave 'er to come 'ome wiv me. I'm 'er bruvver.'

'The boy's right there, miss' one of the footmen said.

'If only grandpapa were here, he would know what to do. How hungry she looks. Are you hungry, my dear?'

'She's starving, that's what she is. An' me along wiv 'er, an' the little ones at 'ome, eight on 'em all starving.'

'You be quiet or we'll 'ave you arrested' the coachman said from his box. 'I knows 'im, I've seen 'im 'itting that poor soul afore this, often an' often as I was passing.'

'Then why did not you stop him? Oh what shall we do for her? Frederick, could we bring food to her?'

'It might be more partic'lar preferable, miss, if we was to give 'er directions to the back door. I 'ave no doubt as what cook would find 'er something 'ot, if I was to pass 'er your instructions.'

'No no, bring her, bring her with us.'

'She's uncommon dirty, miss, an' without a doubt 'as fleas. Mr. Fairbairn would take it very bad if we was to let you come in contac' with a flea, miss, not to speak of Mrs. Gunther nor Miss Arkwright.'

'Grandpapa would not mind, and as for Miss Arkwright, she should be here with me and then we should know what to do. That she should have a headache today of all days!'

Judith hung in their arms. After a moment the two footmen set her down in her doorway, and dusted their white gloves, that were now lightly stained from holding her. They moved back a step or so, as if expecting her fleas to be singularly active after so much handling and beating. She hid her face behind her knees. The girl bent down and reached out a small hand in a mauve silk glove, to stroke Judith's hair. It had grown quite long, and she was able to hide her eyes with it.

'Don't touch 'er, miss! If Mrs. Gunther was to 'ear of this! Best leave 'er to 'er brother, you can't do 'er no good, miss. Get back inside, miss, please.'

'I do not believe he is her brother. I have heard her speak and she has a lady's voice. I have thought of you so often and often since I saw you before, I have not been able to forget you. What happened to you, what is your story?'

Judith lifted her head and looked at her. She remembered the girl in a distant, dreamy way. Thought she did.

'You have been beautiful' the girl said. 'Was it——? Oh, I cannot leave you here.'

'You can't do nothing else, miss' the tallest footman said. Jacky had retreated to a safe distance from the company.

'I can! Are we not Christians? What is the use of going to church and hearing the Gospel if we do not practise what is preached to us? Lift her up, put her in the coach.'

The men stood, not so much in rebellion as dismay. The coachman tried to seem unconnected with the matter, and took a sudden, well-aimed flick at Jacky with his coach whip. Jacky screeched abuse and retreated farther off.

'Then fetch my grandfather!' the girl cried, stamping her

slipper in the mud. 'I shall not leave here without her. Fetch Mrs. Gunther, fetch Miss Arkwright, fetch everyone. I will have my way if it takes until midnight to persuade you. I shall bring you to a warm place' she said, bending lower, 'and you shall be fed, and you shall tell me what is the matter. I shall find a doctor for you.'

'No!' Judith whispered.

There were people gathering, talking, protesting. Jacky crying out 'Me sister, yer can't take me sister away from me, she ain't right in the 'ead, it's kidnapping, that's what! It's again' the Law! I'll 'ave yer up, she's me living!' One of the footmen caught hold of him and began to cuff his head with heavy brutality. Jacky struck the handle of his broom into the footman's stomach, and the man doubled up and let go of him. People were arguing, lifting her, putting her into the coach, on the floor of it. The girl crying, 'No, put her on the seat, on the seat, I tell you!'

Leather, velvet, charcoal burning in a copper foot warmer. Scent of lavender, the girl holding her hand, examining her chilblains, crying over them in a despair of charity. A stable yard. Voices. Lights. Soft depth of hay. The girl saying 'No, no, she must have a mattress, and sheets and pillows.'

A woman with a guttural voice protesting at everything. Another woman crying out in horror. Faces, people, voices. A warm drink. An old man commanding silence, holding a candlestick, the light of the candle warm against a kind but troubled face. The footmen. Servant women. She wished they would all go away and that she was safe in the cellar again. Except that the child was dead.

'She is dead' she whispered. It seemed at that moment all that mattered in the world. Felt tears run.

'Who is dead?'

But she would not tell them that. She wondered where Jacky was, what they had done with him. They brought her food but she could not eat. At last they left her alone, and she lay listening to the sounds of the stable, the mice in the straw and hay, the horses breathing below, stamping occasionally. The girl came back with a lamp, and looked at her. Someone else, whom the girl commanded to go down again.

'Can not you sleep?'

She never slept, but she did not tell the girl that.

'Would you like more covers? Are you warm?'

She began to cry. Could not stop.

'Do not cry! Oh please, you are safe here, God has brought you to safety at last. Say your prayers to Him, and you will sleep then.'

Judith shook her head, rolled it from side to side on the pillow.

'Do not you remember how to pray?' the girl said, her tone shocked. 'What can have happened to you, what can your story be? Did a man abandon you?'

The girl put the lamp on the broad surface of a beam that ran from side to side of the stable loft, and knelt down. She took Judith's hands and joined them together, as if Judith was a child, and she her mother and was teaching her to pray.

'Our Father Who art in Heaven——' she said.

Her mother seemed to be there, in the lamplight, a golden splendour of hair, her face bent down over the bed, saying the same prayer. 'But deliver us from Evil.'

She turned her face against the pillow and cried, went on crying as if all the things that she had seen, all the things she had suffered were in the tears.

Chapter 25

She began to recover. Physically, and even mentally, or at least in part mentally. She could remember things. For whole hours and then days together she was quite clear as to what had happened, although the sequence of happenings was indistinct, and how long had gone by. And things seemed to alter their relative importance, so that one day all that mattered to her was what might have happened to the pig, and whether they had killed it. And another day the pig seemed to her the symbol of all evil, of God Himself, and she dreamed that the pig was lying on a thousand children, and devouring them.

Or she would not know whether she was asleep or awake. She would relive whole days in the mad house, and think that the servants who came to look after her were Poll, or Jenny, or the doctor, or Mr. Barforth, and would cry in despair. The tears gave her relief, and she felt better afterwards and knew exactly where she was, at least for a time.

They had a sick-room for her in the loft above the stables, with a truckle bed, and a mattress, and a side table, and a chair for the girl to sit in when she came to talk to her. Miss Adèle Westmoreland. Small and brown and imperious, although she did not seem to realise that she was that. She had a vivid, heart-shaped face, the blood warm and glowing under velvet skin, and fine, almost grown-up and then in the next moment still childlike eyes, that changed as pools of dark brown water might reflect every change of the sky, according to her emotions.

They had bathed Judith the day after they brought her here, and she had thought, it is beginning. She had prepared her mind for the cold, the shock of it, the pain in her stomach and her bones. Two footmen had carried her down into the stable where the bath tub had been set, and there were two kitchen women in aprons, their sleeves rolled up, waiting to take her from the men. Miss Westmoreland controlling all, and another, older but still youngish woman behind her, with a complaining face, who declared as Judith was brought down the wooden steps that she could not endure the sight, it was beyond all things, and she had run out giving little cries of horror.

The women stripped off Judith's rags when the men were gone and the stable doors were bolted. Now, Judith thought. She would not cry out or resist, she would not give them that pleasure. But there were braziers burning, and the water was warm, and scented. There was soap. The kitchen women muttered and whispered together in horror at her body. And Miss Westmoreland turned away for a moment and leaned against the side of the stairs. Came back and made herself look. 'Be gentle with her!' she commanded. 'No no, I shall show you!' She rolled up the sleeves of her gown and washed Judith with her own hands, against the protests of the women. Washed her hair, the sores of her legs. Touched the bruises. Had her wrapped in great soft towels, and carried up to the bed again, to fresh sheets and blankets, a fresh pillow.

A doctor came, but not like the doctor from the madhouse. He was short and stout and breathless from the climb up into the loft, pursing his mouth, feeling Judith's pulse, writing a prescription for the apothecary, shaking his head.

The old gentleman came, Mr. Fairbairn, Miss Westmoreland's grandfather. He seemed surprised at the change that a bath had brought to Judith's appearance, and to be more reconciled to what his granddaughter was doing. Although he seemed to have little control over that in any case, as if the house was his granddaughter's rather than his. And in one of their conversations, or more accurately, Miss Westmoreland's monologues, Judith learned that it was her house, and that now that she was turned eighteen she was its mistress in all but Law, and would be that too when she was twenty-one. Her parents were both dead, she told Judith, drowned in a wreck on their way to India, where Mr. Westmoreland had been someone of great importance and still greater wealth in the East India Company. And Miss Westmoreland was not only his heiress, but her grandfather's as

[242]

well. All this told with an imperious humility as if her fortune was a heavy burden of which she was determined not to be afraid.

Judith told nothing in return. If they learned who she was the old gentleman would tell the Earl and Mr. Massingham, and they would take her back to the doctor. Or drive her into the streets again. In the next moment she no longer believed that. She knew that they would do nothing cruel, that they were longing to be kind. But she clung to suspicion, hid behind it as if it was protection. To let her mind slowly gather strength, as the bed, and the stable loft, and the quietness, were protections for her body's convalescence. And so she lay quiet, reassembling her life. Remembering. But that did not make her better.

In a way it made her worse. Not in her body, but in her mind. As if the vagueness had hidden things that she could not bear to look at. Now they came out from behind the curtains, one by one. And among all of the shadows, the memories, there was Evergreen in the centre and heart of them. Until the thought of her absorbed all else; the child who had died in the cellar; Jenny; even Robert; Mr. Gaultrip; Guthrum's; Martha and Solomon and all her life before; even her father, even her mother, the memories of them; as if it was too complex and unbearable to think of all those things, all those people, all that loss, and she must take one to stand for all and sorrow for that one alone. And even so it was almost unbearable. She would have to turn her mind from the thought of Evergreen waiting for her, frightened, friendless. Say nothing about her to Miss Westmoreland. Confess nothing. Hide behind her unjust suspicions.

She tried to tell herself that Mrs. Ware would have looked after Evergreen. And knew what would have happened, must have happened. Could see it as if she had been told. A Thursday evening. The carriage, and an old gentleman getting down with eager infirmity, looking for a shy child. Shy and secret and timid and virginal. Taking Evergreen away, while Mrs. Ware got drunk again, and the marquis with her, and Harry and Albertine celebrated after their own fashions in the kitchen. When she thought of that she could not endure to look at old Mr. Fairbairn when he came to visit her, and hid her face.

'She does not improve' the old gentleman would say, 'except in looks. You have taken on a lengthy task, my dear. Pray God she is worthy of it.'

'Do not pay any attention to him' Miss Westmoreland would breathe in Judith's ear when he was gone. 'He is an old bear, but the dearest, kindest grandpapa beneath all, and when you learn to look at him and will speak to him he will love you as I do already. Shall I read the Bible to you to-day again? Do not you find wonderful comfort in it?'

She did not, but she did not say so, and listened with a quiet, still face. Her twitch had almost gone unless she became frightened at anything sudden, or noisy, and here there were few such things to trouble her. She would lie, not really listening to the Book of Job, or the story of the Good Samaritan, or the Woman of Samaria, but thinking of Evergreen and where she might be, and how she might find her again and save her. And tears would run, and Miss Westmoreland would be sure that the Gospel's words had touched her.

Judith even began to trust Miss Westmoreland. She did not trust the servants, or old Mr. Fairbairn, but she began to think of Miss Westmoreland as she had thought of Jenny, as a distant friend. Perhaps trust and distrust were the wrong words, she thought, trying to analyse her feelings. She knew that their will towards her was good and kindly, it was not that that was at issue. But their capacity to carry out their good will? Or would God simply take them away as He had taken everyone else? Or was He taking her away from them? And Miss Westmoreland at least was trying to follow her? But to follow her where? She felt at times as if she was withdrawn deep inside her apparent, outer self; was looking at the world through a narrow window; that everything was far off and not quite in contact with her. She would look at Miss Westmoreland reading to her, and think, how far away she is. And yet she seemed nearer than anyone else. Although that was not very near, and she would think again, how little she knows. She does not know anything of the real world.

The real world was the blind courtyard and its rubbish heaps, and its pale children; the woman lying in the cellar. Sam with his broken back and his legs dragging. And she lay imagining Evergreen sinking down into that reality like a drowned body sinking through green depths of water. The crossing, with its mud, and freezing wind, and Jacky with his broom. The child lying unmoving in the straw, where the pig had smothered her. Small, crushed body, like a doll.

[244]

That is reality, she thought, not listening to the Sermon on the Mount, or the story of Ruth, or of Abraham preparing to sacrifice his son. And she would lie crying, not for herself, but for that real world, that God had made, and that He hated. She had tried to save one fragment of His world from Him. And then another. Loved Evergreen. Loved the child. And one was lost, and one was dead.

'Why are you crying?' Miss Westmoreland asked her. 'Are you in pain? Oh, tell me, tell me, it breaks my heart to see you crying and not know how to help you. You are not afraid here, not afraid that we will let that boy take you back?'

'He is still there' Judith whispered.

'But he cannot touch you now!'

'I know.'

It was a long, long time before she could trust her enough to explain her meaning. And when she attempted it, it seemed very hard for Miss Westmoreland to grasp. 'Of course there are poor children!' she had cried, 'It is terrible, but what can one do? One cannot feed them all.'

'You have fed me.'

'That is different' Miss Westmoreland said, joining her small, determined hands in frustration. 'I heard your voice. Please! Tell me who you are, how you have come to this?'

It was difficult, more and more difficult to resist her kindness. Judith grew well enough to sit up, to move about the loft, even to go down the broad timber steps of the ladder, and stand for a moment in the winter sunshine. The doctor encouraged that, and she was wrapped up in a thick woollen gown and a new cloak that Miss Westmoreland had had made for her, and she walked in the kitchen garden for half an hour at a time, looking at the buds on the apple trees, and remembering Guthrum's, and Martha, and thinking one moment that she must at least send word to her somehow, by some means, and that she must begin her search for Evergreen; and the next moment feeling again that paralysis of mind, as if nothing was possible, everything too hard, too dangerous, beyond hope. And at another moment that nothing mattered at all, except that ultimate reality of the cellar, and death. That the sooner she herself returned to it the better.

She knew it was wrong, cowardly, ungrateful, but she could not help it. If she could have thrown herself quite openly onto Miss

Westmoreland's kindness, answered it, it would have been better, and she knew it, and could not do it. She would be on the point of confidence, and Miss Westmoreland would suggest prayers, or reading the Bible, and Judith's heart would close over in despair. She wanted to scream at her, 'You fool! You spoiled imbecile! What do you know, with your Good Samaritan, and Elijah and his ravens? The ravens would not have fed him! They would have pecked out his eyes!'

She remembered herself with Evergreen, and shuddered. But at least she had not read the Bible to her.

Sometimes she thought of Robert. At first with the same drifting confusion of mind that had brought only Mr. Gaultrip to her in the cellar. And then, one evening, sitting by the loft window, and looking down into the garden, at one of the gardeners digging the black earth round the strawberry bed, and trimming back the low, protecting box hedge, she found herself thinking of him with complete clarity. As if he was there below her. Looking up at her window, as once he had done from horseback.

She could see his face, his thick brown hair. A frost of sea spray on it and his dark eyebrows bent together, above impatient eyes. His mouth determined. 'Come with me!' Reaching up a hand towards her. 'I love you,' his eyes said, 'but I can't wait for you for ever. The world goes on, nothing can stay as it was for ever.'

She wanted to answer him, but she could not. Her tongue would not obey her. She could not move. Could not lift her hand.

'I searched for you,' his eyes said. The line of his mouth told her. Days and weeks of searching. But she could not so much as put her hand to the glass of the window. And if she could have put it there, his ring was gone.

'Answer me!' he called up to her. His eyes growing uncertain. 'Come with me! For the last time, come with me!'

Only the window glass between them. Only the thin glass, the closed window preventing her from leaning down towards him. The gardener straightened his back, putting his fists against an aching place, and the image of Robert vanished. Was no more than a reflection on the glass. A shadow.

Had she really heard anything? 'Come with me.'

She put her hand to her head, lifted the slight, new-growing weight of her hair. Remembered the ropes of it that he had held.

She wanted to cry 'Robert! Come back!' And knew that that was madness, that that was choosing the path back into illness. Yet nothing had ever tempted her so much. She felt her tongue move to shape the words, her lips open. Her body trembling. And something breaking, physically breaking, like a cord in her mind. She was able to turn away from the window and sit down on the bed, her hands still pushed into that growing thickness of her hair. As if she had sent him away. Run from him again.

She felt at once better and much worse. Better because her mind was clearer, and she could think her own thoughts without their being taken and possessed by nightmares. And much, much worse, because that recovered clarity left her mind naked, and defenceless. He was gone. He had been gone before, but she had not thought of it as it was, as it really had been.

She had run away from him. He had tried to tell her the truth and she had not listened. Not because of a greater truth, but because of lies. Her lies to herself. She had wanted the guilt of the old man's death to be Robert's and not hers.

She sat on the truckle bed, facing what she had done. But she could not face it for too long a time together, and she had to put it away, into the back of her mind, and draw the remains of her illness round her. Silence. Caution. But now only a pretence. Day by day she knew that it could not continue, that soon she must give up pretending to be ill. But not yet. When she was well, completely well, then she would have to acknowledge that he was gone for always. Make terms with that. Accept. That he was gone, that she had run away from him, had chosen. That she must live in a world in which she would be alone with the things that she had done, and seen. That there would be no Robert. No one. That that was her punishment; and she could not escape from it forever by pretence of illness. But not yet! Would she not be better dead, to have died in the madhouse, in the cellar, in her doorway? Rather than to live with all that she had done and seen, and there to be nothing else?

She tried to tell herself that where there was kindness, all the kindness she had found here, then there must be a purpose, it must be worth continuing. And—Evergreen? If only she could believe that Evergreen was still alive! That she would ever find her. But she could not. Was terrified at the very thought of searching, of being forced to know, and she shrank away from

[247]

that, too, as she shrank away from Robert's truth, from everything except to stay quiet, here; quiet and still, and secret. One day—one day she must face everything.

But not yet.

The cold weather came back like a whiplash, covering the garden with frost, freezing the water in the stone bird bath, blackening the new buds. They kept a brazier lit in her loft bedroom, a servant bringing buckets of wood and coals for it twice a day. Not very pleased to do such a service for a beggar woman, either, her manner said. The more so because Judith had been afraid to look at her at first, and had then grown into the habit of drawing away to the end of the loft when she came.

A young maid servant, with chilblains of her own, and troubles of her own. Judith knew that she was called Mary, like Jacky's sister, but nothing else about her. She had grown to dread hearing her heavy, tired young footsteps on the ladder, the clank of the bucket with its load of coals, the loose clatter of the armful of wood. Judith would pretend to be absorbed at the frost-patterned window, staring out at the white garden, the whitened trees. And this day as she looked there was a pecking at the window, and a starling was on the other side of the glass. Where Robert's shadow had been.

He cocked his head, and looked at Judith with so strange an expression, so little natural fear in it, such a passion of hunger, of need for help, all shown in a round eye that could not surely reveal anything; in the angle of the tiny head, the lacklustre of the feathers; that Judith held her breath. Thought for a second, he is a messenger from Robert! Thought, I must feed him! But her breakfast had been taken away, there was nothing. She backed softly from the window, afraid of scaring him into flight.

'Mary, look, look at the starling on the sill! Could you—please, please could you fetch me a slice of bread to feed him?' She could not have asked her for it for herself, if she had been starving. But suddenly, for the small bird, Robert's messenger, she was not afraid to ask. And the servant girl stared at her as if she was seeing her for the first time.

Said 'Yes m'm' as if she had heard her for the first time.

Perhaps it was really so, and until then she had never heard Judith speak.

Now she heard the tone of voice that is answered 'Ma'am' and

[248]

by obedience. She went and fetched the bread from somewhere not far off, and the starling waited, as if he was confident that he would be fed. Judith broke the crust into her palm, and very gently, very carefully, opened half the window and laid the crumbs on the sill. The starling ate them. Hopped into the opening and fluttered his wings. He seemed tame.

'He do ha' 'scaped out o' somewheres' Mary whispered, absorbed by his tameness, as Judith was.

'Why, you are from Essex!' Judith said. 'Is not that true? And I am!' And was immediately afraid of what she had told. And then no longer afraid. The maid's voice, her sandy, scraped homeliness, her tiredness itself, were reassuring. Close to reality. And from that day she and the maid developed a kind of friendship, an easiness between them that Judith was able to lean on like a stick.

The starling helped her too. It was folly to think of him as Robert's starling. She knew it, and did not even try to cling to the fancy as a comfort. Yet he seemed like a messenger. To have a meaning. Perhaps not—that he was Robert's starling—but hers? To tell her——What? Within another day he would fly down onto her table and share her meals, and grow impatient for them as if he knew what time it was, and was being kept waiting. Miss Westmoreland brought a pretty cage for him, with a swing, and feeding and drinking bowls, but Judith would not put him into it, and she left him to fly about the loft, and sleep on one of the rafters. One day, when the cold spell broke, and spring came back, he flew out of the opened window and vanished, singing.

To Miss Westmoreland's surprise, Judith did not mind, and grew better and stronger by the day.

Four days after the starling flew away she woke very early in the morning, to hear the birds singing their dawn chorus in the apple trees of the kitchen gardens, as if London had been transformed into countryside. She lay listening and felt as if the last of the curtains had been drawn back from her mind, and she no longer needed even the pretence of illness as a shelter. Like a sick room that for a long time has needed to be close shut, and now may have all its windows opened to the air and the sunlight. She got up and listened to the birds, and almost immediately two starlings flew onto the sill and looked at her. She was quite sure that one of them was hers, the one she had saved. The other had a female's look, a loving possessiveness about her as she hopped and postured beside her mate. They stayed there for a full minute telling Judith of their happiness together, before they flew off again.

I have grown well, Judith thought. And the next instant thought of Evergreen, and gripped her hands together against her shift. What have I been doing? Her mind cried out, what has been the matter with me? Dear God, dear God! She stood still at that careless expression, and sat on the narrow bed and held her head between her hands.

She would have got dressed at once and run out into the streets to look for her, if she had known where to look, or where she was herself. Instead she must wait. Uncountable hours until it was breakfast time. She asked Mary where King Street might be but Mary did not know and looked at her nervously because of Judith's trembling intensity. Soon afterwards Miss Westmoreland came, clearly forewarned of things to be alarmed about, her still childish forehead clouded with adult anxieties. And with something else, like a contained excitement.

'Miss Westmoreland!' Judith cried, 'thank God you are here! I have been so longing for you to come! I—I do not know how to explain it but I seem to myself to have grown well overnight. I—I have been much better for a long time, better every day, every week, thanks to your kindness, but just these last days—last night—I do not know how to explain it, but I am well again.'

Miss Westmoreland looked far from convinced. And still that suppressed excitement in her face, of something bursting to be told. 'I am! I am well again!' Judith repeated, urgently, before Miss Westmoreland could say anything. 'And I have something to beg of you, the greatest favour. I cannot think what has been wrong with me that I have not asked you before, you have been so kind and so patient, I know that you would have helped——'

'You shall tell me in a moment. But please, calm yourself, sit down. I have something to tell *you*. What is it that you want to ask me?' Her eyes filled with what she herself had to tell. Neat and pretty and beautifully dressed in the freshest of white muslins, with a blue satin apron the size of a handkerchief to show that she was mistress of a household and had serious duties in it. She took Judith's hand and made her sit down on the bed. 'You know there is nothing good you can ask of us that we shall not try to do for you. What is it that is troubling you?'

'I had a dear, dear young friend' Judith said, trying to seem calm and to control her voice. 'I looked after her, a—a little as—as you have been looking after me. And—and the day—one day—I left her alone. In a house. Where I should never, never have left her for a moment! And I could not get back to her. I—I was prevented. And now—now I do not know how long has gone by! Or what can have happened to her! I must find her!'

She felt herself growing hysterical, all her new-found recovery threatened, dissolving. As if the clearness of the light was blinding her, and the fresh air choking her. She went down on her knees, and caught hold of Miss Westmoreland's small, frightened hands. 'I am sorry' she whispered. 'I am frightening you. But what can have happened to her? How can I find her again?' She put her forehead against Miss Westmoreland's knees and cried then as she had not cried during all her illness. Cried until she felt emptied, weak again as when she was really ill. The tears soaking into the cloud of white muslin, staining it grey. Miss Westmoreland not moving, not trying to free her hands, not saying anything. If she was praying she did it silently.

'I have ruined your dress' Judith said at last.

'It does not matter in the least. We shall go and find your friend at once, and bring her here. But I told you——I have something to tell *you*.' She waited until Judith looked at her, raising her head. 'Do not be alarmed. There is not the least cause to be afraid. Far from it. But I know who you are. And what must have happened to you. Or at least—at least some of it. I met your cousin Mr. Francis Mortimer last evening.'

'Francis?' Judith whispered. She felt cold and ill, began to shake. Felt as if the curtains were being drawn close again. That she was going to faint. Miss Westmoreland cried out in terror, tried to keep her from falling.

'What have I done?' Miss Westmoreland was crying, 'I have ruined everything! Mary! Frederick! Miss Arkwright! Mrs. Gunther! Grandpapa!'

People came, lifted Judith into the bed. The doctor. Making her drink something. Sleep.

Chapter 26

It took her another month before she was really strong. She lay for days and nights in such a state that Miss Westmoreland dared not so much as attempt to tell her about Francis. She could only sit by the bed, holding Judith's hand, trying to reassure her, calm her. They wanted to move her into the house and she would not be moved. She grew so frantic at the idea that the doctor told them to give up all thought of it for the time being. But he could not prevent there being alterations in the loft itself, to change its character from that of refuge to a part of the outside world. And she could not explain to them why she was crying, why she longed for it to be as it had been before.

It was filled with furniture now, with flowers; everything that could make it as much like a young gentlewoman's bedroom as possible and disguise its former nature. Mrs. Gunther the housekeeper, and Miss Arkwright, Miss Westmoreland's companion, became regular visitors, and devoted nurses. The maids were extravagantly eager to perform any service, with an air of breathlessly respectful curiosity, and wonder in their expressions as if for them to enter the loft was to open a cupboard in a fairy story, and the dear knew what might fly out. While for Judith they brought with them the opposite of fairy stories; a recall to a reality she still could not face without the protection of illness.

Old Mr. Fairbairn himself would visit her for half hours together, accompanying Miss Westmoreland, and while his granddaughter read to Judith, or did her embroidery and talked, he would rest his chin on the silver top of his malacca stick and consider Judith with an eye at once hospitable and interested, until Judith wanted to cry, 'I am no different to what I was before! Before you knew my name.' And was bitterly ashamed of the thought, of answering such kindness with such a foolishly unworldly criticism. And determined to try much harder to get well, so that she might show her gratitude in some practical way.

But these things were less than secondary in her mind. Most of her waking thoughts were for Evergreen, and she could not rest until Frederick had been sent to Mrs. Ware's in King Street to find what had happened, and she lay tense and shivering with nerves, until he returned that evening, having found the right King Street at last, and Mrs. Ware's house, to tell Mary, who was to bring the news up to Judith that the young person in question had run off with herself, it was more nor a year past, and no news nor word of her since, and Mrs. Ware's respectful compliments to Miss Mortimer and regrets as to how she was so ill, but the letter that he had brung back with him, Mrs. Ware would be much obleeged for a answer as soon as was at all convenient.

The letter did not add much to the footman's own words in bringing it. Unlike Mrs. Ware's way of talking it was curt, and the only emotion that it showed was injured indignation—or the pretence of it—and Judith shivered again in horror at what she herself had done, at what must have happened. In the swift space of reading the few lines she could see everything as if it stood there in a series of engravings. Evergreen waiting. Growing more frightened by the hour. Lying alone, not sleeping, terrified, That woman bringing her downstairs. To the dancing class. Cajoling. Bullying. And at the end of it? Had she truly run away? Or had an old man come? And taken her?

With the letter there was a bill for thirty pounds ten shillings, to wit thirteen weeks lodgings at one guinea per week, and a long list of items ranging from dancing and deportment lessons for Miss Evergreen before she ran off; her keep, her laundry; to having the rooms vacant another six weeks in the hope that Miss Mortimer and/or Miss Evergreen might return; to the storage of their luggage, still remaining; 'for to sell up a young lady's goods, no matter *how* inconsiderate they may have seemed to be, was always quite foreign to my practice, my dear Miss Mortimer, and in the hope and expectation of your prompt settlement of this small account, I sign myself you ob:d:t serv:t F. Ware.'

'Is it very bad news, my dear?' Miss Westmoreland said, who had come hurrying to her as soon as she heard that Frederick was returned with news.

'It is, oh indeed it is, the worst—or—no, not the worst, I do

[253]

not know what it is, except that I do not believe her!' She had already told more of the affair both to Miss Westmoreland and to her grandfather, and what her suspicions of the house were. 'And I left her there! To have done that even for an hour! A minute!'

But why she had not gone back immediately, that stayed her secret, and ate at her heart. As if the reason for the wrong was worse than the wrong itself. So that there was no way in which they could console her, because they did not know what it was that most needed consolation. They told her that she must not blame herself. How could she have known that she could not return to her that same day, that same hour? It was not her fault. And as for not having searched for Evergreen before this, how could she have done so?

'You have been as ill as a young woman may be and hope to recover from it,' the doctor told her. 'You must not hold yourself responsible for anything you did not do in such an illness.'

As for their discovery of who she was, Miss Westmoreland had met Francis at a rout, and chanced to tell him of the extraordinary, lost young gentlewoman, surely, surely a gentlewoman, whom she had found and taken home with her. He had recognised the description; the colour of Judith's hair; her face, her voice, her height. But he had not really believed it to be possible, and had wanted to come himself to identify her. And Miss Westmoreland had said no, not yet, that she would prepare the way. 'Oh my dear! I did not dream of how great an effect it would have on you! How sorry I am, how can I ever tell you?'

'It does not matter. The doctor says that if I had gone out that day, as I meant to do, it would have been worse for me, to find Evergreen lost. And as for Francis coming here!'

'He longs to visit you! Would you not receive him one day soon? He has so much to ask and to tell you. And so wishes to explain——'

'No, no, please, no! I cannot see him!'

'He has promised to keep everything a secret, do not you believe him?'

'I do not believe anything they say.'

'But he *has* kept your secret! He has already! Although he swears there is no need, that your uncle the Earl——'

'He is not my uncle! He was my father's cousin, he is nothing to do with me!'

Miss Westmoreland pretended to let the matter drop, but almost every day she or her grandfather came back to it; that she should see him, that she ought at least hear from his own lips his explanations, his promises that neither he nor his father nor his brother had had any knowledge of what had been done to her. Until she gave in at last, and allowed herself to be dressed in the new round gown of pale blue lawn that Miss Westmoreland had insisted on having made for her, along with a dozen, a hundred other extravagances of kindness, and was accompanied down to one of the drawing rooms, her legs trembling so much at the thought of facing him that she imagined she could not support herself another second, and must lean on Mary's arm, must sit down here in the antechamber. Although the doctor had assured her that she was quite well again in her body, as strong as might be expected after such an illness; that she could, she should go out into the air, go shopping, anything. And she had indeed arranged with Miss Westmoreland an expedition for that afternoon. Although not to go shopping. And here she was unable to cross two rooms to meet—to meet Francis. As if it was all her past that was waiting for her.

Going in. She could not see him properly, for a moment. And then only his shocked expression, that tried to hide itself, and failed. Holding her hand, turning it over on his, as though the touch of it, its thinness, robbed him of the ability to say anything in greeting. She sat down in the chair he set for her, and wanted to shut her eyes against seeing him at all. As if—as if in looking at him a thousand things must come back to her that would destroy her frail, new-found balance, and drive her back into illness.

'I am sorry' he said. 'Perhaps it is too soon? But—they told me that you were—were almost recovered.'

'I am quite recovered' she whispered. 'It is very foolish in me, forgive me.'

Looking at him at last. He had not changed. As handsome, as elegant—more elegant, become a man of the world, of Society, his fair hair glistening, tied back and clubbed with a dark blue satin ribbon to match his satin coat. His cream white pantaloons without a wrinkle, as though by a careless miracle they had been moulded on him as he stood. And yet she felt nothing that she had expected to feel. And indeed, what had that been? And with a swift treachery her mind said, if it had been Robert! And the room seemed to turn about her as if the thought could take on immediate substance, and he might walk in, rough coat and jerkin, sea-boots stained with brine, and she would——Crushing down the thought like the threat of madness. Clasping her hands together in her lap. Making herself look at Francis again, smile at him, pretend to be composed.

'May I—may I at least try to explain to you what happened?' he was saying. 'I cannot say excuse it, only explain. Nothing can ever excuse it, I know that. And no punishments of the guilty can make amends. But I promise you that——'

'Please—I beg of you—do not talk of—of amends—of—I want only to——'

'Judith, no! You must hear me out! I have not slept an easy night since—since Miss Westmoreland told me—I swear to you, we knew nothing of what had happened to you. My father, Claydon—nothing in the world. Can I need to tell you that? Can you imagine for one moment, now that you are near recovered, that—that my father—oh Judith! For pity's sake, do not look at me so!'

'I am sorry. I did not mean——'

'We thought——' He put the heels of both his hands to his eyes, as he had done long ago when——And again she must prevent herself from thinking, remembering. No! her mind cried out to him. Stop this, I beg of you! But he would not stop. 'We thought you had—that you had gone off with Barnabas. Oh Judith, I am sorry, it was a monstrous thought, I know it, but—but you had acted so strange and—and he disappeared exactly at that time. Have I mortally offended you?'

She hid her face in her hands and he came and stood contritely before her. 'Please, please Judith. I am telling you only what we thought then. Please look at me, tell me you are not angry. At least—not angry with me for that?'

'I am not angry about anything' she whispered. 'Nor with—with anyone. I want only to forget that—that it happened and——' I must not cry! she commanded herself, and was crying. He knelt beside her, drew her hands away from her face.

'They shall be so punished' he said, 'as shall bring them to you on their knees. The instant that you permit me to tell my father——'

'No! I have told you, begged you, Miss Westmoreland has told

[256]

you—he is not to know, there are to be no punishments, nothing! Do you imagine that I want revenge?'

'But I must tell him that you are found. I must, Judith. And then——'

'Tell him only that. The least possible. And let that be the end of it. Do you think it would help me to know that—those men—I do not want to think of them! There has been enough! Promise me, I cannot bear any more.'

He gave in at last, hedging his promise about with reservations until he saw her grow frantic, and promising again to quieten her. 'You are too good' he said. 'Too forgiving. Miss Westmoreland has told me how she loves you already and loves to have you with her. But my father will not like it, to leave all your care to her, and to Mr. Fairbairn. He will want you as soon as can be to come to us at Matcham and——'

'No!'

'But he will want—he will insist on it!'

'I could not!' And then for fear that too great a bitterness had sounded in her voice, she said 'I must indeed leave Miss Westmoreland's kindness very soon, but that can only be to—to earn my living in some way, and——'

'My father will not hear of any such thing! I know what you must think of him, but you are wrong, Judith! From the beginning he wanted nothing but——Beneath everything he has the kindest heart. Even your servants, Martha and Solomon, he has paid their wages all this while, and seen that Guthrum's——'

'What has happened to Guthrum's?' She had thought that she could not ask him such a question, could not have said 'Guthrum's' aloud. And it was as though she was speaking of someone else's life, something that had scarcely a connection with her. And then with a swift rush of pain she did feel it. Such a sense of loss as left her unable to hear what he was saying and she must ask him to repeat it, her voice unsteady.

'I said that Guthrum's is still yours. It could not be sold up even if my father had wished to go so far. There was some legal matter about selling land for debts that your fellow Terry produced——' He realised what that implied and said quickly, 'It was only Laurence attempting to have things clear cut and now——Now there shall be no question of selling up, or debts, or any such things. I know that my father would want me to tell you that, will you believe me? And—and agree to visit us? My mother——'

She forced herself to be calm, unclench her hands, breathe quiet. She had heard what he said, and understood it, and it meant nothing at all. It was not that loss that she had felt, of bricks and land. Guthrum's still hers? Martha panting after them, carrying their supper tied up in a white cloth. Solomon. The wood. All her life. Her father. Mother. Everything, Destroyed. All destroyed. And he talked as if it could be sold up or given back. She wondered if she could explain that to him, and smiled, with a sad bewilderment for his simplicity.

'That is better!' he said delightedly. 'Have I your promise, that you will come to us? Soon?'

'You are very kind. And your father has—he had much to bear from me, I know that. Please tell him so. But as for——'

At that moment, as though by providence, Frederick came in with Miss Westmoreland's compliments, and would Mr. Mortimer honour Mr. Fairbairn and herself by staying to luncheon? Miss Westmoreland herself following almost at once to prevent any possibility of refusal. And there in the drawing room, and again during luncheon, she was so indignant at the idea of Miss Mortimer being taken away from her on any pretext whatever, that it grew embarrassing.

'And this nonsensical talk of your earning your living, why, I forbid you to speak of it again!' Miss Westmoreland cried, while Miss Arkwright looked down at her plate, her cheeks slightly flushed. Judith tried to think of something she might say that could make Miss Arkwright feel better, and failed. She felt so wretched about it that even Miss Westmoreland noticed, and misunderstood.

'How thoughtless I am!' she said to Francis. 'Here I have promised your cousin my company on a most urgent expedition this afternoon, to seek news of a dear friend of hers, or some way to find where she is gone, and Miss Mortimer is too good to remind me of how time is passing. Grandpapa, may we leave you? And leave Miss Arkwright to supervise your tea tray later on?'

'Poor, poor Miss Arkwright' she said, when she and Judith were in the carriage, on their way to King Street. 'If only I could find her a husband! I love her dearly but she is very tiring after an hour or so. And she looked so cross at being left behind! Yet I know she really wanted to stay and look after Mr. Mortimer. Any gentleman below eighty years old melts her bones, and your cousin——!'

'I should not listen to you say such things' Judith said. 'I am sure she is too generous ever to resent my being in any sense your sometimes companion, but if she did she would be quite right to do so. I am imposing on you, and on your grandfather, and it must not continue. Even now, I—I am taking you away from——'

'Hush!' said Miss Westmoreland, laying her finger across Judith's lips. 'You will vex me. It is quite settled that you shall remain with us and I shall not hear one word to the contrary. You know how wilful, and obstinate, and spoiled I am. When I was a child it gave me hysterics to be contradicted, and now that I am grown up I should most likely faint. So you see how dangerous it would be to cross me?' She had taken Judith's hand into her lap, and held it there with mock severity.

'You will make me cry again' Judith said, and in the face of such kind-heartedness she did cry, and had to free her hand to find her handkerchief, or rather Miss Westmoreland's small and beautiful and useless scrap of Mechlin lace and lawn, smelling of lilac blossom, and so finely made, so gossamer that it seemed dreadful even to dab one's eyes with it, let alone blow one's nose. 'Since I have been ill,' Judith said, 'I seem to have done nothing but cry. I do not know where the tears come from.'

'Nor do I' said Miss Westmoreland. 'But I mean to find out.'

Judith stared at her.

'I have had an idea in my mind for some time' Miss Westmoreland went on, 'that should solve two problems at once. You and I shall become partners in an enterprise.' She looked at Judith with her bright brown eyes and recaptured her hand, inserting one of her own small ones into it. 'I so much want to do good with my money, and you shall help me. Should you be willing to do that? I know so little, and you—oh my poor dear, how much you must know of dreadful sufferings that I cannot even imagine. And I have thought——You see, until now, grandpapa has looked after all such things, both for himself, and for me, and I have had nothing but trifling amounts to give.'

She must have remembered her guinea that at their first

meeting she had given to Judith, and flushed, and raised Judith's hand to her cheek. 'But now that I am grown up, it is only right that I should begin to act for myself. Will you help me? I promise you that I shall make you work so hard that you will be dreadfully exploited. We shall find all kinds of objects for charity, and you shall tell me how best we may give the wisest sorts of help! Oh, I do so long to begin! Is it agreed between us? Will you? Oh my dear Miss Mortimer, please, please! I will not hear no.'

'I do not know what to say, or what help I could give you if I should think it right to say yes. Your grandfather——'

'Oh, he longs for it! He thinks it the most splendid notion!'

'And Miss Arkwright—she—'

'She would have attack of the vapours if a poor person spoke to her. I brought her once into a hospital and she was so overcome she had to be sent home for a month to recover. It was quite the least tiresome month I have had with her.'

'I tell you I must not listen to such things. Nor should you say them, indeed. Nor even think them. It is not only——' Judith stopped herself.

'It is not only?' Miss Westmoreland echoed her, her face grown serious.

'I have no right to rebuke you' Judith said, flushing in her turn. 'I am sorry.'

'But tell me what you were going to say. Please. I should like to hear it.' She had released Judith's hand.

'I was going to say' Judith said, looking down at her lap and flushing redder still, with a fury at herself for flushing, for needing to think twice about speaking her mind; 'that it is not only people whom one finds at street corners who are in need of kindness.'

There was a long silence. Judith looked at the coachman's dark green back, at the street, at the shop fronts they were passing. Miss Westmoreland's small, silk-gloved fingers crept back into Judith's. Judith looked round at her. The great brown eyes in the small, heart-shaped face were at once sad, and amused, and self-mocking.

'I warned you. I am not used to anyone speaking to me like that' she said. 'I think we must make it a condition of our partnership that you shall say such things to me quite often. At least once or twice a month.' And then, the amusement and the smile vanishing, and only the sadness remaining, under the brim of her pale blue chip hat with its mass of darker blue satin ribbons, that looked as if she might have chosen it to match Francis's coat, she gave her face an expression of deep penitence. 'I am very wicked' she said, 'I know it, and oh, how hard I pray to be made better, but it does not seem to serve. Miss Arkwright brings out the very worst in me. And so does Mrs. Gunther. You shall reprove me every day, and twice and three times a day, and I shall love you the more for it, I promise you.'

'That might be too severe a test for both of us' Judith said. 'I shall not try you so hard.' She looked down at the little blue glove lying in her palm. 'I have something else to warn you of. Much, much more important. I do not share your beliefs. I do not know if I believe in God—when I was ill I thought that I did, and hated Him—but I do not believe that He answers prayers. Nor do I think it dignified to pray. For if God can answer prayers He could have made a world in which there was no need for them: where there was no pain nor cruelty, nor hunger.'

'But then there could be no Charity!' Miss Westmoreland cried. She laid all her four fingers this time across Judith's lips, in a gesture that reminded Judith of Robert, and seemed to burn her. Shall I ever cease to be ruined by remembering, she wondered. Miss Westmoreland's voice reaching her from a long way off. 'I have known a long time that you were a great pagan, and I have prayed so hard that you might have the Truth revealed to you. It is quite a destiny that has brought us together, for you shall teach me to be good and patient, who are so good and patient yourself, and I who am nothing at all shall strive to bring you to Our Saviour. And if I succeed then I must surely be forgiven for all my trespasses and short comings, and all Heaven will rejoice over you, as the shepherd rejoices for his lost lamb.' She clapped her hands together in such pleasure at the prospect that Judith had not the heart to answer her sensibly and could only smile. The smile fading as she thought of the errand they were on, and what they should soon hear.

They turned into King Street, close to Mrs. Ware's. Familiar street. Familiar housefront. Harry himself on the doorstep, pretending to rub the brasses, and whistling, showing off his striped black and yellow waistcoat and his polished Hessians to an admiring world. As if nothing had happened, a year and a half had not gone by. As if it was only that day she had left with

Robert; left Evergreen in their small sitting room, with the promise to be back within the hour. She felt herself grow weak with terrors, her heart beating too hard, too fast. She would not be able to stand up, to speak. She wished that they had not come, had left it till another day.

The carriage stopped. The footman sprang down, swaggered across to Harry, prepared to measure liveries, but already the victor in any such contest, he who had never had to soil his white gloves even by pretending to polish a brass knocker, or anything else.

Miss Westmoreland's calling card in his hand.

Chapter 27

Mrs. Ware attempted to take a high tone. To seem the injured party, seem innocent. Then she retreated into hysterics. And within a quater of an hour more had broken down utterly, and told them, or rather told Miss Westmoreland, what they had come to discover. That within six weeks of Judith disappearing she had 'found Miss Evergreen a dear kind gentleman friend.' An old gentleman. A General Pinkney, she had not meant to tell the name, she never, never repeated names, but they had her so upset, so—and he was the most respectable, the most kind and generous old gentleman, the dearest, sweetest creature who had promised to be so fond—like his own daughter—grand-daughter—she would not for the world—such suspicions—what else could she have done? Girls must be looked after—and the expense!—such dreadful, dreadful accusations she had never heard—what was the world coming to when a poor widow—the dear, dear Major—if any man had said such things in his hearing—only meaning to do good—Miss Mortimer flying off, abandoning, seeming to abandon—poor lone waif——A Mr. Barnabas coming like a lunatic—such language as he had used—had rushed off again and come back five times and carried on so until she was in terror of her life—and the young creature, poor lonely child—what had *he* offered to do for Miss Mortimer's little friend? Not thought of it. While *she* had found her a protector—had done all a mother could have done. What more could she—could they have expected?

'So you sold her?' Miss Westmoreland said with a terrible quietness, that had black caps and Newgate Prison behind it. Mrs. Ware had hysterics again. This time so fiercely prolonged that in spite of all her anger Judith thought that they should call for help. But Miss Westmoreland sat gravely waiting as if she was prepared to wait all night to have her way, and at last Mrs. Ware was forced to recover, and tell them General Pinkney's direction.

Miss Westmoreland held up Mrs. Ware's Bill of Account. 'I shall keep this as evidence against you that the girl was in your care' she said. She laid her other hand on Judith's wrist. Said in an even sterner voice to a Mrs. Ware who had become old within the last hour. 'I shall ask my grandfather to deal with you as you deserve. And now have Miss Mortimer's possessions brought down to my carriage.'

Mrs. Ware went on her knees. Albertine at the door, her eyes wide with fright. Harry. The marquis. Half a dozen young girls peeping from the music room doorway. The steps. The street. The old, shabby portmanteau brought down, put into the coach's box.

They drove away.

For a long time Judith did not say anything. She could not. Miss Westmoreland held her hand.

'I am stupid' Judith said at last, 'I knew it must be so. What shall we do now?'

'We shall take her away from this kind old gentleman' Miss Westmoreland said, 'and do everything in our power to make up to her for the wrongs she has suffered. I shall love her as you do. And we shall make her happy again, depend upon it.'

But that was not possible. General Pinkney was dead, and Evergreen was gone from his handsome house, whatever life she had lived there for half a year. A gentleman who declared himself to be Colonel Pinkney, the late General's son, very military, coldly courteous, much honoured to make their acquaintance, he said, but, hem, haw, wather surpwised at their enquirwy, demme, 'pon honour, 'pon his soul he was, he had no ideah wevver sech a cweature hed formed pawt of his fawver's household. Flushing very dark as if even to protect his father's reputation lies came hard to him. The housekeeper called, and yes, indeed, there had been a gypsy girl, an object of her late master's charity. She too flushed, indignant at being questioned on the matter. And by young ladies! The young person had been sent away after the master's death. She had not been at all a suitable young person. The General had been often misled in his kind-heartedness. The young person had been given a quarter's wages and sent away.

[264]

'Where?' Judith cried. 'Where did you send her?' If she had come sooner! Oh, if! But it had been almost a year ago. And Judith wrung her hands together. The housekeeper could only look her astonishment at such unladylike vehemence. 'It was not my duty to enquire where she was going, ma'am. If that is all, sir?'

'That indeed is all!' Miss Westmoreland said. And turning to the Colonel, 'I do trust that when you go to Church this Sunday you will pray that that "all" may be forgiven you. Your father *bought* that girl! From an evil, corrupt old woman who deals in human flesh as butchers do, except less honestly. And you knew it, and turned her away as you would not have turned away a dog. Upon your honour! Upon your soul! Do you have either?'

'Ma'am!'

'We are going. I cannot breathe here. The air around you is corrupt.'

The colonel white-lipped, shaking with fury. The housekeeper turkey red. They went out of the handsome drawing room; and through the hall, with its marble floor, and gilt furniture and footmen, and down steps fresh-whitened and glistening into the street again, and the carriage. 'I feel as Lot felt' Miss Westmoreland said. 'I must not look back at that house.'

They went home, because there was nowhere else to go, and nothing sensible to do. 'Shall we read together?' Miss Westmoreland said. She had the Bible in her hands.

'No!' Judith cried. She felt that she could not breathe here, no more than in that house they had just left. Could not stand still, nor sit, nor listen to anything. Above all not to Miss Westmoreland offering her consolation from the Gospels. 'I must go out and look for her! I must, I must!' She began to gather things together, strong boots, a cloak, as if she meant to make a long journey of it.

'But where? How can we, where should we begin? And you are not strong enough to——' Miss Westmoreland began. And then, seeing Judith's face, said 'I will come. Wait until I am dressed again. Only a moment. And—and let us bring Mr. Mortimer, if he will go with us. He will—he may be—of great—of some help. You mean to go into poor places, do not you?'

'I do not know where I mean to go! How can I?' But she did know. Although why to begin there she could not have explained to anyone. To the crossing where she had begged. And then——

They went in the carriage, Francis very willing to accompany them, and at the same time nervous, and nervously talkative. Or at least so he seemed to Judith, who only wanted him to be silent, to let her gather her courage. Until she had to cry out in desperation, and hide her face in her hands. 'I am sorry' she whispered after a moment. 'You must forgive me. It is more than kind in you to give us your company and I am very grateful.' They completed the brief journey without another word between them.

Jacky was not there, and she felt first only a sick relief, a release of tension that left her sitting quite helplessly in her corner of the seat. She had not known the depth of her fear of seeing him again. Then disappointment, as if his not being there was an ill omen, a rejection of her offering. And what could she hope for? To find one lost girl in this city of a million people? In what cellar, in what other Jacky's hands? Or worse hands than his? If she was still alive?

'We must go on foot' she said. She did not know if her motive was cruelty, or a kind of vengeance on Francis, or even on herself. She scarcely thought about it, beyond that wanting them to see. She led them by the way that she could have gone blindfold, in the dark, summer, winter. She could have found it by the feeling of the stones and the gutters underfoot; the mud, the smells, the corners where she had lain against filthy brickwork until he dragged her on, or hit her in the back to make her move.

She had made them leave the footmen behind, and the three of them went together, she leading the way, through courts and alleys, through the food market with its violence of smells and colour, its slime underfoot, its people staring at this invasion of gentility, drawing back, at once hostile and frightened. More alleyways. And at last the blind court, with its rubbish heap, and death's-head children. The same woman smoking her pipe on the doorstep, as if she had never moved from it. Taking her pipe from her toothless mouth in amazement at the sight of them.

Behind them, blocking the mouth of the alley that led into the court, there was a small, dull gathering of followers; women in rags, a man or two, a cripple with one leg and a wooden crutch too short for him, a dog with him, as starving as its master. Staring. Afraid to beg, to shout insults, come too close to such cleanness, such health and strength.

'God above' Francis whispered. He had protested long before, when they were still in half-respectable lanes, and had grown whiter-faced and more shocked as they went on. Miss Westmoreland had walked quiet and determined from the first, as if she had made up her mind not to be frightened or horrified by anything. But she too looked as if she was feeling faint.

'Here' Judith said. She led the way down the ladder, into the cellar opening. Remembering. Feeling ill herself, shaking. A murmuring in the small crowd in the court, bewilderment.

'Judith!' Francis whispered, his voice low and urgent. 'What are you doing? Miss Westmoreland cannot——'

But Miss Westmoreland was already following. She needed to hold on to Judith's arm as they stood in the half light, in the stench, ankle deep in the filthy, sodden straw. Where the pig had used to lie, in the patch of daylight, the man Sam was lying. Wasted to bone and green shadows. He lifted a hand very slowly to shade his eyes against the light from above.

'Wot—the 'ell?'

'I am looking for Jacky' Judith said, bending down beside him. He stared at her.

'Jacky?' His lips twisted in remembrance. Hatred. ' 'e's gorn' he said finally. 'Gorn off with me blunt.' And suddenly, his voice stronger with fury, ' 'e killed me pig! Sold it on me! Me pig!' The fever burned in his eyes. He put his hand waveringly towards Judith's skirts. 'Give us somefing. Give us some water.' As his wife had used to cry. She too was gone, her corner empty. The man coughed, seemed to clench himself together. ' 'oo are yer? Wot yer want wiv 'em?'

'We cannot stay here' Francis whispered. 'Why have you——I am sorry, I shall——' He turned away and began to be sick. 'I must have air' he said, when he could say anything. 'Miss Westmoreland, please, Judith, for God's sake, come above.' He caught them each by an arm. Tried to draw them towards the ladder.

Judith shook herself free of him. Bent down again beside Sam. 'Is your wife dead?'

'Yes. An' me soon.'

'Is there anyone who will help you? Buy you food? If we give them money?'

"'er wiv the pipe.' Staring. Remembering? "'er up top. 'oo—'oo are yer?'

'It does not matter. I know her. We shall give her something for you.' When she straightened and turned to look for them Miss Westmoreland and Francis had gone up the ladder. Above, in the court, the crowd was slowly closing round them. Not in threat, but drawn by wonder. A child touched Miss Westmoreland's skirts, stroking the cloth. Francis raised his hand in warning and the child shrank away.

'Let us get out of this place, I beg of you. You should not have brought Miss Westmoreland here. How could you?'

'And who brought these people here?' Judith said. 'Give me some money, Francis.'

He emptied his pockets. Miss Westmoreland emptied her purse into Judith's hands. Judith went to the woman with the pipe.

'I want you to buy food for Sam' Judith said, giving her a guinea. 'And drink. It cannot hurt him now. Where is Jacky gone?'

The woman took the guinea and put it in her mouth. 'Jacky?'

'Do not you know me?' Judith put back her hood.

The woman stared, her mouth opening. Shutting, as she felt the coin move in it. She shook her head. It was not possible to tell whether she remembered Judith and could not believe what she was remembering, or could not recognize her. Or was afraid to admit to anything in the face of power. She only repeated in a dull voice that Jacky was gone.

'I wanted him to help me find someone. He might know where to look, where someone might go who was lost and hungry.'

But the woman could not or would not tell anything. Her face grew sullen with ignorance and fear and suspicion. Nor would anyone else there say a word. Not even for money. Judith distributed the silver among the children, who stared at the coins, at her, shrank slowly away. She gave another guinea to the woman Slops, and said in a loud voice. 'That is for everyone, so that you may all have supper.'

No one spoke. When the three of them left, the children were already fighting over the sixpences and shillings. Francis led them at a fast stride, until Miss Westmoreland had to cry to him to lessen his pace, that she could not run any more. Judith

[268]

walking behind them, almost lingering. Ashamed at what she had done, and then savagely glad, and ashamed again. And despair, that Evergreen was lost for ever, that she would never find her.

They would go on looking, she would go on. Knew that Miss Westmoreland would continue with her. She could see already all the blind courts and alleyways, all the lanes and kennels, all the garrets, the hovels, the hospitals and prison cells that they would search in the next year and more; saw them as if she had already experienced them. The starved faces, the haunted eyes, the minds too stupefied with hunger, with drink, with disease, with misery, to answer a question, know a name, remember anything.

As if all had been contained here, to-day, in this one useless journey.

They reached the carriage, and the bored servants, and got in. Miss Westmoreland white and ill. Francis with a look in his eyes as if he too would not recover soon.

'I am sorry' Judith said. 'It was cruel, and it served no purpose. I am ashamed.'

'I did not know' Francis said, not in answer to Judith, or even seeming to have heard her. He looked as if he might get sick again.

'Neither did I know' Miss Westmoreland said in the same, lost tone of voice as Francis. 'But I am very glad to know now. The whole world should know.' She shivered, closed her eyes for a second, and opened them very quickly as if closing them made her feel worse. 'The whole world *must* know!' she said louder. She clasped her fingers in Judith's. 'How grateful I am that you brought us there! I knew before. In a way. A child's way. But now I have seen. I pray God to give us strength for what we must do.' She held Judith's hands against her small, warm breast. 'One day we shall find your friend, I am as sure of it as of Salvation. And whatever she has suffered we shall make good to her, so far as love can. Please believe that! And by her sufferings she will have brought so much good into being, through the things that we have learned, and shall learn, and shall tell to those who must make them right; that she herself will be glad of what has happened.'

And her face glowed with such compassion, such love and goodness, that Judith did not try to answer her, nor wonder aloud why Evergreen must suffer so that men might know what they should have known already. She drew Miss Westmoreland's hands against her own breast in return, and wished that she could believe in something, even if it was a lie.

Chapter 28

She began writing her book to prevent herself from breaking. She had thought, and been afraid of it, that it would be Miss Westmoreland who would break down in the face of what they were trying to do. But Miss Westmoreland seemed to thrive on it, held up by her religion, and by total certainties, not the least of them that money could do anything if she spent enough of it. But Judith, who had believed that she had already seen and known the worst of things, found herself in a world of shadows that grew more terrible by the day, and the week, and the month. And she knew that for many of the shadows money could do nothing.

The first day they went to Newgate, and passed the Bridewell, they saw three women—women? girls, hardly more than children—being whipped, until their backs should be as bloody as the Act required. What could money do for them? And the crowd of idlers watching, jeering, loving their morning's spectacle; what could money do against their viciousness?

'God's children!' Judith cried furiously. 'how can God endure it?'

In Newgate they found women waiting to be hanged, or sentenced to transportation, that was only a slower kind of death sentence, and crueller than the rope. Women who had stolen five shillings' worth of washing from a clothes-line, or something else as trivial and pitiful, so that they could buy food. They went into the debtors' prisons, the Marshalsea, the Fleet; out to Coldbath Fields that was the worst of all of them. They found their way into stews that made the blind court seem like a gentle limbo. Into nests of cellars and tenement rookeries where the Irish lived. If it could be called living. And what could money do in any of those places, except buy a little food, enough gin to bring forgetfulness, bury the children? They spent as much money on babies' coffins as on food. Or seemed to.

They became known. The Grey Lady and the Little Lady. And the Capting, when Francis came with them. He tried to prevent them from ever going alone, and so did old Mr. Fairbairn, but they took no notice of either of them, or their warnings that they would at best be robbed and at worst be worse than murdered. They were robbed more than once, but never attacked, and after a time they were never so much as threatened. The last occasion they were robbed Miss Westmoreland's purse with ten guineas in it was brought back to them by a man with a ferocious squint and a broken-bottle scar that twisted his mouth. He told them that from that out no one 'd touch 'em, nor a ha'penny belonging to 'em. 'Anythink 'appens to yer, or looks like 'alfways to beginning to 'appen to yer, just you ketch 'old of the nearest ragged 'un, an' say as you wants Duke Jacob's 'elp. That's me, Jacob.'

They saw him often after that, a wicked, slouching ruffian surrounded usually by a gang of children, like vicious sparrows, and sometimes with a painted girl, her hair bleached yellow and a raucous voice that could empty a laneway or a courtyard in a few seconds, or else fill it with nightmare creatures who seemed to ooze out of ugly doorways or up between the stones. The girl never spoke to them, but Jacob always saluted them and sometimes told them of people who needed help. Not his own subjects. He helped those himself, or had them helped. But others. And told them at the same time that there was still no news of Evergreen.

'If she was in Lunnon we'd 'ave 'er for yer. She ain't 'ere, my doves.'

He did not say 'She must be dead', but Judith saw it in his face. She made herself work harder, drove herself until she was too tired to think. Tormenting the Directors of Hospitals to allow in more sick paupers; tormenting the staff to let in urgent cases without a letter from one of those same Directors; trying to make doctors come into the stews and the cellars; find more women who would help; bring food, bring medicines, bring common sense.

But she realised very soon that it was better not to bring too much of that because if they were common sensible they would simply go home and abandon everything. It was senseless, what they were doing, and she knew it. Like carrying water in a sieve. Senseless, senseless, senseless, as the lists of their visits grew; the sick, the maimed, the dying, the hopeless, the abandoned; children with eyes that knew too much; mothers with eyes that knew nothing. The beaten, the savage, the whimpering ruins of what had once been human beings.

To go to the prisons, and find them full, and then emptied for the transports, and the next day full again. As if the skies had opened for a new Flood of misery. To find great ladies who thought that Visiting the Unfortunate would be a pretty thing for Friday afternoons, and who expected to do it in the family coach, carrying a lap dog. And other ladies who fainted and had to be taken home and restored, and their husbands pacified. To find Hospitals where the nurses drank all day and slept all night, and the Surgeon stole the money for the patients' food. To find the prisoners in the Bethlehem, chained and naked.

She had thought that she could not go there, and Miss Westmoreland and Francis had tried their utmost to prevent it. But she had had to go. Her hands trembling, her legs threatening to give way. And for a few minutes she had thought she would break, that she could not survive it. But she did. And they began to visit there too, and beg and threaten and wheedle their way into other madhouses. To bring blankets; gentleness; advice to Keepers more bestial than their charges.

None of it was sensible, all of it needed to be done again the moment after it had been done. Except that when she felt that she could not endure the senselessness an hour longer she would remember the starling. Who would have died if she had not fed it. Perhaps somewhere there was a child who would live because of them? A woman who would recover? Perhaps.

She began writing the book as medicine for herself. Old Mr. Fairbairn had at last persuaded them that they could not continue every day, that they must rest. Saturday evening. Sunday.

'But those are the very times we find the most of them!'

Then Mondays? Tuesdays?

Until they promised that at least one day every week they would stay at home and rest. Not always the same day, but at least one. And since Judith could not rest and could not sleep, she began to write to occupy those days. And also very late at night, or very early mornings, before Mary came to bring her tea and toast for breakfast, and help her dress.

She began telling Evergreen's story, like a penance for herself. Remembering her father saying 'You should write it down one day.' She felt sometimes that her father was with her, that he sat beside her at the desk Miss Westmoreland had had made for her, or that he stood behind her reading over her shoulder. He was young again, and full of hope, and at the same time, she thought, very glad of what she was doing.

The story of Evergreen, who had learned to dance and curtsy, so that her father might beg. Who had travelled England on small bare bloody feet. And before she was a grown woman had been bought like a slave by a rich old gentleman, only to be driven out by his son once the old lecher had died of his debaucheries. As if the shame was hers and not the rich old man's. And driven out to what? Into the heart of Christian London, to starve, or steal, or beg, or die, or sell her thin body for a guinea, and then a shilling, and then tuppence, and die at last in a gutter, like a cat run over by a cart. 'Do you wish she had had a longer life, fellow Christians? Or do you wish to see how she once lived? Turn down a laneway, out of the broad street, go into the courtyards, down into the cellars. You will not find her, because she was long ago buried in the river mud, or in the sewers.'But you will find others like her. And you may have time to tell them that God loves them, and His Son died for them, before they too are dead.'

When she had finished the story of Evergreen, she went on writing. She told the stories of those others. Of Jenny, whose husband had loved her sister, and had had Jenny put out of their way, into a private madhouse. She described the madhouse, and the chains, and how the collar felt. The purges, and the laudanum nightmares, the blistering, and the ice-cold baths that made flesh turn to shrivelled marble.

She described the cellar in Blind Court. The child. The woman. Sam. Told stories she had absorbed as she had absorbed the vile air and the stench. That she had not realised she still knew. Of women in Newgate, and why they were there. Of Nosey Grimes, the leper. Of a girl of twelve who was sentenced to death for picking a shilling handkerchief from a gentleman's tail pocket, and was not reprieved. 'My Lord said it was because she was reprobate, she had done it before. And so a child of twelve was hanged. How old is your dear, smiling child, my gentle Christian reader? Is she twelve? Put a rope round her neck and pull it tight. And then imagine that no one will loosen it until she dies. And may your God have mercy on the Judge!' She told stories that she had gathered in the hospitals. In Bedlam. In the workhouses. In the gutters.

None of it succeeded in putting Robert out of her mind. But it deadened the pain of thinking of him, as a red-hot iron can cauterise a wound. She still imagined finding him again. She dreamed of it. Made stories for herself in which he came back to look for her, wrote to her from Leyden. 'I am coming back, coming to find you, I cannot live without you!' All the worn phrases of dreams. She would imagine finding a letter waiting for her in Adèle's house when she came back at midnight; redirected from Guthrum's; although how would poor Martha redirect it? But these things do not follow the rules of reason. She dreamed that Mary would call down the broad, handsome staircase, 'A letter, ma'am! A letter from a foreign place! Oh ma'am, from Leyden!'

Each night as a servant opened the door for her, Frederick, one of the others, she would half expect to hear that news of a letter from abroad, would almost hear the words. And sometimes, often enough, there were letters, and her hand would tremble as she put it out to take them from the salver, or from Mary. But none of them from Leyden.

Or she would turn the corner of a street, and would see him coming towards her. Would be sure, sure as the trick of light and shadow could make her. And a stranger would go by, astonishedly flattered that the tall, beautiful young woman should have looked towards him with such eagerness, and as much cast down when she turned away from him as if he no longer existed.

Sometimes she imagined him walking beside her. Going with her into the alleys and the courts, and the stinking tenements. Already a doctor. Like a rock to lean against. Making all bearable. She would talk to him, hear his voice. One day she had found herself actually talking to him aloud, and the people nearby had stared at her. It was soon after that that she began her book. And the pain of writing down what she knew, what she had seen, and lived through, made the pain of that loss of love—not trivial, oh, not that—but something she could bear, must bear, it was so just and deserved a loss in a world where all the misery that surrounded her, that she saw each day, seemed created from injustice and levelled at those who deserved it least.

And when she had finished the book, sanded the last page, it was as if she had also finished with weakness, and sanded dry the last of her self-pity. She put the manuscript away as having served its real purpose already, whatever she might one day do with it as a book, as an account of things that had happened.

She did not think of it again for above six weeks. And when she did, it was gone.

'I had a parcel of manuscript in my drawer' she said to Mary. 'Tied with a string. Have you put it away somewhere?' But Mary knew nothing about any parcel, and had not touched the desk drawers, and 'never would. Never, ma'am.'

'It does not matter, it was nothing important.'

She wanted to ask Miss Westmoreland, but hesitated even to appear to think it possible that she could have gone to Judith's desk and taken anything, or read private papers. Two days later Miss Westmoreland saved her the trouble of deciding whether to seem so rude.

'Your book is to be published at Christmastime' she said. 'I have just arranged it with Messrs Cameron. You are to get two hundred and fifty pounds, within the month, and another two hundred and fifty when they commence to sell it. It is very little, I told Mr. Cameron, but if it sells as it should you are to get much more. I have had Mr. Pauncefoot look at their contract and redraft it, to protect you.'

'You have done *what?*'

'I have had Mr. Pauncefoot——'

'You know what I mean! You have taken my manuscript and——'

'You did not write it to keep it a secret, I imagine? People write books in order to publish them, or have them published. And so to save all sorts of stupid arguments I have arranged it for you. You could not have arranged it half so well by yourself.'

'You are impossible!'

'It is to be called *Christian Tales*, which I think is quite probable for a Christmas sort of book, do not you?'

'*Christian Tales!* Are you mad! Who thought of such a—such a dreadful——It cannot be published, I shall not allow it!' And yet already a warmth possessed her at the thought of it, mixed with rage at what Miss Westmoreland had taken on herself, and at the imbecile wrongness of such a title, and at being so managed.

'It is a perfect title. Mr. Cameron thought of it, and I quite approved, and there is to be a Subscription List opened at once. I promise you, you will be delighted with everything; we are to have a hundred copies specially bound in red morocco and tooled in gilt, and the rest in plain calf with marbled end papers. He thinks to print fifteen hundred copies as a commencement. The authorship is to be "By a Lady of Quality." In 3 volumes, at 15/- the set. Mr. Cameron is to have it hinted about that you are cousin to an Earl. He says that that will do wonders with the Subscription List.'

Perhaps it did. The fifteen hundred projected copies became five thousand, and within a few weeks of publication those were sold out and another three thousand copies were printed, and they too were sold. And more printed. And more.

'And after this lot is gone' Mr. Cameron said happily, 'we shall sell a thousand or twelve hundred of your little book every year for forty years. It is a Phenomenon, my dear ma'am. A Phenomenon. And one which owes not a little to its title, if I may make so egotistical a claim.'

She herself seemed to have become a Phenomenon. It was known within a week of *The Tales'* publication who 'the Lady of Quality' was, and she found herself half famous and half notorious, at once denounced as a new and worse Miss Wollstonecraft and praised to the skies as the Conscience of the day. A bishop preached a sermon against her in St. Paul's, calling her an Atheist and a Jacobin, and in the same week the Queen directed her Mistress of the Robes to write to Miss Mortimer and say how much affected Her Majesty and the Princesses had been at a reading of Miss Mortimer's book. Perfect strangers wrote to her proposing marriage. Other strangers called in person to explain their projects for doing away with unhappiness. And it was while she was trying to get rid of one such philanthropist, who had a scheme for abating Concupiscence among the poor, that Claydon was announced to her.

She was so shocked at seeing him that she could not greet him properly, or even hold out her hand. And he in his turn seemed no better pleased to see her, his expression of impatient dislike almost unchanged from the last time that they had met, in Guthrum's, three years ago. Until, recollecting himself, he drew out a thick document from his coat pocket and laid it on the table between them. 'My father has bid me bring you this.' He looked at her, and quickly down at the document, his fingers still resting on the table's edge, as if he needed support. He looked even sicklier than she remembered him.

'Pray—pray take a seat' she whispered, 'I—forgive me——I did not know that you were—to call.' All of it returning. Mr. Laurence. That day. The coach. Mr. Massingham. Since her illness her memories jumbled together sometimes, or had gaps in them or came to her out of their proper order. It seemed to her for a moment that Claydon had been there when she was taken to the madhouse. She could see his face. And then she knew that that could not be so, and she sat down in her own chair feeling so ill that Claydon was forced to notice it, and apologised.

'I thought I would take the chance of finding you. I am sorry if——'

'It is of no consequence. You have brought me something I must read? Or——?' She had long ago made a kind of peace with the Earl, allowing Francis to tell him as much as might be necessary, and the Earl had written to her of his shocked outrage at what had been done to her under cover of his name.

'As for the wretches responsible, since you are too generous to allow them to be punished as they deserve, they shall at least have no other indulgence. I have turned them off to find what other employment they can, and if any prospective employer enquires of me about them I shall tell him what sort of villains they are. In Massingham's case I hear that his wife is almost punishment enough, if it was not ridiculous to talk of any punishment being sufficient for his wickedness.

And now, if I may turn from the unhappy past towards what both the Countess and I pray shall be a happier future for you, we do both beg that you consent soon to visit us. When you do we may discuss, among other things, the question of Guthrum's and its ownership. But have no concern about that in the meantime, my dear Judith, for I am determined that all shall be resolved to your complete advantage and satisfaction.'

She replied with proper sentiments of gratitude, and promised a visit at some indefinite time. And there matters had remained. She had not brought herself to visit Guthrum's, let alone Matcham. Martha was safe, and Solomon; and the house and land, all cared for by the Earl's arrangements. One day soon she would go. One day, when she felt more equal to it. But the day had not yet come. And now——She touched the document that Claydon had brought to her. It was tied with lawyer's ribbon, and at that moment it seemed a problem even to open it. She could not decide so much as to pick it up. 'What—is it about?'

'Why do you not open it and see?' Claydon said, his voice sharpening, and as he recollected himself again, 'It is a Deed. Conveying Guthrum's to you Freehold. And cancelling all debts and obligations between you and my father.' He coughed and flushed. 'He has read your book' he said. 'So has my mother.'

'That was kind in them' Judith said uncertainly. Deed? Conveying?

'Well? Are you not pleased?'

She stared at him. 'Why—yes. Yes. I——' She put a hand to her forehead. 'You—you have took me by surprise.' He had begun drumming his finger tips on the arms of his chair, with a sick man's irritability.

'My brother. He is a frequent visitor here, I think?' He was looking anywhere but at her; at the portrait of Adèle's mother over the fireplace, at the fire brasses, the log bucket. He had aged beyond measure in the last three years, she thought. She could almost feel sorry for him. It had been cruel in his father to make him come on this errand.

'I am grateful to you' she said, her mouth dry. 'And—to your father. He is——' She touched the Deed again, took it up. The parchment felt greasy to her finger tips where the copying clerk had pounced it. It made her think of Mr. Terry's desk, its wilderness of documents. She had written him long ago that there was no occasion to continue his searches, that she and the Earl were to find some accommodation between them without recourse to Law.

And now she was given everything. How pleased her father would have been. And thought then, no, perhaps he would not have been. Would have felt deprived of something if victory had come so easy seeming and sudden at the end. Perhaps all victories did. And I, she wondered. How do I feel? But strangely enough all she could think of was how ill he looked. Tomorrow, this afternoon, she might feel glad. Would feel it. Must. I am still not truly well, she thought, as if she was hiding behind something. Realised what she was doing and made herself stand up, and smile at him and hold out her hand.

'I am most grateful to you Lord Claydon. I——I know that you cannot have liked to come here. May I tell you without offending you that—that I have no ill-will towards you? Or—anyone.'

He had also stood up. He took her hand slowly, looking at it rather than at her. His had a sick man's moist chill about it. He seemed not to have heard what she said. When he was gone she sat down and closed her eyes. 'Guthrum's is mine,' she thought. But it seemed immensely far off. As though she was someone quite different from that girl who had run away, how long ago? And come to London to make her fortune. And Evergreen——She put her knuckles against her mouth, bit at them until the pain brought her back to herself, reality, the drawing room, the document lying in front of her on the sofa table.

Frederick came in, putting on the expression of face he had developed for announcing aristocratic callers. 'Lady Augusta Townshend and Miss Townshend, ma'am!'

'My dear, dear Miss Mortimer!' Lady Townshend was crying. 'You wicked, wicked creature to have wrote such a book! I have been weeping all night and poor Seraphina here has not slept a wink with me. And where is dear, dear Miss Westmoreland?'

The very sound of her voice drove shadows flying.

Chapter 29

In spite of all her appearance of folly, it was Lady Augusta who gave their work the practical turn that it needed. 'But you must have your very own hospital!' she cried. 'Those dreadful places! The nurses always drunk! I would not have any servant of mine set foot in one, let alone be cared for. I must introduce you to Mr. Egerton the architect. Quite brilliant! And he has been longing this age to build a hospital, or at least some such thing, and here is his opportunity!'

Miraculously, out of such an unpromising beginning something practical did come. Miss Westmoreland herself had begun to realise what Judith had known from the start, that their work was next to useless from any rational viewpoint. And she seized on Lady Augusta's almost careless suggestion and turned it into reality. Money was found, and land. A Committee formed to raise more money for building. Plans were drawn up, Mr. Egerton proving against all likelihood to be everything his patroness had claimed, and more besides, being quite sensible as well as clever, and willing to take direction on what his employers needed.

There were to be three separate buildings; a hospital, an asylum and an orphanage; all set in wide grounds that would provide gardens for the patients to be quiet in, and others for the children, where they could play without their noise disturbing anyone. The day that the first ground was dug for the foundations Judith and Miss Westmoreland stood beside Mr. Egerton and cried openly, not troubling to conceal their tears from him, or from old Mr. Fairbairn, or the labourers, or Lady Augusta.

'You dear, sweet, sensible creatures!' Lady Augusta whispered. 'I declare you will have me in floods if you go on so. And I wanted to tell you, I have just the person to look after your hospital for you when it is built, a Doctor Parrish. Vastly clever, he is a hydro something, and almost a gentleman, no one could mind speaking to him. I shall have him come to you as soon as you wish, and——'

Mr. Egerton took pity on them, leading Lady Augusta away so that she might advise him about a landscape gardener she knew, who would design the grounds to perfection.

'But it is a thing we must think of' Miss Westmoreland said, when Lady Augusta was far enough off for other conversation to be possible.

'Designing the grounds? I suppose—but——'

'No no! Someone to look after the Hospital and all the staff. It is not a thing we can hope to do ourselves, with under-doctors, and surgeons, and matrons and nurses all to be controlled. We shall need a man. Perhaps her Doctor Parrish may prove like Mr. Egerton?'

Yet even had they wished it they could no longer make such choices by themselves, and there must be advertisements, and interviews. And two months after that day of commencing the foundations Judith and Miss Westmoreland, Lady Augusta and a Duchess, and a General and a Bishop and a Mr. Waterville, who was reputed an expert upon Science, formed a Board that was to spend the day questioning candidates for the Mastership, and for every other important post they had to decide on. The first candidate being Lady Augusta's Doctor Parrish.

He came in stooping and twinkling. Tall, thin, dressed in fashionable blue, eyeglasses glittering, fingers not clicking but seeming ready to snap and click at the first excuse, flexing his knees as he sat down in front of the Board. He stretched out his white silk stockinged legs with a self-conscious elegance, and regarded the Duchess and the Bishop and Lady Augusta with doctorly devotion, comprising the remainder of the Board in his smile as if he was saying of each of them 'Etheric! Positively Etheric Beings! Not an example of Carnality among them!' Judith thought that she would faint, and had to support herself with both hands gripping the table's edge.

She was wearing a bonnet with a deep, coal scuttle brim that shadowed her face, and he had every excuse for not recognising her. After he had distributed his smile of benevolent confidence, he gave his attention to the Duchess, who wanted to talk to him about his attitude towards Religion.

'Mr. Waterville tells me he is a Hydrotherapist' she had said to Judith. 'And often these Scientific men are lacking in Belief. Mr. Waterville himself——'

But Doctor Parrish reassured her with a truly starlike glitter of faith and piety.

I must tell them! Judith thought desperately. Explain——But her voice would not answer, and she imagined herself sitting paralysed, unable to say anything, while they agreed to make this wicked madman their choice. She opened her mouth to cry out at him and could not make a sound. Mr. Waterville was questioning him about his Hydrotherapy.

'Sovereign, sir! I have never known it fail. The most frantic cases of dementia that have took four strong attendants to carry them to the bath are so calmed by it that after but half an hour they can be carried back to their beds by one man. An hour of it, and they are like babies.' He looked round, twinkling.

'Sir' Judith whispered, 'have you—yourself tried out this—this method?'

He looked at her, the beginnings of questioning behind the bright spectacles. Not recognition. Only the mildly puzzled look of someone who has heard a distinctive voice before, and cannot place it. He saw that she was young, and obviously, being seated at the extreme end of the table, of very small significance on the Board. His smile took on condescension.

'Fortunately, ma'am, I have never had occasion for such therapy. But if I should! Why——' He looked as if at any moment he would spring up and snap his fingers, crying 'NEVER HAD OCCASION! WHAT IS WOMAN! LUST AND CAR-NALITY!'

'Then——' Judith said, her voice uneven, threatening to fail altogether, 'you do not know—what it may feel like to the—to the victim? To lie in icy water for an hour on end? Strapped in so that she may not move? In the depth of winter?'

'They do not feel it, ma'am, I assure you. They have not sensibilities as we have.' But the questioning in his eyes had become sharper. He stared towards her, frowning. The Duchess was also looking at her, puzzled by her tone.

Lady Augusta cried from the far end of the table where she was sitting beside Miss Westmoreland, 'Icy water? Surely not? Why, the very thought of it makes my teeth ache! My poor darling little

[283]

pug dog fell into the river once on a quite mild spring day and almost caught pneumonia from it. Cure, indeed!'

'We are talking of lunatics ma'am' the Bishop said kindly, 'Not of lapdogs.'

'They do not feel it, I assure you' Doctor Parrish said again. He could not take his eyes from Judith's shadowed face. 'It—it purifies the spirit as well as——'

She put back her bonnet brim. The doctor's face changed colour, his mouth began to work and he put up one hand to conceal it. 'I know him' Judith said, trying to keep her voice firm. 'I know his methods. I would not allow him to sweep the floors of our hospital.'

'My dear Miss Mortimer!' the Duchess whispered.

'Look at him!' Judith cried, could not prevent herself from crying the words aloud. She felt herself begin to tremble, her own mouth to work as if her twitch was returned. 'Look at him! Can you not see it in his eye, in his face? He is mad himself!'

For a moment, more than a moment, the Committee was almost turned against her. And then Doctor Parrish shouted 'YOU HAVE PLOTTED THIS AGAINST ME!' He dropped his voice to a hiss of anger as suddenly as he had begun to shout. 'She is a Bedlam case, you have fetched her here to injure me!' He had got to his feet, and sat down again, as if his knees had given way. 'Why have you done this?' He dragged out a handkerchief and pressed it against his mouth, his eyes going from one to another of them at the long table. His face yellowish, sickly as jaundice. The Board stared at him, surprise turned to astonishment, to a suspicion that Miss Mortimer must be right.

'Jealousy!' Doctor Parrish whispered, his voice muffled by the handkerchief. And then 'IT IS JEALOUSY, THEY ARE TRYING TO DESTROY ME AND YOU ARE THEIR DUPES! THEIR DUPES, DO YOU HEAR ME?'

No one spoke. Mr. Waterville went round the table to him and took his arm. 'Come sir' he said. 'You are not quite well I think. Someone shall attend you home.'

'The mad creature!' Lady Augusta cried, before he was well out of the room. 'And how clever in Miss Mortimer to recognise it! Icy baths indeed!' She seemed to have forgotten that he had been her protégé. An air of self-congratulation spread from her along the table. Judith sat shivering, her bonnet drawn forward again, her eyes shut, closing her ears against the sounds of screaming, the crash of iron, *Cherry Ripe*.

Two more candidates came and went without her being truly aware of them. I must be calm, she thought. I must control myself. She made herself look up, pay proper attention to what was happening. To the next candidate.

It was Robert.

For a moment she thought that she had tricked herself again, been tricked by shadows. Closed her eyes. I am not ill! she told herself. I will not let myself be ill!

Robert's voice, answering a question. Of Mr. Waterville's. 'In Leyden sir. And I've been in Switzerland most recently. In Basel.'

'No!' she whispered, 'No! I shall not let it happen!' Ordered her mind to obey the laws of reason, the voice to become whatever it ought to be. Doctor Smith's of somewhere. Doctor Brown's of somewhere else. Not his, not his!

For the first time that morning she looked at the agenda paper Mr. Waterville had given her. And saw his name. Doctor Robert Barnabas. From Leyden.

She looked at him then, and he was staring at her, his face almost as pale as hers must be. His voice lost. Trying to say something, shape a word. What was he trying to say? And the echo of her name seemed to come to her. But from very far away.

'Robert' she whispered. And wanted to hide her face from him, still not able to believe. And at the same time to hold out her hands towards him. And she could do nothing. Not move. Not speak. While the Duchess began to ask him about his Beliefs and Mr. Waterville wanted to know what he had done in Basel.

Robert. She was crying as she sat there, her face hidden again by the deep bonnet brim. Her hands locked in front of her, clinging to the table's edge.

Doctor Barnabas. Doctor—Barnabas.

Whispering the words to herself as if they were echoes, that she was hearing in her mind.

He was still looking at her as if he too was seeing ghosts. It is truly him, she thought. He is truly there. And did not know how she managed not to faint. Not to fall.

'My dear' the Duchess was saying to her. 'Miss Mortimer? Have you no question for Doctor Barnabas?'

Chapter 30

They went to Guthrum's from the wedding. A clergyman. Another ring. A church, quiet and empty in the early morning. Adèle Westmoreland and Francis for witnesses. No one else. They wished it to be like that. Robert, because he was a man. Judith because—because I do not wish them to see, she thought. Without being certain whom she meant by them, or what it was she did not wish to be seen. Memories of that first ring, that first betrothal in a hackney coach with muddy straw under foot, and broken cushions, and a smell of mice and staleness. Of the Dutchman's house. Of——

Kneeling before the clergyman, before the altar, her hand on Robert's arm. And her heart beating, beating. As if from one moment to the next she expected to hear someone crying out, 'No! Stop!' And it would be her voice.

I love him, she thought. I have never ceased from loving him. And still she was afraid to look at him, kneeling beside her. Remembered his taking her, in that squalid room, that grey darkness under the dusty skylight. And it would be like that again? No, nothing like! Nothing! Robert!

Someone lifting her hand, separating the fingers. Warm gold. 'With this ring——'

What have I done? WHAT HAVE I DONE? I CANNOT!

And if in that second she could have trusted her strength she would have run out of the grey silence into the streets, looked for refuge anywhere. But she had no strength, and could only lean on his arm as they walked slowly out of the quiet church, into the sunlight.

Mrs. Barnabas, her mind whispered.

Mrs. Robert Barnabas.

I am his wife.

And then clinging to him, holding him so desperately that he looked at her with the beginnings of surprise. I have found him again. Robert.

The words like echoes. Of her voice saying long, long ago, 'Doctor Barnabas. Doctor—Barnabas.' Beside a fire. Shadows. And she held his arm as if without its strength she would fall.

Adèle had given them her coach for the journey. And the coachman. Four horses. And sent other horses ahead to wait for them so that nothing should trouble them, not even to rely on posting horses for their changes. The coachman would return at once, and sleep in Urnford on his way back to London. And Adèle had had hampers packed with wine and all that they might need, things that they swore they would never touch as they kissed her for them. Who can imagine eating cold venison pasty and pressed ducklings and jellies and fruit tarts at such a time? Or imagine drinking burgundy, and champagne, and liqueurs?

But they did eat, and drink. And came at last to Guthrum's.

There were only Martha and Solomon to meet them there, and Mary accompanying them, riding beside the coachman, wrapped up close against the autumn chills. Familiar house. Familiar rooms. It was not her first return here since she had left with Evergreen all that time ago. And she was determined that it should not seem like it, that she should not feel as if she was going back into the past.

Only to look forward, only the future. Only love. The loving bride who was so proudly showing Robert all that should now be his. Gift of herself, gift of everything. And did feel all of that, holding his hand, pressing it against her side, as if to say, here, take, all this is yours.

But one cannot give one's self without the past.

And in the house there was no corner that did not have its shadow. She could not bring Robert into a room to show it to him without seeing a place where——

Where she had stood, so quiet, so shadowlike. So obedient and frightened. And trusting.

Robert, hold me!

How had she died? Where? If she could know even that. Even be certain of her death. Know that it was over for her, all done with. And knew as she thought of it that it would only make things worse. Did it help to know how old Mr. Gaultrip had died? To feel the sea choking her, the weight of iron chain bound round her body? The terror? And yet she still thought; if only I knew! *If*.

But this is madness, she told herself. What is the good of it? And she kissed Martha, and held Solomon's hand and told him how handsome he was grown these past few months, while he scraped his boots on the kitchen floor and turned scarlet with pleasure. She asked after Mrs. Locke, and Mrs. Rigg, and all the cottagers. Was the lady of the house, as if she was two people, one talking, smiling, sitting down to supper by the fire in the small parlour, holding Robert's hand in secrecy when Mary's back was turned to bring them more wine or another dish; thanking Martha for all the cleanness of the house, the brightness of everything, brasses and coppers, floors and wainscot shining with polish and loving welcome; saying, yes, oh yes, I am home at last. Even though we must go away again, to London, to our work there, this is our home, and always shall be, and you are our Martha, our dear, dear friend.

One woman who said and did all that, and held up her glass to Robert's, to touch them together. And another who was standing aside from everything, scarcely knowing what was said, what was being done. Only—waiting. For what? All the waiting is over, I have found him again, he has found me! My love! And yet it was as if that other self was shivering in fear of something, setting her hands to her hair to lift its weight from her. While a voice said, 'To your health, my dear, dearest Robert. And to our future, yes, oh yes to that!' And her shadow self stood waiting, shivering. For what?

For Martha to go to bed. And Solomon. And Mary.

Leaving them alone at last, by the fire in the parlour, touching hands, saying again and again all the things that they had said already a thousand times in these past weeks. Do you remember this? And that? And I. And you. How thin you've grown! But it makes you more beautiful, I swear, I promise. And how was it in Leyden? Your grandmother? How I searched for you! I was like a madman.

Over and over. Promises, love, remembering, explaining. Lovers' talk. Hands touching. Her heart beating. And that shivering in her mind.

He set his glass down, looked at her. Now, she thought. Her

lips dry. Now. He stood and held out his hands and took hers. And again she must hold fast to him to support herself, for fear of falling. Now.

If he let go of her hands she would fall.

'Go into the kitchen' he whispered.

Not—and she was able to let go of him. To walk out of the room, not asking him why. Go slowly down the passage. The kitchen dark except for the firelight. The shivering grown quieter, as if she knew that whatever was to follow would not happen immediately, that she would be alone for a little while. Safe.

She drew a stool to the fire, and sat quietly, thinking of nothing but the firelight, and the shapes the embers made. No longer distant journeys in them. Seas and islands. Instead, journeys done. Homecoming. Quietness. Oh please! Let us be quiet now. Let us love.

There was a soft scratching sound and the smallest of shadows moved on the other side of the hearth. The mouse. Was it the same one? She wished that she had a crumb for him. He sat up, small and dark and neat, like a tiny gentleman, washing his face with his paws.

If I could sit like this for ever.

There were no sounds except the rustling of the mouse, the fire's whisper. Quiet. Dark. She forgot the mouse, and when she looked for him he was gone. Hiss of flames from a log. Fall of embers into the red heart of the fire. Shadows moving. Silence.

She lifted her head and listened. Was that a footstep? Outside? A knuckle tapping the glass of the window? She felt her heart-beat quickening, and went in the dark to the passage; to the door. Put one hand to the bolt that Martha had pushed home two hours ago.

'Who is there?' Whispering.

'Won't you open to me?' Whisper in return, against the thick timber.

Her hand hesitating, drawing the bolt very slow and quiet. Lifting the latch. His shadow in the dark. The smell of tar, and oilskin, of leather jerkin and coarse wool.

'Who is it?' Her heart trying to escape.

'A friend.'

Closing the door behind him Pitch dark when it was shut. She put out her hands to feel for him. Touched his jerkin. The coldness of the leather. His hands felt their way along her arms, came to her neck, her face, her hair. Loosened the knot of it. It had grown so long again she needed to knot it up. Letting it fall round her face. Touching the neck of her dress, the buttons of it, that buttoned down the front, from neck to hem. Unfastening one, and then another, and another.

'What are you doing?' Still whispering.

'What I've dreamed of,' he breathed. Until her bodice was opened to the waist and he could touch her, hold her as she had so long wanted to be held. And the traitor walked like the mistress of the keep, giving her orders to the garrison. Surrender. Lay down your arms.

I remember that room, her mind whispered.

Remember nothing! Obey! Obey! And she no longer knew whether they were playing a game, or who he was, or what day and year it was; this year of 1803 or that long, long ago year when they met first, or when. Or when.

Remember nothing! Think of nothing!

And she did think of nothing, except that they were in the dark together, in the cold stone passage as if it was long ago, and time had turned back and the smugglers were outside, only their two selves there. His hands holding her, sliding on warm cambric under her arms, holding her closer to him.

'Will you belong to me?' he whispered.

'I do not know who you are. How can I tell in the dark?'

'I can tell who you are by the beating of your heart. And the softness of your hair. Can't you tell me by my coat?'

She laid her head against the leather jerkin. 'I love you' she breathed, the leather cold on her mouth. Such a child's game to play. Or was he trying to cancel out that room in the Dutchman's house? That other wedding day? Undoing the remainder of her buttons, stooping down in front of her, until he could open out her dress. Catching up her shift and chemise and under skirts from their hems and lifting them. The cold air against her nakedness.

And a dreadful memory came of that happening the day she was taken to the madhouse, and she almost cried out. The waist of the underskirt was too tight to lift as he wanted it to, and he broke the waistband and she was naked to the throat, a thick ruff of silk and cambric round her neck, covering her face. He bent down and put one arm behind her knees, and brought her slowly and carefully into the kitchen, to the fire, that seemed almost brightness after the dark of the passage. He sat down on her stool, and held her against him, settling her on his knees. Like a loose woman with a sailor, in a tavern. That image that had haunted her. The woman naked by the fire. She hid her face with her hair. Against his face. The fire warm on her skin.

As if he had stripped away not only her clothes, but her life since they had lost one another. Layer on layer of her life until they were once more two strangers, sitting by this fire and wondering; who is he, who is she? Shall we become lovers, what will happen to us? Or perhaps it was much simpler; just that it gave him pleasure to play such a child's game of make-believe. But she did not want to think that, and thought instead; he is doing this to be gentle. To give me time. To ask me to remember not the bad but the good. For surely this was always good, and only good, to sit loving one another? If only I had gone with him. When he first begged me to! To run away with him to Leyden! If I had brought——

She tried not to think of Evergreen, of bringing her with them, having her safe now. If! Oh, if! I must not, must not think of the past. Only that I love him, that he is gentle, I did not think he would be like this, so wise in such a foolish, foolish way. Touching, stroking, kissing her mouth through strands of warm hair, smoothing it away and kissing. Kissing her breast so that his head was bent under her mouth and she could press her face down against it.

Until as they sat by the fire she began to shiver under his stroking, not from cold, not the room's cold, not that earlier shivering in her mind, but something else. 'I belong to you' she whispered. 'Take me. Is that terrible to say?'

He lifted her again, her opened dress trailing its skirts against the stone floor. Against the floor of the passage. Against each tread of the stairs. The corridor. The step down. Her room, that she had written to Martha was to be their room, at least for now. At least for this first time of coming here as Mrs. Barnabas.

A fire burning, warm and red and welcoming.

'Pull the covers down by the fire' she whispered. 'The mattress, everything.' Her heart like a living creature, beating at its cage. Not to think of anything, of anything but this. Of love, his body and mine, the firelight. Take me, take me! What are you doing, spreading the covers out like a maid making a bed? Throw them down, take me, I am here for you, don't wait, don't try to be gentle any more!

The traitor shouting in triumph, raising her traitor's flag.

TAKE ME! and she stood still and quiet, her hair covering her face, as if she was Niobe. But her arms so contriving that her chemise and underskirt did not fall, did not cover her. And then with a sudden shame she let them fall. But in that second he had turned to her. Gripped her by the arms and pulled her down beside him. And he took her as she wanted to be taken, as she had wanted five years ago when she had first seen him, and felt that sweetness, that treachery in her blood. And while they were making love she did think of nothing, wanted to think of nothing except loving, being loved.

Until they lay quiet, and he was asleep, his arm across her breast, holding her as if somewhere in his sleeping mind he was afraid that she would get up, escape from him.

But I do not want to escape, she told the darkness, the fire. Told the shadows. I have come home.

Except that one shadow would not answer her. Sitting quiet and still and frightened just out of her sight, at the corner of her vision. And there was another shadow like a drowned man floating just beneath the surface of the water. And the whisper of the fire was a child's breathing, and the weight of Robert's arm grew light, like a child's.

She wanted to cry out, 'Robert! Save me! Make love to me, keep them away!' But he would think that she was ill again. She turned towards him, kissed him, held him, and he stayed asleep, murmuring.

'Love me' she breathed against his sleeping face. 'Love me!' But he did not wake.

The wind cried in the chimney. 'Jenny Wren, pretty Jenny. Save me! Save me!' The firelight a fragile island in the dark.

Robert's breathing, Robert's dark head lit by the flames, Robert sleeping.

The shadows bent down towards his head, towards her. All the shadows she had seen. How can one dare to love in such a world?

Evergreen! Evergreen!

But that shadow could not answer her.

Chapter 31

She walked slowly towards the wood through the summer fields.
Corn growing, and clean pasture; cows; sheep; the hedges
trimmed, and white with blossom. A labourer with a bill hook,
cutting back the quickset. Touching his forehead. 'Good morrow
Mistress. That's a fine day for the babe.' Mary behind her,
carrying the baby, already grown out of her first babyhood;
fifteen months old, and delighted with the bright sky, and the
hedges, and the butterflies, and the sheep, and the ribbons that
floated behind her mother's hat. Calling 'Mamma! Mamma!'
until Judith turned round to smile at her. Her mind absent,
thinking how beautiful the day was. Wishing she could fold it like
linen and take it back with her to London, where Robert was
waiting, and the Hospital, and all that she and Miss
Westmoreland had begun. And that she and Mrs. Francis
Mortimer were continuing.

Mrs. Robert Barnabas. Mrs. Francis Mortimer.

And now poor wretched, sickly Claydon was dying, still
unmarried, and Adèle would one day be Countess of Matcham,
and had said, in a burst of stupidity and tears the day after
Judith's child was born, in their own Hospital, because that was
where she and Robert lived in London, in the Master's House;
had said, 'I—I did not take him from you? Tell me that you
truly, truly did not want Francis for yourself?'

'It would be a trifle late now if I had done' Judith had
answered her, holding the baby against her breast, while the
nurse hovered. 'But extraordinary as it may seem to you, I really
do prefer my own husband to yours. I know you do not believe
me, but it is really so.' And they had both cried, and Miss
Westmoreland—— It was hard to think of her as Mrs. Francis

Mortimer—had been wonderfully jealous of the baby, and enchanted by its handsomeness.

'It is not meant to be handsome' Judith had whispered, 'it is meant to be beautiful. It is a girl, not a boy.' And had tried not to remember that other girl baby who had lain fumbling against her breast.

'You're destroying yourself' Robert had warned her, not long before, very gravely. 'It's my business to judge minds, and try to heal them, and I tell you, you're endangering yours, and your life with it. You can't go on like this, remembering, and tormenting yourself. You're doing no good to anyone. And least of all to me.' He had held her as if she was Venetian glass, and he felt that a breath might break her.

'I am stronger than you think.'

'You're too strong. That's your danger. You're holding all this inside you and pretending you're well, and that nothing is the matter. It can't go on.'

She did not know what to answer except to tell him again, 'I love you. Love me! Forgive me! I—if only—— But I will try! I promise you I shall try to be—to be well again. Soon! Very soon!' And she had taken his hand and pressed it against her body where the baby lay, now quiet, now stirring.

'There! Can you feel her moving? She is alive! Alive in there! When she is born——'

Oh, how wonderful everything would be. All the shadows would be gone.

'Perhaps it will be a boy,' Adèle had once said, trying to tease her, forgetting, not understanding.

And she had been so shocked and frightened, that Robert had had to come running to her, to swear on his doctor's knowledge that it would be, must be a girl. The way it lay. The way it moved. On his oath.

'Tell me again! Promise me!'

Because if it was not a girl—— And the baby crawled towards her in her dreams, held out blind hands, whispered, 'Let me live!'

And she herself would reach out to find Robert. 'Hold me! Love me!'

'Hush, there's nothing there!'

'Love me. Please.'

And for a time the shadow would be held at bay.

Her time came, and it was a girl, and for a brief while that was enough. To lie with the small weight in her arms, warm, soft, alive, complete. 'Is she—?' Crying the first instant she could cry anything except with pain, 'Is she—? It is—it is a girl? And she—she is all right?'

'Yes! I promise! Perfect! There never was such a perfect child!'

'Show me! Give her to me!' And she had lain holding her. Then the terrors had come back. She could hear the sounds of an animal's grunting in the night and would go a dozen, twenty times to the cot to see that the baby was not dying, that no gaunt, emaciated creature with huge jaws lay on her.

She herself grew so thin she frightened everyone, and had to allow herself to be sent away from London, down here to Guthrum's to get strong, away from the bad air and smoke of London.

But here there were other things to frighten her, to come creeping, threatening. The sea, and the wind, crying with an old man's frightened weeping. Shotton, and the knowledge that the smugglers were still there. Robert's father, Slipgibbet, all of them.

She had refused to meet Robert's father, or even his mother. Had grown frantic at the thought of it, no matter how many times Robert gave his oath that his father had known nothing of the old man's murder. That it had been Slipgibbet's doing, with two other men. They alone had decided it, and carried it out. They had done it for his father's safety, perhaps for cruelty as well, 'but I swear to you as God's my judge, my father knew no more of it than I did.'

'But Slipgibbet is still there! And that old man is dead!' And in a low whisper, like a dreadful afterthought, 'And I am still here.' But he looked so frightened in the face of such unreason, that she held his hands and begged his forgiveness, promised again to become well. 'I shall, I know it. Only give me time.'

They both pretended to believe her, and she stayed in Guthrum's for close on three months, and did seem to grow stronger, until she could not keep herself from her work, and Robert, and her real life, any longer. Went back to walk in the wide, cool rooms of the Hospital; in the garden of the Asylum, where the gentler lunatics walked by themselves, and the more difficult with their keepers. Even the ones with their keepers knew her, wanted to touch her. Even the ones who must be kept locked safe in their quiet rooms seemed to know her, to grow happier when she came to them. She went throught the classrooms of the Orphanage that they called Nazareth, the name of it not her choice but Adèle's, and she could feel again, did feel, that these things were something gained, were lit candles. She felt as if her father was with her, and her mother.

Until she would turn a corner, go down a corridor, see a shadow; and it was Evergreen. For that second it was truly Evergreen, with her dark, secret head, her silence, her fears. And Judith's heart would stop, she would catch her breath with the pain of it. Need to stand still, lean against something, shut her eyes in terror that anyone would see her, see how ill she was, and tell Robert or Adèle. Have her sent away again to rest. To rest! And she would gather up her strength to go on, to pretend.

Or in the wards of the Free Hospital, where the babies were that they found sometimes in the streets, and doorways, or sometimes in orange boxes and nests of papers laid on the Hospital steps. In the wards she would see the dead child of the cellar, still holding out its arms to her, for her breast, as if it was jealous of the living baby who lay there to be fed. If she looked into water, into the fish pond in the garden, into a well, into a hospital basin filled with bloody water and pus and bandages, she would see the old man's face reflected, his eyes in terror. 'I am a dead man! Why did you mix yourself up in such a business? They will murder me!' She did not need to be in Guthrum's to hear his voice.

Or she would hear a woman singing, that high brittle voice that the demented have, like a cracked bell of cheap, foolish metal; and hear the echoes of *Cherry Ripe*. She longed for the other days when she and Adèle had gone into the laneways and the courtyards alone, bringing their stupid, foolish, useless charities, and there had been no time for thinking of anything but tomorrow. Now work was committees and writing reports, and letters, and memorials, and addresses to Parliament. She could be spared from all that too easily, and they had made her go down into Essex again, on the pretence of wanting her to finish her new book, that was to follow *Christian Tales*. The *Tales* themselves had had such a success as seemed to have taken them out of her possession, and she could no longer think of them as hers. Mr. Cameron predicted that within another few years, when the first furies had had time to be forgotten, the *Tales* would be given to children to read in their schoolrooms as a pious work. 'With certain—ahem—passages adapted to their tender understanding of course.'

He had annoyed her so much that she had refused to write a preface for the newest edition, and would almost have burned it rather than see it have such a destiny. But her new book, if she ever finished it, that beyond all question would have to be seen for what it was. No one would twist *that* into a snivelling agreement with the Mr. Carterets of the world.

She set her fingers deep into her hair that had grey in it now, and yet had kept its flaxen shimmering, like pale, living gold, so that the labourers and the smugglers' men still whispered 'Silver Tail' behind her back. And she walked like that towards the wood, Mary carrying the child behind her. The baby cried with pleasure, 'Mamma!' And then to Mary, 'Nanna, Nanna!' How wonderful her world must be, Judith thought. She does not know that winter comes, and the small birds go hungry.

She came to the wood, where now the undergrowth was cleared, and the ash saplings cut, and there was a broad path winding among the trees.

That too she was sorry for, although it had needed to be done or the wood would have died into scrub. She stopped for a moment and shut her eyes, imagining she smelled woodsmoke. And held her hands together against her breast, before she went on slower still towards the clearing, and the mound, and the summer house. Turned the corner of the path. There was no fire burning. How could there be? Not so much as a circle of cold ashes. How could there be even that? Grown over long ago, become green again.

The stone temple cleaned and swept, fresh with air and summer, and a vase of flowers that one of the men had put beside the bronze statue of Aphrodite, Love rising from the waves. Field flowers, and hawthorn blossom that must not come into a closed house, but could be brought here, where the building was open to the sun. She sat on the bench with its heavy cushions, Mary beside her, the child struggling towards Judith's arms.

'I will take her' Judith said, and held her close. A shadow lay on the floor at her feet, on a heap of bracken that long, long ago had been swept out and burned. Another shadow bent down beside it, touched its leg, and the summer air was filled with the smell of death. She held the baby against her heart, and did not know which of them she was protecting.

And then, from a hazel tree, flying down, there came a starling. Strutted, walked about and looked at them. 'I am alive' his bright eyes said, his tilted head, his small pointed beak. 'How wonderful that is!' And flew away, into the stillness of the summer evening.

Judith continued sitting there, thinking about him, although it was growing cool, and was already twilight. Almost cold in the stone summer house, with the statue of Love behind her, and the stone pillars on either side. Almost dark. As if she was hidden there, Mary beside her, and the child on her lap, wrapped in her white merino shawl, asleep now, her eyelashes fringes of bronze-gold on the smooth, full cheeks. The clearing in front of them was like the empty stage of a theatre, waiting for a play to begin. The starling its Prologue, its Messenger. What message? What play? But it was pleasant to sit quietly there. Looking at nothing. As near to happiness as she ever came, except in Robert's arms, for a moment, a half hour of forgetfulness. What message? What play? She sat expecting nothing, knowing that there was nothing to expect. Yet she stayed sitting quietly, dreaming of nothing, of impossible things. Remembering the starling.

'We should goo back ma'am' Mary said. 'You'll catch cold. An' t' baby.'

'Yes. We must. In a moment.' But she did not move. And the silence grew round them again. A living silence. Bird sounds, and rustling of leaves, and beyond the dunes the sea's murmur against the sand. A living quietness that seemed to grow, fill the evening with expectancy. And in the quietness a sound like a cracked bell. Cheap, foolish metal. Judith held her breath, her heart missed its beat. A strange rustling among the trees. And the quietness stilled. The birds' voices, the wind in the high branches stirring the dry autumn leaves, all holding their breath, or seeming to. And then beginning once more on a different note as the donkey entered the clearing. A grey, small donkey under a load of pots and pans and tinkering stuff and gypsies' gear.

Two gypsies walking behind him, guiding him forward. One a man. Dark and watchful, although he did not see Judith watching him from above, from the shadowed entrance of the summer house on top of the mound. And behind the gypsy, a gypsy woman, carrying a child. No older than Judith's child, a small dark head against the woman's ragged dress. Her skirts brushing the grass, her feet bare. Her head a tangle of black hair, hiding her face. Coming softly behind her Rom. It could not be! And Judith clenched her hands together in her lap.

Even that small movement caught the man's eye, or his ears. And the woman's. They stood looking up, at the summer house, at Judith, sharp with fear. But after a moment, the woman came slowly forward, step by step, lifting the tangle of her hair with one hand, the baby in the crook of her other arm. And it was Evergreen. Her face as secret as it had always been, worn with five years of the roads, and the woods, and God and she alone knew what else. But it was Evergreen. And life there. And freedom. And the starling's song.

Judith stood up, holding her own child, and came down the steps towards her.